SKINGRAFTERS

INDIES UNITED PUBLISHING HOUSE, LLC
P.O. BOX 3071
QUINCY, IL 62305-3071
www.indiesunited.net

For Monali, the Sadiya to my Maadhini

"Love is its own reward." – Mario Puzo

Acknowledgments

Before I thank my wife, editor, and my cover artist, a big thanks to you, dear reader. What a blessing it's been to have written a 30,000-word novella four years ago and yet, thanks to the support of my readers, 30,000 words has become 200,000+, and I can tell you now, for the first time, that more is on the way (you'll have to read the Afterword for more details on that).

Of course, my acknowledgements wouldn't be complete without thanking some others as well:

Monali Krishnan: My "alpha reader," who never makes me feel uncomfortable in my own skin.

Shaylin Gandhi: My editor, who continues to know just what questions to ask to get the best product possible out of me. One of these days, we'll meet in person.

Amrita Raja: The best cover designer a person could ever ask for. The exact wrong example for those who say to never mix friends with business.

To the mom and four sisters who taught me that vulnerability is strength and kindness is the great equalizer: thank you.

And finally, to the aunties: There are so many of you that to list you all would be ridiculous. You are my "second moms" who raised me to believe that strong women will save the world.

BHARAT KRISHNAN

SKINGRAFTERS

A WP DUOLOGY

INDIES UNITED PUBLISHING HOUSE, LLC

BHARAT KRISHNAN
PASSION
A WP NOVEL

Chapter One

Even now, a year after Maadhini had left India for New York City, she still couldn't sleep without playing the phone recording she'd made of Bangalore traffic. NYC called itself the city that never slept, but the noises outside her shared studio apartment paled in comparison to those she'd grown up with. Honking was India's national pastime, and the shouting of street vendors and drunken frat boys outside her window here just didn't measure up.

After the first few weeks of their freshman year, Sadiya had insisted on buying Maadhini wireless headphones for listening to what they both affectionately called "the allure of home."

Sadiya could do without it.

Now sophomore year started tomorrow. Maadhini needed a good night's rest. Turning over, she saw her roommate tightly bound in a pink faux fur comforter, fast asleep. Truthfully, she was just as happy to have the headphones as Sadiya had been to give them. She'd never tell, but Sadiya was a loud snorer.

Look how peaceful she is, perfectly comfortable with

herself. They were best friends, had been since primary school in Bangalore, but now Maadhini sometimes felt a chasm between them as deep as Chicago pizza. *I still haven't even told her I prefer it to this New York shit.*

Sadiya hadn't had any trouble fitting into NYU, making friends in her Urban Design and Architecture Studies program, even dating. For Maadhini's part, she'd taken Bharatanatyam dance classes last year, thinking she'd make some other friends and maybe even meet a boy, but all she'd gotten was a twisted ankle. Their apartment complex had a dance studio in the basement, but she doubted she'd ever go back to what was once a passion of hers dating back to their preteen years.

I might stay a virgin forever. When they'd first moved to New York, she'd hoped it'd be like their favorite show growing up, *Friends.* But if her life did resemble the sitcom, it was only because she was Fat Monica and Sadiya was glamorous Rachel.

Maadhini sighed. She wanted to ask Sadiya what a penis looked like. If they'd still been in high school, she might've been brave enough to ask whether Sadiya had lost her virginity yet. Here, though, things had changed. Blowing her lips in frustration, she shoved her bangs out of her eyes and reminded herself she needed a haircut soon. *I'll have to check my social calendar, first. Might have too many engagements to do it this weekend.*

Laughing to herself to keep from crying, she closed her eyes and begged for sleep to take her away from this place.

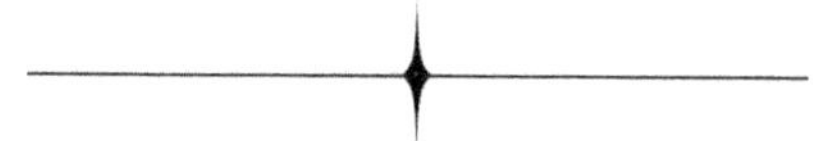

Maadhini woke several minutes before her alarm went off. It wasn't even eight a.m., but she could tell

Sadiya was up. The curtains were open to let in the sun, and her roommate's day planner sat on their kitchen table.

Getting up, Maadhini walked toward the table to find a half-empty cup of chai and a big circle drawn around an event happening on Saturday night: "DDD." *Some weird bra thing?* Looking down at her own full chest, her heart raced as she wondered if Sadiya was considering a boob job. *Is this what Hema Aunty meant when she said to make sure her daughter didn't do anything "too American?"* She was saved from her thoughts by a flush and the smell of vanilla-scented soap as Sadiya emerged from the bathroom.

"I made chai," Sadiya said. She retrieved a mug from their cabinet and handed it to Maadhini before sitting down and taking out a pen to start marking up her day planner.

Leaving her friend to her work, Maadhini took a long sip of her drink before muttering her thanks and taking out her flip phone. Her parents had many rules, and one was that there was no need to waste money on a smart phone when, in her *appa*'s words, "a dumb phone is perfectly fine." The other rule was to call each morning. She could speak with her *amma* anytime she liked, but Vir Kedilaya, graduate of the elite Indian Institute of Technology, now attended Mercer County Community College each morning in pursuit of his Associate of Applied Science, since America wouldn't recognize his engineering degree. Consequently, she could only speak to him before he left for classes and his job at the local Indian grocer, Patel Brothers.

A pang of guilt hit her stomach, like the spicy tacos she and Sadiya devoured on Taco Tuesdays. Her *appa* hadn't wanted to leave India, but there had been no stopping her *amma* from moving to America once

Maadhini had decided to attend NYU. The family had settled in Iselin, New Jersey.

"You better eat something," Sadiya said, interrupting her thoughts. "I can't be late on the first day. Grab a bagel because you know I will leave you."

"In a minute." Maadhini didn't bother suppressing her grin. Sadiya wouldn't tolerate being late on any day, be it the first or the final. Warming up a bagel and taking a swig of her chai, she called home.

"Vir! Stop this nonsense!"

Maadhini could barely hear her mother over the sound of a lawnmower.

"Huh?" Her *appa's* shout came over the line as the machine stopped. "What are you saying?"

Maadhini had the phone pressed to her ear, but moved it away to avoid the booming voices of Vir and Tanvi. *Is an immigrant household truly happy if there hasn't been a fight by eight a.m.?*

"Vir! Get over here!"

"Don't shout, woman. It's like I say when you call India; you don't even need the phone. Open your mouth and all the world can hear!"

"You are one to talk! You can't run the lawnmower at this hour! Our neighbors will hate us!"

"Our neighbors already hate us! At least this way I can get some work done before leaving."

"Ah yes, leave." Sarcasm dripped from her *amma's* side of the conversation (*can you call this a conversation?* Maadhini supposed so, even if she wasn't part of it). "While you're gone, I get to endure passive-aggressive taunts from the other housewives about how something loud woke them up."

Passive-aggressive? Endure? Maadhini raised an eyebrow. She'd have to compliment her *amma* on her

English when this was over.

"You want to trade places?" Vir asked. "Come, go to Patel Brothers after hours of schooling. See if you can impress Mr. Pandya at the shop."

Seeing Sadiya tap her foot and point to a clock hanging across from their fridge, Maadhini tried to end her parents' bickering. "Guys..."

"*Sharm karo!*"

Though she couldn't see her *amma*, she knew the woman was out of steam when she uttered that phrase. A look of resignation no doubt colored her face.

"I have plenty of shame." Her dad's voice dropped several octaves as he said his final piece on the matter of *Suburban Mornings with a Lawnmower*. She'd heard this particular play a number of times; it was substantially more embarrassing to witness in person.

Her *amma*'s voice softened like nothing had happened, as if Tanvi Kedilaya had just picked up the phone. "Hi, *beta.* Did you sleep well?"

"*Amma?*"

"Yes?"

"What was all that?"

A loud sigh passed through the line, long enough to strangle them both. "Your *appa* is getting worse. The grass, the snow, the idiots in his classes, the idiots in the store. You know"—she dropped her voice to a whisper —"white people have started coming to the store."

"That's not a crime." Maadhini laughed. "I mean, who can resist Maggi Hot & Sweet?"

"Some of these white people, they live in our neighborhood. They see your *appa* in school. They make their snide comments when they think we can't hear, about the 'brownie' who smells bad and works at a grocery store."

Snide? "Your English really has improved so much."

Changing the subject was the only thing to do in these cases. Vir refused to talk about his challenges, leaving Tanvi to voice them and Maadhini to internalize the guilt of uprooting her family until it devoured her soul and left nothing but a husk for her parents to marry off one day.

The circle of life. She made a note to herself that this year she'd save up enough money to see that show. She loved *The Lion King.*

Sadiya opened the door to their apartment, which Maadhini took as an opportunity to end the conversation.

"*Amma*, I've got class."

"Okay, *kanne.*" Tanvi only used that term of endearment when she was disappointed in Maadhini, wielding kind words like daggers as only an immigrant mom could. "Will you come home this weekend?"

"I'm not sure." She threw on some faded white sneakers as she stepped out of the door with her best friend.

"Okay, *kanne.*" A pause filled the silence, long enough to connect them back to Bangalore, India.

"*Amma*, I gotta run. I can't be late on our first day. I'll call you tonight."

"*Thik hai. Thik hai.*"

She could picture her *amma* waving her off, her head bobbing in satisfaction. Two calls a day wasn't sustainable for the long term, but it would keep the peace today. Maadhini hung up just as the elevator doors whisked shut.

"They shouldn't guilt you like that," Sadiya said.

Maadhini sighed. The four narrow walls surrounding a toilet or an elevator shaft that could plunge them to their premature deaths provided her only refuge from the obligations of living.

"They shouldn't," she agreed. "But since when has that mattered?"

Leaving Coral Tower, the two women jumped on the M101 bus outside their building as it rushed toward the College of Arts and Sciences. After paying their fares to the driver, the pair walked to the back, only to find there were no seats left. Standing, holding a pole for support, Maadhini let her eyes wander to the yellow taxicabs, brownish street stalls, and multi-colored storefronts that made up New York City.

"So much activity, and yet it's so different from the streets of Bangalore."

"Eh." Sadiya shrugged. "Noisy here, noisy there. At least here, you can get a decent slice at midnight."

Maadhini rolled her eyes and wondered if she should go ahead and say Chicago pizza was better. Her thoughts were interrupted when a young boy and his mother shoved right past them and approached an old Black lady who was seated by the rear doors.

"Excuse me, Miss," the boy said. "Can my mommy and I sit there, please?"

The elderly woman smiled. "What a charming, polite young man."

Young man? He can't be older than four. A hostage to her inner monologue once again, Maadhini strained to hear the rest of the conversation as the woman got up and let the mother sit with the boy on her lap.

What the hell? If she'd been a braver woman, she would've said something. The old woman had calloused hands and wrinkles on her forehead. *So much for respecting your elders.*

"Look at the boy's shoes," Sadiya whispered.

Composing herself as the bus idled at a traffic light, Maadhini saw that the boy's laces (so tiny!) had flecks of white in them. WP.

The magical drug was doled out to Caucasian children

at birth, entrusted to generations of "real American" families by the government. She'd read about a few immigrants who'd moved to America and founded companies and secured the drug in exchange for equity in their firms. Some people traded it like stocks. But there were only two ways to get a hold of it legally: be white or be rich.

And one usually necessitates the other.

In a city filled with immigrants, Maadhini's daily interactions with the drug were still jarring. It was so obvious where the fault lines were; no one could pretend WP was distributed in any kind of a fair manner.

And yet they do. When she'd first landed in America, she hadn't known about the drug. Maadhini had read up about so much of this country, but none of her history books had mentioned the elephant in the room. Neither had her parents. It'd been left to Sadiya to explain. Sadiya, who had stumbled upon the term "WP" when reading about the sororities on campus.

Thank god she gave up that dream. Maadhini couldn't bear to lose her best friend to some exclusive club, even if the club did grant WP to its best recruits—be they white or not.

"'Dhini," Sadiya hissed, using the pet name only she could. She kicked Maadhini's shins for emphasis. "Do you see it?"

"Ow! Yes!"

"You can feel the energy rush through you, can't you?" Sadiya couldn't seem to tear her eyes away from the boy's shoes.

People will think she's a kidnapper. "All I feel is nauseous."

"Do you think he can run super fast? Is that why it's on his shoes?"

"Who knows?" Though the bus chugged along on its

route, Maadhini risked falling on her face to move farther away from the mother and her boy.

"Wait up." Sadiya joined her. "Why'd you move?"

"That stuff," she whispered. "It does things to me…"

"I read it affects different people differently," Sadiya said. "Some people get super-speed, some get super-strength, others become super-smart. You never know how it'll interact with your system until you get some."

Standing farther away, Maadhini could finally bear to look at the boy. Sitting on his mother's lap, he played with his laces, making noises to himself and ignoring the people around him, totally lost in his own world.

"It's so gross," Maadhini whispered. "This country says it stands for equality, and yet what could be less equal than giving some people magic and denying it to others?"

When Sadiya didn't respond, Maadhini continued. "It must be so lonely to admit to yourself that you aren't enough. To have your happiness, your personal fulfillment, be dependent on some drug."

"There's nothing wrong with a little enhancement," Sadiya said. She smiled, and Maadhini saw the boy smile back at her.

When the bus halted at the next stop, the mother and son disembarked along with them. Maadhini watched as the boy raced past his mother to Washington Square Park. The shoelaces did, in fact, give him super-speed.

"Speaking of enhancements," Maadhini said. She grabbed Sadiya's arm and pulled her to her side as they walked to the College of Arts and Sciences. She leaned in so that their noses were touching.

She smells so nice. "'Diya." She used her own pet name, the one she'd had for Sadiya since they were kids. "Are you getting a boob job?"

Sadiya frowned in confusion, then shifted to gut-busting laughter. "Are you insane?"

"Um…"

"Okay, I know no one's about to motorboat these things, but they can still draw attention in the right dress." She laughed again, and it felt like butterflies were suffocating in Maadhini's stomach.

Me and my big mouth.

"'Dhini, why would you say that?"

"I saw your planner," Maadhini offered weakly. "…it said DDD on Saturday."

Sadiya laughed so hard she snorted. "It's a sorority. The Tri-Delts."

"…oh." *I'm not sure that's better than getting a boob job.* "I thought you changed your mind on rushing."

"That was just an act for our parents," Sadiya said. "This is what I want. That's why I had that part-time job last year. And why I worked during the summer. *Amma* and *appa* said 'no' last year, but now I have enough money to pay the fees on my own. They don't need to know about it."

Lying to your parents? Maadhini couldn't bear the thought, but masked her judgment.

"God, 'dhini." Sadiya laughed again. "Thanks for the laugh."

"Are you joining because you want WP?"

Sadiya ignored the question, but Maadhini suspected the answer was yes. Sororities and fraternities distributed the drug at parties in private rooms, making it clear to all college-aged Americans that there existed elite societies worthy of privileged treatment. And then those students graduated and built lives based on that exclusivity. As much as the thought repulsed Maadhini, she'd be lying if she said it didn't also intrigue her just a little. *If everyone could do it, if everyone could live their best life this way, is it worth dismissing?* It was a silly question to ask, she knew, because not everyone could do it. *And yet…*

Entering their building and making their way to a classroom, Sadiya offered up one last thought. "That was a cute kid, on the bus. I can't wait to meet a guy and have some of my own."

Maadhini didn't meet her eyes as Sadiya continued.

"Once I'm a Tri-Delt, we'll get into all the good parties. I'll bring you along, of course. We'll both have awesome boyfriends by the end of the year."

Is that what's missing from my life? Maadhini held the door to SCA-UA 601, Approaches to Metropolitan Studies, for Sadiya to enter first. It was an advanced course for two sophomores, but they'd tested well and made a personal appeal to the professor last year. Her parents knew she was taking a 600-level course, and that meant she was gifted. They didn't have to know what she was gifted at, exactly, until they saw her semester grades in December.

So not exactly a lie, she reasoned.

"Take your seats."

Professor Wilson Pryzbylewski had his back to the class as he spelled out his name on a white board with a different colored marker for each letter.

"It's going to take you awhile if you insist on writing with different markers."

The remark came from a woman in the front row. She had alabaster skin, blonde hair, and for some reason, was wearing a white pantsuit to go with her flats.

"Should we have dressed up?" Maadhini whispered to Sadiya as they took their seats, also in the front row, on the opposite end from the blonde.

"India has a dress code, not here." Sadiya settled in an upholstered chair with a foldable arm for their laptops or bags, pressed so close against Maadhini's chair that their legs were touching. The vanilla-scented soap from her morning shower had mixed with the smells of the city and were doing something to Maadhini's stomach that she didn't understand.

Whatever discomfort and joy she felt was broken by Professor Pryzbylewski's response to the student's comment. "Your consideration for my time is noted, Ms. Steinbeck."

He said the words with a smile, but the crow's feet around his eyes and the way his shoulders slumped when he turned to face them revealed his true thoughts: *will this be yet another class of disappointments?*

Maadhini was determined to show him that this would be his best class yet. After all, that's why he had agreed to have her and Sadiya: because they had proven to him last spring that they had the intellectual fortitude and curiosity to keep up.

This Steinbeck girl looks young, too.

"Now then," he continued. "My name is Wilson Pryzbylewski."

"Hey, Professor!" A white kid in cut-off jeans and a baseball cap called out from the last row. "Can we call you WP?"

Laughter rippled through the room like ocean waves, growing with each row until it hit Maadhini. She rubbed the back of her neck instinctively.

"Quiet," Wilson said. He didn't shout, but his tone reminded Maadhini of her father's when he gave the final word on a family matter. "We can go by first names here, Chad. I don't wear my WP on campus because I want to make this a safe and fair environment for *all* of my students, and I've avoided that nickname my entire life because anything explicitly designed to keep out a portion of our American brethren is antithetical to our founding principles."

"Hear, hear," the blonde girl whooped. Her enthusiasm earned a nod from their professor.

"So," Wilson continued, "this is Approaches to Metropolitan Studies, and over the next fifteen weeks, you'll be learning the dynamics of capitalist urbanization during the early and mid-20th century. We'll be talking about things like racism in infrastructure and labor rights."

"Hold on." Chad snickered. "We're going to read about racist highways?"

"I can see the spark of genius in you, Chad," Wilson said. "Racist highways are exactly what we'll be discussing today."

Maadhini observed that half the class had their laptops flipped open by this point, typing words that were probably more related to Instagram than the class. Still, some, like an East Asian woman behind her and the Steinbeck girl, leaned over in enthusiasm. Sadiya had already begun scribbling into one of her notepads.

"He's trying too hard," the East Asian girl whispered, loud enough for her and Sadiya to hear. "Making a show of not wearing WP he owns, of not going by WP…does he want a cookie? Another 'woke' white guy looking for brownie points from the coloreds."

I'm not sure we're allowed to say that? Maadhini pretended not to hear.

"*Si monumentum requiris, circumspice,*" Wilson said. "If you seek his monument, look about you. Those words adorn Sir Christopher Wren's tomb, and no other phrase could speak to the legacy of Robert Moses. He designed New York City, and let there be no doubt that he was an appalling racist and that his personal beliefs motivated the construction of the greatest city in the world."

Now he had the entire class's attention. Sadiya's lip

quivered as she chewed her pencil a bit too enthusiastically.

Is she wearing lipstick? Should I start wearing it, too?

For the next ninety minutes, Wilson taught them how Robert Moses had designed New York City explicitly to keep Blacks and Hispanics segregated from whites and therefore unable to reap the benefits of urbanization. Saying this class was his own form of social justice, he demonstrated on the white board with pictures of highways cutting through what were once vibrant Black neighborhoods, bringing air pollution, traffic, and increased accidents.

"There were secondary consequences, too," he said. "Who wants to build a park near a highway?"

The words flew over Maadhini's head, but the blonde girl raised her hand.

"Yes, Ms. Steinbeck?"

"It's structural racism. Clear as day."

"Yes, well said."

"Teacher's pet," Sadiya muttered so only Maadhini could hear. "Ask me about Bangalore architecture, I can tell you everything. This woman is probably a native New Yorker and didn't even know about its racist design."

Maadhini willed herself not to smile. Sadiya hated the possibility that someone could compete with her academically, could pull at the heartstrings of a teacher more than she could. More than once growing up, she'd been referred to in India as a "teacher's pet." Still, this Steinbeck woman, there was something about her...

"He destroyed whole city blocks to build a half-dozen bridges and over thirty expressways and parkways in the city." Wilson's words broke Maadhini from her air-headed thoughts. "As many as a quarter-million New Yorkers were displaced in the name of progress. He built overpasses that were too low to accommodate city buses that would've otherwise provided low-income neighborhoods with access to the beach. If you couldn't afford a car, you couldn't enjoy his city."

The whole class leaned in, rapt. Chad whistled. "Sounds like a powerful guy."

"Yes," Wilson agreed. "Probably the most powerful unelected American in the post-war era. But power always comes at a price."

"For those who don't wield the power," the Steinbeck woman added. "People who have power, they treat it like it's their birthright. It's nothing to them."

"Well said, Ms. Steinbeck."

"Like I said," Sadiya muttered. "Teacher's pet."

This time Maadhini couldn't stop herself from giggling. The sound drew the blonde woman's attention, and when their eyes locked, she found herself blushing and abruptly stopped.

"Well," Wilson said, "that's time. I'll see you again Thursday evening. Make sure you've read chapter one."

Maadhini's growling stomach agreed with the clock above the school building. It was already nearing eleven a.m. She'd always been a rabid eater, pecking at food throughout the day as her stomach seized control of her mind and body every few hours.

"No need for a watch," Sadiya teased. "I could just listen to your stomach to keep time."

Blushing, Maadhini said nothing. *I'll never have her lithe frame.* Another reason she'd wanted to come to America. Boys here didn't care about skinniness as much as they did back home.

Maadhini wandered in her own world, not realizing Sadiya had crossed the street to Washington Square Park until she called out.

"Earth to 'dhini!"

"Right!" Though her colleagues flowed around her, Maadhini still looked both ways before joining Sadiya. The red hand sign was on, after all.

New York City's smells changed with the seasons, with the hour of day, with the tempo of its people. Every day offered something different. Today, Maadhini detected cheese melting (pizza and quesadillas being prepared by nearby vendors) and perfumes reeking (who would set up a shop now, with the August humidity?). The soundtrack of the city flared with orders being called out and students gossiping about who was sleeping with whom and who'd gotten fat over the summer. Subconsciously, Maadhini brushed her hand over her ass as she stopped at the Shake Shack food truck. *Boys here like some 'junk in the trunk.' They've written songs about it.*

Standing in line, she thought about ordering the excellent ice cream they called "concrete" for some reason, then immediately wondered if she really needed the extra calories. She couldn't take her eyes off Sadiya's more proportional butt...

"Ugh, you can see the outline of my thong, can't you?" Sadiya asked, turning around.

How hard was I staring at her? "Um..."

"You know how humid this city gets in August," Sadiya explained. "Thongs mean no swamp ass. You should try them sometime."

Maadhini rolled her eyes. "That'd go over great when *Amma* does my laundry."

Sadiya offered a weak smile. "We both know you can do your own laundry. Why do you let your parents guilt you like this? You don't have to go home every weekend."

Maadhini guffawed as people ahead of them stared. "Oh, man. Thanks for that. I needed a good laugh." She continued, despite Sadiya's puzzled look. "It's easy for you to say, *yaar*. Hema Aunty and Sahit Uncle are still in Bangalore. You talk to them, what, once a week? Last year you only went home once for a couple weeks."

Sadiya brushed aside the comments like they were nothing. "Are you going home this weekend?"

"I don't want to," Maadhini said, "but how to avoid it?"

"I know it's different with your parents living here, but you could try being honest with them."

It was their turn in line. The man at the truck was waiting for Sadiya when Maadhini let out another loud laugh. "You should be a comedian," she said.

Turning away with a frown, Sadiya placed her order.

Maadhini continued. "Don't worry; I'll come up with something more believable than the truth."

The rest of the day passed without incident, save for the fact that their math class was filled with other Indians and East Asians.

"They're going to mess up the curve," Sadiya complained on their way back to Coral Tower that evening. Stepping off the M101 and opening the door into the building, Maadhini nodded in agreement.

"I can't believe our parents insisted on us taking the class." Sadiya walked past her. "We already fulfilled the gen-ed requirement!"

"Always need backup plan, *beta*," Maadhini teased, adopting an exaggerated Indian accent. "Maths always good in case architecture thing falls through."

"Tanvi Aunty's English isn't that bad," Sadiya said.

"No," Maadhini agreed, "but your *amma*'s is!"

Sadiya snorted in delight as the elevator arrived, and

Maadhini beamed at knowing she'd made her best friend laugh.

Even after a year of being on their own, neither of them knew how to cook, so they ended up ordering in for dinner.

"It's my parents' fault," Maadhini said as she tipped the delivery guy in cash and set the bhindi masala and malai kofta on their kitchen table. Sadiya nodded as she got out plates and doled out the rice. "When they send food home with me every other weekend, what do they expect?"

Sadiya laughed and a flutter ran up Maadhini's spine. "Don't worry," she said. "I'm hardly going to blab to Tanvi Aunty that we can't even cook rice."

"She'd buy us a rice cooker," Maadhini said. "Come to think of it, it's strange she hasn't given me one already."

Turning on the TV as they ate, the two saw a campaign ad for Barack Obama's re-election campaign. "How pathetic," Sadiya said.

"I thought you liked Obama," Maadhini said.

"Yes, definitely. This Romney guy is shifty AF."

"AF?"

Sadiya grinned. "As fuck."

Choking on her bhindi masala and rice, Maadhini struggled to hold back tears of laughter. "Sadiya!"

"What? I heard it in some rap song."

"Yeah, but do real people say it?"

"Who cares? Gimme some of yours, mine isn't spicy enough."

Letting Sadiya scoop out some of her bhindi, Maadhini repeated her question. "What's wrong with Obama?"

"He's got some good ideas, and it's cool he's Black…"

"But?"

"But he's a bit milquetoast."

Maadhini rolled her eyes again. "We know you scored high on your SATs. Stop bragging."

"No, I mean, he talks a big game, but his position on WP legalization is nonsensical. Establish a bi-partisan commission to examine the status quo and make recommendations? The entire history of this country has been an examination of the status quo! Not one Democrat in Washington is fighting for people who look like us."

"Neither of us are history majors, and we just got here last year," Maadhini said. "I'm sure he's given this a lot more thought than us, especially given his background."

"Whatever," Sadiya said. "Politics is boring, anyways."

They ate the rest of their meal in silence. Maadhini fidgeted. *Does Sadiya wish she was somewhere else? Should I have invited someone over, like that Steinbeck girl or something?* College was about finding themselves, Maadhini knew, but what if the cost was losing each other? Because unlike Sadiya, she didn't want to join a sorority. Or lie to her parents. Or wear a thong. *A thong looks like it hurts!* Struggling to chew with her mouth closed while a rerun of *Friends* played in the background, she was saved from delving deeper by a ringtone coming from her back pocket.

"Is that '*Chaiyya Chaiyya*?'" Sadiya laughed as Maadhini dropped her phone to the floor and had to bend over to pick it up.

Me and my fat ass. She hoped Sadiya wasn't staring the way she had that afternoon. "Instantly recognizable as home," Maadhini explained. She answered the call and put it on speaker. "Hi, *Amma*."

"Maadhini?" Tanvi shouted. As Maadhini pulled the phone away, Sadiya frowned. *One year in this country and she's forgotten that when your parents call, you have to pick up, no matter what?*

"*Amma*," Maadhini said, "you don't have to scream."

"You sound thin," Tanvi said, ignoring her.

"What exactly does that sound like?" That comment, at least, drew a smile from Sadiya.

"Don't be smart," Tanvi said. "Did you eat dinner?"

"Yes, *Amma*."

"None of this American-schmerican food, I hope. Something substantive."

"America has an obesity problem, *Amma*. All of their food is substantive."

"Filling and substantive are two different things," Tanvi snapped. "Please learn that. Now, where is Sadiya?"

"Hi, Aunty," Sadiya said. Scooting her chair closer to the phone, she sent a wave of scent into Maadhini's nose.

"When are you going to come home, *beta?*"

Sadiya's head bobbed, her American accent fading faster than Maadhini's romantic prospects. "Soon, Aunty, soon."

Maadhini smiled. Even after a lifetime, they both still "code switched" when speaking to their elders, adjusting behavior for the sake of someone else's comfort. It was why every time they spoke to their parents, they became "more Indian" in ways that even they couldn't really control.

"*Beta,* you do me one favor, okay?"

"Name it, Aunty."

"You take my Maadhini to the gym with you, yeah? You have such nice figure. We find her a good boy from good family this year, yeah?"

Forget a boy; the silence between them could have gotten Maadhini pregnant.

"It's important," Tanvi said, not waiting for a response. "Like her *appa* says, this college thing is about fun. She have fun."

"*Amma*, I'm right here," Maadhini complained, coming to her senses and pulling the phone to her ear as if that would show how upset she was.

"Yes, you are right there," Tanvi agreed. "That is problem. This weekend you don't come home."

"...what?"

Sadiya bit her lip, and her wide smile let Maadhini know she was doing her best not to laugh.

"You don't come home," Tanvi repeated. "Stay there, go to party, find boy."

Another silence filled the room.

"Just don't get pregnant. And don't do drugs. Or alcohol."

"...okay?"

"But you go have fun, you find boy."

"*Amma*...when did you become my pimp?"

"*Ayyo Rama!*"

Maadhini dropped the phone on the floor again at the shrieking from her *amma*. When she picked it up, the conversation had continued without her.

"...so I talk to your *appa* during lunch, and he say important for you to live 'full college experience' since we bring you here. He make sense. Just don't end up like that Serena girl."

"...Serena?"

"Oh, *kanne.*" She could hear the disappointment dripping from her *amma*'s lips. "You watch more TV, learn up on pop culture. Serena is big character on *Gossip Girl.*"

Maadhini spit out her bhindi, smearing their white table. Chuckling, Sadiya took a napkin from their food bag and cleaned it up.

"Important to know pop culture, stay hip."

"Yes, *Amma*," Maadhini said. "You are the first thing I think of when I think of a hip person."

"Thank you, *beta.*" Her mother hadn't caught her

sarcasm. "Okay, see you."

"That's all you called to say?" She wasn't sure whether to be relieved or annoyed; usually these calls lasted at least half an hour.

"You have schoolwork, I'm sure. And maybe Sadiya take you for blowjob."

Sadiya turned as white as a ghost and Maadhini dropped the phone yet again.

"Hello! Hello!" Her mom's voice flooded the room, as if she were physically in the apartment.

"Um, what did you say?" *She couldn't possibly have meant what I think she meant...*

"For your hair, to impress boys. Blowjob."

"Do you mean a blowout? You want me to get a blowout for my hair?"

"Ah, yes," Tanvi said. "Blowout."

Looking over at Sadiya, Maadhini knew she had to get off the phone ASAP or they were both going to lose it and have to explain. "You're right, *Amma*. I should go work on my hair. Okay, bye!"

The second the phone call ended, both friends busted out laughing. It lasted for minutes, until Maadhini's guts threatened to burst from the food and fun.

"Man," Sadiya said, "your mom is a riot."

"Could you imagine if she and Hema Aunty both lived in Jersey?"

"We'd have to bail them out of jail."

"Either that or bail out our *appas* for murdering them."

Sadiya snorted before excusing herself to go to the bathroom. She acted like it was a secret, but Maadhini knew she'd peed herself by laughing too hard. Knowing she could still do that, could bring such delight to her best friend, reassured her. *So what if we drift apart a little during college? We'll always find our way back to each other, because we're family.*

She cleaned up, and by the time she heard a flush and the run of the sink, the dishes were done.

"Thanks for cleaning up," Sadiya said.

"Thanks for keeping it together until my *amma* got off the phone."

"She was right about one thing. A blowjob *would* impress a boy."

Maadhini shoved her friend in jest; the touch of Sadiya's skin sparked her imagination.

"Hey," Sadiya said. "Don't listen to your *amma* so much."

"Huh?"

"What she said about the gym. It's nonsense. I'd kill for your curves."

Heat flooded Maadhini's cheeks as she looked at the floor, avoiding her best friend's eyes. "...thanks."

Once more, Maadhini lay in bed, listening to the recording of Bangalore traffic on her phone and trying to block out Sadiya's snoring.*Next time Amma brings up how perfect Sadiya is, I'm going to tell her she snores.* Turning over, she looked at her best friend. Even in sleep, Sadiya looked as peaceful and grand as a full moon.

Chapter Two

Maadhini hardly had time to think as Tuesday morning turned into Friday night. Besides Wilson's class, she had four others (only one of which Sadiya shared, and which they both dreaded—math). Sadiya mapped out their study schedule at the library, and it was as good an excuse as any for Maadhini to spend her nights there instead of talking to her mom about "blowjobs." She'd even discovered that academic libraries carried DVDs. She'd made it half an hour into James Cameron's *Avatar* before realizing it was very much not *Avatar: The Last Airbender.* When Sadiya came searching for her, curious why her "bathroom break" from studying together was taking so long, her friend was both annoyed and amused.

"One made a billion dollars," Sadiya explained. "The other is a cartoon."

"One is immensely enjoyable, has universal appeal, and makes you think without even realizing you're learning," Maadhini rebutted. "The other is about blue aliens."

"'Dhini." Looking bemused, Sadiya seized Maadhini's hand and dragged her back to the quiet room. "Come on, we've got to get through chapters two and three for Metropolitan Studies. I'm not scoring lower than that Steinbeck girl. We'll be here all night if you take off like that again."

That didn't sound so bad. Their different schedules and priorities had kept them apart since Monday night. When they were together, it was at the library under a cone of silence, with Sadiya staring at her notecards so hard Maadhini thought they would catch fire. Bored, looking around, she couldn't help but notice the lack of white people in the quiet room. Certainly, the Steinbeck girl was nowhere to be seen. *And why would she need to be here? She's got WP to focus her.* Letting out a sigh so loud it made her bangs flutter, she caught another glare from Sadiya that meant she should at least pretend to study, so she went back to reading about the racist history of highways.

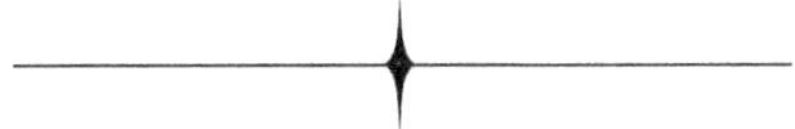

Maadhini slept in Saturday morning, waking only around ten thirty to the sound of their Keurig machine whirring and her best friend leaving the bathroom freshly showered and dressed.

"'Diya?" She could tell Sadiya had used some kind of almond-honey shampoo today. Stretching her hands over her head, she let out a moan and kicked her bed covers off.

Sadiya smirked at the sight of her *Spirited Away* pajamas. "What even is that, 'dhini?"

"Leave me alone, it's anime."

Rolling her eyes, Sadiya walked to the kitchen and added some milk and sugar to her coffee. "Tanvi Aunty would be horrified, but I know some guys think the cartoon thing is cute."

When Sadiya winked, Maadhini felt a gurgle in her stomach that could be hunger, nausea, or excitement. *Time to change the subject.* "Why are you up? Studying again? At this rate you'll have read the entire library by the end of the year."

"Don't think I haven't calculated how long that would take," Sadiya said. "Longer than a year, but I could finish everything before we graduate."

Maadhini howled with laughter as she entered the bathroom herself. Though she closed the door, she could still hear Sadiya as she brushed her teeth.

"Did an hour at the gym," Sadiya said. "Breakfast now. Then maybe I actually will get a blowout before tonight."

Spitting into the sink, Maadhini let the sink run. "What's tonight?"

"I can't hear you," Sadiya said, opening the door.

"'Diya!" Maadhini had to restrain herself from jumping back. "What if I'd been on the toilet?!"

"So? I've seen you poop before."

"When?!"

"Primary school. Field trip to a farm. You had to go on our walk back to the bus, but we were outside, so I positioned you between myself and a sleeping cow to hide your body."

Maadhini stared. "...I'd convinced myself that was a nightmare."

"Nope. It happened. I'm not sure what smelled worse, you or the cow."

Mortified, Maadhini came to her senses and shoved the door shut in Sadiya's face.

"I emptied my water bottle over your stinky ass!" Sadiya shouted gleefully through the wooden barrier.

Mother of God...

By the time Maadhini left the bathroom after her extended shower, Sadiya was gone. She found a note, written in the distinct penmanship that had won Sadiya an award in high school. *Decided to get a blowjob. Hope it impresses boys. Meeting up with some Tri-Delts for lunch before tonight. Back around 5.*

In her embarrassment, Maadhini had never asked Sadiya what was going on tonight. Whatever it was, it was clear she wasn't invited. *One week in and she's already got other friends?*

She wanted to call her parents, but they'd just worry. And maybe call her fat again. She flopped into a chair. *Why am I even here?* She'd fought so hard to come to NYU; *Appa* hadn't wanted to send his darling daughter abroad. The only reason *Amma* had advocated for her was because Sadiya was coming, too. And it wasn't just them. Her parents had uprooted their lives. She owed it to them to make it count. *I'm not giving any blowjobs tonight, but maybe a haircut wouldn't be a bad idea.*

Maadhini had splurged with her *appa*'s credit card, hoping he wouldn't mind, since apparently it was his idea to "have fun" in college. When Sadiya returned to their apartment, the smile on her face was as radiant as the sun.

"'Dhini!" She squealed. "What a cute bob! And you kept the bangs!"

"Thanks." Maadhini couldn't even keep her friend's gaze, instead looking at the ground.

"The boys are going to be all over you!"

Ignoring that, Maadhini remembered Sadiya's comments about tonight. "Um...where are you going?"

Looking Sadiya up and down, she noticed her friend had gotten work done today, as well. She had gotten the blowout; long hair rolled down past her shoulders like waves, streaks of blonde interspersed with her natural black color. A shopping bag was in her hands.

"I have a recruitment party tonight," Sadiya said. "Well, not so much a party as speed dating, ha. The Tri-Delts I met this afternoon prepped me; I should be a shoe-in."

"You're really going through with it?"

"Of course! 'Dhini, this is going to be a good thing, for both of us."

"And your parents?"

Dropping the bag, Sadiya adopted an Indian accent and waved her hands theatrically. "Why you want to do something so expensive? These white people, always making up clubs to take your money."

Maadhini couldn't help but laugh. "Was that Hema Aunty?"

"*Amma* just doesn't understand. But hey! I got you something." Sadiya took clothes out of her bag and started laying them on their beds. A floral camisole top rested on her bed, and a black crop top and matching skirt made its way to Maadhini's.

"For me?"

"It may not get you laid, but it's definitely gonna help."

Maybe I should get a job? The idea exited Maadhini's mind as quickly as it entered. Her *appa* would take it as a personal offense, as if his money wasn't enough.

"Earth to 'dhini..."

Shaking her head, Maadhini apologized for her airiness and thanked Sadiya. "But where am I going to go in this?"

"There's a college Dems party tonight; I heard that Steinbeck girl talking about it in class on Thursday."

Maadhini frowned. "You want me to spy on the Steinbeck girl for you?"

Sadiya grinned. "Maaaaybe."

"This top shows my tummy."

"Are we still on this? Guys here like curves. Come on, I even bought you something extra special. Look inside the bag."

Picking it up, Maadhini put her hand inside and retrieved a black thong. "'Diya!" She dropped it and the bag like they were contaminated.

"Don't worry, I'll do it with my laundry." Sadiya laughed. "You just go out tonight feeling your sexiest and see what happens."

Maadhini couldn't speak. After a few moments, Sadiya excused herself to the kitchen and returned with two shot glasses and a bottle of Bombay Sapphire.

"Here, this'll help."

Maadhini had only had a drink a handful of times, and only then on special occasions her parents had known about, like when she'd gotten accepted to NYU or on New Year's Eve.

"It's not like I'm offering you WP," Sadiya said. "Just do it, *yaar*."

Maadhini laughed before taking one of the glasses and letting Sadiya pour her a shot.

"To blowjobs," Sadiya said, clanking their glasses together.

"Or at least to fun," Maadhini agreed. Downing their shots in one go, they each changed into their new outfits before doing another round of shots and stepping into the night together.

Maadhini almost jumped when they walked out the doors of their complex. Sadiya's fingers were like silk as they grazed her arm and snatched her phone.

"Relax," Sadiya said, "I'm just putting in directions."

Before Maadhini was able to tell her the code to unlock it, Sadiya had already opened up Google Maps and was typing in the address.

"You know my password?"

"'Dhini, come on. What don't I know about you?"

Searching for a clever retort, Maadhini paused as a guy from one of her classes raced past them on a skateboard.

"S&M! I like it!" He whistled and disappeared before either of them could respond.

Maadhini scowled. "Was that guy checking us out?" *And is it okay that I'm more offended than flattered?*

"Take it as a compliment," Sadiya said. "Cat-calling isn't all bad."

Maybe not, she thought, *but that guy is gross.* "Why S&M?"

"It's a double entendre," Sadiya explained. "Our names are Sadiya and Maadhini, plus the fetish thing."

"Fetish thing?" She thought her face would turn into a tomato at how red it was getting.

Sadiya laughed as she handed back the phone, directions to Midtown typed in. "Like, blindfolding. Spanking. That kind of thing."

Maadhini stopped walking, causing an elderly woman behind them to bump into her.

"Sorry," Sadiya said on her behalf as the woman sneered at them before walking off.

"How do you know that? What exactly was this 'summer job?'"

Sadiya burst out laughing. "'Dhini, nothing like that. I just...we both read *Fifty Shades of Grey*."

Some of us still read it, I guess. Desperate to change the topic, Maadhini said she'd call a cab. "This place is kind of far off."

"Cool, cool." Sadiya gave her a hug before turning around. "I'm actually the other way. I just wanted to hang out with you a bit longer."

Maadhini smiled. *How can she be like that? Like we weren't just talking about crazy stuff?*

Sadiya called over her shoulder as she walked off. "Hey! I want to hear all the details when you're back!"

"Same!" Holding her hand out, Maadhini stepped into the street and waved a taxi down. Sliding in, she pulled at her thong as it wedged between her cheeks. *I hope no one saw that.*

Maadhini heard the nostalgic tunes of the '90s playing from a balcony above her as she stepped out of her cab in front of a building at East Fifty-Fourth and Fifth. Tipping the nice Pakistani driver who'd insisted on testing her Hindi (she'd passed, something she'd brag about to her parents at some point), she walked into the apartment complex and found that the doorman had no problem waving her up to the fourth floor.

"Ms. Steinbeck said to expect a young, diverse crowd."

Well, that's a weird thing to say. Maadhini hadn't known this was the woman's personal party and wondered if she was about to get kicked out. Knocking at the door, she was surprised when her classmate answered, wearing not a pantsuit but a red summer dress with white polka dots and a black belt.

"Hey, I know you from somewhere." Pulling Maadhini inside, the girl handed her a red Solo cup. When their arms touched, Maadhini noticed her host had on earrings with white flecks embedded in them. Closing her eyes for just a moment, Maadhini heard nails on a chalkboard.

The hairs on her arm stood upright. Opening her eyes, Maadhini's stomach turned as those earrings pulsed with energy.

Nothing's wrong with my stomach, she told herself. *It's just the alcohol.* She'd never heard of WP before coming to America, and believing in magic seemed silly, but what else could she call the substance? A physical manifestation of white supremacy? An unequivocal marker of the divisions that were ripping this country apart? It disgusted her to the point that she thought of leaving the party right away.

"It's Maadhini, right?"

The girl's voice pulled Maadhini back to the present, a lifesaver amidst the typhoons that governed her innermost thoughts. Maadhini nodded. "You know you can hear the music from outside?" She practically screamed to be heard.

"Really?" the girl asked. "That's cool." She hadn't let go of Maadhini's hand yet, pulling her toward a crowd on the balcony, stumbling as she walked. To access the outside, they had to go through what was obviously her bedroom. Though the A.C. was on, heat shot through Maadhini's face and downward.

"Who's the new girl, Rebecca?"

Ah, Rebecca. At least Maadhini wouldn't have to embarrass herself by asking the party's host for her name.

The East Asian woman from their Metropolitan Studies class had asked the question. The party was like a Model U.N. conference—white, Black, East Asian, South Asian, South American. People stood all around the apartment and balcony, drinking alcohol and listening to "If You Wanna Be My Lover" by the Spice Girls. A couple was dancing on a table inside. Maadhini worried they'd fall and break it.

One of Rebecca's friends popped Maadhini's thoughts like a bubble. "What are you?"

Maadhini turned. "...what?"

"You're dark, but I don't think you're Black. Are you, like, one of those Indians from Trinidad and Tobago?"

Maadhini mumbled her response. "No, I'm like one of those Indians from India."

"Vanessa!" Rebecca scolded. "That's not cool. Sorry about her. Want the tour?"

"God, yes." Worrying she'd answered too enthusiastically, Maadhini quieted as Rebecca said her goodbyes and led her by the hand through the bedroom again.

"This is where the magic happens." Rebecca waved at her room theatrically and Maadhini noticed a desk with plenty of open, scribbled-on notebooks. The TV in the corner had a DVD player with every season of *Gilmore Girls* next to it. The bedside table had a copy of some book, *The Power Broker.*

"It's all about Robert Moses," Rebecca explained, watching Maadhini take everything in. "You know, the racist guy Wilson talks about in class?"

"...oh...yeah."

"By the way, cute bob."

Feeling another rush of heat, Maadhini looked down at the floor and crossed her legs. "...thanks."

"You can drink that, you know." Rebecca pointed at Maadhini's untouched cup of beer. "I made sure no one roofied that one." After several moments of a blank stare in response, she clarified that she was kidding.

"Oh...I know," Maadhini said.

"So, where's your friend?"

Maadhini wished she was out on the balcony again, or right next to the speakers so she could feign deafness. "Um, she's at a sorority thing."

"Really? I wouldn't have taken her as the type."

Who was this woman? "And how would you know her type?"

"Easy, Maadhini." It was the first time she'd heard the woman say her name. Unlike every other white person she'd met, Rebecca knew the dh was a "th" sound instead of a hard D.

"You said my name right?" She hadn't meant for it to come out as a question.

"It's so disrespectful to mangle someone's name, don't you think?"

Maadhini's blank stare was apparently enough of an answer, since Rebecca just continued talking. "You know I didn't mean any offense about Sadiya." Again, she knew the "d" was really a "th." "It's just that she seems a lot like me. You know, super studious and confident. Those sororities are great for people who need focus in their lives, but people like us already have that."

People like us? Looking at the crowd around her, the dancing, the kissing, the drinking and joking, she wondered if she was making things harder on herself. Rebecca's earrings, the white glint in the rings and watches of some of her colleagues around the apartment, no one else minded them. Not even the other nonwhite people. She hadn't been here a half hour, but already that nauseous feeling was being replaced by something else. Belonging? Happiness?

Realizing she was actually excited to be here, she stared again at Rebecca's earrings. *Maybe magic isn't silly or hateful, but a tool to fill your deepest needs.* And her deepest need was to belong.

"You zone out on me?" Rebecca laughed, pulling Maadhini back to the present, saving her from the storms of her mind again. "Honestly, just take a drink. Loosen up."

Whether it was the fact that this woman could say her name right or the idea that taking a drink would give her an excuse to leave the bedroom for a refill, Maadhini gulped down her beer in one swig.

"Whoa." Rebecca laughed again.

The sound did things to Maadhini's stomach. *Or maybe that's the beer.*

"First time?" Rebecca said.

"Is it that obvious?"

"It's as cute as that skirt. Lemme get you a refill."

Biting her bottom lip, Maadhini said she wanted to get it herself. As they left, the dancing couple stepped off the table and eyed the bedroom.

"Hey!" Rebecca snapped her fingers and looked right at them. "Uh uh, take her to your own apartment, Steve."

Moving to the kitchen, she scooped out two Jell-O shots from a large silver tray and handed one to Maadhini. "To fun," Rebecca said.

Should I really just lighten up? Is it that easy? Watching the party go on around her, Maadhini resolved to just get out of her head. She downed the whole shot and reached for another one. "To fun." The second shot reeked just as strongly of vodka, but there was an air of freedom in the taste as well.

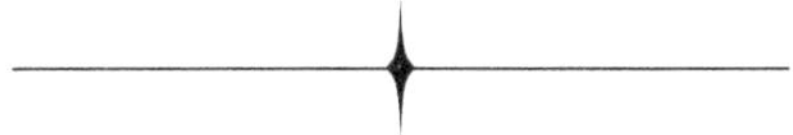

The sun had set and the party was over, yet Maadhini stayed behind to help clean up.

"Thanks again for staying," Rebecca said.

"It's only polite. Thanks for hosting." Maadhini stumbled from side to side as she threw half-full red Solo cups and empty Jell-O shots into a black Hefty bag. She wondered if this was the first time she'd been to a party without Sadiya. Rebecca's friends were cool, talking about things like WP legalization and the presidential election. They were topics she'd only heard her parents discuss. She wasn't even sure if she was allowed to have an opinion. Straining to reach a cup under the couch, Maadhini pressed her four-foot-eleven frame against the sticky floor. When she got up, her skirt suffered a small rip.

"That sucks, Maadhini." Rebecca's voice came from the kitchen, strong over the sound of running water. "I'll buy you another one."

"Oh, you don't have to..." Standing up, her bare hip came into view. She thought she saw Rebecca smile from across the room, but it must have been the light. "Just, um, do you have a sewing kit?"

Turning off the water, Rebecca came and waved her into the bedroom. "Maybe somewhere around here."

The room felt like a palace with just the two of them here now.

"You can actually see Trump Tower from the balcony," Rebecca said as she rummaged through her closet. "I want to book him later this year for a college Dems speech."

"Oh? You're the president, right?"

It was dark, but Rebecca's alabaster skin shone in the moonlight. Her blonde ponytail moved with her head, shifting back and forth with the speed of her voice. She'd talked all night about social justice and Barack Obama and how she wanted to travel to India someday and how she spoke Spanish and French and Italian. Most importantly, even though it was her party, she'd never left Maadhini's side. She'd made her feel like she was the most important person there.

"Why are you being so nice to me?"

Taking her head out of the closet, Rebecca turned.

"Are people usually not nice to you?"

Maadhini pondered the question for what was obviously way too long because eventually, Rebecca just laughed again. "Sorry, no sewing kit. How about another round of beers?"

Giggling, Maadhini asked if the Jell-O shots were all done.

As it turned out, there were three shots left.

"You take two," Rebecca said, downing one as they stood in the kitchen. She smiled when Maadhini finished both in a row.

"You know," Maadhini slurred, "I'm actually here to spy on you." The alcohol shot up through her skull as something else burrowed deep into her heart and further below. Walking toward the couch, she stumbled and fell onto it.

Rebecca let out another laugh.

That laugh is as infectious as the common cold, and yet how could anyone call it common?

"What?" Rebecca joined her on the couch, so close their legs were touching.

Before answering, Maadhini leaned in conspiratorially, placing her hand on Rebecca's bare thigh. "Sadiya said I should chill out for once, but she could've taken me with her to the Tri-Delt party. Why'd she send me here?"

Laughing again, Rebecca leaned in so that their heads were touching. She took Maadhini's hand in hers. "You two are close?"

"Inseparable!" Maadhini screamed the word, making a dramatic gesture to cover the whole room.

"Yeah?"

It was amazing how Maadhini could shift her voice back and forth from a pitch only dogs could hear to the baritone certain Indian women back home had. *Is this what having WP feels like? I can change my voice at will?* It took all her willpower not to brush her hands against Rebecca's earrings, to feel that rush of magic connect with her bare skin. She knew now, without a doubt, she had to at least try some WP. How could she have been so judgmental about something she hadn't even experienced?

Maadhini whispered into Rebecca's ear, using the opportunity to brush a hand against the woman's bare skin. Just being this close to the earrings was enough; she worried an actual touch would scald her. Speaking each word made her feel powerful and also like her head might split in two. "We grew up together in Bang-bang-Bangalore, India. Where honking is a national pastime and cow piss is sacred enough to bathe in."

Rebecca smiled again and her perfect teeth did things to Maadhini's nether regions. She smelled like Sadiya, like vanilla. Staring at her earrings, hearing the thrum of energy those inanimate objects exuded, Maadhini continued. "Best friends since primary school. It was our dream to come to the Big Apple!" Her whisper turned to a roar, and she pointed at the stack of apples on Rebecca's kitchen counter.

"Maybe we should get you something to eat," Rebecca suggested.

"No, don't go," Maadhini whined. She pulled Rebecca closer, though the woman hadn't actually gotten up. "Stay with me," she whispered.

"I'm not going anywhere." Rebecca adopted Maadhini's reverent tone.

"You're so nice," Maadhini said, and tears formed now at her eyes. She let out a sniffle, grabbing someone else's half-finished beer and gulping it down in an attempt to mask her reaction. Her mouth was wet, as were other parts of her body.

"I think you're really nice, too," Rebecca whispered. She placed her hand on Maadhini's thigh, now.

"Sadiya fits in." It was a statement of fact. As Maadhini said it, she craned her neck so that her face was now buried in Rebecca's shoulder. The woman stroked her hair as Maadhini confessed. "We both came here, but she found herself and I'm still searching. How fair is that?"

"Life isn't about fairness," Rebecca said. "It's about getting whatever you can by any means necessary, seizing happiness wherever and however you find it."

Maadhini couldn't hear the words, her whole self caught up in her first ever drunken soliloquy. "And you know what's even more messed up? My parents came with me."

"That's nice of them to shift their whole lives for you." Rebecca stroked Maadhini's hair. When the woman touched her ears, Maadhini's heart rang with a sound she thought was only reserved for pizza.

"Nice, huh?" Maadhini exhaled with such force that her bangs caught in her eyes. Rebecca brushed them aside and the look they exchanged caused both of them to sit upright.

"I can tell my *appa*, my dad, isn't happy here," Maadhini continued. "He could've stayed in India, like Sadiya's parents. But my *amma*, mom, wasn't having it. So now they're both here and I've got to make sure it was worth it."

"That's a lot of expectation," Rebecca cooed. Their legs were still touching, their hands were still touching. At any moment, Maadhini thought she might fall over and into the arms of this wonderful stranger.

"Expectations everywhere," Maadhini agreed. "Even Sadiya. She buys me this skirt and says 'go out! Have fun!'"

"Are you?" Rebecca leaned in as she whispered. Her earrings were so pretty, the thrum of them even louder than the music of the party.

How to resist? Did she even want to? Maybe not.

Maadhini leaned over and fell into Rebecca's arms. Within moments, she was on top of Rebecca, their tongues twisting together, Rebecca's hands moving over her torn skirt. Rebecca shifted, cupping her full ass and pushing her back as they made out, until Maadhini's head hit the upholstered couch arm. She noticed her position, spread-eagled on her back, and sat up before crossing her legs and scooting backward on the couch.

Rebecca pulled away. "Did I hurt you?"

Maadhini stared. *Holy shit! Holy shit! Holy shit! My first kiss is with a girl? A woman? A young lady?*

Okay, focus, Maadhini! What you call her isn't important!

What will my parents say?

What will Sadiya say?

Should I lie?

Am I gay?

Am I bi?

Would my parents think being bi was worse than being gay?

She heard her *amma*'s voice in her head. "Why you can't choose? Gay or straight. What this bi?"

"Am I that bad of a kisser?" Rebecca's voice was strong, unapologetic. It pierced through Maadhini's thoughts like they were made of gossamer, her words a lifesaver amidst the monsoons of Maadhini's mind. Her grin melted Maadhini's insides.

"You are the exact opposite of a bad kisser." Maadhini stated the words like a student trying to impress a teacher, hoping for reassurance as the noises within her stomach sorted each other out.

Please don't burp. She wished she hadn't drunk so much.

"Am I the first woman you've kissed?"

Woman. Okay, she calls herself a woman. "Um…you're the first human I've kissed." Maadhini adopted an Indian-style pose on the couch, now. Then she laughed to herself at the irony of that pose. Then she scolded herself for choosing the word "human," as if Rebecca might now be imagining her kissing a frog or a cow or something.

"That's cool," Rebecca said. She didn't scoff or tease.

Maybe in America. Maadhini's mind raced with the lies she could tell Sadiya and her parents, but for now she had to respond before Rebecca thought she was too much of a weirdo.

"Hey!" She was shouting again. "What did the shy pebble say?"

"…what?"

Maadhini ignored Rebecca's confused expression. "The shy pebble said: I wish I was a little bolder!"

Rebecca didn't laugh, but Maadhini did, so hard she did end up burping in the woman's face.

Shit. "I'm sorry," she said.

"It's okay." Rebecca's laugh convinced her that it really was okay, that she wasn't just saying that.

"So…um…are you my girlfriend now?" God, she was bad at this.

"From no kisses to a girlfriend in one night, huh?" Rebecca grinned again and Maadhini couldn't breathe. "Sure."

"Cool." Leaning in for another kiss, Maadhini grasped the nape of Rebecca's neck and as their lips touched, her fingers brushed against those white earrings. They sent shivers down her spine. Her entire life, she'd been the shy pebble. She'd never been around WP, and now the drug had transformed her life in just a few hours. It'd given her first ever unfiltered view of happiness. "Those earrings…" She'd been so foolish to scoff at what she didn't understand.

"Yeah," Rebecca said, breaking the kiss. "Those are flecks of WP. I don't always wear them, but my parents expect to see me out and about with them on. They knew I was having this party and I knew they'd want to see pictures, so I brought them out."

"Did they…did they have anything to do with the kiss…" *Fuck. Don't cry. Don't cry in front of your first girlfriend the first time you kiss her. Or whatever this is.*

Rebecca bit her lip. "WP can influence a person's mind at times, but we still don't know much about the science, especially how it affects people like you."

Ouch. It was true, there wasn't much research at all into the effects of WP on minorities. But the phrase "people like you" always stung.

"Anyways," Rebecca continued, "it can't create something that doesn't exist in the first place. It can only enhance or shrink existing emotions."

Maadhini sighed in relief. That meant she'd wanted to kiss Rebecca.

"So, Sadiya is your sister from another mister?"

Maadhini nodded, hoping the gesture conveyed her gratitude at the change in topic.

"I've got a sister, Claire."

"Are you close?" Rearranging herself, Maadhini sat on the couch right next to Rebecca. Their legs were stretched out on the wooden table, their toes touching.

"We talk a few times a month. So, yes, I guess?"

A few times a month counts as close? "Does she go here?"

"No," Rebecca said. "She's a year above us; she's a junior at Harvard."

"Wow."

"I guess? Legacy admissions are a bitch."

Who is this woman? Maadhini had heard about legacy admissions, of course, but it had been abstract. The way you hear about celebrity sightings in NYC but never happen upon one yourself. Sometimes she walked around New York just to try and see someone famous.

Focus. She smiled at Rebecca, hoping it wasn't her creepy smile. And hoping that the alcohol trying to force her eyelids closed wouldn't make her fall asleep before she got home.

"As Steinbecks, we grew up as princesses," Rebecca explained.

"I thought America didn't have royal families."

Rebecca giggled. "No, babe. It's just a figure of speech."

Babe? Her heart melted and she felt a warmth in places she hadn't yet mapped. *Am I about to pee myself?*

"We were Boston Brahmins, noted participants of high culture in the city. As famous as the Kennedy brothers in the 1950s."

Maadhini seized on an opportunity to impress this woman. "I'm a Brahmin, too."

"It's not really the same thing," Rebecca said, laughing.

Maadhini's head shrank, but when she tried to get up to go home, she found her lips on Rebecca's once again. The woman pulled at her like a magnet, refusing to let go. Now Rebecca was atop her and kissing her neck and moving her hands across her breasts like a violinist.

Can I be like this forever? Maadhini let the thought consume her, let it creep into every region of her body, and when it had left roots across her entire being she forced herself to see reason and get up. "It's getting late…" Out of breath, she half-hoped Rebecca would suggest she stay over because of the late hour.

"I get it," Rebecca said. "We don't have to rush. Call me tomorrow?"

"Okay." *She knows. How does she know?* Maadhini wasn't sure how she felt, but she knew she liked it. She knew it was worth fighting for. *And yet...*

She wondered what she'd tell her *amma* and *appa*.

Rebecca walked her to the door and offered to call an Uber.

"I'm okay," Maadhini said, "but thanks." As she stumbled into the elevator, she felt Rebecca's eyes on her. They were the last thing she saw before the doors closed.

Her stomach churned with butterflies. Rebecca's kiss had been better than pizza, better than the most decadent cake. *Is this what love feels like?* When the elevator doors opened and she walked out of the building, she saw a trash can at the corner of an intersection and ran toward it to throw up. *No, this is what too much vodka feels like.*

Wiping her mouth as neighbors looked on with disgust, she ran off into the night alone.

It was past midnight by the time Maadhini returned to the apartment. To her surprise, Sadiya was already there.

"What took you so long? Did you get laid, or what?" When Maadhini didn't answer immediately, her best friend squealed. "Shut! Up!"

"It wasn't totally like that," Maadhini said.

"God, I hate you. The Tri-Delt party was a total taco fest. It was just a bunch of catty biddies fighting for attention."

Maadhini was unable to stop smiling, until Sadiya shoved her and the two retreated to their respective beds.

"Come on, spill," Sadiya said.

The tastes of alcohol and vanilla still tingled on Maadhini's lips. A new sense of satisfaction and pride acted as a charger for her heart, rejuvenating her, sending her senses into overdrive. After so much time in the darkness, she couldn't wait to share with her best friend. Maybe, just maybe, Sadiya would even be jealous of her for once. There were notions of shame, of embarrassment, but they felt like grains of sand compared to the tapestry of joyful living that sat in front of her for the first time in her life.

"...'dhini? Are you still drunk?"

Shit. How long had she been gone this time? She was such an airhead. "Sorry?"

"Must have been some night," Sadiya said.

"'Diya...something wonderful has happened." She didn't know what else to call it.

"What's up?"

While Maadhini's brain had been frozen on the cab ride home, labeling the feeling churning inside her now calmed her locomotive heart. *Wonderful. It was wonderful.* "I'm wonderful."

"...good?"

"Great!" Uh oh. Her voice was changing again.

"Why are you being weird?"

Maadhini giggled. *Why* am *I being weird? Does being happy mean being super weird all the time? And you just realize the people you love also love you in spite of your weirdness?*

Or do they love you because of your weirdness?

Did Rebecca actually drug me?

How would I even know?

Thoughts raced through her system like bad tacos.

"'Dhini..." Sadiya held up a trashcan. "Do you need to puke?"

"I'm gay!" Maadhini blurted.

With the trashcan still held out, Sadiya looked like one of those three-year-olds down at Kips Bay who'd just witnessed a seagull fly off with their ice cream cone.

"At least...I think I'm gay," Maadhini added.

For a long moment, no one spoke. Then Sadiya's face adopted the widest grin Maadhini had ever seen. "I knew it!"

What?

"I always said to your *amma*, no guy is good enough for 'dhini. Whenever she worried about why you weren't dating or anything, I told her you just hadn't found a guy good enough, that she raised you to have high standards."

...what?

"'Dhini." Sadiya moved to Maadhini's bed, setting the trashcan down and sitting next to her. When their hands touched, scents of vanilla drifted up again and Maadhini couldn't help but grin as the memories of Rebecca flooded through her system.

"It's okay," Sadiya said. "I still love you."

Is this love? If so, then what do I feel for Rebecca? Maadhini didn't know much, but she was confident her feelings for Sadiya were *not* similar to the ones she had for Rebecca. When she closed her eyes, she saw Rebecca's blonde hair, felt her breath on her neck as she pinned her down on the couch and explored her body like an archeologist, mapping the most precious finds.

"I know that look."

Opening her eyes, Maadhini saw Sadiya still grinning. She watched as her best friend walked back to her bed, rummaged underneath, and returned with a brown package.

Maadhini narrowed her eyes.

"Open it."

Lifting the cover, Maadhini picked up what looked like a back massager. Halfway down the unit, it said, "Magic

Wand." "What is this?"

Sadiya laughed. "It's a vibrator."

Maadhini dropped it in shock.

"Careful!" Sadiya grabbed it from the ground, wrapping the white cord around it. "This was sixty bucks!"

"Oh my god! When did you get that?!"

"I bought it for you. I got mine last year."

"And you use it?! In this room when we're together?!"

Sadiya answered with a noncommittal shrug. "It's good for like, if you're nervous or can't fall asleep. You know how rough finals were for us."

Maadhini's voice jumped through pitches like a soprano singer training to break glass. "Is that what that noise was during finals week?! You told me it was cicadas?!"

Sheepishly, Sadiya admitted that cicadas only came once every seventeen years, but she came a lot more than that, thanks to her toy. "Anyways," she said, "do you want it? You look like you need it."

Maadhini felt like a tomato as she stared at the ground. "I, uh, don't do that often."

"What, masturbate? 'Dhini, you gotta know what makes you feel good so some guy isn't in charge of your pleasure."

Oh my god! How did this conversation get like this?!

"Er, I mean, some woman, I guess."

Flustered, Maadhini got up and walked to the kitchen. As she poured herself a glass of water, she heard Sadiya stepping behind her.

"Hey." Her friend's voice wasn't much higher than a whisper. "I just, I care about you. Tell me about this girl."

"She made me feel safe." Maadhini couldn't admit the truth directly, but staring at the sink made it bearable. "I feel better than ever and also like I might throw up."

"That's how it felt for me, too."

...what? "Sadiya, have you...?"

"No."

Maadhini avoided looking at Sadiya. She gulped down one glass and refilled it.

"His name was Mahesh."

"From high school?" Gulping down her second glass, Maadhini finally turned to face her friend. The water and the news of this guy sobered her up.

Sadiya shrugged. "It was lust, not love. Our parents never taught us the difference; society never taught us the difference."

Maadhini didn't say anything. She could see the tears welling in Sadiya's eyes. *She never told me, which means she never told anyone.*

"He broke my heart. That's why I followed you here."

She followed me? Sadiya always made it seem like NYU had been a joint dream.

"Don't get me wrong, I love New York. And I always wanted to come to America." As Sadiya stepped closer, Maadhini put the glass of water down and allowed herself to be led back to the bedroom, where the two sat on Sadiya's bed again. "But my first motivation was to get away from Mahesh."

"What happened?"

"He was...he was really controlling. He was so wonderful in the beginning, such a gentleman...but he was so controlling."

Maadhini frowned. That was the same word she'd used. *Wonderful.* But then again, that was in India. Mahesh didn't have WP. It really wasn't a similar situation.

"You don't have to tell me about the girl, but you should keep the toy." Wiping the tears from her eyes, Sadiya laughed again. "Learn the difference between love and lust."

Ignoring that, Maadhini returned to her bed, tucking the toy underneath it. "Good night, Sadiya."

As Sadiya turned off the light and got under the covers, she had one last thing to say. "...'dhini...thank you."

"For what?"

"For trusting me with the truth."

As Maadhini tried to think of what to say, Sadiya started snoring.

Maadhini lay in the dark thinking. She'd never had an orgasm. *Is Sadiya right? Should I really leave my first time to another person?*

Ignoring her friend's snores, she slid her pants off and slipped off her thong. It had a wet spot right at the gusset. Had she pissed herself and not realized it? Shrugging, she threw the underwear on the floor and returned to exploring her body. Moving a hand under her covers, she slid a finger inside and to her surprise, her body accepted it easily.

That didn't happen last time we tried this.

Great, I'm talking to my vagina now.

Is this normal?

For a brief moment, she thought about asking Sadiya the next morning, then decided she'd never discuss this with anyone. Closing her eyes, she began moving the finger in slow circles inside her. Her breath hitched. Squeezing her eyes closed, she pictured the night again.

Rebecca, wearing that red dress.

Rebecca, with that kind laugh.

Rebecca, her hands on my breasts, her lips pressing against mine.

Rebecca, who likes my fat ass.

Rebecca, who can pronounce my name properly.

Her mind told her to try inserting a second finger and

her body listened, inviting it inside. She moaned in pleasure as her hips began bucking against the mattress.

Wooh! Wooh! Wooh! The inconsistent, loud sirens and red and blue lights outside her window told her police vans were making their rounds on a Saturday night. The noise brought her back to Earth as she put her panties back on, flopping over and trying to find her phone recording to go to sleep.

So much for that. As she listened to the whirr of Bangalore traffic, squeezing her comforter just to feel something, she wondered if Rebecca was thinking about her, too.

Chapter Three

Maadhini tossed and turned through the night, eventually needing the trashcan Sadiya had left by her bed. Sadiya snored through it all. When Maadhini finally got up the next morning, the clock confirmed it was past noon. She was alone; Sadiya was at the library per her texts.

Stepping into the bathroom to shower, Maadhini embraced the hot water on her skin to purge the poison of last night. The moment she snapped the water off, her phone started singing *"Chaiyya Chaiyya."*

Shit. Her mom would want to know how last night went. *Thank god we don't have video on our phones.* Maadhini hadn't looked in a mirror, but she imagined she looked severely hung over. Her eyelids weighed as much as boulders. Her mind churned like a child shaking a snow globe as she remembered the touch of Rebecca's skin against her own. She smiled, realizing how happy she'd been last night, then bit her tongue to push the memory away so she wouldn't have to explain it to her mother. Even without video, her *amma* could sense emotions like a bloodhound.

"Hi, *Amma*!" She answered enthusiastically, pushing all other thoughts and feelings in her head aside.

"*Kanne,* you haven't called all day," Tanvi scolded. "I was about to go to bed."

"Sorry, *Amma*, I had studying this morning." *Which isn't a lie,* she told herself. She needed to read that Moses book for Wilson's class.

"*Thik hai, thik hai.*"

Sadiya arrived back at their apartment, saving Maadhini from having to fill the silence. Sadiya, all of five foot one and built like a twig, was struggling to carry two upholstered chairs into the apartment.

"Need help?" Maadhini said.

"What nonsense," Tanvi said. "Why would I need help?"

"Not you, *Amma*." Setting the phone down and turning it on speaker, Maadhini helped her friend bring in the furniture. "Sadiya found some chairs we're bringing in."

"Good, good."

Maadhini pictured her mom bobbing her head from side to side, nodding approvingly.

"Now you can entertain at ho…" Tanvi trailed off.

Sadiya grinned as she put the chairs down in their kitchen, moving the kitchen chairs to their living space. "At home, Aunty?"

"Don't be silly!" Tanvi snapped. "This is your home while you're here. So, you come next weekend."

Still grinning, Sadiya assented. "Yes, Aunty. I'll check my workload and get back to you. For sure we'll see each other in September."

"Where's *Appa*?" Maadhini cut in.

"That man!" Her *amma* was always upset with someone these days, but as long as it wasn't her, she enjoyed their talks, nonetheless.

"What did he do now?" Maadhini rolled her eyes as Sadiya patted her shoulder in thanks before heading to the kitchen to start brunch.

"Always out with friends, like some big shit."

Maadhini almost choked. "...do you mean big shot?"

"Yes, yes, your English better than mine," Tanvi said. "Not good to brag. I raise you better than that."

"*Amma.*" She whispered her next words, as if speaking them aloud would shatter any notion of them being true. "You have friends in Jersey, too, right? We picked Iselin because of all the other Indian families there."

"Tsk." Tanvi's dismissal was absolute. "Why I need friends? I have you and *Appa.*"

I could use another drink. The pressure was too much for anyone to bear, let alone Maadhini. *I can't be responsible for her happiness. I don't even want to be responsible for* my *happiness.*

"...*kanne?*"

The moment had to have lasted longer than acceptable. Maybe she should take something to help her focus. "Sorry, *Amma.*"

"You coming home this weekend, right?"

"Yes, *Amma.*"

"Good, good." Her mother already sounded more cheerful. Sadiya's nickname was 'diya, but as far as her mother was concerned, it was Maadhini who was the *diya*, the light that made life worth living.

I can never be anything but a good, dutiful daughter. She pictured telling Tanvi Kedilaya she was gay. If her mother was cooking, she'd burn herself in shock. For sure, there'd be yelling. And crying. Her parents would pull her from NYU. She imagined her *amma*'s voice: "New York City? What else could you be but gay in a city where everyone thinks they're gay?"

She pictured a whole life ruined after she'd insisted

on moving to America. After her parents had given up everything to make this dream come true. No, she'd keep this dream as long as she could, for *Amma* and *Appa.* She would be the dutiful daughter who studied hard to bottle prosperity and bring it to her parents.

"You so good," Tanvi said. "*Rhumba chamata.*"

"Thanks, *Amma.* I'll see you in a few days."

Hanging up the phone, Maadhini turned to see Sadiya breaking eggs over their skillet and empathized with the eggs. *If only it was that easy to break out of your shell.*

"Eggs and plenty of water," Sadiya said, handing her a plate as they sat on their new chairs. "The sisters told me about it."

"You got in!" Maadhini's voice jumped an octave. Sororities weren't her scene, but if her best friend wanted it, that was enough for her, and she welcomed the distraction.

"Not officially, but I should be getting a bid soon."

"That's so exciting." Taking a bottle of hot sauce out to drip over her scrambled eggs, Maadhini paused upon seeing Sadiya's bulging eyes. She dabbed at her lips with a napkin. "What? Do I have drool on my mouth?"

"We're seriously not going to talk about what happened last night?"

"...um..."

"'Dhini!"

"Okay," Maadhini said. "Maybe we should use our inside voices."

"You're gay! This is so exciting!"

"Is it?" *And am I?*

"The way you talked about that girl, that's how it's done in the movies."

"Hollywood or Bollywood?" Maadhini joked.

"Does it matter?"

"I don't even know if I'm gay, really," she said. "What

you said last night, about how love and lust can be confused..."

"Forget what I said." Ignoring the food, Sadiya took her by the hands and shifted them into their newly furnished living space. "You could have said this woman was hot or whatever, but you didn't. You said she made you feel safe. That's some real shit."

Neither of them spoke as Maadhini contemplated this. Closing her eyes, she realized Sadiya was right. She couldn't even picture Rebecca's body right now, not the specifics at least. All she saw was safety and compassion. But she couldn't be gay. Remembering her conversation with her *amma,* she searched for an explanation for her behavior. *I was drunk. And high on WP.* That had to be it. Because if it was something else, if it was her real, authentic self, then it would be the straw that broke the camel's back. Clear, undeniable evidence she was different, foreign to anyone and anything she'd ever know.

"It's terrifying," Sadiya said, breaking the silence. "I won't insult you by pretending to know what you're going through. But you owe it to yourself to take a chance on happiness."

And what do I owe to Amma *and* Appa? No, Rebecca could never be anything more to her than a youthful indiscretion.

"Your parents will understand," Sadiya said, reading her mind. "Even Krishna believed in gay rights."

Maadhini laughed. Her mom's favorite stories involved tales of that mischievous god's exploits. Growing up, they'd celebrated his birthday with plenty of sweets, then recounted tales of how he'd saved wives from abusive marriages by marrying them himself and then allowing them to do as they wished. "Yeah," Maadhini chuckled, "but Krishna never met a hole he didn't want to stick it in."

Sadiya slapped her hand in jest, and for a moment it was like they'd never left India. Here they were, two friends being real and enjoying life. *Can't I just find my happiness in this?*

Somehow, Maadhini doubted it.

Sadiya unpacked other purchases from her morning out as Maadhini did the dishes after brunch.

"You bought a whiteboard?"

Sadiya hoisted it above the chairs in their living space. "We needed something bigger to display both our schedules."

"The 'we' is doing a lot of work there."

"Oh, shut your face," Sadiya said. "You'll thank me after midterms. I can't believe they're in just five weeks."

As Maadhini soaped and scrubbed, she watched her friend reference her day planner and copy tasks onto the board. "You won't forget to schedule some fun on there, too, right?"

"Ha, ha," Sadiya said. "You laugh now, but proper planning prevents poor performance."

"...did you find that in an Etsy store?"

Ignoring the question, Sadiya finished writing. "You need to finish the reading for Wilson's class tomorrow."

"And what will you be doing?"

"I read this morning." Lacing up her shoes, Sadiya headed for the door. "I just came home to say hi and eat with you. I've got to meet the Tri-Delts for some follow-up stuff. Drink some more water and take a shower, but make sure you actually do some work, too. I'm gonna quiz you tonight."

"Okay, *Amma*." Maadhini threw a dish towel as Sadiya closed the door behind her.

Alone at last, she joked to herself.

Maadhini paced back and forth, unable to contain herself in that empty apartment while memories of Rebecca and those earrings bombarded her. Sadiya would have WP too, soon, after joining the Tri-Delts. And then what? The thought of answering that question was too much for Maadhini, prompting her to retreat to the dance studio in the basement of Coral Tower. It was designed for ballerinas in training, but she hoped it could serve as a refuge for her and her lost dance craft, as well.

Nothing is ever really lost, is it? She'd been such a devotee of Bharatanatyam once upon a time. Adopting the moves, feeling the music flow through her, she hoped it would give her focus. Help her figure out what she wanted.

Closing her eyes, she heard her mother, Sadiya, and Rebecca shout differing responses to a question only she could answer. Their voices swirled in her head, each adopting a different dance style and manifesting in the room.

Rebecca's legs flailed in an Irish jig.

Her mother jumped forth, suddenly adept at Bhangra.

Sadiya, clothed like a ballerina, pliéd and leapt through the air effortlessly. Everything Sadiya did was effortless.

If only my life was as easy.

Shaking the thoughts out of her head, she opened up YouTube on her phone and turned on some classical Karnatic music. Adopting the *sama* stance, head forward and feet facing front, she allowed herself to get lost in the music.

That much really was easy. The muscle memory from what had once been her escape from the pressures of living returned. She let the past control her body, finding comfort in its familiarity.

Aramandi. White people called it the half-sitting position. Spine erect, legs bent at an angle, toes pointing out diagonally.

Now *adavus.* She moved her hands and legs in all directions, as the music demanded. Arms right, legs bent. Arms left, straight as an arrow, toes pointed.

Abhinaya. Her facial expressions changed on command.

Happy.

Laughing.

Shocked.

Sad.

Ashamed.

She fell, launching her hands at the bar to keep from cracking her head on the wooden floor.

Ashamed. This emotion didn't pass as easily as the others, instead burrowing into her and refusing to let go.

She wept, underground and alone where no one could hear. She ugly-cried to her heart's content, and when nothing was left, she dug her nails into her hands to feel something as dangerous and painful and thrilling as she had last night. Through it all, the Karnatic music played, a reminder of the familial and cultural expectations she'd never escape.

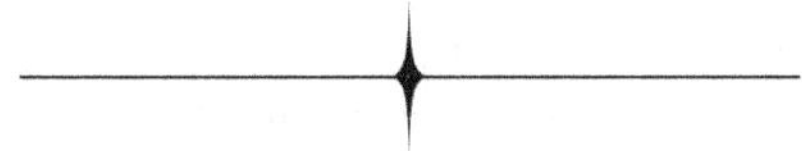

Maadhini composed herself well before Sadiya returned that night. As they watched a *Friends* re-run together ("The One With All the Thanksgivings"), she subconsciously brushed a hand over her tummy when Monica overheard Chandler calling her fat. Sadiya chose that moment to offer another taco filled with sour cream; biting the inside of her cheek, Maadhini declined.

By the time Monday came around, Maadhini had convinced herself Saturday had been nothing but a thrilling distraction. Thankfully, Professor Pryzbylewski had rescheduled class, so she didn't have to face Rebecca that morning. Sitting in the kitchen as Sadiya prepared lunch, she thought of what convincing lies she could tell Rebecca when they eventually did meet. *Maybe I'll just say it was a phase.*

After lunch, they'd have to head to their math class. "What even is Stochastic Calculus?" Maadhini asked as Sadiya tried (and failed) to make a proper dosa for them to eat before they left the apartment.

"Beats me," Sadiya said. As she set a broken one aside, she poured out more batter on their skillet.

"Just give it to me," Maadhini said. "I don't mind if it's a little broken."

"Sometimes broken tastes better," Sadiya said, handing her some milagai podi to go with it. The podi, AKA "gunpowder," transformed the meal from simple to exquisite. Mixing the spicy reddish powder with sunflower oil resulted in a dining experience that had to be vocalized.

"Mmmm," Maadhini sighed. "Screw pancakes and crepes, this is where it's at." Closing her eyes, relishing the food of her ancestors, she told herself to be content with what she had.

The Hudson bus line dropped Sadiya and Maadhini off at Broadway and Third. From there, it was just a short walk to the Courant Institute, where NYU's math department was centered.

"Were you just being polite when you said I was the opposite of a bad kisser?"

Oh no. Maadhini's heart sank. Turning, she found

Rebecca walking toward her. Rebecca, wearing an ocean-blue maxi dress. Rebecca, whose lips were redder and more dangerous than the gunpowder Maadhini had eaten with lunch. Rebecca, who wasn't supposed to appear in her life for another few days while Maadhini came up with a believable lie.

"Hang on," Sadiya said as the woman approached. "*Rebecca* was the girl you kissed?"

"There's no girl here; I'm a grown-ass woman, Sadiya," Rebecca said. "I guess I made a good impression, since she mentioned me."

Sadiya glared. "You've got the ass part right."

"Whoa, there," Maadhini said, putting her arms between the two. "No need for tempers."

The sneer on Sadiya's face confirmed that Maadhini should've just told the whole truth last night, but she knew she hadn't been in the right frame of mind.

Rebecca propped a hand on one hip. "You said you'd call."

"I wanted to talk in person," Maadhini lied. Turning to Sadiya, she begged for a few minutes alone.

"Five minutes," Sadiya said. "I'm not enduring a lecture on tardiness from Professor Chen for *her*."

As Sadiya walked off, Rebecca took Maadhini aside. "What's up? Why are you avoiding me?"

Maadhini flinched. She'd handled this so poorly. She knew by Sadiya's tone and pacing that her best friend was livid. Rebecca was justifiably mad at her, too. *When all else fails, try the truth.* "I cried yesterday," Maadhini said.

"So, I really am that bad of a kisser?"

"No!" Fuck. Her voice was doing that thing again. "No," she whispered. "You were great...but I'm not actually..."

"Good thing you're not in my creative writing class," Rebecca said, her tone flat.

Torn between wanting to end this relationship before it started and wanting to take Rebecca right then and there, it took all Maadhini's strength to not cry again. But when she dropped her eyes to the pavement, inviting it to suck her into the ground, Rebecca caught at her chin and tilted her face up.

"Hey," she said. "I get it. My family didn't sign on for some woman who couldn't carry on the family name. Dad was already bummed he got two daughters and no sons. Now he has to pin all his hopes on Claire."

Maadhini let out a deep sigh, one she hadn't known she'd been holding since that fateful night. Part of her longed for Rebecca to push her against the building next to them and kiss her. She desperately tried to shove the urge down.

"We can take our time," Rebecca said.

"You don't have to—"

Rebecca's voice rose. "I know I don't *have* to do anything. If I wasn't sure about this, I would've kicked you out of my apartment that night. You're worth waiting for."

That made Maadhini pause. "How do you know?"

"I don't," Rebecca said, her voice gentle as silk once again, "but I have faith."

Faith... Lost in her thoughts, Maadhini didn't even realize her phone was missing until Rebecca handed it back to her.

"I listed my number in your favorites. Now you don't have any excuses to not call." Turning away, Rebecca met Sadiya's stare. "And don't worry about Sadiya."

She pronounces her name correctly, too. Was there anything this woman couldn't do?

"I'll win her over," Rebecca said, "and then maybe I'll be allowed upstairs."

Maadhini blushed. Rebecca walked away, her dress

flowing behind her like a royal's gown as she crossed over an air vent from the subway below.

"You better text me soon," Rebecca said, looking over her shoulder with a smirk, "before I get distracted by something else."

Maadhini couldn't make eye contact when she returned to Sadiya's side. They walked silently to the math department, until finally Maadhini broke the silence. "I'm not even sure what's going on."

"You're happy, aren't you?"

"What even is happiness?"

"It would be so much easier to hate this," Sadiya said, "if you weren't so fucking happy."

Maadhini bit her lip. "Even if I was, what would I tell my parents? There's no future here."

"You talked to her quite a bit for there being no future."

Tears started to form in Maadhini's eyes before she blinked them away. "I don't know what I'm doing. Why did you even send me to that stupid party?"

Sadiya sighed. "I thought you'd have fun and get some good gossip on her."

"I did."

Sadiya's voice was flat. "Yeah?"

"She's super fun and she has a sister. There."

Sadiya looked hurt. "Was she your first kiss or just your first kiss with a woman?"

"That's...um...personal."

"I bought you a vibrator!"

Students stared as they stopped outside the Courant Institute doors.

"Keep your voice down," Maadhini hissed. "And I never asked you to do that...and I never used it."

"Whatever. It was your first kiss ever. You would've

told me if you'd kissed someone before."

That's true. Sadiya could always read her like a book.

"You're being emotional; I understand," Sadiya said, more gently this time. "I just don't want this to turn into a Mahesh situation."

"What do you mean?" Stepping through the door, guiding Sadiya toward their classroom, Maadhini squeezed her friend's arm. "'Diya…I didn't even *know* about Mahesh."

"Only *Amma* knew…" Sadiya's voice broke, and Maadhini's eyes found the floor as she let her best friend collect herself. "His kindness was toxic, eventually stripping me of my free will. Ordering food for me, laying out clothes for me to wear, telling me who I could and couldn't hang out with."

"I could've helped…"

"I didn't want you to have to share my pain."

Is Rebecca controlling me? Would I think I was gay if not for her? Maadhini heard Professor Chen calling roll, pulling her, at least temporarily, from that line of thinking.

"We're gonna be late," Sadiya whispered.

"It's never too late," Maadhini said. "Let's make a promise: we'll trust each other with the truth from now on."

"Yeah?" Sadiya sounded hopeful.

"Yeah," Maadhini said, steel in her voice. "You're my best friend."

"You're *my* best friend."

"That means I want to know everything from now on," Maadhini said. "The good, the bad, and the ugly. And I'll tell you everything, too."

"Deal."

"And give Rebecca a chance, for me, okay?" Maadhini wasn't sure if it'd end up like Sadiya and Mahesh, she wasn't sure what she'd tell her parents, but seeing Rebecca again had reopened whatever door she'd tried to shove closed.

Sadiya nodded before heading through the classroom door. "Okay."

"Who knows, you may end up liking her more than me."

Sadiya laughed as they sat down. "You're the gay one, not me."

Maadhini shuddered on the bus ride home. "Isn't being good at math supposed to be in my blood? I'll never pass Chen's midterm."

"You will if you keep to my study schedule," Sadiya said, adopting a sing-song voice that bugged Maadhini more than the smell of piss percolating in the back where they'd managed to find two seats.

"Stochastic Calculus got you in an annoyingly good mood?" she said. "What's up? I know you aren't any better at this dumb subject than I am."

Sadiya rolled her eyes. "God. We dishonor thousands of years of Indian mathematicians on a regular basis, don't we?"

As the bus drove through Ukrainian Village, Maadhini noticed an old man in front of her looking at his watch. The piece of jewelry was encrusted with WP. If she closed her eyes, she could hear its energy. She got the same lurch in her stomach that she'd had when first kissing Rebecca. Leaning closer, she found she wanted to touch the man's watch. She wanted it to give her the answer to how to navigate her parents and Rebecca and still come out ahead and happier than ever. WP could do that, right?

Sadiya grabbed Maadhini's arm. Maadhini opened her eyes, shocked by the sudden touch. She realized she'd risen from her seat, trying to lean over as if she could just ask the man for his watch.

"Maadhini? What the fuck are you doing?"

"That man," she pointed. She thought she was going to hurl again. "He's got WP on his watch."

"Were you going to ask him for it?"

Maadhini composed herself and sat back down.

Sadiya bit her lip. "I guess now's as good a time as any to tell you I've made a decision."

"What are you talking about?" Maadhini's legs shook like pistons. As the bus stopped to pick up a passenger, she didn't protest as Sadiya took her by the hands and brought them to a different section. Standing at the front next to some Hispanic kids, her stomach eased. *But I could handle it around Rebecca…*

"Hey," Sadiya said. "It's different for everyone."

Maadhini nodded blankly, her mind elsewhere. *Should I really have asked Rebecca to be my girlfriend the other night?* She'd been so confident of the decision at the time, but she'd never have a chance to see if things could work out if she couldn't handle the drug. If her parents would be against it, and she couldn't handle being around WP, was Rebecca worth fighting for?

Would she ever stop thinking herself in circles?

Sadiya's words saved Maadhini from her thoughts once again. "I got a text when we were in class. That's why I'm chipper."

"Yeah?"

"'Dhini…I'm getting a bid."

It took Maadhini a moment to process what Sadiya was talking about. "…a bid? You're gonna be a Tri-Delt?" Before Sadiya could answer, Maadhini squeezed her arm in delight. She knew the sorority handed out WP, that Sadiya would have some. She'd been right; getting in would help both of them. Sadiya could wear hers around the apartment, help Maadhini get used to being near it.

Maybe Rebecca isn't worth fighting for, but I am. If she got used to WP, if she and Rebecca were on even footing and she still wanted this, then she'd know it was worth protecting. She'd be able to handle her parents and have it all.

"…'dhini?"

Shit. Focus. "'Diya, that's so exciting!"

"No, I mean—" Sadiya started.

"What's the matter? This was what you wanted for so long, right?"

"I wanted to prove I could get in…"

As the bus arrived at their destination, the pair stepped out and walked to Coral Tower.

"You're in!" Maadhini said. "You'll get into all the cool parties; you'll get WP!"

"'Dhini…"

"What?" Maadhini's eyes narrowed. "What's the problem?"

"You were right, at the start of term, when you said your personal fulfillment shouldn't be dependent on some drug."

"What are you talking about?"

"Talking to you, thinking more about it, I changed my mind. I think what I really wanted was to show those dumb white girls I could compete at their level. That's all."

It was as if a gunshot ripped through the air. Maadhini felt its impact like a bee sting mixed with a ton of bricks to her head. *Who says no to WP? To that kind of power?* "So…you're not going to join the Tri-Delts?"

"It's so expensive, and really, what's the need?"

Always so easy for Sadiya. Perfect Sadiya, who doesn't need WP to fit in. Maadhini couldn't mask her disappointment. Opening the door to their building, taking the elevator up, she silently stared at her friend the whole time.

"…what?" Sadiya said. "Do I have a booger?"

Maadhini scoffed. "When you said this would be a good thing for both of us, I was dumb enough to hope that might actually be true."

"'Dhini…"

"I didn't believe you at the time, but now…you'd have WP."

"Keep your voice down," Sadiya said, opening the door. "It's a secret they dole it out to people like me. And anyways, I'd only get some at parties, under supervision."

"Still," Maadhini said, "that exposure."

"Why do you care all of a sudden?"

Maadhini's silence filled the gap forming between them as they entered their bedroom.

Sadiya's expression went flat. "This is about Rebecca."

"I think I like her."

"You think?"

"Yeah. Believe me, I wish I knew for sure. But for the time being, my thinking is going to have to be enough."

Sadiya's eyes dropped as Maadhini emphasized that last sentence with her finger before collapsing on her bed in shame.

"But you can't be around WP," Sadiya reasoned slowly, "and you're afraid that'll mess it up." She rubbed Maadhini's shoulders as the woman flopped on her mattress.

"You don't get it…"

"'Dhini…"

"No!" Maadhini's voice rose. She plunged her face into the pillow to avoid having to look Sadiya in the eyes.

Sadiya's weight lifted from the mattress. All Maadhini heard was the running of water in the kitchen and Sadiya's returning footsteps as she placed a glass of water by her bed.

"You don't get it," Maadhini repeated. Pulling her face out from her pillow, she looked at Sadiya with puffy eyes.

"What don't I get?" Sadiya whispered as she sat in the study chair next to Maadhini's bed.

"Am I gay? Am I bi? Am I just going through teenage angst? Is WP just making me *think* I'm gay? Or bi? And if I am gay, is Rebecca really the one or do I just think that because she's my first? And because she wears WP?" Maadhini's voice climbed an octave with each question.

"Slow down," Sadiya said.

"You're fair-skinned. I remember when we vacationed around Europe and Asia over school breaks growing up; people thought you were white." Maadhini continued, refusing to let Sadiya butt in until she'd had a chance to say her whole piece. "It's a kind of privilege I'll never know. Maybe it's why the drug doesn't affect you as much."

"...I didn't know." Sadiya pulled Maadhini into a hug. "What I do know is that you should explore this thing with Rebecca, as much as I hate it."

"Yeah?"

"Something's different about you, and you owe it to yourself to explore it."

Maadhini sighed in response, as if she was blowing out the weight of her ancestors.

"It's going to be okay," Sadiya said.

Maadhini didn't believe that, but what else was there for her but to have faith?

Just like every other night, Maadhini called her mom after brushing her teeth. Reassuring her for the fifth time that she'd come over that weekend, she finally hung up after half an hour.

"Whatever excuse you gave *Amma* to get out of coming home on Friday, it's not going to hold up for next weekend."

Wrapping herself in her pink comforter, Sadiya pulled out her day planner to check off the last things on her to-do list before going to bed. "Yeah, yeah, I'll come home then."

"And we're agreed, right? Neither of us is going to mention Rebecca."

"My lips are sealed," Sadiya said. "Your *amma* is going to get it out of you eventually, though."

"How's that?"

"You've got *lovestruck* written all over your face."

"I do not!"

"I can count on two hands the number of times your face lit up like the Rockefeller Center during freshman year."

"And?"

"And it's already done it more times than that this year, and it's hardly been a couple days." Laughing, Sadiya turned off the lights.

It's that obvious? Maadhini had to find a way to mask her emotions if that was true. Part of her wanted her parents to find out, to give them a chance to tell her who she really was because she didn't know herself. But a larger part of her knew they'd never understand. How could they understand when even she couldn't?

I'm not gay.

Maybe if she said it enough times, it would become okay. Eventually.

I'm not gay.

Her stomach gurgled as she pulled the now-clean trashcan by her bed close in case she needed it again.

In the three days since she'd run into Rebecca, Maadhini had thrown up four times, convinced herself twice that she wasn't gay because she had a crush on this guy in her Race and the Neoliberal Metropolis class, and texted Rebecca exactly zero times. In Approaches to Metropolitan Studies yet again, she closed her eyes and took a seat next to Sadiya. She bounced back and forth between wishing Rebecca would show up and hoping she wouldn't.

"'Dhini, you need another trashcan?"

Opening her eyes to wave Sadiya off, Maadhini saw Rebecca enter the classroom. *Sundresses should be illegal.* Rebecca's legs shone like temple columns, and when she sat next to them her perfume enveloped Maadhini like a noose.

"Hey," Rebecca said.

"Hi." Maadhini was spared any further awkwardness by Wilson's appearance.

"Folks," he said, "put your books away and leave a space between each other. Pop quiz time."

As Sadiya fretted at the unplanned event, Maadhini placed herself further away from her friend and Rebecca. *I've never been more grateful for a pop quiz in my life.*

Maadhini wasn't even sure she'd answered all the questions. Handing in her quiz, she took her seat and tried to focus on Wilson's lecture. The whole time, her eyes never left Rebecca's ears. A feral longing grabbed her heart and worked its way down below her waist.

It was a choice to wear those earrings. As if reading her thoughts, Wilson chose that moment to address Rebecca's fashion choices.

"They're nice earrings, Rebecca, and you didn't know, but I don't allow WP on test days."

"It won't happen again, Wilson." Rebecca smiled and

Maadhini's stomach growled.

"But let this be an official statement," Wilson said. "Anyone caught wearing WP during the midterm in a few weeks will be given an F. We don't believe in unfair advantages in this class."

Chad snickered from the back of the class. "Gravity exists whether you believe in it or not."

Whether Wilson heard, he carried on with the class as if he hadn't.

After class, Sadiya stopped Maadhini when she tried to hurry out of the room. Thinking about those earrings, recalling that feral instinct they lit inside her, she felt as though she couldn't get home fast enough. *See?* she announced to herself. *I'm not gay. I'm just horny.* Maadhini frowned as Sadiya blocked the door. "What?"

"'Dhini, stop avoiding your happiness."

Maadhini narrowed her eyes. "Excuse me?"

"I said I'd make an effort, right? This is me trying," Sadiya said. "I don't want to see you again for a few hours, at least. Take Rebecca out to eat or something."

Behind Sadiya, Rebecca idled by the door, playing on her phone. Maadhini glanced away. "She looks busy..."

"Anyone with a brain can see she's stalling to leave. Do you have a brain, Maadhini?"

"...yes."

"Then *jao*," Sadiya snapped, waving her hand.

Maadhini knew she shouldn't need Sadiya's permission to explore whatever this was, but she grabbed it, nonetheless. Sadiya's blessing was only second to her parents'. *Maybe I don't need to be ashamed to take what I want.* Walking to Rebecca, engaging in some bullshit small talk, Maadhini embraced that animalistic longing inside her and left Sadiya behind.

Holding Rebecca's hand as they left the College of Arts and Sciences together, Maadhini noticed Chad watching them.

"Mmmm," he sighed, "check out Becca rubbing the mad genie."

Rebecca rolled her eyes as Maadhini turned red.

"Get it?" Chad leered. "Because Maadhini sounds like mad genie."

"Your insults aren't even clever, Chad," Rebecca said. "And it's Maa-thin-ee, not Mad-din-ee."

Maadhini had been feigning fascination with the color of the tiles below them, but now she lifted her gaze to meet Chad's. "Shove off, mouth breather."

"...what?" Confused, he unlocked his skateboard from the bike rack outside the building and left.

Maadhini squealed in delight. "Where did *that* come from?"

Rebecca grinned. "You're adjusting to being around my WP."

Staring at the earrings again, Maadhini held a hand over her mouth. "What?"

"You didn't text, you didn't call. But you were so into me at the apartment."

"Rebecca..."

"And then it hit me, duh! I gotta level the playing field. Help you out a little bit."

"You wore the earrings...for me?"

Rebecca nodded and Maadhini's smile was brighter than the sun.

"Confidence, calmness, focus, it's all right there in front of you," Rebecca said. "You just have to be able to recognize it and seize it. That's what WP does. I've been around it so long I forgot why we treasure it in the first place. It seems so obvious to me, but not everyone has the right stuff."

"The right stuff?" *Don't white people need to get that confidence, that focus from the drug, too? It's not like they're born with it...*

"Don't worry," Rebecca said. "Stick with me long enough and it'll rub off on you. In just this short time, you were able to tell Chad to piss off."

As they waited for the bus, Rebecca kissed her and all of Maadhini's doubts were shoved aside by the woman's tongue.

"So...dinner?" Swiping her card to pay her fare, Maadhini sat at the front of the bus with her girlfriend.

The women found a Mediterranean food truck outside Coral Tower. After enjoying roasted chickpea gyros (though Rebecca said Maadhini would love beef if she gave it a try), they walked through Union Square Park and visited a Barnes & Noble.

"How do you find time to read for fun?"

"You have to make it a priority," Rebecca said. As they walked around the bookstore, past a section called "LGBT Fiction," Maadhini noticed a high-school aged girl browsing the shelves. Maadhini smiled, watching the girl read something. Just then, a woman who must've been the girl's mother ripped the book from the girl's hands and shoved it back on the shelf before dragging them both past Maadhini and Rebecca.

She felt the blood drain from her cheeks. *That would be me and* Amma.

"It's so sad seeing that kind of intolerance in the 21st century," Rebecca said, eyeing the mom with a judgy stare until both mother and daughter left the store. Taking

Maadhini's hand, she walked them into the same section, handing her the book the girl had been holding: *The Price of Salt.* "This is a cult classic among lesbians."

Maadhini shot a panicked glance around. "Rebecca!" *Will I ever be able to control my voice around her?*

"What? No one knows, do they? No one except me and Sadiya?"

Eyes to the ground, Maadhini handed the book back and bolted from the store, ashamed of how happy she was and ashamed for feeling ashamed.

"Will you slow down?"

Maadhini was approaching Coral Tower when Rebecca grabbed her arm and swung her so that their eyes met. "Jesus Christ, just stop."

"What?!" Maadhini snapped.

"I know you're into me. Just let yourself be happy."

"I can't!"

"Why not?"

"Because I'm not like you!"

Rebecca gritted her teeth. "Yeah, I get that. I'm white; you're so dark you could pass as Black. I'm rich; I guess your family isn't. I'm skinny; you've got curves I want to sink my teeth into."

"You're forgetting the most important part of this!" Maadhini was furious, and yet the woman's voice woke things hidden deep within her soul.

"Yeah? What's that?"

"You have WP!"

A silence stretched on, and as onlookers stared at them, Rebecca took her to the side of the building. "I want to try and make this work. Who convinced you that you weren't worth fighting for?"

"...no one had to convince me..."

Their voices were whispers now, as if they both had secrets to keep from the world.

Rebecca sighed. "What's something you do just for you?"

"I dance..."

"Show me."

Maadhini wavered, but eventually took Rebecca to the basement of her building, to the place that had been her refuge freshman year. She looked at where she'd tripped last time and promised herself, she wouldn't let one stumble stop her from doing what she loved.

Sama stance. Pulling up some music on her phone, she tried the same routine as before. As her hands and feet swayed, as her face changed, Rebecca giggled.

"What's wrong?" Maadhini stopped her routine.

"It's pretty," Rebecca said. Her words were nice, but her tone rested on the edge of laughter.

"But?"

"What about me scares you?" Rebecca said.

"What do you mean?"

"You're still holding something back. I can tell."

This was so dumb. I shouldn't have let her inside. Tears welled in Maadhini's eyes, and it took all her strength to keep them at bay. "It's not you; it's me."

"Hey," Rebecca said. "It's just you and me; you can let your guard down. You deserve to be happy. Let me show you."

And when her girlfriend hugged her, Maadhini let the walls come down. She cried so hard her whole body heaved, and through it all Rebecca ran her perfect fingers down her cheeks and across her blouse. Rebecca refused to let go, smelling her hair and resting her hands on her waist.

"I told you I wanted to sink my teeth in these curves..."

Maybe she was high on the proximity to WP, or maybe she'd gained some post-cry clarity, but before Maadhini knew what she was doing she shoved Rebecca against the bar ballerinas used. Their tongues danced the tarantella, and she didn't protest when Rebecca threw her shirt aside and cupped her breasts over her bra. Now Rebecca was on her like a predator, cornering her small body and pushing it to the ground. On top, Rebecca kissed her neck and plunged a hand beneath her panties. Maadhini heard a wetness and gasped as their two bodies joined.

"'Dhini...'"

Maadhini didn't stop Rebecca from calling her by that nickname. She'd never be able to stop Rebecca from doing anything she wanted—

"Hey!" A security guard at the front door brought both women to their senses.

Maadhini leapt to her feet, grabbing her blouse from the ground as Rebecca stammered and blushed. As the pair talked, Maadhini escaped out the side door.

In the twenty-four hours since she'd last seen Rebecca, Maadhini hadn't said anything to Sadiya about the dance studio. What could she say? Her thoughts and feelings bounced against the walls of the only world she'd ever known, her passions sunk by the weight of her heritage. Was it Rebecca or was it the drug that made her feel more alive and happier than she'd ever been? Was that feeling enough to sacrifice the dream her parents had built for her? She didn't have an answer yet. And so, when her friend had asked what happened, Maadhini told her they'd had dinner and kissed. *Not a lie,* she told herself.

"Your mom's okay with you going to Jersey tomorrow morning instead of tonight?" Sadiya whispered as they sat in the library together.

"I let her know we were studying."

"Shh!" Someone shushed them. They were in the quiet area, but this was the first time someone was enforcing that rule.

"Oh, suck it," Sadiya responded. "I guess we're done studying. Pizza and *Gilmore Girls* reruns?"

"Only if it's season one," Maadhini said. "Max is so dreamy."

"Max?"

"Who cares about Rory? Lorelai's the one with the carefree lifestyle and glamorous sex life. She should've ended up with Max instead of Luke."

Sadiya laughed as they exited the building together. Outside, Maadhini heard a familiar voice. "What gives, 'dhini?"

Oh no. Turning, she saw Rebecca's eyes narrowed like pointing guns.

"Excuse me?" Sadiya put herself between the two lovers.

"I need to talk to her," Rebecca said, pointing at Maadhini.

Maadhini's mouth went dry. *Those earrings...*

"That's a pet name for me to use," Sadiya said. "Just me."

"Well," Rebecca said, her pearly whites gleaming, "college is all about adjusting, isn't it?"

"'Diya, give me a minute, huh?" Maadhini felt Sadiya's eyes boring through her skull as she and Rebecca walked off. "What is this?"

"Are you ever gonna use that number I gave you?"

"You know you can't rush me," Maadhini hissed.

"I know you're hot and you want me."

Maadhini searched for words and found none.

"Look," Rebecca said, "I'm done chasing you after

tonight. You can come back to my place, and we can try and figure this out, or that's it."

As Rebecca turned to walk away, Maadhini closed her eyes and saw a future without Rebecca in it. A future where she'd be cold and trapped and confused forever. Every single time she'd been around those earrings, she'd experienced earth-shattering clarity around her wants and needs. A feeling she wasn't familiar with, and so she'd rejected it. She still wasn't certain, but she knew now that a risk had to be taken. Opening her eyes, seeing Rebecca's earrings glint in the moonlight, she acted without hesitation. Grabbing Rebecca by the arm, she swung the woman around and locked lips with her. Having WP may be illegal, but having Rebecca wasn't. "I'll be there when you get home."

Sadiya's sneer could have its own Twitter account. Maadhini took her time returning to her best friend, as if she could delay the inevitable.

"Why does she call you 'dhini?"

"I don't know." Maadhini blushed. "I'll tell her to stop."

"What happened last night? Why's she so obsessed with you?"

"I don't know. She said that's it if I don't go after her tonight."

"What are you going to do?"

"Sadiya..." Maadhini felt her face fall as she whispered her friend's name like a prayer.

"What!"

People around them stared at the outburst.

"I have to...I have to give this a chance." Raising her head, she met Sadiya's eyes. She'd known true happiness each time she'd brushed against Rebecca's earrings and kissed those lips and felt those hands on her body. Whether that feeling was tied to WP or to Rebecca herself, what did it matter?

"...okay."

Maadhini paused. "Okay?"

"I'm proud of you for realizing this is worth a couple fights with your parents. I said I'd be supportive, and I meant it. You deserve happiness."

Tears prickled at Maadhini's eyes. "I don't deserve you."

"Ain't that the truth." Sadiya smiled and relief swept over Maadhini.

"But tell her to stop calling you 'dhini. That's all I ask."

"Right away. Tonight."

"And tell me the truth about what happens tonight."

"You'll hear all the details," Maadhini said.

"Promise?"

"Promise."

Rebecca's door swung open the moment Maadhini knocked. Inside the apartment, sirens blared through the open windows.

"I wasn't sure you'd come," Rebecca said.

"I want to be happy. For once in my life."

"And what about the rest of your world?"

"I don't know." As Maadhini stepped past the threshold, Rebecca's smile hardened. "I don't know, Rebecca. That'll have to be enough. This is all new to me."

"...I guess I can understand that."

"But I know I'm worth fighting for." Maadhini lifted her chin. "You and Sadiya taught me that."

Rebecca offered her a drink, but Maadhini waved off the suggestion. "I shouldn't need alcohol to enjoy you." As she spoke, she noticed Rebecca's earrings.

"There's nothing wrong with a little enhancement." Rebecca pulled Maadhini's head to hers. Their lips brushed, and the wailing of cop cars outside transformed into the sirens of myth and wonder in Maadhini's ears.

"It's my first time..." Maadhini whispered.

Rebecca unbuttoned both their shirts, throwing the garments onto the couch. Navigating their bodies to her bedroom, she tossed Maadhini's skirt aside and brushed her fingers across a black thong. "I'll be gentle."

Rebecca's breath made Maadhini's leg hair stand on end. She wished she'd shaved. "I thought this wouldn't happen...but it makes me feel free."

Pushing her against a wall, Rebecca kissed Maadhini from her chest to her hip before slipping her panties down and helping her step out of them.

"You can be free within these four walls, if nowhere else."

Free...

Maadhini sighed as Rebecca's mouth moved between her legs. Closing her eyes, she felt her legs buckle after just a few moments, and let Rebecca move her to the bed, where she allowed herself to get lost between bedsheets and bliss.

Chapter Four

The competing thoughts within Maadhini's head rattled inside her with the ferocity of the Amtrak train taking her and Sadiya home to Iselin, New Jersey.

Do I tell them tonight?

Is Diwali the right time?

Is there such a thing as the right time?

I wonder if Rebecca talks about me to her parents?

Almost two months had passed since she'd given her virginity to Rebecca. In that time, Maadhini had learned to draw upon Rebecca's strength to make her opinion heard, speaking up in class more and even pushing back if Sadiya wanted to buy something for the apartment she didn't like. Even being around other people wearing WP didn't affect her as much anymore. What had once been the sound of nails on a chalkboard, a nauseous pit of despair in her stomach, now resembled the humming of cicadas. Annoying, but simply part of her background once she accepted it as reality.

"'Dhini?" Sadiya asked. The pair sat across from one another, Sadiya's eyes peering over her day planner as she reviewed their midterm schedule.

"Sorry, what were you saying?"

"We've got Wilson's midterm next week. Does my study schedule sound all right to you?"

"Oh...yeah."

Sadiya displayed a color-coded study schedule, but Maadhini simply nodded.

Sadiya raised an eyebrow. "What's got you more engrossed in your thoughts than usual?"

Maadhini sighed. "Sorry, just preoccupied. Thinking about Rebecca again."

"I'm surprised at her resilience."

"What do you mean by that?"

Sadiya snorted. "You told me all about your sexcapades that night, but it's October and nothing's happened since, and she's still happy to take things slow."

Maadhini's brow furrowed as she bit her bottom lip. "I don't know if she's happy..."

Rebecca was so good for her, she knew that. But the intensity of their relationship scared her. After the night she'd lost her virginity, she'd said she wanted to take things slow, and Rebecca had respected her wishes. *She hears me.*

Rebecca had even offered to stop wearing her earrings, but Maadhini insisted on them. *It's good to push my boundaries...* Plus, Rebecca didn't mind when Maadhini left for weekends with her parents. She didn't mind that they held hands and sometimes kissed but hadn't been naked together since that night. *Or maybe she does mind and just isn't saying anything about it yet...*

"Earth to 'dhini..."

Again? "Sorry, what?"

"Our stop is in a couple minutes. We gotta get our stuff."

Getting up, Maadhini got on her tiptoes to retrieve her suitcase. In addition to insisting on doing her laundry, her *amma* had demanded she bring home a handful of items from a few shops in the city because "better quality than Jersey."

"Work it, girl." A boy around their age wolf-whistled as Maadhini's shirt rode up, exposing her stomach and the fabric of her underwear.

"Ignore him." Sadiya took the suitcase and put herself between Maadhini and the rude boy.

"Hey, where you going? You want to party?"

Maadhini didn't look back as they walked into the adjacent chamber where they would disembark upon the train's arrival.

"You look hot," Sadiya said. "I'm sure Rebecca agrees."

"It's like you're either chubby and they make fun of you for that, or you start working out and you get stretch marks they tease you for..." Maadhini's voice quivered as she ran her fingers over the permanent reminders impressed within her skin.

"I know," Sadiya nodded. "Sometimes it seems like there's no winning for women like us."

When the train stopped, Maadhini was the first passenger to exit. Helping Sadiya and the luggage down, she scouted the station for her *appa*. "I hope he hasn't been out drinking."

"He found a bar that carries Kingfisher?" Sadiya asked.

"Oh, yeah, he's made so many Indian friends from work. You'll meet most of them tomorrow at the party. Sorry in advance when they hit on you."

Sadiya laughed. "Pervy, old Indian men hitting on you is basically a rite of passage."

Not for me.
Wait.
Why am I sad about that??

Shaking the thoughts away, she grasped Sadiya's hand. "Seriously, thanks for coming this weekend."

"Are you kidding me? My *amma* would disown me if I skipped Diwali with the Kedilaya family."

"How is Hema Aunty, anyway?" Maadhini said.

"She wishes I called more. She threatens to move here once a month. Same old, same old."

"And Sahit Uncle?"

"He drinks too much. He makes the same bad jokes every time we talk. Same old, same old."

"Yeah…" *But even for a culture as old as India, things can change…right?* Fearing her thoughts, yet wanting to speak them into being, Maadhini changed the subject. "*Amma* asked for your help specifically to get things ready tomorrow morning."

"Oh yeah?"

Adopting an over-the-top accent, Maadhini continued. "*Kanne,* we all have our own strengths and weaknesses."

Sadiya raised a brow. "And?"

Maadhini grumbled. "And I guess cooking isn't one of mine. She's put me on cleanup duty after the party and basic house maintenance beforehand."

"Lucky for you," Sadiya said. "Cooking the food and desserts is tough enough, but the real pain in the ass is drawing the *kolam.*"

"I've seen *Amma* draw it on the front porch a thousand times," Maadhini said. "I just wish she trusted me."

"Well, trust is a two-way street."

The hair on Maadhini's neck stood up. "What's that supposed to mean?"

"'Dhini, just tell them. They'll be fine with it."

Maadhini just stared. "You know, *Amma* is going extra crazy about Diwali this year because she has friends here now."

Sadiya looked confused. "...that's...nice..."

There was venom on Maadhini's lips when she spoke. "*Amma* tells me about them once in a while, about one in particular. Jayanthi Aunty. See, she has a daughter that just came out as gay."

"Oh!" Sadiya's eyes widened. "That's...good?"

"I guess it's good if you want to be kicked out of the family." Maadhini hissed like a snake, her tone just as deadly. "Jayanthi Aunty asked for the others to pray for her, so *Amma* does, every night."

Sadiya's expression softened. "'Dhini..."

Blinking back tears, Maadhini snorted loudly, forcing calmness back into her throat. "You don't get it, so please don't act like you do. If and when I decide to share this part of my life with them, it'll be on my schedule. Not yours. Got it?"

Sadiya nodded silently as a red Toyota RAV4 parked in front of them and Vir Kedilaya got out to help them load their bags in the trunk.

It's ironic that such a colorful society is so conservative, Maadhini thought.

Saturday turned into night, and by the time Jayanthi Aunty, and Varsha Aunty, and all the other aunties and uncles arrived at the Kedilayas' split-level house, the *kolam* had been sketched on the front porch with chalk. The sambar and idlis and rice had been cooked. *Amma* had kept Sadiya in the kitchen all afternoon as they'd set trays and trays of gulab jamun and carrot halwa next to the chikki (peanut brittle) and almond burfee.

Pity the one Indian here who'll inevitably go into

anaphylactic shock before the end of the night. For a brief moment, Maadhini considered whether someone dying would make it easier to come out to her parents.

"I may be gay, but at least I didn't kill anyone."

That was stupid. She could hear her *amma's* response.

"So what, people die all the time. India, over one billion people. Me? Only one chance at a grandchild."

"Maadhini, have you been working out?" Varsha Aunty's words pierced her thoughts and sent them out of mind.

"Hi, Aunty."

"Beta, you've lost weight since the last time I saw you. You must share your secrets."

Maadhini almost laughed. *A steady diet of self-loathing mixed with the occasional skipped meal and treadmill run.*

"But where is Sadiya?"

Taking Varsha Aunty's light coat at the door, Maadhini put it in the adjacent closet and pointed to the kitchen. "She's just laying out some snacks."

"That girl, first-rate. And so fair!"

The comment on Sadiya's skin tone stung like a scorpion bite. Controlling her instinct to pull at the aunty's saree and not stop until all of the woman's fears and anxieties were exposed, Maadhini instead complimented it. "What lovely colors you're wearing, Aunty." She hoped the sparkle in her eyes masked her anger.

"Oh, thank you, *beta.*"

Sadiya's work was done within minutes of the party starting, thankfully, and so Maadhini had a partner to walk through the house with as she made her awkward hellos to the uncles and aunties who filled their home.

Her *amma* showed off some jewelry and regaled the other women with the latest gossip from India as they all sipped tea in the kitchen. The uncles were in the basement, watching the final games of the MLB season. Deciding it was safer down there than with the aunties who would undoubtedly poke and prod at her love life, Maadhini made their way down the stairs with Sadiya.

"*Ayyo Rama!*" Prakash Uncle sounded like he might throw something at their plasma TV.

"*Chup!*" Another uncle waved at him to sit back down on the couch. "Have another Kingfisher and just enjoy the game."

"*Kanne?*" Maadhini's *appa* spotted her and Sadiya approaching. "You didn't want to be with the women?"

Maadhini flushed. *Just one woman in particular...*

"It's cooler down here, uncle," Sadiya said. "Besides, we like baseball."

"A woman after my heart," Rakesh Uncle said. "Are you single?"

"Rakesh!" Now it was her *appa* who'd gotten up. He slapped the man's back.

"Kidding, *yaar!* You think Jayanthi would let me bring home someone so young and fair?"

So this is Jayanthi Aunty's husband? Maadhini wondered what would happen if she asked about his daughter.

Waving Rakesh off, Maadhini's *appa* continued. "Sadiya, you'll have to come home more often."

"Why's that, Uncle?"

"So that I can tell you all the many reasons this sport is garbage compared to cricket."

At that, all the uncles' heads bobbed up and down in agreement.

They couldn't hide in the basement forever.

Eventually, the suggestive comments from the uncles shifted from merely inappropriate to outright sexual harassment and Maadhini and Sadiya found themselves upstairs again. The aunties fawned over Sadiya's lithe frame and borderline white skin, of course, and Maadhini leapt at the chance to excuse herself when the sun set.

"Yes, Aunty," she said, waving one off. "I can't wait to get the recipe for that spinach smoothie. I'll be right back; I do need to pick up the sparklers so we can celebrate outside."

Halfway up the stairs to get fireworks from a closet, she heard one (*Nilam Aunty?*) tut-tutting about her thighs.

"Some meat on the bone is not always bad," another said. "That Mindy Kaling girl has her own show now! South Indian, chubby, and successful! Triple threat!"

Maadhini bit her tongue to keep from snorting in laughter. *If only that counted as a triple threat.*

"That Mindy girl is funny, though," Varsha Aunty said. "Maadhini not so funny."

Thanks, Aunty. Rolling her eyes, she hurried to get the sparklers before her scoffs became too loud for the aunties to ignore.

Insisting the uncles abandon the game on TV ("What does it matter? Tigers are up 3-0 in the series anyways. Yankees are doomed."), Maadhini's *amma* started handing out boxes of sparklers outside.

"Come, *beta,* you help with this."

Really, Amma? I can be trusted to hand out sticks that catch fire? Maadhini smiled at the thought until she realized her *amma* was giving her only unlit sticks while Sadiya went around actually lighting them for people. *Of course.*

With the sun down, Maadhini saw the stars shining

above her. Walking away from the crowd, she closed her eyes and pictured what it might be like to live on the moon or some other planet, far from the constraints of her life. She waved her sparkler. It was full of boundless energy and a light that could cast out the most pernicious darkness, but she knew it would eventually give out.

"Hey." Sadiya tapped her on the shoulder.

Maadhini turned. "Hey." Their words were like whispered prayers.

"I'm sorry about last night."

Maadhini kicked at the ground. "Forget it."

"No," Sadiya said, strength in her voice. "I won't. You're right; I can never understand what you're going through...but I do want to try and help."

"I appreciate that."

"Rebecca seems nice..."

"Don't just say shit."

Sadiya sniffled. "No! It's...it's true."

Maadhini looked up. She felt her eyes asking questions she was still afraid to voice.

"Fine," Sadiya admitted. "You're right...I'm not one hundred percent sure about her. But she clearly makes you happy. I'd have to be blind not to see it."

Maadhini nodded. "So where does that leave us?"

"'Dhini...I just want you to be careful. She talks smooth and she makes you feel gushy inside and I've just been down this road before..."

"With Mahesh." A statement, not a question. The crispness in Maadhini's voice reflected the October air.

Sadiya looked away. "...yeah."

"You talk about trust, about looking out for me. You're my best friend; I love you. But you gotta tell me what happened."

"...you're right," Sadiya said.

The conversation could've lasted an hour for all Maadhini knew. By the time Sadiya was done telling her about how this man used to pick out what clothes she should wear to school, what movies they should watch and what friends she was allowed to hang out with (no men), most of the aunties and uncles had gone back inside.

"*Kanne!*"

Maadhini sighed. She knew her *amma* was disappointed in her. God forbid an aunty leave without saying bye to her. *Oh, shucks. I can't believe Varsha Aunty didn't get to make another crack at my weight before going.* "In a minute, *Amma!*"

"Anyways," Sadiya finished. "When he said he wanted sex or that was it, I knew I had to end it."

Maadhini refocused on her friend. "You've never had sex?" *But she's so...hot! And I'm...me.*

"No," Sadiya said. "That was another reason I didn't want to rush. Those sorority girls look down on you, but I'll know when I'm ready and I'm not gonna be pressured when I'm not."

Maadhini looked at Sadiya like she was an alien. "You never even saw Mahesh naked?" *How am I the first one of us to...*

A warmth filled her stomach and made its way into her heart. *Am I the cool one now?*

"Well..." Sadiya's words burst through her thoughts. "I wouldn't say that..."

Maadhini smirked.

"But honestly," Sadiya finished, "lady parts are much more attractive."

The two shared a laugh, one of those gut-busting laughs they hadn't had since their days in high school.

"*Chup!*" Her *amma*'s voice rang through the night. "You want to wake neighborhood? Get back here and help wash dishes!"

Holding hands, the two women walked back inside.

"So...we're good?" Sadiya ventured.

"We're good," Maadhini said. "I'll be careful. I promise." *And the next time I'm home, I'll tell* Amma *and* Appa *about Rebecca.* Because with her friend at her side, with the confidence that she was finally cool, she knew that her happiness was worth fighting for.

Chapter Five

Even though the Yankees had lost, Maadhini's *appa* counted their party as a rousing success. Maadhini knew this because he'd told her multiple times over the last two days, continuing to do so now as she walked to the library with Sadiya and thanked her stars it was him on the phone and not her *amma*. She'd need to hang up soon; she couldn't afford to be kicked out of the quiet room again.

"Your *amma* is so proud," he said. "You know what this means?"

Maadhini tapped her pencil on the desk. *She's finally happy in America?*

"If I stay out drinking, it's fine, as long as it's with Jayanthi's and Varsha's husbands! She want all gossip."

Maadhini rolled her eyes. *Men are so dumb. No wonder I like girls.* "...but Dad, does *she* ever go out?"

"*Ai.*" He made a dismissive sound. "Where she gonna go?"

"*Appa*, when's the last time you two went out together?"

"Why go together? Spend enough time at home."

"Some couples like going out together, like on a date."

"Maadhini, we are not some couple. We are your parents. Now, give the phone to Sadiya."

Sighing, Maadhini handed the phone to her best friend, putting it on speaker so she could sort through her notes. Midterms were in two weeks, and Sadiya's day planner was marked up with so many different colors it could pass as a Benetton ad.

"Sadiya?"

"Yes, Vir Uncle?"

"You tell Maadhini: dates are for you two. Her *amma* and *appa* happy as is."

"Why don't *you* tell her, Uncle?"

"*Ai*, you two go to college, yet not so smart."

"Sorry?"

"Kids are all same, even when I was kid. Listen to friends, not parents."

Sadiya laughed as Maadhini rolled her eyes. "I'll tell her, Uncle."

"Good. Study hard."

Maadhini took the phone back to say goodbye, but he'd already hung up. She made small talk with Sadiya as they entered the building and took an elevator to the quiet floor.

"Your dad seems happier," Sadiya said.

"Only because he can go out drinking after night classes now."

"I'm sure your mom would say something if it really upset her."

You only think that because Hema Aunty would one hundred percent say something. But Maadhini's *amma* was different. Once, when Maadhini had been seven, her *appa* had forgotten their wedding anniversary. When Maadhini had asked her *amma* about it, she'd been told that anniversaries were skipped in odd-numbered years, so actually her *appa* was being respectful. *She'll lie to protect me, to protect herself.*

As they stepped into a room, Maadhini's phone buzzed with a text: *Come to the apartment.* Her mouth went dry imagining what she and Rebecca would do once there.

"Hey," Sadiya said, snapping her fingers. "Eyes up; we gotta focus."

Maadhini stashed her phone. "Er...I'm gonna go study with Rebecca." *Now I'm lying to protect myself, just like my mom.*

"You're not helping yourself," Sadiya said. "Wilson's midterm is gonna be brutal."

That's where you're wrong, best friend. For once, I am helping myself. "No, really," Maadhini said. "She and I are gonna quiz each other."

Sadiya huffed, putting her bag on a desk and taking out some color-coded notecards. "Here." She handed Maadhini a handful.

"Really?"

"I just have one question."

"Anything!" Maadhini didn't rein in her tone. Her voice had no chill when Rebecca was concerned, and she was finally fine with that.

Sadiya narrowed her eyes. "Does she still call you 'dhini?"

Maadhini gulped. "I'm gonna tell her to stop. I promise." As she walked away, she could feel Sadiya's eyes boring into the back of her head.

Thursday evenings meant Metropolitan Studies. Maadhini tried to focus on Wilson's lecture as Sadiya buried herself in a notebook, scribbling notes so hard a pencil tip broke, and she had to get a new one from her bag. On her other side, Rebecca kept "accidentally" rubbing their legs together. *I wish I'd shaved…*

"Maadhini?" The professor's question poked through her thoughts.

She snapped her head up. "Yes?"

"Would you care to offer an opinion?"

"Um…Robert Moses is bad…"

As the class laughed, Wilson nodded indulgently. "You're not wrong, but that answer would still get you an F on the midterm. What was Robert Moses's lasting legacy?"

Biting her bottom lip, Maadhini caught Rebecca sharing a laugh with Chad. Her stomach plunged. *She'd laugh with that douche?*

"Professor?" Rebecca raised her hand.

Maadhini fumed. *And won't even let me answer my own question?*

"Yes, Rebecca?"

"Moses crafted the city, and that's a legacy that'll stand forever, but anyone who studies New York's infrastructure would have to agree that absolute power corrupts absolutely."

Smiling, Wilson nodded. "Correct. They say near the end, as anti-discrimination laws passed despite his disapproval, he used his considerable wealth to secure more and more WP. Eventually, the drug permanently compromised his immune system, and he died one winter of the common cold."

Maadhini froze. *What?*

"Too much of anything is a bad thing," Wilson continued. "Even, and perhaps especially, power."

Maadhini didn't always do the assigned readings, but she knew enough about life to know that was a lie the powerful told the powerless to try and keep them at bay.

"No way." Chad snorted in derision.

"You have a different take, Chad?"

"No offense, Teach, but I can't believe this badass Moses ever became some common skin grafter, too high on his own supply."

The room went silent as Wilson's eyes bulged. "Say that again, and you will get an F on your midterm." Moving on, pretending it hadn't happened, he turned around and started drawing on the whiteboard as he continued with his lecture.

"What was that about?" Maadhini whispered to Rebecca.

"Chad may as well have used the N-word," Rebecca replied. "*Skin grafter* is a really foul thing to call someone who wasn't born with WP, someone who stole it."

"But Moses was white," Sadiya said, trying to insert herself in the conversation.

"Ladies, would you like to leave class to carry on your conversation?" Turning around, Wilson scolded them.

Sadiya slumped in her seat as she redoubled her note-taking efforts, only to break another pencil.

"Anyways," Rebecca continued, this time in a whisper so low only Maadhini could hear, "the slur refers to someone so desperate for WP that they're willing to graft white skin onto their body to convince the government they deserve it. Can you imagine? They're willing to deform their body permanently for just the possibility of better living?"

How's that different from plastic surgery? And that's legal. Maadhini thought about asking Rebecca after class but decided against it.

"You promised you'd get dinner with us," Maadhini said. Class was over and Sadiya was trying to excuse herself to go back to the apartment.

Sadiya gazed at the door longingly. "I've gotta study."

"You've gotta eat, 'diya. We've never shared a meal with Rebecca, and you promised you'd make an effort."

At the front of the classroom, Rebecca stood asking Wilson about the midterm as the two best friends talked in low voices.

"You're right." Sadiya sighed. "One meal. I can ask Ms. Perfect Little Democrat why she supports a president who's anti-gay rights."

"'Diya!"

"Oh, come on," Sadiya said. "Why'd Obama only come out for gay rights this year?"

"Why are you constantly looking to pick fights with Rebecca? If I didn't know any better, I'd say you were jealous."

"Jealous?! Of her?" Sadiya's nostrils flared as her hands curled into fists at her sides. "What's happened to you?"

"What do you mean?"

"You ditch study dates. You lie to your parents. You're having sex."

Maadhini frowned. "Slut-shame, much? Don't get your panties in a bunch because I'm getting some and you're not."

"'Dhini, you hardly know this woman," Sadiya hissed.

"I know I'm happy..."

I am, right?

No, I am.

"It's like, ever since you got with her, you're..."

Maadhini propped her hands on her hips. "I'm what? Confident?"

When Sadiya didn't respond, Maadhini shook her head. Sadiya had been her best friend her entire life. Maadhini had always been content to let Sadiya direct things, decide where to go for dinner or what to watch on TV. But now that she was happy and doing her own thing? *Sadiya feels lost.* Without Maadhini's constant presence in her life, Sadiya must've felt like a ship without its anchor, drifting into uncharted waters. *I understand; I used to be lost, too.* "Calm down," she said. "Come to dinner. Make an effort."

Sadiya's lip quivered as she nodded. Was she about to cry? "It's an adjustment, 'dhini, that's all."

Maadhini gentled her voice. "I just want us to all be friends. Rebecca didn't even wear her earrings tonight because she knew we'd all be going out together." Taking Sadiya's hand, she guided the two of them to the front door where Rebecca waited.

They ended up at a diner in Midtown near Rebecca's apartment. Maadhini slid into a booth next to her girlfriend, leaving Sadiya the entire booth across from them.

"Can you believe Chad?" Rebecca asked. "He's such a tool." When Sadiya didn't respond, she idly spun her plastic straw around in her glass of water. A waitress delivered the drinks to their table. "So, how do you like America?"

Coolness entered Sadiya's voice as she answered. "It's like a second home."

"What's your favorite color?"

"Red and gold. Favorite book?" Sadiya shot back.

Rebecca leaned away; her arms crossed. "Richard Ben Cramer's *What It Takes.*"

"I'm not familiar with that one," Sadiya said. "What's it about?"

"Guys, what is this?" A month ago, Maadhini might've hid behind a menu as the two traded barbs, but not anymore.

"We're just getting to know each other, babe." Rebecca smiled at Sadiya.

Sadiya smiled tightly back. "Any siblings?"

"One: Claire. You?"

"Only child."

"Must've been lonely growing up."

"Not really; Maadhini was always around."

Maadhini gasped as Rebecca stroked her bare thigh under their table.

"Can I get you anything?" Their waitress returned, temporarily saving them from further awkwardness.

"An order of loaded tots for the table," Rebecca said.

"Hang on," Sadiya said as the woman jotted it down on her notepad. "No beef, right?"

"Well, it has bacon." The waitress sounded bored.

"Can we get it without bacon?"

The waitress nodded, adding a notation before leaving.

"Oh, right," Rebecca said. "Sorry; I forgot."

Sadiya narrowed her eyes. "You forgot your girlfriend doesn't eat meat?"

Maadhini winced. *Fuck.*

"Um…" It took a lot to render Rebecca wordless, but Sadiya had done it.

Be brave. Be brave. Be brave. "Sadiya…"

"What?"

Maadhini fidgeted. "I…uh…I eat meat now."

Sadiya looked like she'd been slapped. "'Dhini!" Hissing the words, she kicked her under the table.

"Ow!"

"Oh! Sorry! Reflex." She continued as Maadhini rubbed her shin. "But seriously, you just decided one day to flush twenty years of vegetarianism down the drain?"

Opening her mouth to apologize, racking her mind to come up with a convincing lie, Maadhini shut her lips.

Honesty.

I am a strong, confident woman.

That's what Rebecca told her, and that's what she had to convince herself of if she was ever going to get out of her parents' shadows. From Sadiya's shadow. "Are you upset I eat meat, or are you upset I didn't tell you?"

Sadiya stared blankly as the waitress left a plate of cheesy tater tots in front of them.

Before she could leave, Maadhini spoke. "Ma'am, we're ready."

"What can I get you, sweetheart?"

"A cheeseburger. Medium-rare." Her cheeks burned as the waitress went on to take Rebecca's order. Things had changed and Sadiya needed to know it. There was nothing to be embarrassed about. Yet Maadhini couldn't quite convince herself. All she knew was the look of hurt on her best friend's face as Sadiya put in an order for a grilled cheese, tomato soup, and a strawberry milkshake.

As the meals arrived, Maadhini wondered how early she could end this dinner without seeming rude. Then again, Sadiya was likely already convinced the dinner was an awkward disaster. And if she went home with Rebecca instead of Sadiya afterwards?

She could've been a Formula One racer for the way she navigated through her thoughts as everyone chewed their food in silence. Each time Rebecca tried to play footsy with her under the table, she pretended to be super into her food or the décor on the walls.

I just wanted to share my happiness. It'd been naïve to assume her best friend and her girlfriend would naturally like each other, but how could she choose?

"So," Rebecca said, pausing from her own burger, "you can't eat beef because you're Hindu?"

Maadhini stifled a groan, wishing her girlfriend

would shut up for once. All this awkwardness was giving her a stomachache. *Or maybe that's the beef.* She'd only eaten a burger a couple times and wasn't even sure she liked it. Pangs of guilt ate at her as she thought of what her parents would say if they knew. Would they view eating meat as better or worse than being gay?

Whatever. Eating meat is a safer way of rebelling than becoming an alcoholic.

Sadiya's voice pulled her from her thoughts, a lifeline against further despondency. "Cows are such sacred, gentle creatures. Bhumi, Surabhi, these are goddesses who took on the forms of cows at one point or another in our ancient tales."

When did she learn all this? Maadhini crossed her legs, reminding herself to re-read the Hindu texts in her parents' house next time she visited. Sadiya had even mentioned that some of those books had passages praising gay rights. *Was Krishna really gay?*

"Would you eat your gods?" Sadiya asked.

Finishing her burger and taking a loud sip of her vanilla milkshake, Rebecca responded. "That's literally what receiving Eucharist is."

"...what?" Maadhini felt Sadiya's confusion reflected on her own face.

"You go to church, and you listen as the priest says his bit and then you go up to him and he gives you a wafer that symbolizes the body of Christ."

"So, you...eat your god?"

"Don't make it weird," Rebecca said.

"It is weird," Sadiya said.

"Whatever."

Maadhini recognized the hurt in Rebecca's voice, surprised to learn anything could embarrass her. As the check came and the three of them paid up, she shifted her feet to play with Rebecca's under the table.

"You coming over tonight?" Rebecca asked as they all exited the restaurant.

"I should get back to our place," Maadhini said. "I need to call my mom before bed." The two stood together as Sadiya waved down a cab.

"I understand. Just don't keep me waiting too long."

Rebecca turned to walk away, and Maadhini found her heart controlling her body. Grabbing Rebecca by the hand, she spun her around and kissed her lips. She turned her brain off and allowed her fingers to run across the woman's body like it was a violin, strumming the notes she knew elicited the most pleasure. Closing her eyes, she lost herself to the music and only stopped when Sadiya tapped her on the shoulder.

"Um, I'm not paying this guy to watch you make out."

Blushing, Maadhini excused herself to the cab.

"See you around, 'dhini." Rebecca closed the car door behind them.

As they sped away, Maadhini saw the look of hurt on Sadiya's face.

Neither of them spoke the entire ride back. Sadiya was halfway through the door to their building by the time Maadhini paid their driver and raced to catch her. "Would you slow down? You know I can't run."

"You promised!"

The doorman interjected as Sadiya pushed the button for the elevator. "Ma'am, is there a problem?"

"We're fine," Maadhini said. Grabbing Sadiya by the shoulders, she forced her to make eye contact. "I'm sorry."

"For?"

Jesus, she can't make this easy. "For not telling her to stop calling me 'dhini."

Sadiya's bottom lip quivered. "I just...I feel like I'm losing you. Everything is happening so fast."

"'Diya, you couldn't lose me if you tried. You're my best friend!"

Sadiya sniffled as the elevator arrived and the doors opened. Maadhini recognized two guys from their Stochastic Calculus class get out.

"Hey," one drunkenly slurred, staring at Sadiya's tears. "What's wrong, Sad-iya?"

The other let out a belly laugh as he dragged his friend outside. He added his own two bits before disappearing around the corner. "You'd look better if you smiled."

Maadhini lifted her chin. "...ignore them."

In the elevator, Sadiya began to cry as soon as the doors closed. "I'm making an effort, 'dhini. I am."

"I know..."

"But you start eating beef, and that's fine, really, it is, but then why don't you tell me? I have to learn about it from *her*?"

"She just..." Maadhini trailed off.

"What?!"

"It makes me feel special..."

"...what?"

The elevator doors opened, but neither of them moved.

"Our pet names...they're something special," Maadhini said. "A secret. Proof that we have our own special world where we reign as queens."

"Yeah..."

"I wanted Rebecca to be part of that. Because when we're all in this world together, it's not so scary."

Sadiya sighed. "'Dhini..."

The elevator doors closed again and returned to the lobby.

"I know it's stupid..." Maadhini began.

"It's not..."

"When I'm with her, I feel special. Sex, secrets, steak, what could be more American? I feel like I finally belong." Maadhini wiped the tears from Sadiya's face as she continued. "You've been the cool one, the smart one, the pretty one for so long. It's just nice to have this to myself."

Sadiya hesitated. "That makes sense."

The two friends had composed themselves by the time the doors opened.

The doorman grunted when he saw them. "Elevator not working again?"

"Don't worry," Maadhini told him. "Broken's not always a bad thing. If it doesn't break, how can you fix it and make it better than before?"

Maadhini went to bed that night without listening to her soundtrack of Bangalore's streets. Closing her eyes, she remembered Rebecca's breath on her neck, her lips on her face, the way she grabbed at her body like she owned it. *I deserve to be happy.* Tracing a finger down into her panties, she gasped and let her pleasure guide her to sleep.

Chapter Six

Maadhini woke with a clear head and a smile on her face. She was going to do something today just for her. It was going to hurt her parents, but it would make their relationship stronger in the long haul. She started her day by repeating an affirmation she'd read on a calendar somewhere: *I define myself, not anyone else.*

She only had one class on Fridays, in the afternoon. Making her way to the bathroom, she noted that Sadiya was already gone. For some reason, her best friend had scheduled back-to-back classes on Friday mornings.

Flushing, Maadhini washed her hands and shed her clothes before stepping into the shower. Closing her eyes, she applied Sadiya's shampoo to her hair, inhaled the vanilla scents, and repeated another affirmation from that calendar: *Do something for yourself today.*

Maybe it wouldn't be this weekend, but she was going to have sex with Rebecca again. Soon.

I am a sexy person who enjoys doing sexy things. Maadhini would tell herself that until she started to believe it. Getting dressed, she tucked her wallet in her jeans pocket and left the apartment.

She took the 4 subway line to the Victoria's Secret on Broadway. Just stepping inside made her blush.

No big deal. Just chilling out like I belong here. She'd been in this store once, with Sadiya, during their freshman year. They hadn't been able to stop giggling at the sight of a headless mannequin wearing a thong. *But now I'm going to buy one of my own. Because I'm cool.*

"Can I help you?"

Maadhini practically jumped out of her skin. The saleswoman had earrings with WP embedded in them, just like Rebecca's. The energy pulsing from them sounded like bongos at first, but quickly faded to background noise.

"Yes, um, what do you have in my size?" It took all of Maadhini's strength to hold a straight face.

Curves are sexy.

Curves are sexy.

Curves are sexy.

"Of course." The woman guided her to a section deep within the store, right by a dressing room.

This is the farthest inside I've ever been.

...that's what she said.

Maadhini laughed to herself.

"Sorry?" the saleswoman asked.

"Nothing," Maadhini said. "I'm being dumb. Thanks for your help."

"No problem," the woman said. "Personally, I think our XL stuff is some of our sexiest. My girlfriend just bought this."

Girlfriend? She barely registered the woman handing her a dark-blue teddy with a neckline that wouldn't leave anything to imagination.

"Go ahead," the woman said, "treat yourself."

Girlfriend.

I am somebody's girlfriend.

Smiling, Maadhini took the clothes into the dressing room.

An hour later, she left the store with not just the teddy, but also a matching thong and bra.

Maadhini Kedilaya: Sex Goddess. Racking her brain to try and remember if there was a Hindu sex goddess, she called her mom as she made her way underground to the subway. *Time for the second thing I'm doing for myself today.*

"*Beta?*"

"Hi, *Amma.*"

"Why you call now? I'm seeing you in a few hours, no?"

"...no."

"*Arre yaar!*"

Maadhini held the phone away from her ear as her *amma* shouted. "I'm not kidding. I had something come up last minute." *Not a lie.*

"What comes up? You study here; bring Sadiya, too."

"Sadiya has her own life, *Amma.*" Staring at the electronic monitor that told passengers which trains were coming when, she saw hers would arrive in just a couple minutes. Then she could honestly say her phone had lost its signal.

"Sadiya has life, you have life, what about me?"

"We were just there last weekend, *Amma.* Why don't you hang out with your own friends?" She asked the question just a bit too forcefully.

"*Thik hai.*" Pain filled her *Amma*'s voice, as if someone had knocked the wind out of her.

"*Amma...*"

"*Hogona,*" she said.

"I don't have to go just yet..."

"*Kanne,* I have to go. Actually, now that you mention it, Jayanthi is coming for tea in little while. Her daughter doesn't visit either. I'm sure we'll talk about that."

"Okay, Mom. I'll call later." Closing her eyes, Maadhini compelled herself to not throw her phone at the speeding train that ground to a halt in front of her. Jayanthi Aunty's daughter didn't visit because she knew she wasn't welcome. She should've told her mom that. Instead, her stomach ached knowing she'd hurt her mother. And then ached more when she realized she'd done nothing wrong. *I'm entitled to a weekend alone. I can't be responsible for entertaining* Amma *constantly.*

On the train, Maadhini had to grab a metal pole to keep from falling. Her nose crinkled in disgust. *Did someone pee on this?*

It was noon by the time she returned to the apartment. Rather than wait for Sadiya to return from class, she called down to the Chinese place a block from their building. "Can I get the General Tso's chicken?"

She hadn't asked Sadiya if it was okay to have meat in their place, but it was her place too, and it was past time she acted like it. Waiting for her food to arrive, she unpacked her clothes and tried them out. She snapped a few selfies on her phone and debated sending them to Rebecca before deciding against it. *I wonder if Rebecca's ever sexted anyone?*

The question ate at her, and she was about to change her mind about sending a selfie when the doorbell rang. She threw on an oversized T-shirt to answer the door, hoping it hid everything.

"Damn, baby." The man at the front door handed her a plastic bag with a Styrofoam container in it. As he looked her up and down, she remembered she had shorts on, so the oversized shirt made it look like she wasn't wearing anything else underneath. "You're really wearing that shirt like you're doing it a favor."

She chuckled nervously and looked at her feet,

handing him some cash.

"Later, baby. Next time you order from here, ask for Larry."

Closing the door, she felt violated and flattered at the same time.

Hunger sated, Maadhini looked again at her new clothes, laid out on the bed. They called to her as loudly as the WP in Rebecca's earrings. *Fuck it.* Throwing the shirt off, she snapped a few selfies of herself lying down on the bed.

What's that thing called? Duckface? She tried doing it before deciding it was lame and deleting the pic. Before she could change her mind, she sent the others off to Rebecca, then changed into school clothes and left for class.

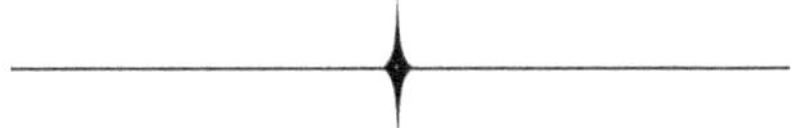

It was past five by the time Maadhini got back from class. Sadiya had left a note about going to the library. Not for the first time, Maadhini wondered why Sadiya bothered to pay rent since the library probably had a bed and shower somewhere on its premises. Checking her phone, she saw a missed call from Rebecca and called her back.

"Hey, sexy," she said when Rebecca answered, then immediately regretted it. *Stupid. Why did I call her sexy?*

Rebecca laughed, and Maadhini closed her eyes. *See? She agrees it's stupid.*

"Hey, babe."

Maadhini flailed for a response. "Um, what's up?"

What's up?

Jesus Christ, Maadhini. What's up? You just sent her a

nude.

Well, almost a nude? A semi-nude?

Focus!

Clearing her throat, she heard the end of Rebecca's question. "...coming over, right?"

"Sorry, what?"

Rebecca's laugh cut her heart open and buried itself inside. "Honestly, babe, you're such an airhead. I asked if you were coming over so we could finish that photo shoot."

Opening her mouth, Maadhini almost accepted the invitation before stopping herself. *I need to take care of my parents before I can focus on her.* "I've got some stuff to figure out...rain check?"

"Seriously? Babe, the rain is here. Those photos are full of thirst." The hardened edge of Rebecca's voice did things to Maadhini's stomach. "Are you going to your parents' this weekend?"

"No," Maadhini said. "That's actually the stuff I've got to figure out. I need to focus on myself. Talk to my parents about the importance of healthy boundaries."

A pause large enough to make them both pregnant filled the line. Finally, Rebecca spoke. "...I get it."

"Really?" Maadhini heard how hopeful she sounded.

"Yeah. Good for you."

"...thank you." Maadhini blushed at the praise.

"You're quite the enigma, 'dhini."

Despite what she'd promised Sadiya, she found herself smiling at the nickname.

"One moment you're a total wimp, and the next minute you're sexting me and kissing me all over like a total badass."

Maadhini snorted. "Well, I promise I won't make you wait too long to see that stuff in person."

"I'm getting pretty thirsty myself, but you're worth

the wait."

Maadhini's insides quivered as Rebecca hung up.

For all her talk about "establishing boundaries," Maadhini had as much interest in speaking with her parents as she did in Chad's penis. Focusing on herself tonight meant junk food and reruns. Halfway through eating leftovers for dinner and watching the same episode of Friends for the hundredth time ("The One With Ross and Monica's Cousin"), Maadhini got a text from Sadiya at the library.

Hey, Tanvi Aunty texted me.

A moment passed. Maadhini looked on in horror as her best friend kept texting in small snippets.

She seemed really upset.

She said you'd know why.

I thought I'd escape this drama after leaving the fam in India, but I'm here if you want to talk.

Sadiya was here…

Maadhini gripped her phone in anger. *That's the fucking problem.* Sadiya was here and her parents were there. Sadiya was so selfish, indulging them to stay in India, leaving Maadhini's parents all alone to do nothing but watch her like a hawk.

Getting up, she turned off the TV and laid out the lingerie again on her bed. Repeating her morning affirmation to do something for herself, she resolved to go to Rebecca's this weekend.

I can't be a good daughter.

I can't be a good friend.

I can't be a good girlfriend.

She let out a scream, primal to its core. The person in the adjacent apartment applauded, probably thinking she was getting laid.

Tomorrow. I'm going to see Rebecca tomorrow. The

answer wasn't in anyone but herself. She knew that, and she knew what she had to do next. Sadiya was frustrating, but her best friend held that title for a reason. She was right; she couldn't let someone else be in charge of her pleasure, her happiness. Though she was home alone, she still looked behind her and locked the door before going under her bed to retrieve her vibrator.

Satisfied, Maadhini had hid the toy under the bed by the time Sadiya returned for the night.

"'Dhini?"

Maadhini feigned sleep as her friend entered the bedroom, but caught Sadiya looking at the floor beneath her and remembered she'd left the toy unwrapped near the front of the bed. Whether Sadiya suspected she was actually asleep or not, Maadhini was grateful that she played along.

Leaving the room to study in the kitchen, Sadiya turned off the light and left Maadhini alone.

The next morning, Sadiya kept looking at her like the Cheshire cat from *Alice in Wonderland*.

Maadhini ducked her head. *She knows.*

Of course she knows.

Who cares if she knows? She bought it for me! "Why are you being weird?"

Sadiya grinned. "How was it?"

"I don't know what you're talking about."

Sadiya replied with a wink, but she dropped the topic.

The concept of a lazy Saturday was foreign to Sadiya Murthy and Maadhini Kedilaya. Both had study sessions for their other classes during the day, and of course Maadhini had to budget two hours to listen to her *amma* tell her how sad she was to be alone this weekend. She was so sad to be alone that to make up for her comments yesterday, Maadhini had to speak not just to her parents, but to Jayanthi Aunty, Varsha Aunty, Nilam Aunty, their husbands, and the mailman who happened to arrive during her call.

"Yes, I'll come by soon so we can do this in person," Maadhini said, trying to get off the phone with Rakesh Uncle. The man was under the impression that she liked both baseball and him because she'd hidden out in the basement with the uncles rather than face the aunties during Diwali. Hearing the door open, she saw Sadiya return from the library. "Okay, then, I have to go now."

"*Kanne,*" her mom said, taking the phone back, "you'll come next weekend?"

"I'm not sure." Maadhini knew whatever she decided would disappoint her mom. "I'll call you tomorrow, *Amma.*" Hanging up, she noticed it was already 6 p.m.

Sadiya squinted. "Weren't you just about to get on the phone when I left?"

Some of us have to deal with our obligations here... "She had to tell me how lonely she was."

"Ah. I've had that conversation before. Sorry."

"The conversation featured guests who could attest to how lonely she was."

"Yikes." Throwing her bookbag in their room, taking a seat on the couch, Sadiya continued. "Well, I got us pizza to eat while we prepare for Wilson's test, and some trashy DVDs to relax with afterward."

Standing from the kitchen table, Maadhini interrupted her as Sadiya began pulling out discs of *The Bachelor.* "Um, yeah, I'm actually about to leave…"

She might as well have hit Sadiya with a car for the way 'diya looked at her.

"Are you mad at me? We've barely said two words to each other all weekend."

"You've been studying," Maadhini snapped.

"And you don't want to talk about what happened last night, which is totally cool. I bought it for you. Totally cool."

Maadhini had endured hours of listening to her mother and the aunties. Now this from Sadiya. If she'd been in a pit of despair, her mom and Sadiya's solution would've been to haul her out by knotting a rope around her neck and pulling. She'd had enough. "Just leave me alone!"

Sadiya stood up in shock. "…'dhini?"

Maadhini looked down as she continued, knowing she wouldn't be able to finish saying what needed to be said if she focused on the tears forming in Sadiya's eyes. "I gave myself an orgasm, okay! You were right, I shouldn't leave my pleasure up to someone else without pleasing myself first."

"…'dhini."

"Is that what you wanted to hear? Thank you very much for your assistance. Now I'm going to see Rebecca."

Sadiya's eyes darted to their trashcan. The Victoria's Secret bag from yesterday was still peeping out from the top. "You bought something for her, right? Can I see?"

The anger building in Maadhini over the last two hours with her *amma*, the last two semesters seeing Sadiya happy every day while she languished, the last two decades of thinly veiled critiques from her loved ones about her body—they all simmered to the forefront of her mind like a perfectly cooked mug of chai. "I bought that for me! So that for once I can feel as sexy as you get to be every day."

Sadiya opened and closed her mouth. Pain switched to confusion as she looked like she'd just seen a dog talk. Finally, she spoke. "...I never knew you felt that way."

"Why wouldn't I? I'm fat; you're not. I'm dark-skinned; you could pass as white. I have to visit my parents every weekend or endure their scoldings; you get to be free." She spewed word vomit as if she were a bird shitting in a parking lot.

"That's your choice," Sadiya said. "We all have it in our power to change the relationship we have with our parents."

"How can I change that?"

"I did."

Maadhini fisted her own hair, as if to rip it out. "It's easy for you because your parents are eight thousand miles away! You're so selfish, you told them not to follow you here because you wanted America all to yourself!"

Sadiya looked like she'd been shot. She fell back on the couch. "That's not fair."

Maadhini stepped right up next to her friend. "Who said any of this was fair?" Taking her phone out, she texted Rebecca that they were on for tonight and walked to the door.

"I'm sorry!"

Maadhini heard the words being hurled out as a weapon, a last-ditch attempt to guilt her into staying. "For what?"

"For making you go to that stupid party. I should've never asked you to spy on Rebecca. This is all my fault."

Maadhini scoffed. "Not everything revolves around

you, 'diya. You don't have such control over my life. I made this decision because it makes me happy. You can accept that, or not. But I hope you do." Grabbing the clothes from her bedroom and a toothbrush from the bathroom, she told her best friend not to wait up.

Maadhini stormed through Rebecca's door the moment she opened it.

Rebecca blinked at her. "Babe?"

She entered Rebecca's bathroom, connected to the bedroom, and set her toothbrush down before acknowledging her girlfriend. "I'm ready."

Rebecca trailed after her. "To...?"

"To spend the night."

Rebecca took Maadhini by the hands, guiding her to the couch in the living room, where they both sat down. "You said you needed time..."

"Didn't that frustrate you?"

"It did...but why the sudden change?"

Maadhini stared at the ground. "It's time for me to grow up."

Rebecca was quiet a moment. "Did you and Sadiya have a fight?"

Maadhini gritted her teeth, refusing to answer.

Rebecca sighed. "Angry sex is only hot if it's with the person you're upset with. I'm not here as your fallback because you got in a fight with your best friend."

"It's just..." Maadhini stood up, grabbing at her hair again. Her bangs dangled between her eyes, and she made a note to book herself a haircut. "For so long, I didn't know who I was without her. I let her define my life."

Rebecca leaned forward as Maadhini paced around the table next to the couch.

"I let others determine what I did. Not just Sadiya, but

my *amma*, my *appa*..."

"That must have been suffocating." Rebecca's words dropped to a whisper.

"It was. And then Sadiya and I made this decision to come to America and I thought things would be different."

"And it wasn't..." Rebecca knew it wasn't a question.

"With you...I can breathe."

"Me?" Rebecca stood now, too, taking Maadhini by the shoulders so that the two locked eyes.

"You make me feel like I can do anything, be anything."

"So why the hesitation?"

Maadhini bit her tongue, repeating another life affirmation to herself: *I define myself, not anyone else.* She couldn't mess this up, not now. She had to be honest. "You have these relationships, like you and your sister, and they've lasted so long that you both think the rules are set. But what if they aren't? What if, one day, you decide to change?"

Rebecca's smile pierced her heart, burrowing deep. "Sadiya doesn't want to change?"

"For so long it was me and her, and now I want it to be you and me and her."

"You don't have to be a genius on WP to tell she doesn't like me."

Maadhini sniffled. "She's my best friend; I just want everyone to get along. I don't know why she's so threatened..."

She let herself be pulled into Rebecca's embrace, listened to her heartbeat as Rebecca stroked her hair and kissed her forehead. "She's an alpha. She's had her way for so long. But now you're an alpha, too, and alphas rarely play well together."

"And you?" Maadhini looked up, into Rebecca's eyes.

"What about us, if two alphas can't get along?"

"Don't worry," Rebecca said. When she smiled, her teeth practically sparkled in the moonlight. "I'm on a whole different level."

Maadhini let Rebecca grip her wrists and pull her into the bedroom. She didn't protest when Rebecca spun her around, biting her neck before pushing her onto the bed, pulling down her bottoms, kissing each inch of her legs as she removed her thong.

"You bought something for me?" Rebecca murmured.

Seeing the hunger in Rebecca's eyes, Maadhini had to admit it then: she'd bought it for her. Rebecca spanked her before turning her on her back, playing with her body as if it was a harp in need of tuning. Each stroke of the woman's fingers elicited new sounds from Maadhini's mouth. Closing her eyes, she let herself drown in the sensation.

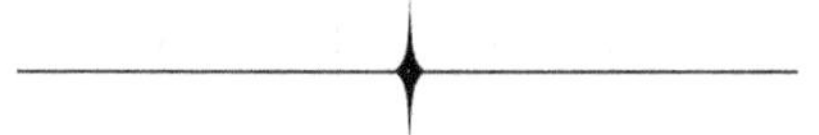

Maadhini woke naked and in the dark, self-conscious of the fact that she hadn't brushed her teeth. Lying on the bed, she noticed Rebecca's arm around her and smiled at seeing her lover as nude as she was. Lifting the comforter, she noted Rebecca's slender frame, the way her skin seemed to shine even before sunrise, without any makeup. A fleeting pang of jealousy was replaced by pride.

She let me have sex with her.

She'd been clumsy, but Rebecca had assured Maadhini that her enthusiasm more than made up for her inexperience. Burying herself under the covers, she started kissing the back of Rebecca's legs from bottom to top.

"Mmmm." Rebecca sighed in pleasure, turning over and opening her eyes. "Use your fingers."

Maadhini followed her lover's commands, tracing her body just like Rebecca had instructed her last night. She smiled at seeing Rebecca's eyes widen in pleasure when their two bodies connected.

I did that. I made her smile.

The ringing of her phone broke the morning's glory. Glancing at the bedside table, Maadhini saw it was Sadiya.

"Pick it up," Rebecca said.

"Really?"

"She's your best friend."

How can she be so cool? Maadhini stopped what she was doing and answered. "Hello?"

"'Dhini...'"

"Yeah?"

Sadiya sighed. "I didn't like how we ended things..."

"Me either..."

"I'm sorry..."

Maadhini's heart leapt. "Yeah?"

"You...you were right."

"About what?" Engrossed in the conversation, she hadn't noticed Rebecca throwing off the bedsheets and sneaking up behind her until the woman began tracing her tongue over Maadhini's bare back. Her breath caught as she struggled to process Sadiya's response.

"I moved here for you, and to see America...but I also moved here to avoid my parents. It was selfish."

"We're allowed to be selfish sometimes..." Her voice wavered as Rebecca's hands grabbed her waist. She gasped when the woman kissed her hip.

"'Dhini? Where are you?"

Maadhini tried to shush Rebecca, but only a moan came out as her lover worked her hands further south.

"Are you with Rebecca right now?!"

"'Diya…" She tried pushing Rebecca off, but the woman's hold was as commanding as the worst addiction.

"You're being so gross, Maadhini." Her friend hung up before Maadhini could think of a response.

"Why did you do that?!" No longer trying to hold it together for Sadiya's sake, Maadhini turned around and pushed Rebecca back on the bed.

"Relax," Rebecca said. Her laughter enveloped Maadhini's whole being, forming walls around her psyche. "It's fun."

"Fun? I think some people would call that sexual harassment."

"Boring people, maybe."

As Maadhini searched for a rebuttal, Rebecca opened a drawer in her bedside table. "Put these on."

The earrings… The sight of WP rendered her speechless. From just a few inches away, she could hear their deafening roar. Closing her eyes, she could've sworn they called her name.

"I've never offered these to anyone." Rebecca pushed the jewelry into Maadhini's hand.

The pulsing in her head made its way through her entire body. She arched her back, licking her lips. *Am I flying? Am I dying?* She knew all the answers to questions she'd never even contemplated before. She knew she'd get an A on Wilson's midterm and she understood why Sadiya was mad. She knew she would only ever love women and she understood why WP had been made illegal for people like her.

Real power is confidence. She would never be afraid again. No wonder the government guarded this drug so closely.

"You think you're happy now, but just wait." Guiding Maadhini's hands, Rebecca placed the earrings right at her ears. "This'll only hurt for a moment."

Blood dripped from Maadhini's ears as her lover shoved each earring through the holes she hadn't used since childhood. She winced, but Rebecca was right. After a moment, she couldn't believe she'd ever not felt like this. The drug was in her bloodstream now, shaping her in ways she'd never understand.

"It's different for everyone," Rebecca said.

Maadhini couldn't answer, couldn't speak.

"But sometimes it even stops you from getting your period. This'll be our little secret, 'dhini."

What a wonderful secret…

She had nothing to say when Rebecca kissed her lips and when Rebecca kissed down her chest and when Rebecca buried herself under the covers and used her mouth to make Maadhini shriek in pleasure.

Throwing her head back, Maadhini closed her eyes and let the darkness take her.

Chapter Seven

Maadhini had been told by Tanvi when they'd left for America that her college years would feel like decades condensed into the span of mere months. She hadn't understood what that meant until the weeks that followed her first taste of WP. The drug took the fleeting experiences of adolescent rebellion and shaped those accompanying emotions into a world of their own, complete with walls and windows to keep out unwanted intruders.

The pleasure never has to stop. That's what real power is...

Rolling out of bed one morning, she saw an unread notification on her phone. *Sadiya.*

Class was about to start. Wilson would be returning last week's midterms. Sadiya hadn't understood why Maadhini was spending so little time in the library with her until Maadhini had told her the truth, that her grades hadn't suffered thanks to Rebecca's help. *Rebecca.*

Closing her eyes, she thought of the previous day's activities, wishing she was still tangled in Rebecca's bedsheets. The passing of Halloween had brought an end to all her fears and anxieties as she'd embraced a new lifestyle, one only designed to please her.

And it's about damn time.

She studied her school subjects during the day and the female anatomy at night. Instead of being locked in a room on Saturdays studying with Sadiya, she could go to Rebecca's and devour some WP to hone her senses and prepare for their upcoming finals. The drug ensured she never forgot facts or figures, it whispered her name as seductively as the woman she loved. WP transformed a boring Saturday of studying into an unbridled bacchanal.

Her phone buzzed again as she reminded herself to ask Rebecca if she could take some WP home this coming Wednesday. She'd never let Maadhini touch it outside of the four walls of her apartment, but they loved each other...right? While Rebecca spent Thanksgiving with her sister and parents in Paris, Maadhini would be stuck in Jersey with her parents and Sadiya.

Sadiya. She let her phone ring until it fell silent. She still answered any time her *amma* called, but in the past month she'd grown used to ignoring Sadiya's calls if they came at an inopportune time.

Rebecca was so helpful, showing her that only she could determine her own worth. *"If someone calls you and you drop everything to pick up, you're telling not only that person but also yourself that they are more important than your own activities,"* she'd said.

Maadhini always called Sadiya back, and she never ignored her *amma*'s calls, but now when they spoke, she chose to center herself before all else. So, when her *amma* clucked that Jayanthi Aunty had found "such a nice dress she was going to buy for you, but they didn't carry it in a size that big," Maadhini thought of how Rebecca's earrings made her feel and replied that her mom should thank Jayanthi Aunty for her consideration, but that it was tough to find a dress that could fit her big personality. "It must be so much easier to be as small as her."

Her mom had howled with laughter at that. It was the first time a parent had acknowledged her wit, had smiled when she'd stood up for herself against someone's bullying.

Power respects power. Brushing her fingers against her ears, remembering the drug that had accompanied the earrings in them yesterday, she wondered for the hundredth time why she'd ever allowed herself to be walked all over by the Jayanthi Aunties of the world.

By the time Maadhini had changed, brushed her teeth, and left Coral Tower to head to class, she only had ten minutes until it began. No normal human would be able to avoid tardiness, but instead of waiting in the rain to catch the M101 bus and texting Sadiya back to let Wilson know she was on her way, Maadhini snuck behind her building and took out some white powder from a pocket in her dress.

Who needs the bus when you can run? In a surprising act of defiance against the world's unrelenting power structures, she'd swiped the smallest amount of WP from Rebecca last night. *Would a billionaire miss a dollar?* The logic was flawless as far as she was concerned. Looking to confirm she was alone, she snorted it like pixie dust before running toward the College of Arts and Sciences.

Maadhini saw individual raindrops falling all around her. She spotted people walking around the top floors of Coral Tower as clearly as an eagle in the air would. Bending her knees, she launched herself toward class and tried not to throw up as traffic and birds carried on in slow motion all around her. Racing faster than her body was built to manage, she wondered how there weren't more robberies in the city. She knew the answer, of course. One of the main arguments against distributing WP to minorities was that the crime rate would increase. As racist an argument as ever, yet it had been her first thought, too. *What does that say about me?* She arrived outside her class building before she could think of an answer.

Opening the door to Wilson's room, Maadhini collapsed as the drug's aftereffects took their toll on her knees.

"Oh my god!"

Feeling someone take her by the hand, she opened her eyes as Sadiya forcefully hoisted her up against a wall. "'Dhini?"

Wiping her nose, Maadhini saw blood dripping on the linoleum floor.

"Professor?" Sadiya sounded shrill. "We need a minute."

Wilson waved them off and Maadhini tried to force feeling into her legs so that Sadiya wasn't dragging her to the bathroom outside.

Sadiya was yelling as soon as the door closed behind them. "Where have you been?!" Her voice carried all the subtlety of a cannon.

Maadhini waved her off. "Shh…"

"Don't you dare shush me!"

Opening her mouth to speak, Maadhini threw up instead. While most of it found its way into the trashcan Sadiya shoved her toward, the new color of Sadiya's sneakers confirmed not all of it had.

"…sorry."

"For what, 'dhini? What are you sorry for this time?"

As the drug exited her system, memories from that night after her first true encounter with WP took its place.

The two of them yelling at each other as Sadiya commanded her to never do WP again.

Sadiya threatening to tell her parents about Rebecca.

Maadhini throwing Sadiya's day planner down their building's garbage chute.

Tears. Their fights always ended in tears and ice cream. Tears as Maadhini promised to replace the day planner and never do WP again and Sadiya promised to be less judgmental.

Sadiya had been a true friend in the weeks that followed, making up stories to explain to Tanvi why Maadhini wasn't coming home every weekend. She'd even visited Jersey by herself once. *But we outgrow even the best of our friends if they can't grow with us...*

Sadiya slapped her back. "Did you at least remember to bring a pad like I asked?"

Maadhini threw cold water on her face and wiped her mouth with a paper towel. She hoped Rebecca wouldn't be too grossed out once she returned to class. "What?"

Sadiya rolled her eyes. "My text? I'm on my period. Did you bring a pad?"

Grabbing the sink with her hands, looking down as if the drain held some secret deep within it, Maadhini shook her head.

"God, I thought I'd left this dumbass solution back in India." Sadiya sighed as she ripped off several strips of paper towels and tucked them into her underwear. "I can't get back to class before dinner. These will have to do if my last pad gives out."

Maadhini stared blankly, still trying to assess what was going on. Her head might as well have been connected to a helium tank. Her legs shook with the strength of willow branches.

"Easy, there," Sadiya said, grabbing her as her arms slipped from the sink. "You're still taking WP, aren't you?

I've read about the effects on people like us. It's why the sororities can't pass it out willy-nilly anymore."

"People like us." Maadhini spit out the words like poison before leaving the bathroom and Sadiya behind.

"Hang on," Sadiya said, racing to catch up with her as they walked back to class together. "Why aren't you on your period, too? Our cycles are pretty consistent."

Maadhini shushed her as she opened the door back to the classroom. "Don't worry about it." Taking her seat next to Rebecca, she let herself get lost in the bustle of class, happy to turn her brain off and pray the drug wouldn't fail her again.

"A little disappointing from some of you," Wilson said. He handed an exam to a woman who looked as if she might cry. "And a lot disappointing from others."

Chad scoffed as he took his exam from Wilson's hand. "Yo, Prof, I aced this stuff!"

"You did answer all the questions correctly," Wilson acknowledged, "but I saw you pulling at your watch during the exam. I saw it sparkling with WP-enhanced stones."

"It's not against school policy to use WP during exams," Chad whined.

"That's true, but it is against my policy."

"In fact," Chad continued, ignoring him, "some teachers encourage WP use. It helps keep the strong strong."

"And the weak weak," Wilson said. "That's why I don't allow it in my class. How can we ever achieve equity if some people are given an unfair advantage?"

"This is bullshit!"

"Watch your tongue, Mr. Thompson."

Sadiya pretended not to hear the argument, but Maadhini grinned and leaned in.

"No, this is garbage," Chad said. "We're supposed to rough it with the muggles because you're hot for skin grafters?"

Sadiya pressed a hand against her mouth. Rebecca's nostrils flared.

"Out," Wilson said. "Do not return to my class."

Standing, kicking at his chair before grabbing it in pain upon remembering it was connected to an entire row of chairs, Chad hopped right out the door.

The rest of class was uneventful, save for a girl named Julia snorting in indignation as Wilson told them his final was right after Thanksgiving. "Why's it called a midterm if it isn't given in the middle of the term? A final right on the heels makes no sense," she said. "In what world is it fair that eighty percent of our grade is decided in the final two weeks of class?"

Wilson sighed. "Sometimes we do things that don't make much sense just to keep the peace with the powers that be."

Sadiya confronted Maadhini after class ended. "We're really not gonna talk about what happened?"

Maadhini groaned. "'Diya, can I have just one day of peace?"

"What is wrong with you?"

"I'm suffocating," Maadhini said. "I have to talk to you every day and I have to talk to *Amma* every day and I have to keep Rebecca engaged."

"You don't *have* to do any of those things. You're an adult; those are all choices you've made."

"Yeah, right," Maadhini said, rolling her eyes. "I have a choice."

"Yes, you do. I didn't call my own parents often; now I do. Honestly, I used to think Tanvi Aunty was a little annoying. Now I think she's awesome. Your *appa*'s jokes are getting funnier, too."

Maadhini gritted her teeth. Sadiya's own family's approval wasn't enough? She had to steal her *amma*'s approval now, too? She smirked as she remembered she had one thing Sadiya didn't, though. "Whatever. I promised Rebecca we'd get lunch."

Sadiya grabbed her arm as she turned to leave. "Are we okay?"

"How many times are you going to ask the same questions? Yes, we're okay." They were alone, now. Everyone else had left the classroom, and perhaps that's why she'd decided to voice the cruelest thought in her head. "Don't be so insecure."

"You think that woman cares about you?" Sadiya's voice shook like an old car, but she kept going. "It wasn't so long ago that you were the one crying on my shoulder about whatever your *amma* had said or some boy or some teacher. Even now, where was Rebecca when you were literally bleeding from your nose and collapsing in front of everyone?"

Maadhini's cheeks burned. She reached for insults as if a lion had cornered her, throwing whatever she could think of at Sadiya in the hopes that something would stick. "It must suck that you look like that and yet you're still a virgin. I'd be pissy too if I wasn't getting laid."

Sadiya stepped back as if she'd been slapped. "'Dhini…"

"And on top of that, it's that time of the month for you, too."

"Having sex doesn't make you cool." Sadiya spat the words. "And losing your virginity to a woman like that? You devalue yourself, Maadhini."

Now it was Maadhini's turn to step back. She couldn't remember the last time Sadiya had used her full name. Hands at her sides, she balled them into fists. "A woman like what? Successful? Beautiful? Powerful?"

Sadiya chuckled, wielding her laughter like a scimitar, the sound tangling deep in Maadhini's body. "A woman who isn't interested in pursuing a real career. We're going to be architects. Vir Uncle is an engineer. What is she doing?"

"Politics isn't a real career? Public service isn't a real career?"

Sadiya chuckled again, each note of laughter burying itself deeper within Maadhini's psyche. "She isn't going into public service! She's a Steinbeck, one of the elites. Their job is to debate with a bunch of other assholes and decide who's going to wield power today to screw everyone else over."

Maadhini wondered what would happen if she punched Sadiya in the face.

For sure, Amma *will disown me.*

Might still be worth it.

I'd need a new best friend.

Rebecca, right?

I'd have to tell my parents about all this, then.

But if they've disowned me at that point, will it matter?

"You think you understand power because Rebecca let you sniff some WP?" Sadiya's voice burst through her thoughts like they were nothing. "You have no idea. People like them will never, ever let us taste real power."

On the verge of tears, Maadhini uncurled her fists. Their friendship had changed in this room. Forever. But that didn't mean she had to change to accommodate it. If happiness was what mattered and being in this room wasn't making her happy anymore, she could leave. She repeated another affirmation to herself: *I am worth fighting for.* Rather than thinking of a clever riposte, she chose to save her energy and simply left to be with the woman she loved.

The crisp November air of New York calmed Maadhini's mind as she made her way to Rebecca's apartment in Midtown. She'd tried running, like she had before, but it was no use. Calling a cab instead, she brushed a hand over her bare ear. The magic of WP was gone, and she was shaking with the need to get more. If her brain was a 108,000-piece jigsaw puzzle, the drug had allowed her to put it together for the first time, unlocking secrets about her body and mind that no one knew. Yeah, sex was great, but have you ever been treated special?

I need Rebecca. She prayed her lover would lend her some. Every moment without her and her WP made Maadhini's entire body ache.

"That's $17.57." Her gruff cab driver looked back through the transparent barrier separating them, expecting cash before allowing her to leave. She handed him a twenty-dollar bill, closing her eyes and saying a silent prayer upon seeing the picture of Ganesha on the driver's dashboard. Acknowledging his thanks, she got out and entered Rebecca's building.

Rebecca answered the door with a sigh. "I didn't wait up because it looked like you needed to say some stuff to Sadiya."

Grasping the woman's face with both hands, Maadhini kissed her as soon as she walked in. Rebecca's eyes widened as Maadhini brushed her ears, touching the earrings. Maadhini's heart quickened, and she wondered if it was due to Rebecca or the drug.

You can't feel love for an inanimate object. She whisked the notion from her mind as if it was useless clutter, its only aim to distract her.

"Er, a little forward for you, isn't it?" Breaking the kiss,

Rebecca tilted her head. "Grabbing and kissing me before we even close the door?"

"I've learned what I want and what I don't." Maadhini followed Rebecca's eyes as they went to a jewelry-encrusted box on the table near the couch. Her heart raced even faster as she wondered why the box was out. Did Rebecca realize Maadhini had stolen from her?

The next thrust of Rebecca's tongue pushed the thought out of her head. "I know we said we'd get lunch, but how about dessert first?" She shoved Maadhini's full body against the door, making it slam shut.

As they explored each other's mouths, Maadhini spun Rebecca, then seized her wrists and pinned them above her head. Rebecca's expression showed Maadhini how thin the line was between lust and fear.

"I'm in control today," Maadhini whispered, tugging Rebecca's skirt down and biting her hip. Pushing Rebecca into the bedroom and back onto her bed, Maadhini shoved her green panties to the side and disappeared between her thighs.

Their bodies stuck to each other and the sheets as they lay sprawled, naked and sweaty, across the bed. Rebecca's fingers traced figure-eights across Maadhini's full bottom. Each touch made her tingle.

"That was nice," Rebecca sighed. Her breath brushed the back of Maadhini's neck, as alluring as the whispered promises of the Devil. "I love that we can do nice things for each other, trust each other."

Maadhini froze. *Shit.*

She knows?

Should I admit it first?

Rebecca's voice pierced her thoughts before she could answer herself. "There's been some WP missing. Any idea where it went?"

Maadhini's stomach rumbled. *Oh god, please don't fart.* Deception made her gassy. Growing up, Sadiya could always smell her while playing hide and seek. "Um…"

"It's okay, 'dhini." Rebecca's voice was as calm as a silent brook. "I just need to know."

Propping herself up on the bed, covering herself with a blanket, Maadhini nodded silently.

"Hey," Rebecca cooed, "it's okay." Embracing Maadhini, she pulled their bodies together, letting the blanket fall away. Pushing Maadhini back, Rebecca took in the sight of her, biting her bottom lip. "You're lucky you're so fine."

Blushing, Maadhini let her lover grab at the folds of her skin, at the fat under her breasts. Rebecca made her feel as if she was Michelangelo's *David*. She gasped as Rebecca pinched a nipple.

"It's just that I saw your nose bleeding today." Rebecca's voice was as syrupy as a Starbucks Frappuccino, but her eyes narrowed to tell a different story.

"Rebecca…you're hurting me."

"Well, 'dhini, sometimes passion hurts."

Maadhini gasped again as Rebecca let her go.

"If I could figure out that you stole from me, someone else could, too."

Rubbing her sore nipple and sniffling, Maadhini stood up and put her clothes back on. She covered as much of her body as possible as she dressed. "I'm sorry." The words came out masked by choked tears.

"Oh, 'dhini." Rebecca got up, stopping right behind her and pressing her hips against Maadhini's as she whispered in her ear. "It really is okay. We all make mistakes." She kissed Maadhini's neck, licked her earlobes. "You just need to understand how your actions can affect other people now that you're with me. That WP was for me to bring home to my parents this weekend, my sister, and now it's all gone, isn't it?" Her hand rubbed against Maadhini's mound.

"Yes..."

"My family's a big deal, and, well, a story like this, you know what the media would say. Some skin grafter stealing from American royalty."

Maadhini inhaled sharply as she heard the wetness around Rebecca's fingers.

"Of course, I think that's all horse shit. What a foul phrase. But CNN would use the term, and then where would that leave you?"

She's right.

She's always right.

She just wants what's best for me.

"I'm so sorry..."

"Don't worry," Rebecca said. "I have an idea."

When they were both dressed and in the living room, Rebecca opened the jewelry-encrusted box on the table. A sea-blue necklace sparkled inside.

"It's for you," Rebecca said.

Maadhini gasped. "For...me?"

Giggling, Rebecca picked it up and unclasped it, walking behind Maadhini to put it on. The moment it touched Maadhini's skin, a familiar energy thrummed through her insides.

"You feel that? I told you my family's a big deal. Claire's going into high finance, but Daddy is a scientist. They've found ways to mask WP's physical properties. It's all over that necklace, and you can't even tell. No one can unless they have specific equipment. Now we can go out in public like this, like equals."

"I love you." Maadhini said the words without hesitation. She knew it more than she knew anything else. It was as unassailable a truth as gravity. And she knew Rebecca loved her back. She didn't need to hear the words; this gift was enough.

"…you're sweet."

When Maadhini turned to face Rebecca, she saw her throwing some objects from the adjacent bathroom into a bag.

"You really should go," Rebecca said. "I need to pack. I leave to meet Claire and my parents in Utah tomorrow morning."

I thought we'd spend the night…

Did I say "I love you" too early?

But then why give me this necklace?

She's nervous. I can be strong for her, just like she's strong for me.

Thoughts bubbled up through Maadhini's head like a carbonation through soda, consuming every inch of free space, rising until her head threatened to burst open. Rebecca walked to and fro, packing like the world wasn't melting around her. Only when Maadhini grabbed the kitchen counter for support did her girlfriend notice her unsteadiness.

"'Dhini?"

Maadhini opened her mouth to respond and couldn't breathe, collapsing to her knees instead.

"Oh my god, 'dhini?!"

Rebecca raced to the kitchen sink and returned to shove water into Maadhini's hands. Gripping the glass with both fists, Maadhini somehow managed to gulp some down before the glass slipped through her fingers and shattered on the floor. Shards bounced into her hair, cutting her nose and cheeks. Jagged edges found their way as far as the window on the other side of the room. She grabbed at her neck, unable to breathe, and vomited the water back up. It wasn't until Rebecca yanked the necklace off and threw it across the room that her mind was able to reorient itself. Tears glinted amid the shattered glass as she looked at Rebecca.

"It was instinctual," Rebecca said, staring at the now-broken necklace on her floor. "I thought it might help…"

She broke it for me? "How much did that cost?"

"It doesn't matter," Rebecca said.

Maadhini avoided staring at the creases in the woman's furrowed brow, evidence of the shocked pain at having destroyed something so precious.

"What matters is that you're safe," Rebecca said dully.

"What, uh, what'll you tell your dad?"

"Don't worry about that." Rebecca's answer was a whisper. She was hesitant at first, but by the time she stood and began sweeping her floor, her voice had a new strength in it, colder. "It's okay. Some people just weren't made to handle WP."

Do I just leave? It felt so incomplete. One minute they'd been naked in bed, the next Maadhini was just staring blankly as Rebecca cleaned up her mess.

"Tell your parents I said hi," Maadhini said. "I mean, if you've told them about me. I know some families are weird about those things…"

Rebecca's answer was as crisp as the November air. "I make a habit of telling my family about anyone I'm sleeping with."

Maadhini looked at her feet as she replied. "Um, how many people would that be?"

"Don't be so insecure, 'dhini. You're the person I'm with right now; why can't we just enjoy the present?"

It's okay.

We're okay.

I'm okay.

Forcing herself to believe it, she wished Rebecca a happy Thanksgiving and returned to the city alone.

Chapter Eight

Maadhini's cluttered thoughts bounced around her mind as the Amtrak train sped out of the city and into Jersey. Crossing her legs, she stared out the window and did her best to ignore Sadiya. The Wednesday before Thanksgiving was always packed leaving Penn Station, and the two women were forced to sit next to each other.

Perfect little Sadiya, she thought. *Even had time to shave her legs this morning.* The smoothness of her skin made Maadhini's stubble all the more noticeable as their limbs bumped against each other.

Sadiya stared at her lap, earphones attached to her iPad as she watched some romcom with Ryan Gosling and Steve Carrell.

Crazy Stupid Love? Well, that's ironic.

They'd barely spoken since Maadhini had returned from Rebecca's apartment. Sadiya had suggested that morning that they table their fight and try to be civil for the weekend, a sort of truce to keep the parents off their backs. It was a good idea.

So, naturally, I didn't think of it. Only Saint Sadiya did.

If there had been space to navigate around the train, Maadhini would've gone right up to the front, opened the door, and flung herself out. As it was, she wasn't even brave enough to risk sliding through the crowd and bumping into people to try and go to the bathroom. Something was trying to rip its way out of her stomach, but no doubt she'd have to wait in a long line. *And pooping in that toilet? No, thanks.* Checking her phone for the fourteenth time, she let out a deep sigh. Nothing from Rebecca.

"What's wrong?" Sadiya took out one earbud. It almost looked like she cared.

But why would she? I was horrible to her. When Sadiya had asked last night why her eyes were red, Maadhini had ignored the question and said she was thinking of moving out to her own place next year.

"It's nothing."

Sadiya huffed before putting her earbud back in. "Suit yourself."

Seated, cornered between Sadiya and the stranger on her other side, Maadhini pumped her knee like a piston. As much as she hated how she'd left things with Rebecca, she hated even more that she couldn't talk to Sadiya about it. She was convinced, though, that 'diya would just lord it over her, anyways. No, she couldn't let Sadiya think she was right.

"Next stop: Metropark." As the Amtrak conductor announced their imminent arrival to Iselin, NJ, she stood with the rest of the crowd and retrieved her baggage.

Vir's red Toyota RAV4 was already waiting for them when they walked off the platform.

"Hi, Uncle," Sadiya said. She rolled her suitcase over and he waved her off when she tried to help him throw it into the trunk.

"All good?" he said.

"All good." Maadhini forced a smile and shared an awkward one-armed hug before getting in the backseat. He'd definitely think something was up if she sat shotgun instead of next to Sadiya. *Everything's just great.*

"How are classes, Uncle?" Sadiya said.

"They are not challenging, but I have made friends and the degree will be good for me."

"That's great."

He gazed at them in the rearview mirror. "And how are you girls keeping your time?"

"We have finals coming up," Maadhini cut in. Sadiya had promised not to bring up their fight, but things could spill out in anger. Things about Rebecca.

"I know my little 'diya is keeping you on track with that day planner she always carries around."

Maadhini winced. *When was the last time I called her 'diya?* Her parents could call them whatever pet names they pleased, of course. By the look on Sadiya's face, she clearly liked it. "Yes, *Appa*, we practically live in the library."

"Study hard," Vir said, his voice losing its playfulness. His brow furrowed. "They did not recognize my degree, but it must be better for you now that we're here."

Guilt ate at Maadhini's insides. She couldn't waste four years trying to "find herself" like the others at school, or even Rebecca. Her time at college had to mean something.

"I talked to your *appa* last night, Sadiya."

"Really, Uncle?"

"They say you've been calling more and more. *Rhumba chamata, beta.*"

Maadhini frowned. She could be very sweet too, if only her parents noticed. "Any news from Hema Aunty and Sahit Uncle?"

"They're thinking of coming for Christmas."

The news hit Maadhini like a bag of bricks to her gut, increasing her bathroom issues.

"Yes," Sadiya said. "*Amma* and *Appa* mentioned that to me a few days ago."

Maadhini bit her lip trying not to scream, wondering why Sadiya hadn't told her. The last thing she needed was two Indian mothers patrolling her every movement during the winter break. Growing up, Sadiya had told her how Hema Aunty had once logged into Sadiya's email account and told a boy she was talking with that "she" had decided to become a Catholic nun. When Sadiya had confronted her, Hema Aunty had said, "I do you favor. If he still interested, must be gay. Only gay guy not care about sex. If he not interested, was shallow. Who would stop talking just because gay or Catholic?"

When Sadiya had pointed out that Hema Aunty didn't have any gay or Catholic friends, her response was as brief as it was obvious. "I'm shallow."

Her *appa*'s words pulled Maadhini roughly from her thoughts. "...they wanted to go after a week, but we convinced them to stay for three."

Three weeks?! She grabbed her stomach as it growled. *Maybe I should've risked the train toilet.*

"Aunty must be thrilled," Sadiya said.

"Yes," Vir nodded, making a turn into their neighborhood. Oak trees and fountains and children playing basketball at the park in the distance littered Maadhini's view as she stared out the window. "It will be good for her to have her best friend around."

That's what one would think...

"New York must have been ecstatic," Vir continued. "Obama being re-elected. Did you go to Times Square and celebrate?"

"No, Uncle, it gets so rowdy and crowded during

those parties."

Closing her eyes, Maadhini remembered Election Night. As head of their chapter of College Democrats, Rebecca had been slammed in the days leading up to it, coordinating canvassing trips into Philadelphia and even sending some students as far south as northern Virginia. She'd tried to get Maadhini to come on a trip with her to canvass voters, but talking to strangers about American politics? Her stomach gurgled again just thinking about it. She tried picturing that night again, trying to get her mind off the fact that she felt like her insides wanted to become outsides. Not only had Obama won, but Democrats had expanded their majority in the Senate, too. It had been the only time Rebecca had shown up at her apartment. Drunk and horny, she'd taken Maadhini back to her place. Maadhini wasn't sure she was a Democrat, but when she'd woken up the next day, she knew she liked them winning.

"I heard this guy from California could be majority leader one day," Vir said. "Manish Nagaraj."

Maadhini opened her eyes. "*Appa*, some Indian liberal is never going to rise to power."

"But it would be super cool if it happened, Uncle," Sadiya interrupted. "And you never know. He is a senator now, no? So why not leader one day?"

Sandbagged by the revelation that she'd be sharing her winter holiday with Sadiya's parents, irritated at how she'd left things with Rebecca, silently furious she couldn't talk to her best friend about any of this, she lashed out the only way she knew how.

"*Appa*, I have a friend who's the head of College Democrats at school. He knows U.S. politics better than Sadiya ever will."

Turning into their driveway, Vir nodded his approval and waved off her words. It was clear he wasn't listening, but the comments hit their intended victim full force. Maadhini tried not to smile as she saw Sadiya blinking away tears as they exited the car and Vir popped the trunk, ready to carry their baggage for them.

Vir carried their bags into the house as Maadhini touched her nose behind the car.

"Something's wrong," Sadiya said, spotting blood smearing Maadhini's nails.

She tried wiping them on the inseam of her black skirt. "It's nothing."

"I knew there was a reason you were being such a bitch."

It was no less than Maadhini deserved after what she'd just pulled, what she'd been pulling this whole time. Still, Sadiya hadn't been so upfront when they'd fought in the past. "I don't feel great, but it's fine. Let's move on."

"Move on?"

Grabbing her stomach with one hand and the top of the car with the other, Maadhini stumbled a bit.

"You want to throw up, don't you?"

"I just need a minute."

Sadiya smirked. "Whether upstairs or downstairs, the blood has to come out somewhere."

This is worse than a period. Closing her eyes, she pictured late nights and early mornings in Rebecca's apartment, but she no longer saw Rebecca's naked body splayed across hers like a harp she could pick at and admire. When she pictured the apartment, she saw earrings and a necklace.

"I thought as much during class, but it's true, isn't it?" Sadiya seized her by the shoulders, leaning her against the SUV. Though it was in the fifties, the car burned against her back. "You lied to me. It didn't stop with that one time. You've been taking WP this whole time."

"...yes."

"'Dhini..."

Maadhini opened her eyes. "What? Are you going to call me a skin grafter? Fine. But you don't know, 'diya!"

"What don't I know?"

"When I'm on it...I have the confidence of a mediocre white man!" Her stomach rumbled again, and as Maadhini crossed her legs she knew the next interruption wouldn't end peacefully.

"Must not be too confident, since you just told Vir Uncle that the head of College Democrats is a man and not your girlfriend."

Maadhini balled her fists before uncurling them. The murmurs in her stomach were becoming yells. The fight was leaving her, and other things wanted to leave as well.

"Leave *Appa* out of this!" She shouted the words as she ran inside, past her *amma*, and slammed the guest bathroom door behind her. Yanking her bottoms down to sit on the toilet, she heard her *amma* through the walls, speaking to Sadiya as she entered the house.

"*Beta,* what was all that about? You all took so long, I got worried."

"Oh, nothing, Aunty. You know how embarrassed Maadhini gets. She's been a bit unwell and didn't want anyone to know she's having diarrhea."

Maadhini bit her lip again to keep from screaming in frustration. Sadiya knew talking about bathroom issues made her crazy, especially when they were *her* bathroom issues.

"*Thik hai,*" Tanvi said. "I'll make mosaranna for dinner. Curd rice is always good for the system."

Maadhini hated mosaranna. And she hated Sadiya. And she hated WP if this was what it did to her. Trying to ignore the sounds and smells coming out of her body, she focused on the conversation outside instead.

"Come, *beta,* I need help in the kitchen." Her *amma* shouted to her through the bathroom door before they left. "Maadhini, remember to turn the exhaust on when you leave!"

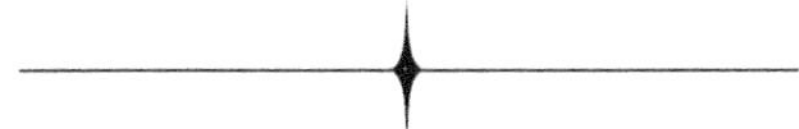

Maadhini's *amma* insisted she and Sadiya sleep in the guest room that had its own bathroom, "in case you need it during the night."

Maadhini did, but that didn't stop her from cursing her mother's boldness. By the time she woke up the next morning, Sadiya was already downstairs. Tanvi's voice carried all the way from the kitchen, instructing Sadiya on the proper way to make Mysore Pak. Maadhini smiled, touched her mom had remembered that Mysore Pak was the only Indian sweet she liked. Walking down the stairs in her pajamas, she watched Sadiya stir chickpea flour with ghee and sugar in a heated pan.

"*Beta,* did you wake up in middle of night?"

"No, *Amma,* I slept well, thank you." *Maybe this weekend won't be a disaster.*

Her *amma*'s smile wilted as she looked from her to the pan. "Oh, *beta,* I had separate dessert made for you."

"...what?" Maadhini couldn't believe her eyes as her *amma* took some cookies out of the fridge.

"Chocolate chip zucchini!"

"What the hell is that?"

"*Ayyo Rama,* language, *kanne.*"

"...*Amma*...why?"

"Nilam Aunty worked so hard last night."

"Last night?!"

"Your stomach. Can't give Mysore Pak. Too much ghee and sugar. Bad for digestion."

"What did you tell Nilam Aunty?!"

Sadiya failed to stifle a giggle as she continued to stir the ingredients in the hot pan.

"We all supposed to pretend you don't poop? I tell her truth; your stomach delicate. Just like your sensibilities."

Maadhini wondered when her *amma* had learned that word, sensibilities. Instead of responding, she grunted in frustration and went down to the basement to see her *appa*. Closing the door behind her, she heard Tanvi ask Sadiya, "It's that time of month for her?"

The Giants were playing the Rams. Vir sat in a recliner, Kingfisher beer in one hand and remote in the other. He muted the game upon seeing Maadhini. "Don't tell me; you've finally decided to learn about football?"

Maadhini smiled. "Who's winning?"

"It doesn't matter who's winning in the first quarter; only who's in the lead at the end of the fourth."

"So, the Rams are winning?"

"You should've majored in comedy, *yaar*. What are you doing wasting my money trying to become an architect?"

She knew he meant it as a joke, but it still stung. Her smile flickered, as evanescent and steady as a candle in the wind.

"Besides," he continued, not noticing, "this is a highlights reel. Games won't start for a couple more hours."

"Oh."

"Your *amma* banished you down here? I thought she wanted you to actually cook some things today."

"...really?"

"Some American food she planned."

Maadhini paused. *American food?*

"She figured since it's an American holiday, let's eat

American food."

"Then why the Mysore Pak?"

"*Ayyo Rama,* we are still good South Indians. How should I pass up an opportunity for Mysore Pak?"

Maadhini's smile returned.

"And don't worry, I'll protect you from those gross cookies. I can sneak you some Mysore Pak."

"Thanks, *Appa.*" She gulped, remembering the promise she'd made herself last time she was home. She knew she could tell her dad about Rebecca. He was so cool about things. He'd understand. Gathering her confidence, rubbing her hands over her ears, she wished she was wearing the earrings. "Do you want another beer?"

"Thank you, *kanne.*"

Her breath caught at the word. Her *amma* used terms of endearment as weapons, but *Appa* had never been anything but genuine. *Beta* meant you were someone he liked and respected. *Kanne* was reserved for loved family. Walking to the mini fridge near the wet bar, she noticed a half-empty bottle of Johnnie Walker Black. "Scotch, *Appa?*"

Vir rolled his eyes. "Don't tell your *amma.* She never comes down here anyways."

Maadhini let out a nervous laugh, biting her lip as she pumped herself up.

You can do this.

You can do this.

You can do this.

"You're so good, *kanne.*"

"*Appa,*" she said, "there's something I have to tell you…" Her hands were so clammy she almost let the bottle slip from her fingers as she handed it to him.

"When I hear about Jayanthi Aunty's daughter, I think how lucky we are to have you." Maadhini's insides froze as her dad continued. "She spoke with Tanvi this morning. Her daughter isn't even in Jersey with her today. *Paavam.*"

Paavam? There's nothing sad about Jayanthi Aunty's situation. Maadhini's hands curled into fists. She shoved them in her pockets in case the universe shifted and her *appa* actually observed his surroundings.

"Instead, the girl is in California with her 'girlfriend.'" Vir put his hands up in quotation marks. "Who knew a good Indian daughter was so rare?"

Unmuting the game, he took a long sip of his beer as Maadhini swept a tear from her eyes. "Yes, *Appa.*"

"Hey," Vir said. "Don't tell your *amma*, but you can have a beer if you want. It's your vacation, too."

Nodding, she took one from the fridge and used it to drown her sorrows.

Her *amma* refused to walk more than a few stairs down toward the basement when she summoned Maadhini back up hours later.

"As long as she is up there and I am down here," her *appa* explained, "she can pretend the beer and scotch don't exist."

Upstairs, Tanvi assigned Maadhini the task of roasting carrots, sweet potatoes, and parsnips as Sadiya prepared a green bean casserole. "This our second year here," Tanvi explained. "Okay now to wade into some American traditions."

Maadhini bumped elbows with Sadiya and her *amma* as they all navigated the kitchen. She sighed in relief when the home phone rang and her *amma* raced to the living room to get it.

"Tanvi Aunty has me cooking so much that I feel like we're married," Sadiya laughed. "There's nothing more American than the annoying mother-in-law who puts you to work all day."

"Oh, you think this is funny?" Maadhini put her pan down to ensure she didn't throw it at her best friend.

Sadiya frowned. "'Dhini, relax. It was just a joke."

"I'm glad you find being gay funny."

"What are you talking about? Are you still sick?"

Maadhini ignored the question. "I almost told *Appa* just now."

"That's...that's awesome."

"Yeah, I was all ready until he started talking about Jayanthi Aunty's daughter."

"...oh..."

"Right. Oh..."

"'Dhini, I'm sorry..." Despite everything, Maadhini's heart lifted when Sadiya squeezed her shoulder in solidarity. She opened her mouth, ready to talk, but her *amma* returned before anything more could be said.

"That was Varsha Aunty," Tanvi said. "She wanted to know why we call Thanksgiving an Indian holiday. These white people so confusing."

They'd snacked on Kurkure until eating around three in the afternoon.

"These are so much better than Cheetos," Sadiya said. Maadhini murmured in agreement.

"Vir, come up to eat."

The fact that her *appa* came immediately told Maadhini all she needed to know about the score. "I thought it only mattered who was winning at the end of the game?" she said.

"Even the Giants can't come back from that whooping," he sighed.

As they all sat around the table, Tanvi said that Nilam Aunty had told her yesterday about the American tradition of saying what you're thankful for before eating. "Let us try, huh?"

Maadhini gazed around. *Are they doing all this for me?* The casserole. The beer. Even telling her to get out more, pushing her to that party where she'd met Rebecca in the first place. *And what am I doing for them...*

Her head throbbed as thoughts raced through it. A familiar ache started in her gut.

"'Dhini?" Sadiya blinked. "You okay?"

"...sorry?"

"I said I'm thankful we're still together after all these years."

"Oh...yes..."

"*Beta?* Are you okay?"

"It's my stomach again. Diarrhea." She raced upstairs. It wasn't, but she'd rather have her parents picturing that than what she knew was about to happen. She'd hardly opened the bathroom door when vomit and blood erupted from her throat and splattered into the toilet. She hadn't made it to their bedroom's bathroom, but luckily this floor had one apart from the master and guest rooms.

"'Dhini?" She heard Sadiya close the bathroom door behind her. "I told your *amma* I'd check on you."

"Go away." Maadhini waved a hand in protest.

"You've been taking it this whole time, haven't you? Not just a little, but a lot."

Maadhini hugged the toilet bowl. "I just wanted to be like her..."

Sadiya came and held her hair back as she continued

to paint her own version of a Jackson Pollock. She was ready to spill her guts in more ways than one. "She gave me a necklace, that night. It had WP. I wore it."

"Oh, 'dhini…"

"Imagine how that feels. This perfect woman you love hands you unlimited power. And I couldn't handle it. I felt like I couldn't breathe. She had to tug it off me before I passed out."

Sadiya hugged her, and she knew she was being honest, she knew it was the only way she could endure in this world. "I've given everything to her…"

"And what has she given you?"

"She's made me feel safe, and loved, and special." Maadhini whispered the words.

"Then that's worth holding onto." There was no smile or glint of teasing in Sadiya's eyes. Her best friend spoke with steel in her voice and fire in her heart.

How can she be like this after I've been so terrible? "I'm so sorry…"

"Hey," Sadiya said, taking a tissue to wipe snot and vomit from Maadhini's face, "this is new for both of us. It's okay; I just want you to be happy."

"You're my best friend."

"I know; you're mine, too."

Hoisting herself up, Maadhini flushed before turning the faucet on and wiping her mouth.

"Think you can manage?" Sadiya asked.

"WP addiction is a bitch." They shared a laugh before Maadhini continued. "Remind me never to do this again."

"I'll help you through the withdrawal, if you'll let me."

"Deal."

Tanvi was right outside the door as the two emerged.

Maadhini shrank back. "*Amma*…" She was a deer in headlights as Tanvi hugged her.

"*Beta,* I'm sorry I couldn't figure out what was going

on."

"*Amma…*"

"We not so different. So what if you like girls?"

Maadhini stared at Sadiya as her *amma* continued to hug her, sharing a silent conversation with her best friend over her mother's shoulder.

"When I first married Vir, sometimes I wondered if a woman would've been better."

Maadhini gasped. "*Amma!*"

"No, no, I like him okay after a few years. He good man."

"Aunty?" Sadiya ventured, her eyes wide.

"*Kanne.*" Breaking the hug, Tanvi turned to Sadiya, whose jaw was on the floor.

Kanne…

Maadhini had never heard her mother use that word with anyone else. Her tone was nice enough, but she may as well have stabbed Sadiya with the butter knife, they'd use to cut dessert. "We wanted you here to look after Maadhini." She was somehow smiling and frowning at the same time. "How she get into drugs with you looking after her?"

Sadiya buried a sniffle.

"*Ayyo Rama,*" Tanvi said. "Crying not help anyone. You just do better from now on, okay?"

"…yes, Aunty. I'll look after her."

"Good." Turning to Maadhini, she finished saying her piece. "You think you so important, in charge of all our happiness?"

"I, uh…"

"Maybe I'm not as smart as my genius daughter, but still pretty bright. I make friends, enjoy all kinds of food, good living here. Because that's what's important."

"*Amma…*"

"You embarrass to tell us? I understand. Not always

easy. But we came to America so you could dream bigger. Bigger means gay? Okay. As long as you're happy."

"And *Appa*?"

Tanvi waved a hand as if swatting a fly. "Don't worry about *Appa*. His bark worse than his bite. I can take care of him."

Maadhini flung herself at her *amma* with all the feelings she'd bottled up since September. The impact almost bowled them over.

"Okay, *beta*." Tanvi tapped her daughter's back. "Enough sappy stuff. You come down now. Vir will think we all got sick."

As she left, Maadhini and Sadiya could only stare at each other. "...what the fuck was that?"

"Dude," Sadiya said. "Tanvi Aunty is a baller."

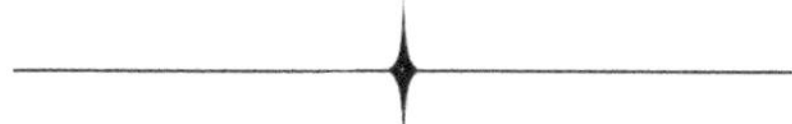

"I'm just saying, I'm not sure my *amma* would ever be that cool." Sadiya's words pierced the reverent silence of Amtrak's quiet car.

"Well, you can always turn gay and we'll find out." Maadhini bumped Sadiya's leg playfully as they sat pressed against each other on the ride back to NYU. "We talked more that night, after *Appa* passed out from drinking too much scotch and *Amma* was pretending he was just tired."

"Where was I?"

"Upstairs studying. I can't believe the end of term is so soon."

Sadiya scoffed. "You don't deserve it, but I'd be willing to let you back into my study group."

Maadhini giggled. "The exclusive study group of two?"

"With prizes awarded for every correct question."

"...thank you."

The two friends shared a look, a squeeze of the hands, before the passenger behind them shushed them into silence. Pointing at each other and grabbing their luggage, they ventured to another car.

"Studying in the quiet car has never been our deal," Maadhini said as they left.

"Speak for yourself," Sadiya replied. "America has solidified my love for notecards over most humans. Anyways, what did your *amma* say?"

Maadhini found them new seats before explaining. "She said she knew I'd been acting out of character all semester, that she was just happy I hadn't been raped or anything."

Sadiya's eyes widened to the size of saucers.

"Yeah, she was so afraid I'd met someone at the party she pushed me to attend, and that night had ruined my life. I guess guilt works on *ammas* and *appas* as well as their kids."

Sadiya rolled her eyes. "Yeah, but what about Jayanthi Aunty?"

"*Amma* didn't mention it, and I wasn't about to bring it up." Maadhini giggled again before finishing her story. "*Amma*'s only real comment was that between watching Modern Family and Ellen, she's a little sad I'm not funnier."

Sadiya snorted. "For real?"

Maadhini adopted an overly thick accent before answering. "Gay people so funny. Why I not laughing all weekend?"

"What did you say?"

"I said, 'You weren't laughing all weekend because you were worried about *Appa*'s drinking.'"

"Oh my god!" Sadiya slapped her arm as the train pulled into Penn Station and they exited to rejoin the hustle and bustle of the city.

"Yeah, *Amma* had the same response." Maadhini laughed.

As the two girls wheeled their bags to a cab, Maadhini's pants pocket vibrated.

"Your butt's buzzing."

"What?"

Sadiya pointed to the back of Maadhini's jeans. Retrieving her phone, Maadhini saw a text from Rebecca.

Just got back. Can you swing by the apartment?

"Rebecca?" Sadiya guessed.

"...yeah..."

"It's okay. You take this cab. I'll grab another one."

Maadhini bit her lip. "Yeah?"

Sadiya's eyes conveyed understanding, but her tone was weighted with expectations. "'Dhini, it's okay. Just... please don't wear any WP. You can't handle it...and that's okay."

Hand in her pocket, Maadhini pinched her thigh to keep from huffing at the statement. She couldn't handle it? "I told you addiction is a bitch, didn't I?"

"You also told me to remind you to never do it again..."

My amma *accepts me as gay and I'm having sex with a white woman. I can handle anything.* Maadhini forced a smile as she got into the cab. "Thanks for the reminder. I got this." She didn't look back as the car pulled away onto the mean streets of the Big Apple.

Rebecca's door was open when Maadhini arrived. She was wrapping up a phone call with her sister. "I know, Claire."

Maadhini hesitated at the sight of Rebecca's furrowed brow. She knocked on the door to grab the woman's attention, thinking the sight of her would soften her frustration, but if anything, it looked like her presence made Rebecca even more exasperated.

"Okay, Claire. I gotta go."

Maadhini stared at the floor as what was undoubtedly an awkward conversation wrapped up. She made figure-eights across the flooring with a shoe.

"Yes, she's here. I'll call you later." Hanging up, Rebecca smiled at Maadhini. That smile mocked her, the same one she always used when she just wanted her *amma* to shut up about something.

"What was that about?"

"How was home?"

Maadhini looked Rebecca in the eyes. The first thing she noticed was the earrings.

"Oh...yeah..." Taking the earrings off, Rebecca set them on the kitchen counter before wrapping her arms around Maadhini, moving her to the couch to sit. "We...we need to talk."

Had anyone ever delivered good news after saying those four words? "Um, what's up?" Maadhini forced steel into her voice.

Whatever Rebecca said, they'd get past it together. She was a South Indian lesbian sleeping with a white woman, and she had her mom's approval. She could handle anything.

"The break was good...it gave me the chance to think about a lot of things, about life, about family..."

"Yeah, me too, actually. I told my *amma* about us."

Rebecca's eyes widened. "How much about us?"

"I mean, she doesn't know I'm not a virgin anymore."

"WP?"

Maadhini fidgeted, sitting on her hands, and pretending to be fascinated with the shape of her shoe. "Um, yeah...she guessed that."

"Claire was right..."

"About what? Rebecca, what was that phone call about? What's going on?" Maadhini had been keeping her emotions in check since she entered the apartment, but when she looked up at her lover's face, she saw tears and couldn't hold back her own anymore.

Rebecca's expression crumpled. "I'm sorry, 'dhini."

"Sorry about what?" Maadhini leaned in, hugging Rebecca for support.

Rebecca pushed her aside and stood, turning her back to face the windows and Trump Towers. "I told Claire what happened, you know, about the necklace breaking…"

"Babe." Maadhini got up as well, reaching out to hold Rebecca's hand. After a moment of contact, Rebecca pulled away as if her touch was toxic. "That was in the past…"

"Thanksgiving, Utah…I had time to sort out my feelings."

Maadhini froze. "And?"

"It's not just the necklace. Just…our families are too different…"

As if Rebecca's tears held Maadhini's lifeforce within them, pain lanced through her every time Rebecca brushed the droplets aside like obstacles blocking her way.

Sniffling, Rebecca delivered her next words with the force of a bullet. "We need to break up."

Maadhini's heart stopped. "…what?" She fell back onto the couch as if she'd been punched in the gut.

"During break, Claire told me about this Korean guy who's a senior at Harvard. He had a good job offer and everything." Rebecca turned to face her, calmness now oozing from her being. Her words were deliberate, and Maadhini suspected she'd rehearsed this. "The guy tried to run through Commerce Street during rush hour."

"Oh…babe…"

"WP. He'd taken some to get through finals, to get his dream internship…he had so much promise, but in the end, he turned out to be nothing but a skin grafter."

Maadhini cringed at the slur, even though she'd heard Rebecca use it before. Could one weekend with her family really have changed her so much? Or was this who she'd been all along?

"I know, it's terrible to call him that. But it's worse than just being a drug addict, in my opinion. People like him…chasing a temporary high isn't enough. They want to play God with their genetic makeup, they want to dream bigger than they should."

"You mean bigger than white people think they should?" Anger in her voice, Maadhini stood again, putting her hands on her hips. "What happened to your lofty ideals?"

"I don't know…" Rebecca's voice cracked, and it looked like she might cry again. In the next moment, though, she choked down whatever uncertainty was in her soul. "Claire told my parents about the necklace, about everything. They won't press charges."

"Charges?!" Maadhini shouted a question and accusation together. "You *gave* me that WP!"

"They can bury the truth, make sure no one finds out. Please, you don't want a Steinbeck as an enemy. They just want you to go away." Rebecca's voice was as dead as the beef she ate.

Maadhini wondered if her girlfriend was a sociopath or merely past the point of pain, someone to be pitied because they'd decided feeling nothing was better than dealing with reality. Balling her hands into fists, she took a step toward Rebecca. "You're nothing but a hypocrite. WP legalization, LGBT rights, they're all under the same umbrella of equality."

"That's not true," Rebecca said. Their silhouettes cast shadows against the wall in the empty apartment. Short and plump versus short and thin. So similar, yet destined to be different. "I'll always promote equity, but sometimes that's in direct contrast to promoting equality."

Maadhini opened her mouth to scream and found that she'd lost her voice. Instead of producing words, tears streamed from her eyes. Her bangs fell in front of them, blurring her vision further. Rebecca looked like one of the *rakshasas* she'd read about in epic stories about heroes and villains. She tried matching her voice to the steel in Rebecca's, but when she opened her mouth, it was with the fortitude of a frog. "That necklace...was a gift...for me."

Rebecca stared past her, like she didn't exist.

It'd be easier if she hated me. "Do you...do you have another one?"

Rebecca touched her at last, holding Maadhini's hand and steering her toward the front door. Maadhini thought Rebecca's skin would soothe her but found that the woman's coldness took on a lifeforce of its own. It threatened to suffocate her as easily as the necklace had.

"Even if I did, you know I can't give it to you."

Maadhini dug her heels in as Rebecca opened the door and tried pushing her out.

"'Dhini..." Rebecca warned.

Maadhini should've never let her use that pet name. She feared it was ruined forever now. *What about me makes me unlovable?*

Rebecca handed her a napkin, pulling her from her thoughts. "Your eyes aren't red from crying; you look like you need a fix."

Maadhini wondered if Sadiya was right, if she really was becoming an addict.

"I really did love you," Rebecca continued, "but you're

better than becoming some skin grafter. And if we were together, that's exactly what you'd turn into. You're shaking. For Christ's sake, you had trouble breathing with the stuff on."

The fight in Maadhini's body gave out, and she let her lover shove her across the threshold of the apartment. The gap between them stretched a thousand miles.

"Use this as a learning opportunity and go live your best life."

The moment Rebecca shut the door in her face, Maadhini crumpled to the ground.

The sun had long set by the time Maadhini returned to their place. Unclear how she'd walked home, eyes still red and teary, she entered the kitchen to see Sadiya cleaning dishes.

"I didn't wait up for you since I wasn't sure if you'd be spending the night at Rebecca's..." Sadiya turned mid-sentence and dropped the dish. It clanged against the sink.

Maadhini almost laughed. *I look like shit, but what else is new?*

"'Dhini...what's wrong?"

Maadhini recoiled. *That name...it was ours and I threw it away. And for what? To feel like I was cool for a hot minute?* Bottling her despair on the walk home had been unbearable, but now all her emotions spilled out like water bubbling from a kettle left on the burner too long. "I just...Rebecca just..."

Sadiya grabbed her, guiding her to their bedroom and sitting them both down. The only sound for a long time was Maadhini's muffled howls against Sadiya's T-shirt.

Finally, when nothing was left, Maadhini spoke.

"I don't want to live."

Sadiya stiffened. "You don't mean that."

"Maybe I do."

Sadiya wiped her tears, and when they locked eyes, Maadhini was relieved to find that her best friend wasn't putting on a happy front. She was smiling, but her eyes told the truth. She knew how deeply Maadhini hurt, which made the pain all the worse.

I'm no good for anyone.

"Your *amma* has shown you the true meaning of love, a meaning you could never get from a woman like Rebecca," Sadiya said.

"How did you know?"

Sadiya's tone made it clear she was barely hanging on from crying herself. "I've been in love before. I know that look."

"Mahesh?"

"Yeah…"

"How long did it take you to get over him?"

Whatever resistance Sadiya was holding onto must've broken, for she spoke her next words with silent tears streaming down her face. "I'll let you know when it happens."

Maadhini pushed Sadiya aside to get a better look at her. "What?"

"I was so eager to leave India, to leave him and start anew. But the past follows you wherever you go, an echo you're forced to listen and react to constantly."

Maadhini snorted. "So, it never ends? That's depressing."

Sadiya shook her head. "It's not. Echoes remind us of what once was. Their beauty lies in the fact that we can use the past to build a better future. The Japanese call it *kintsugi.* They take broken pottery and make it even better, spotlighting the broken parts to enhance their beauty." Sadiya parted the bangs from Maadhini's face, clearing her eyes.

"But you're not broken," Maadhini said. "I've only ever seen you smile. For as long as I can remember, you've raised the sun with your smile."

"We're all broken, 'dhini." Sadiya tilted her body away but didn't break eye contact.

"What do you have to be sad about?"

"My best friend's heart was just broken."

Maadhini laughed, one of those belly laughs she was famous for back in India.

"And I do doubt myself," Sadiya said. "I never used to call *Amma* because I didn't want to hear ten minutes of how I could be a better daughter."

"You've always seemed so brave, so strong."

Sadiya smiled, brushing her hand down Maadhini's arm. "Our culture…it's taught us to view each other as enemies. To believe there's only so much beauty in the world. That there's only so much smarts in the world. That you have to fight for it, especially if you're a woman, especially if you're a minority. But that's all bullshit." Standing up, Sadiya pointed to some pictures of them from various trips. The Grand Canyon. The Taj Mahal. Italy. "You're telling me there's a finite amount of beauty in the world? Nah, that's the white man's game. To pit us against each other so we can't recognize the power in ourselves. Because if we did, then nothing could stop us."

Maadhini wiped her wet nose on her arm. "What?"

"The whole appeal of WP is it can unlock something you need, something that's scarce. But beauty isn't scarce. We both got As on our midterms. For one of us to succeed, the other one doesn't have to fail. Life isn't a zero-sum game; it's a team sport."

Maadhini wondered what she'd done in life to

deserve such a friend. Already, she regretted ever considering ending her own life. She wanted to live, to be with Sadiya. And her parents. She even missed Jayanthi Aunty. "I lied to you."

Sadiya glanced at her as she sat back down on the bed. "Yeah?"

"I asked Rebecca for more WP. Even…even after she dumped me." Saying it out loud made it hurt worse than ever, and she plunged her face between Sadiya's arms.

"It's okay."

"I'm sorry."

"There's nothing to be sorry about."

"Why do you even want to be friends with a fat loser like me?"

Seizing her by the arms, Sadiya forced her back so that their eyes locked again. "Maadhini Kedilaya, you're a lot of things, but you're not a loser."

"Maadhini's eyes were glued to the floor. "You're just being nice…"

"You're the bravest fucking person I know."

Looking up, Maadhini saw how serious Sadiya's face was. Her insides fluttered and she knew as much as her life sucked right now, she also couldn't wait to spend another day with her best friend. She'd pray to every single one of her Hindu gods for forgiveness at ever considering suicide. "What?"

"Did you not hear a word I just said? You call your parents every day. Even though you know Tanvi Aunty is going to judge you and Vir Uncle isn't going to remember half of what you tell him. Because you understand that family is forever, that it's the only thing that matters. I envy your bravery."

Maadhini sat back. *Envy…me?*

"You're so comfortable with yourself, coming out the way you did."

"Yeah?"

"To be honest, I was jealous. I thought I was losing you. Especially when that woman started calling you 'dhini."

"I'm so sorry..." Maybe she hadn't been searching for Rebecca. Maybe she'd just been searching for belonging and validation, even though it'd been right in front of her for her whole life.

"'Dhini, it's okay. Don't let one person ruin what we've built over decades." Sadiya kissed her forehead. Warmth flowed from Maadhini's face down through her entire body. "It's you and me, forever." Sadiya held up a finger. "Pinky swear?"

"Pinky swear." As two hands united, Maadhini sniffled again. "Why can't I just be happy?"

"Want another vibrator?" Sadiya asked. "That's usually a good start."

Chapter Nine

Four days after the breakup, Maadhini was still hugging the toilet in her apartment at all hours of the day. "Withdrawal is such a bitch," she moaned. "I'm never touching this stuff again."

Sadiya entered the bathroom to see if there was anything she could do.

Maadhini waved her off. "You're going to be late to Wilson's class. Just go ahead without me."

"And leave you here? I don't know how, but your *amma* would figure it out and convince my *amma* to move here to keep a closer eye on me."

Maadhini chuckled as she heaved again. "*Amma* has been unusually cool."

"That's one way to put it. I can't believe what you told me last night."

Wiping her mouth and flushing the toilet one last time, Maadhini got up and splashed water on her face. She closed her eyes and smiled again upon remembering how her *amma* had taken the news of the breakup.

"*She no like you anymore? Is okay. I no like her.*"

"*Thanks,* Amma.*"

"What's her address? I write her note."

"Oh god, Amma, that's okay."

"Ayyo Rama, you just tell me. Then, I tell her how boring Grapes of Wrath *is."*

"Amma...I think she enjoys her family's book royalties whether you find the book boring or not."

"No, no."

Maadhini pictured the small woman shaking her head back and forth in disagreement.

"If book boring and old, no one buy. No royalties. It on Amazon?"

Maadhini giggled before answering. "Yes, Amma. The Grapes of Wrath *is on Amazon."*

"Good. If you not give me address, I write note there. Maybe she read."

"Thanks, Amma." Her mom was trying. That was more than she could say for her father, who must've thought she was just about dehydrated with the amount of diarrhea and nausea they'd both told him she was suffering from. The fact that finals were next week had helped convince him it was just stress.

"Don't worry, beta. *I tell the aunties too. They also write notes on Amazon."*

When they arrived to Wilson's class, there were only two seats left near the front. Maadhini groaned as she realized they were in the sight line of Rebecca and some guy she'd never noticed before. Her ex-lover's legs dangled close to his.

"Don't jump to conclusions." Sadiya squeezed her hand as they took their seats.

"Ladies," Wilson said, frowning. "Thanks for joining us."

"No problem!" Sadiya squeaked.

"You're so enthusiastic; maybe you can take the first

review question. Remember, the final is next Wednesday."

Sadiya sputtered out some type of explanation, but for the rest of class Maadhini's eyes never left Rebecca. She saw how her alabaster skin shimmered under the fluorescent lights and how her leg bumped against this boy's and how her white earrings sparkled, emanating an energy that still called to her...

"I don't want to do Indian food again for dinner." Sadiya pulled at her as soon as class ended, but Maadhini planted her feet and pretended to pile things into her backpack, waiting for Rebecca to walk past her.

"Hey, Maadhini."

Maadhini looked up. She noted how it was no longer "'dhini," both happy and sad that that was the case. Rebecca's fingers were interlocked with the guy's. There was no doubt what was going on.

Was she cheating on me with him?

We never said we were exclusive, did we?

Should that matter?

Yes!

"Are you okay?"

Maadhini blinked before responding to Rebecca's question. "Um, yeah...sorry."

Why am I apologizing?!

"I said that there's no reason to look so serious. This final isn't the end of the world. You should smile more."

Maadhini's teeth clenched. She kept Sadiya next to her until she was sure the new couple had exited the building. "It'd be easier if she'd just called me a skin grafter. At least that kind of hate, a person can understand."

"I can't believe she cheated on you," Sadiya said. "No way did she hook up with Ben so fast."

"Oh," Maadhini said. "That's his name?"

"Yeah. He's fairly quiet in class. I think he wants to go into finance. He took this class for fun." When Maadhini didn't respond, Sadiya narrowed her eyes. "Not that I don't love that smile, but what's up?"

The two left the building together to catch the bus home. "She found another guy," Maadhini mused.

"So?"

Jumping on the M101 toward Coral Tower, she explained. "It's not that she thought I couldn't handle it or that she thought I was ugly or anything. She just wasn't gay." *It wasn't me...*

"Okay...but...you're still not going to do WP again, right?"

Closing her eyes, hearing the bus rattle forward and the humming of passengers' energies from various WP-encrusted jewelry, Maadhini took a deep breath. She could see the energies around her, could feel their warmth. They were so close, and yet so devastatingly far. *Hit me, baby, one more time.*

Just one last hit, and she could end it on her terms. Not Rebecca's. "Of course," she told Sadiya. "I'm done with that stuff."

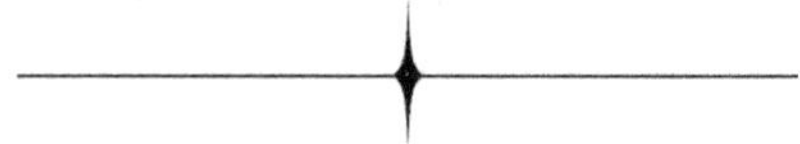

With less than a hundred hours before Wilson's final in Metropolitan Studies, Maadhini found herself at the library once again. Laid out on a table in the quiet room were color-coded notecards Sadiya had labored over in an attempt to create a Jeopardy-style practice exam for them.

"Queens for $200," she said.

Sadiya read from the back of the notecard. "This landmark became the home of the Mets after Robert

Moses failed to convince the Dodgers and Giants to play here."

Maadhini bit her lip before answering. "What is Shea Stadium?"

"Hey, that's right!"

"You sound surprised," Maadhini grumbled.

"Oh, it's not like that, 'dhini. I just never see you doing the readings."

"Sometimes Rebecca and I did actually have study dates…"

The quiet room earned its moniker as the two friends stared at each other.

"It's okay," Maadhini said. "It's not like I'll fall apart from saying her name."

Sadiya handed the notecard over. When Maadhini took it, their hands lingered.

"Hey," Sadiya said, "no one thinks you're some delicate wallflower. A couple more questions and we can go back to watching *Friends* re-runs and order some Grimaldi's Pizza."

Maadhini pinched her thigh through her pants leg. She'd promised herself she'd be more honest with Sadiya, with her mother, with everyone. One small step at a time. It was their last Saturday night before finals and going home for the holidays, and she wasn't going to spend it eating shitty pizza. "Actually…I prefer Chicago deep-dish to NYC pizza."

"What?" Sadiya's tone prompted a librarian across the room to shush them. The elderly woman wore bangles that jangled as she shook a finger. The jewelry was encrusted with WP, and even from across the room, Maadhini heard a thrumming all around her, encouraging her to close her eyes and let the music take her. It took all her energy to resist.

"'Dhini, why didn't you tell me sooner?"

Maadhini remained amazed that Sadiya's "quiet voice" seemed louder and more intimidating than her actual yells. The tone was enough to pull her from her haziest thoughts and meanest impulses.

"We've been ordering from Grimaldi's since Welcome Week freshman year!"

Maadhini looked at her feet. "I just...I never wanted to rock the boat."

"Consider the boat rocked." Sadiya laughed. "But that's a good thing. We're in America now. We don't have to settle for anything less than exactly what we want."

Maadhini smiled as Sadiya pulled up the menu of Chicago-style pizzerias in the area on her phone. "Two more questions and we're done with the game. Then we can order whatever you want."

Whatever I want...

Sadiya understood, deep down, even if she'd told her to forget about WP. Closing her eyes, sighing contently, Maadhini dared to dream that she didn't have to resist the music, that what she wanted and what she deserved were the same thing.

Sadiya bounced her leg as if it was a piston, sitting in Wilson's class and wondering where Maadhini was. She'd assumed Maadhini had gotten a head start on the day when she woke up and found the apartment empty, but now she was worried. She'd texted her three times in the span of ten minutes, each one more frequent than the last.

Earth to Maadhini?!
Did you forget Wilson's final is today?!
Seriously, where the fuck are you?!

They'd gotten past Stochastic Calculus on Monday somehow. Their Metropolitan Studies exam was the last barrier between them and winter break. She'd be ordered to put her phone away in minutes. Scanning the room, she saw Chad, Ben, Rebecca.

Rebecca...

She'd rather break the woman's perfect nose than ask her for help, but for Maadhini's sake, she made an exception. Getting up from her seat, she walked over to the woman and her new boyfriend.

"Um, Rebecca, have you seen Maadhini?"

"Sadiya, hey, how are you?"

Ignoring the question, she pushed through. "I can't find her and, you know, the exam is starting soon..."

"Oh, yeah, I haven't heard from 'dhini since she texted me last night."

Sadiya clenched her fists. *Call her 'dhini again, bitch. See what happens.*

Rebecca continued. "Can you tell her to stop texting me? We were busy last night..."

Sadiya suppressed a desire to gag as Rebecca and Ben kissed in front of her. "Thanks..." Returning to her seat, she checked her phone, hoping to see a response from Maadhini and trying not to focus on the fact that her friend had texted Rebecca yesterday.

Tuesday nights meant *New Girl*, but Maadhini had said she'd wanted to do some Bharatanatyam, instead, to shed some nervous energy before the final. Sadiya had hoped it was proof she was getting back to her old self by reclaiming the dancing that'd once made her so happy. Sadiya fell asleep without confirming Maadhini returned to bed.

"Okay, class, notes away, please. I won't ask a second time."

Wilson's voice shook her from her thoughts. Looking

at her day planner, she saw a note written in the passage, instructions from Tanvi Aunty she'd committed to performing over any school work: *Take care of Maadhini.* Hesitating for only a moment, she got up and began walking out the door.

"Sadiya?" Wilson asked. "What's up? If you leave, I'll have to fail you."

She bit the inside of her cheek to keep her composure. The exam was 35% of their final grade. She'd fail the class, even with her perfect record thus far.

"I understand," she said, "but I need to find my best friend."

Sadiya didn't remember getting on a bus or getting her shoes wet as she ran through some snow and almost tripped. She did remember rushing up the elevator to her apartment, throwing the door open, shouting Maadhini's name, and finding her friend keeled over on her side, vomit and toilet water stuck in her bangs. "Oh my god, 'dhini! 'Dhini!"

Maadhini didn't budge. Dropping to her friend's level, Sadiya slapped her face. Hard. She heard a gurgle. Placing her finger under Maadhini's nose, she felt air and slapped her again.

"...what...?"

"Thank fucking god!" Seizing her, Sadiya wiped at Maadhini's face, trying to clean it up a bit before pulling her into an embrace. Flushing the mess down the toilet, she propped Maadhini up against the bathroom wall. "What the hell just happened?"

Snorting, huffing, coughing, it seemed like hours before Maadhini finally answered. "I just wanted to end it on my own terms..."

"You tried committing suicide?!"

"What? No!" Maadhini shuddered as she spoke.

Relief flooded through Sadiya's veins. She'd never taken WP, but she imagined the high the drug gave paled in comparison to the joy she experienced knowing her friend's sadness wasn't deadly.

"I did think about it when she first dumped me...but I want to live..."

"Rebecca said you texted her last night..."

"...we were about to start *New Girl.* I just wanted to see how she was doing, but..."

"...she didn't even respond." Sadiya imagined breaking Rebecca's nose and smiled. "We've been finishing each other's sentences since primary school."

"You must think I'm so pathetic."

"You're not pathetic, 'dhini. You're just sad, and that's okay. You just got your heart broken."

"I didn't lie about going downstairs to clear my head."

"What happened?"

Maadhini couldn't look Sadiya in the eyes. "I was dancing, and that's when I saw it in the carpeting. White. It didn't sparkle, it didn't call out to me like her earrings, but I knew what it was. I snorted it."

Sadiya clamped a hand to her mouth. "Oh...'dhini..."

"I dug around the edges of the room and just kept finding more and more. I must have somehow made my way up here this morning, because the next thing I remember you were slapping me awake."

Sadiya shook her head before placing it in her hands. It was true, she thought. *We're all just one day away from becoming the worst versions of ourselves. But that also means we're all just one day away from becoming the best versions, too.* "The building manager told me a few days ago..."

"Told you what?"

"'Dhini...they're shutting down the basement at the end of the week. They found white mold under the carpeting. It's dangerous stuff..."

Maadhini ugly-cried and the sound pierced Sadiya's heart. All she could do was bring Maadhini into her embrace as her best friend spoke in muffled gasps. "I thought I could just do it one last time, ace the finals and go out on my own terms."

Perhaps Sadiya would've feigned strength if this had happened near the beginning of term, but their friendship had deepened over the past weeks, even now, after decades of knowing each other. Anger had served as fuel for their relationship, the way fire tempers steel, making it stronger. She let her tears run over Maadhini's bangs, wanting her friend to know she shared her sorrow.

"I'm so weak..."

"You're not weak, 'dhini, you're human." Hugging her tight, Sadiya took out her phone and called a Lyft to take them to Jersey. "Don't worry. I'm going to take care of you, just like I promised your *amma*."

Sadiya guided her friend between the patches of ice outside their apartment complex. Maadhini let herself be pushed and prodded into a stranger's car. Silence as heavy as their parents' expectations filled the air, until finally Sadiya grew tired of the quiet as they passed Holland Tunnel into Jersey. She sighed in relief that it was the middle of the day. Vir Uncle wouldn't be home. She knew Aunty would help them come up with a believable lie. "It'll be okay," she told Maadhini. "At least you aren't drunk."

Maadhini stared out the window. Snow capped the top of the cars racing around them. Winter had finally arrived.

"Hey," Sadiya continued. "Speaking of alcohol, do you know where *idlis* go to get drunk?" Nudging Maadhini to ensure she was still awake, she noticed her friend's hair was littered with not just snow, but crumbs from their dinner last night. "*Idlis* go to *sambar* to get drunk."

Silence reigned for a moment, until finally Maadhini chuckled, her cheeks expanding as she tried to hide her amusement. "Leave the bad puns to me." She didn't say anything for the rest of the drive, but held Sadiya's hand as her best friend called her mom and told her to prepare lunch for three.

The tall oak tree outside Maadhini's house was quite beautiful on this December afternoon, its multi-colored leaves weighted down by snow but resilient enough to withstand the pressure. Unlike others, they changed color later in the season and insisted on taking the additional time to accept their new forms. They made no apologies for being late bloomers, confident that they were worth the wait.

"*Beta.*" Tanvi's voice was ghostlike, echoing in Sadiya's head as she held Maadhini's hand and led her over some black ice into her *amma*'s arms. She waited for the Lyft driver to reverse out and drive off before following the pair inside the house.

"Why are the girls here?" Vir's question hung like a noose. Sadiya's insides seized as she wondered why he wasn't at work.

"Sadiya, Uncle came home for lunch. I will take Maadhini upstairs; you explain to him." Without apology or a second look, Tanvi took her daughter by the hand and went upstairs.

"Well?" Vir asked. He held a strip of roti in his hand, a curry of eggplant and cauliflower on his plate.

"Uncle, it's a good thing you're already seated."

Sadiya told Vir everything, only replacing Rebecca's name with "Robert." She figured the thought of his darling daughter dating a white boy would make him angry enough. He'd stopped eating after three minutes and began pacing after ten, hands behind his back as he made long strides across the living room, mumbling to himself.

"...Uncle?"

"America wasn't built for people like us. I knew coming here was a mistake."

Was this really worse than never leaving India? She wished she knew the answer. Maadhini was free from the expectations of heteronormative behavior that would weigh her down in India. Tanvi accepted her. She'd experienced love. *But everything has a cost...*

"I came to America for you girls. How could I separate you two? How could my 'dhini shine as bright as possible without her 'diya by her side?"

Despite herself, Sadiya smiled, her eyes scanning the oil lamp on their mantel. It wasn't lit.

"Now a boy has gone and broken my 'dhini's heart." Grabbing his plate of half-finished food, he launched it at a wall and watched it shatter. The noise prompted a shouted admonishment from Tanvi upstairs. "I let my temper get the best of me," Vir said, frowning. "Forgive me."

"No need, Uncle. I'm also quite emotional about this whole thing. Just this morning, I wanted to break Rebecca's nose."

"Rebecca?"

Sadiya winced. *Fuck.*

"Sadiya." His words sucked her from her thoughts and placed her firmly in front of his stern eyes. "What is this behavior?"

The truth came out like diarrhea: messy and in spurts, but at the end of it all, Sadiya felt a weight lifted from her very being. She was glad he'd already broken his one plate. As it was, he'd curled his hands into fists and taken a walk outside despite the blizzard that had begun raging in full force.

Vir returned from the backyard after several minutes. "We will not speak of this."

"Are you okay, Uncle?"

His glare gave her all the response she needed. "I wish I didn't feel this way. Perhaps more time in America will change my mind." He spat the country's name out like a curse.

This is all an adjustment for him. It's been unending shocks to his life since moving here.

"Maadhini is going through withdrawal," Vir Uncle said.

Sadiya raised her eyebrows. "You've read about such things?"

"Yes. It will be quite painful, but it's good it happened now. Perhaps she will be able to return next month as if nothing happened." His nostrils flared as he continued. "I was right, the first time Maadhini asked to move here. America is not meant for people like us."

As Sadiya searched for a response, Tanvi emerged from the stairs. "I gave her something to sleep. *Beta,* why don't you go up and check on her and get your things settled?"

Mouthing a thank-you, Sadiya took her bags upstairs and pretended not to hear Vir and Tanvi's whispered arguing in Tamil and Kannada. Opening Maadhini's door, she could tell by the sniffling and shivering that whatever her *amma* had given her hadn't kicked in yet. Placing the luggage on the ground, she started to leave, but stopped when Maadhini called out.

"Will you stay with me?"

"Of course." Moving to her friend's side, Sadiya pulled the sheets over both of them and hugged her tight. She kissed her forehead and brushed the tears from her eyes and stroked her hair as Maadhini shook with the crushing weight of disappointment and disgust.

Vir Uncle is wrong. America was literally built by people like us, an unfinished experiment birthed from immigrants. As Sadiya listened to the whispered shouting of parents below and the stifled cries in her arms, she watched the oak tree through the window. It swayed in the wind, refusing to break.

Next season, it would be even stronger.

BHARAT KRISHNAN
PATRIOT
A WP NOVEL

"If you're going to live by the river, make friends with the crocodile." - Hindu Proverb

Chapter One

June 7, 1986

A child born in America has unlimited potential. As Puli Shetty stared at his newborn child through the looking glass of Hoboken General, he knew Aditya would grow up to accomplish things he couldn't even imagine. Placing a hand on the glass, he took in his son's full head of hair and devilish smile, then returned to his wife's room to reassure Deepika that their child was well, that moving from Bangalore to New Jersey to start a family had been the right choice…

December 24, 1990

In chaos and in calm, Deepika's heart filled each time she saw her son smile. This particular moment saw Aditya's mouth agape at a spread of Christmas cookies and kheer. Tucked away in a corner of the motel his parents worked at, the boy spent most of the night ignoring his mom's calls to comb his hair or stop running inside, or playing tag with his best friend, Karthik, while Karthik's parents also helped turn the motel's conference room into a suitable place to host a party. Now that the food was out, though, the two boys stopped their game to eye the sweet treats.

"Not until you eat some real food," Deepika chided, grabbing her son by the shoulders, and steering him toward chafing dishes set atop canned burners heating butter chicken, pulao, aloo gobi, rice, and naan. Her boss, Jason Cooles, was the owner and manager of The Śānta Stay and the restaurant connected to it, Curry in a Hurry. He'd insisted on an all-Indian spread to commemorate the five-year anniversary of Puli and Deepika coming to work for him.

"Karthik will split his head open running around like that," Swapnika, Karthik's mother, said, rubbing her sweaty palms against her green *lehenga*. A red *choli* finished her Christmas-themed outfit. "It's virtually guaranteed he'll spill food on his new clothes, and I'll have to go upstairs and get him changed, but what to do?"

Deepika shrugged. "Help me bring out the plates and silverware." She smiled as they walked together past the hallway connecting the motel to the restaurant. "That's a pretty dress."

"You know I prefer pink, but Karthik wouldn't stop crying until I changed. Something about Christmas spirit." Swapnika bit her bottom lip. "Are we indulging them too much?"

Deepika laughed. "It's the American way, no? And speaking of indulging, don't you dare leave the party early to go work. You aren't a dishwasher today; we hired cleaners, remember?"

"And what if I like washing dishes?" Swapnika teased,

a smile reaching her eyes.

"You'd have to explain yourself to Jason, who I know for a fact complains about how much you work, and then you'd have to find a new best friend because I'd leave you if you left me to make small talk with the others."

Swapnika sighed. "If only all bosses could be as sweet as Jason."

Returning to the holiday party, the two stopped at the front door to watch their husbands try to lug a tree into the motel by themselves.

"Push the door open with your back," Puli grunted, his calloused, sweaty hands threatening to let the seven-foot tree slip and break his toes.

"We should've waited for Ryan or Bob or someone else to help us," Ramesh said. The man's back pressed against the door, trying to move the handle to let them inside from the cold.

"We don't always need their help," Puli said. "Grip the tree tighter. I gotta readjust."

Deepika watched Swapnika open the door in an attempt to help Ramesh, then heard her friend scream as her husband collapsed into her, bringing the fir tree down on top of them. Puli and Deepika laughed out loud.

Their best friends scowled from the ground. "Are you going to help or just watch?"

"Sorry, Ramesh," Deepika said, bending down to lift the tree as the married couple wiggled out from underneath. "I'll tip you tonight, for sure. I'd hoped Jason would hire a comedy act."

"Seems like you've got the joking covered," Ramesh grumbled.

"That's my wife," Puli said, his grunts replaced with a broad smile. "She got the looks and humor."

"And where's that leave you?" Swapnika teased.

"Damn blessed," Puli said.

After the four of them carried the tree into the party room, the women set up the tree and tended to their children as they returned to the lobby to retrieve the silverware and plates they'd left. Brushing remnants of the tree off their clothes, Deepika saw Jason arrive through the front door, his hands overflowing with Christmas gifts.

"Let me help you," she said, opening the door as boxes tumbled to the ground. The man was pushing seventy yet bent over without a problem to pick them up. His hands touched Deepika's as she joined him on the ground; she didn't pull them away until Swapnika cleared her throat.

"Who are all these gifts for?" Swapnika asked, popping the tension as if with a safety pin.

Jason's eyes crinkled at the corners. "What kind of Christmas party would it be without gifts for the boys?"

"You shouldn't have," Deepika protested.

"Nonsense, and I've got gifts for you all, too."

"You really shouldn't have," Swapnika said, hardly louder than a mouse.

"We're celebrating more than just Christmas tonight," Jason said. "I can't believe it's been five years since Ramesh brought Puli to work here."

"And just like a real Santa, you were good enough to take us in and make our dreams come true," Deepika said.

"I thought about dressing like Santa," Jason said, "but thought better of it. With the gut and beard, I'm practically there anyways." Laughing as loudly as Deepika imagined St. Nick himself would, he led the ladies back to the party.

Jason's arrival marked the official start of the celebration, with Swapnika setting the plates and napkins out and Deepika playing the soundtrack from *Mr. India*, the recent smash hit starring Sridevi and Anil Kapoor. No sooner had "Zindagi Ki Yahi Reet Hai" started blaring through the sound system than Ryan, Bob, their wives, and a half dozen other employees showed up. Their kids joined Deepika's own to play Hungry Hungry Hippos in a corner of the room as she tried her best to avoid making small talk and ignore Bob's wife's comment on how spicy butter chicken was. Making herself a plate of naan, aloo gobi, and butter chicken, she retreated to a corner with Swapnika.

"She brought her own sugar with her, I swear," Swapnika whispered. "I saw her mixing it on her plate with the rice and subji."

"Well, if she insists on sprinkling it in all her food, perhaps she's actually Gujarati," Deepika teased. "She's not much lighter-skinned that me, and she does lather on a lot of makeup. How are we to know if she's really white?"

Swapnika choked on the mango lassi she was drinking. "You're so bad."

"And you're so good." Deepika's tone sank to a whisper, her heart filling with the weight of honesty.

"What's with the melancholy?" Swapnika asked. "We were laughing just minutes ago!"

"Forgive me," Deepika said. The moment was over as quickly as it had come, her voice already filled again with life. "Perhaps I really should embrace the American way and get a therapist."

Swapnika tilted her head to the gods and recited a quick *sloka* before staring her friend in the eyes. "Deepika, what's all this?"

"It's just what Jason was saying, I suppose. And it's Christmas."

"Just spit it out." Exasperation filled Swapnika's voice.

"You changed our lives five years ago, and I haven't even gotten you a gift."

"What nonsense is this?" Swapnika asked, brushing her hand in jest. "Your friendship is the greatest gift. Everything else, the gods provide."

"Life in India feels so long ago, as if decades have passed." Deepika's voice trembled with the burden of centuries of familial expectations. "My parents married me off to a man I'd never met, and within five months he'd made the decision for both of us to move here."

Swapnika took her friend's hands, kissing them before placing them to her eyes. "Our husbands spent so much time being ordered around by others. Puli was a driver in India, wasn't he?"

Deepika nodded, swallowing a particularly large bite, and glancing around to ensure they were alone in their corner of the room. One of the other wives could eavesdrop at any moment, or her son could run by and pull on her *lehenga* and demand to be carried. It was only with Swapnika that she could admit how very tired she was all the time, and only then for a few stolen moments. To be a woman was exhausting, and to be a poor immigrant woman even more so.

"Puli spent so long driving that CEO around, being reminded on a daily basis of what he lacked in terms of smarts or wealth," Swapnika said. "But every man wants to be a king, and so these men feel the need to take us halfway across the country just to prove they can. But we all find agency in our own ways, huh?"

"What do you mean?"

Swapnika adopted Deepika's whisper. "Don't tell me Puli taught himself English. Who tutored you? Jason?"

Blood drained from Deepika's cheeks. She grabbed Swapnika by the arm and pulled her into a nook of the party room. "Him, yes And the library has great resources." Realizing she'd seized her best friend in a vise, she let the woman go. "Sorry, it's just you know how prideful Puli is."

"Relax," Swapnika said, "your secret's safe with me. But like I said, your friendship is the only gift I'll ever need."

"How lucky we were that we stayed here our first night."

Swapnika's eyes twinkled. "Luck is just a term the gods gave us to describe their will."

"I might've died of loneliness without your constant presence," Deepika sighed.

"Well." Swapnika smiled. "You're not lonely anymore, are you? I see how Puli dotes on you."

"He had a good example in seeing all Ramesh does for you."

"And to me." Swapnika giggled like a schoolgirl. "It's a good thing our rooms are on separate floors, or I'd feel self-conscious at night."

Deepika slapped her friend's arm, shrieking with laughter so loudly that Bob's wife turned and began to walk over to join them.

"Don't be so modest," Swapnika whispered again, apparently trying to get one last remark in while they were still alone. "Anything that makes you that happy on a Monday morning should be flaunted proudly."

Deepika shushed her friend as Bob's wife approached. She hoped Swapnika would remember the woman's name.

"Great party, huh?" The woman offered the question innocently enough, but Deepika saw the way her nose scrunched up in sync with the Hindi music. The refusal to dance with some of the other employees and her mostly filled plate was proof she was only here as a favor to Bob.

"Are you having fun, Barbara?" Swapnika said.

Barbara. Thank the gods for Swapnika's memory.

"Having a blast, Nikki."

Deepika cringed at hearing her friend's "white name."

"I do hope we open presents soon, though," Barbara continued. "It's a bit boring just watching the men play."

Looking over her shoulder, Deepika saw the men had found a whiteboard and were keeping score of their Ping-Pong games. They'd formed two teams of doubles, with her husband and Ramesh leading 2-0.

"They're playing best of five," Barbara said. "I suppose I should go back. I'm scorekeeper. Just came to say hi."

"We'll join you in a bit," Swapnika said. "I'll bring you some lassi."

Barbara smiled as if a dentist was forcing her lips apart before walking back to the other side of the room. The two best friends broke out laughing as soon as she was out of earshot.

"Thank the gods I met you, Swapnika Thakur." Setting her now-empty plate down, Deepika wiped her hands on a napkin and embraced her friend for several moments.

Swapnika patted her on the shoulder, kissing her head before responding. "We were just happy to find another brown family with a kid our age. We can't just rely on nice white people like Jason, bless his soul. After all, he grew up in Sedona and I've heard that place is filled with hippies."

Deepika snorted in laughter. "What's a hippie?"

"Oh? They didn't teach you that word at the library? Maybe you should ask Jason."

The pair continued to laugh as they put their plates and glasses away, finally joining their husbands across the room.

The third game was underway when Deepika and Swapnika joined their husbands, but Bob and Ryan had taken a break.

"One more game and this is over," Puli said.

"Have you checked on your son?" Deepika tried for a stern expression but couldn't hide a smile. She loved seeing her husband like this, in his element. She wondered if Swapnika would take Aditya for a sleepover tonight.

"He's my son when he's running around like a monster, huh?"

"No, he's your son when I've been entertaining him all day," Deepika said.

Puli shrugged toward the corner. "He's still playing with Karthik and the others."

Deepika watched Aditya slamming his right hand down to control a plastic hippo as he continued to play that board game from the motel's reserves.

"Did Bob and Ryan give up already?" Swapnika asked.

"Oh, honey," Barbara said, sympathy in her voice, "they're just getting their own paddles."

"Why—" Deepika started at seeing the two men return. A chill ran up her spine as they drew closer. Putting a hand to her forehead, she realized she was sweating.

"Okay," Bob said, "now we're ready for game three."

Deepika shivered. White dust lined the perimeter of these new paddles.

"Is that WP?" Swapnika's whisper plunged Deepika back in time, to the silent room of the library where she'd first read about the magical drug—government-regulated, limited to Caucasians for its magical properties, and always unpredictable. She'd heard tales of people using it to gain strength, speed, intelligence. Some could even turn invisible or fly or spit fire from their mouths. But it affected everyone differently, and it was particularly dangerous for "some people." That's how the textbook had described it. That was why the government had criminalized its ownership by nonwhites after the

Civil War. "For their own protection."

Bullshit.

WP was a tool of the white supremacist. The most effective way to keep immigrants in their place. It wasn't about white or Black or Asian or anything like that. It'd been legalized for the Irish less than a century ago.

And one day it'll be legalized for people like my son.

That's what she hoped, but for the moment it was still going to be a tool to humiliate her husband and Karthik. Still, despite everything, she couldn't help but admire the way Bob and Ryan played.

"Zero-zero," Bob announced, tossing the ball into the air to serve.

Watching him and Ryan play was like listening to two harpists strum in tandem to the tune of Mozart's 9th. Like watching Rishi Kapoor and Tina Munim sing in a Bollywood movie. It was as beautiful and delicate as Michelangelo painting the Sistine Chapel, worthy of tears. The match seemed to stretch on in slow motion, with the two men dancing around the table as they returned the ball.

They're toying with Puli and Ramesh, Deepika thought. A few times, they smashed the ball faster than the eye could follow, but more often than not they took their time, placing the ball on the perimeter of the other side to make her overweight husband run in desperation, only to fall just short of success.

"I can't believe the government would allow such a drug, especially just to some people," she whispered to Swapnika.

"It's just the way it's always been and always will be," Swapnika sighed. "No use fighting it. At least Jason doesn't parade his around."

Deepika opened her mouth but stopped when she

noticed Aditya and Karthik walking toward them. "You got tired of Hungry Hungry Hippos?"

"What are they playing?" The young boy's eyes gleamed and his mouth fell open as he watched the dance of domination in front of him. Deepika checked the scoreboard and saw her husband had lost the third game.

Who can resist such beauty, even if it means to destroy you?

Aditya wrapped his small hands around Deepika's legs, and she noticed his palms were clammy. She wondered if WP exposure was healthy for someone so young and considered asking Bob and Ryan to stop before talking herself out of it.

"Mister, can I see that paddle?" Aditya asked Bob, his gaze never leaving the match. His eyes widened upon seeing Ryan spike the ball so hard it cracked on his father's side of the table. Everyone present knew how the fourth game would end.

"Guess I don't know my own strength," Ryan laughed, fishing another ball from his pocket.

"You don't want this paddle, kid," Bob said. "Someone sees you with it, they'll think you're just a skin grafter."

Deepika bit the inside of her cheek. Ramesh was charging toward Bob with his fist raised when Jason balled his hands into fists and shouted. "That's enough!"

Deepika winced. She couldn't remember a single instance in her five years of living here where Jason had raised his voice.

"It's Christmas, and you've had a few drinks, so I'm not going to fire you for saying that," Jason said. "But if I ever hear that word come out of your mouth again, you're done here."

"Aw, come on, boss," Ryan argued, "it's just a word."

"It's disgusting, from the word itself to the dark history behind it."

Deepika didn't know what'd happened, but she smiled upon seeing the stricken look on Barbara's face. Swapnika nudged her, sending Aditya back to play with the others. "That word, it means someone who stole WP," she whispered. "It's a term used to justify violence against nonwhites. Almost no one uses it today."

"How do you know this? I didn't read about it in the library's history books?"

"There's more to history than what's taught in books," Swapnika said. "Some people have called Ramesh one over the years. And after...after that happens, it's always bad."

As Swapnika turned pale as a ghost, realization hit Deepika like a cold shower. "He still hits you? I thought things were better."

"They are," Swapnika said, rushing her words and reaching for Deepika's hand. "He can actually be quite sweet. And he's a good father. It's just when he feels run down, helpless."

Deepika didn't know what to say, and so said nothing.

"Have I ever called out sick after that one time? Have I ever shown up with bruises on me? My life's not so bad." She continued before Deepika could respond. "Being around WP gets easier over time. If more white people came here, you'd probably have built up some tolerance by now. Jason doesn't usually wear his, and it's not like Bob and Ryan spend that much time around us."

Deepika's cheeks heated. *If his own colleagues embarrass Puli like this, thank the gods I never told him about Jason's tutoring sessions.*

Jason's voice pulled Deepika from her thoughts. "Game's over."

"What?! We were about to win!"

"It's my motel, Bob. Besides, it's time to open presents."

While the party had gone on, the hired help had decorated the tree with lights and ornaments. Deepika even saw a Radhakrishna placed on the very top instead of a star. Other workers had moved gifts from Jason's office and placed them underneath.

"The Thakurs first," Jason said, his eyes gleaming as he picked up a small box wrapped in red and gold and handed it to Ramesh. At over six feet tall, Jason towered over him.

Ramesh opened it to find an envelope with a check inside. "Mr. Cooles…"

"Don't you dare hand it back, Ram," Jason said. "You deserve it. Take it from an old fart like me, you'll never regret the vacations you take and the time you spend with that little one."

The next package took up half the space under the tree. Jason handed it to Aditya and the boy wasted no time in tearing it open.

"Unreal!"

Aditya tossed the torn box aside. A Nintendo. Deepika had read about the gaming system from Japan that was sweeping the country. She watched as Karthik jumped in to help his friend unwrap the smaller gift next to it, all decorum gone.

"Super Mario!" Karthik screamed.

"Mr. Cooles…" Puli's tone wouldn't reveal to anyone but Deepika how hurt he was. "This is way too much…"

For once, Deepika agreed with her husband's pride. It was bad enough that Jason insisted on packing "extra fruit" when he ate snacks in his office, throwing an apple or orange to the boys as he wandered the halls greeting guests.

As if I don't know how to feed my son.

"Nonsense," Jason said. The boys had embraced his

legs in a vise grip of a hug. He patted them both on the head. "They'll need an outlet since Puli won't be able to spend as much time with them."

"What?" Puli's question echoed across the room.

Everyone gathered now to hear Jason's announcement.

"I told your wife we were celebrating more than just Christmas." Jason's eyes radiated with the warmth of a summer breeze upon the ocean. When he spoke, the lilt in his voice reminded Deepika of Puli's kisses and her body warmed. "I'm announcing my retirement tonight."

Barbara gasped, and she was not the only one. Bob and Ryan exchanged a smile, no doubt thinking they had a promotion in the bag.

It's amazing how dumb people can be even when given every advantage. Only she knew what Jason was about to announce.

"I'm stepping down as manager of The Śānta Stay at the end of the year, and I do hope my good friend, Puli Shetty, will grant me the honor of becoming my successor."

The room fell silent, filled only with the Bollywood music that blared from the sound system. As "Chanda Hai Tu" came on, Deepika became aware of the irony of a mother/son wedding dance song playing this night, when all their lives would change irrevocably and result in the perfect wedding being possible for her darling boy. She would miss seeing Jason every day, but her son's future was far more important than anything else.

Apna time aayega. Their time was coming, and she would not shrink from it.

Puli bent to touch Jason's feet with his hands before bringing his fingers to his eyes. "Blessings upon your entire family, Jasonji."

Cheeks red, Jason placed his hands upon Puli's head

before speaking. "Blessings for you, my son."

When her husband stood again, Deepika saw he was close to crying. She hoped Jason wouldn't embarrass him like that, and indeed he spoke again, pulling everyone's attention away from Puli.

"When I was a boy in Sedona, my parents had a large statue of Radhakrishna in our veranda. The eighth avatar of Vishnu was constantly paired with his consort, Radha, instead of his wife. I always found that fascinating."

Jason navigated the room like he owned it, and Deepika reminded herself that he did. He knew which employees to touch on the shoulder, which to smile at, which to embrace. She made a mental note to convince Puli to get his MBA one day, just like this wonderful man.

"Hindu poets knew marriage wasn't the same as love, especially for women back then, so they wanted to separate the notions as best they could. Krishna couldn't succeed without Radha at his side, and everyone knew it. Remember that, Puli. Society advances, thank god, and now marriage and love are tied together. But love your wife like Krishna loved Radha, and I have no doubt this motel will blossom beyond my wildest imaginations." Raising a glass of mango lassi, Jason indicated everyone should cheer his successor. "I'm proud of you. To Puli and Deepika!"

"To Puli and Deepika!" Everyone cheered, and Puli bit his bottom lip so hard it bled.

Deepika knew it was to prevent himself from crying. As people patted her and Puli on the back, she saw Ramesh head to the bathroom and prayed this wouldn't impact their relationship. If Jason had asked her who should get the job, she'd surely have said the man who'd recommended Puli in the first place. Any doubts the Thakurs were jealous were cast aside, though, as Swapnika embraced her.

"Congratulations, sister!"

"We succeed together, *akka*," she replied, using the deferential term for an older and wiser sibling.

The party stopped soon after, with Deepika and Swapnika refusing to let their boys stay up to set up the Nintendo.

"It's already past ten, *kanne*," Deepika told Aditya. The boy didn't have the strength to argue, falling asleep the moment she took him in her arms. Walking past the front door, she interrupted Puli saying his goodbyes to Jason.

"I'm putting Aditya down," she said. "Thank you again, Jasonji, for everything."

Jason kissed the boy's forehead before addressing both of them. "I meant everything I said. And call me if you have any questions; I'll be around for a few more years."

Deepika smiled. "You'll outlive us all, Jasonji."

As she waited for the elevator, she overheard Puli. "I owe so much to my wife. I don't know how she does it: caring for Aditya and still having time to tutor me in English and accounting."

Though the elevator opened, Deepika couldn't move. Her palms were as clammy as if she'd been around Bob's WP, and she almost dropped Aditya.

Please don't expose me. She hoped Jason understood the importance of bridal secrets and Indian pride. Spending so much time alone with a white man—it wasn't good for anyone to know she'd done that.

Jason chuckled. "She spends a lot of time at the library, that one. Might not be a bad idea to bring her on as a bookkeeper next year."

"That's a great idea," Puli said.

Exhaling, Deepika entered the elevator and pressed the button to take her upstairs so she could put Aditya to bed and await her husband's return.

They made love that night, with Aditya fast asleep in the corner and the TV on for white noise. Puli wasn't unskilled with his fingers and mouth, moving around her body like a violinist eliciting notes with a bow. It hadn't been like this the first few years, but now they had a routine, and it quenched her thirst. When she was sated, she mounted him and kissed his neck as their hips rocked in tandem. He grabbed her as he finished, digging his fingernails into her bottom, and when she returned from the bathroom they lay in bed and dreamt of a brighter future unlocked by Jason's kindness.

"Don't return the Nintendo tomorrow," Deepika whispered, her head on Puli's chest.

"Why not?"

"Jason needs to see the kids use it at least once. Wait a week, and then sell it with the game."

Puli crooked his neck to look his wife in the eyes. "You want to buy another dress?"

Annoyed, she slapped the fat around his stomach. "That's a hundred dollars, with the game."

Pulling himself upright, Puli leaned against their bedframe. "How do you know all this?"

"The library. With that money, plus what we've saved this year, plus the promotion, we can afford to lease a used car."

Puli grabbed her in an embrace, kissing her deeply and biting her neck. She felt his excitement grow against her slender chest. "Easy, Krishna," she teased. "Radha needs a break."

He bit his bottom lip, fire in his eyes. "We're lucky you're so smart."

Checking on Aditya one last time before turning off the lights, she responded with her best friend's wisdom.

"Luck is just a word the gods gave us to describe their will."

Chapter Two

August 6, 1993

"I'm just saying," Swapnika said, "who does he think he's going to fight? I'm sure it's offending some guests."

Deepika sighed as she continued cleaning one of the motel rooms in anticipation of the Friday night rush. "Ajeet is a great employee," she said, folding some towels to place in the bathroom. "That dagger on his belt is called a *kirpan*, and it's for religion."

"And the bracelet around his right arm?" Swapnika asked. "That's religion, too?"

Deepika chuckled as she flushed the toilet and put in an air freshener. "Yes, actually. It's called a *kara*. Personally, I think Sikhism is beautiful."

"It's weird," Swapnika said.

Deepika frowned as she exited the bathroom and watched her friend make the beds. "You realize plenty of people think Hindus are weird, right?"

"Only idiots," Swapnika said. There was no amusement in her voice.

Deepika sighed. She had discussed this with

Swapnika enough times to know she couldn't be reasoned with when it came to the new hires Puli had made. Personally, she thought Swapnika might be jealous at how young and fit Ajeet and his wife were.

"Anyways," Deepika said, trying to change the subject, "it wouldn't kill you to be nicer to him and Kiara. They're a great couple and we were lucky to find them last month. Puli wants to expand the restaurant side of the business and there aren't that many qualified chefs in Hoboken."

Swapnika's nose crinkled, and for a moment, Deepika was ready to shout, but then she noticed the marijuana cigarette at the edge of the window near the TV. "Disgusting!"

Swapnika sighed. "We really should start reporting these things to the police."

"Just help me get rid of it," Deepika said. "Business will suffer more than it already has since Puli became manager if we get a reputation for being the narc motel in the city."

Using a napkin, Swapnika picked it up and tossed it into a container they called their "gross problems bag"—filled with cigarettes, needles, used condoms, and other collectibles. "Karthik is so excited about tonight," she said, changing the subject. "So nice of Puli to take him in his car."

"Oh, please," Deepika said. "Aditya has been bugging us about this movie for weeks. Of course he's going to take his best friend."

The two women shared a knowing smile. Puli and Ramesh away with the boys all night to see *Jurassic Park* meant Deepika could tutor Swapnika more about finances. One day soon, Swapnika assured her, they'd have two cars to use between them.

Deepika had feared that the Christmas when Jason

had announced his retirement would fracture her friendship, but it'd only grown stronger. As best she could tell, Swapnika harbored no resentments over Puli having been promoted instead of Ramesh.

"Stop by our room around six thirty, okay?"

"Sure thing," Swapnika said. "I'll bring the okra subji I cooked yesterday."

"Sounds delicious. I do wonder if the boys will have nightmares after this movie, though. I know they're going through a dinosaur phase, but it's PG-13 for a reason, no?"

Swapnika smiled. "We have to let the boys indulge somehow, right? I hear from Karthik that Aditya's still a little sore sometimes that you returned that Nintendo."

Deepika snorted in derision. "Let him walk all around town to get his ice creams and go to these movies instead of sitting in a nice air-conditioned car. Then he'll really be sore."

Aditya Shetty fancied himself prince of the world—Coca-Cola ICEE in one hand, bite-size chocolate Crunch bites in the other, and flanked on all sides by his dad, Ramesh Uncle, and his best friend, Karthik, as if he was a celebrity with his entourage. On the cusp of entering first grade, he had it all.

"*Nimage bēre ēnādru bēkā?*"

"No thanks, Dad," Aditya said. "I don't need anything else." He knew his dad was stretching their dollars on movie snacks and tickets as it was.

He can't resist pretending to be a big shot. His dad wouldn't speak Kannada normally, especially not in public. He was too proud of being an American. But his father always chose his words deliberately and if he was speaking Kannada now, it was because he was prouder than usual.

And why shouldn't he be? Sure, the movie had been out for a while now, and they'd gotten cheap tickets at the discount theater, but there was nothing more American than seeing a Spielberg epic on the weekend while munching on movie snacks. They'd made it. His dad was a king, and he was a prince.

"We gotta sit midway up, right in the center," Aditya said. At his insistence, they'd gotten to the theater a half hour before the show started. He and Karthik grinned next to each other as he offered his best friend some Crunch bites.

"Ah," Karthik sighed, smacking his lips. "This is the life."

As they waited for the previews to start (the best part of some movies, in his opinion), Aditya heard Ramesh Uncle grunt. Turning his head, he saw the man sitting in the row directly behind Ramesh Uncle put his feet up on the chair.

"Excuse me," Aditya said, raising his voice.

"Aditya," Ramesh Uncle started, "don't worry about it." He grabbed Karthik's hand, no doubt warning the boy to not say anything.

Princes don't tolerate such disrespect.

"Hey," Aditya shouted, "can't you see your feet are right next to his head?"

"Whatever, man," the guy said. "Shouldn't you be wearing a turban?" He did withdraw his feet, but his comment stuck with Aditya through the entire movie.

As the end credits rolled, Aditya looked around and saw the hooligan (a word his mom had taught him to impress his teacher) had already left. Walking out, he stopped with the others at the bathroom before heading home.

"Do you need help?" Ramesh Uncle asked.

Aditya rolled his eyes. "I'm seven." Escaping into a stall, too shy to pee in front of everyone during a post-movie rush to the restrooms, he thought about how a dinosaur would never tolerate someone putting their feet up on their chair.

"What was your favorite dinosaur?" his dad asked Karthik as they strolled into the parking lot to search for their red Subaru Justy.

Aditya didn't know much about cars, but he thought Japan was cool, and the Justy's red paint job reminded him of Raphael, his favorite ninja turtle. That made their car the best one in the whole world as far as he was concerned. Between their cool car, the movie snacks, and the movie itself, he wasn't gonna let some joker (another word he'd picked up from his mom, though this one she used when she thought he wasn't listening) ruin his weekend. Besides, tomorrow was Saturday morning cartoons, which meant Batman.

"The T-Rex, obviously," Karthik said. "Nothing can stop that kind of raw power." His smile reminded Aditya of the Joker's.

"What about you, Aditya?"

Ramesh Uncle's voice sounded far away, and Aditya wondered if he'd talk to Swapnika Aunty about what happened. He wasn't dumb; he'd overheard his parents discussing racist guests at the motel from time to time. But grownups got upset when you spoke above your age, so for now he just answered the question. "I loved the velociraptors."

"Really?" His dad sounded surprised.

"Something that small that can still do that much damage? And working together to spit poison and rain chaos upon others? That's special."

Smiling as his dad ruffled his hair, Aditya let himself into their car and dreamed of a gang of velociraptors tearing that stranger apart as they drove home.

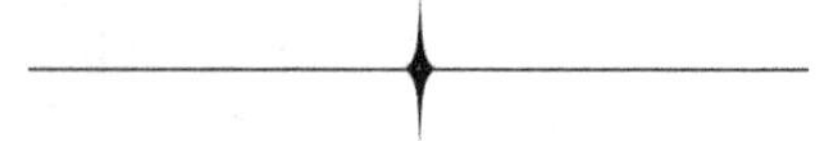

August 7, 1993

Aditya's and Karthik's parents swapped responsibility for the kids each weekend. This Saturday morning found Aditya in the Thakurs' motel room at 7 a.m., waiting for Batman cartoons to begin.

"Hey," Swapnika Aunty chided, "don't you dare turn that TV on without praying first." She pointed to the Ganesha statue next to their second-floor window.

"Yes, Aunty," Aditya said. He prostrated himself in front of the god before jumping onto the bed, causing Ramesh Uncle to grunt in exasperation. "Get up, Uncle! You can't still be sleepy!"

"I'm pretty sure the Shettys cheated us to get an extra morning alone," he said.

"Oh, come on," Swapnika Aunty whispered. "We can't afford better birth control than these demons on Saturday mornings."

"What's birth control?" Aditya asked.

Swapnika Aunty laughed before shooing him and Karthik into the bathroom to brush their teeth. "I'm setting a timer for two minutes," she said. "You better not return before then or there'll be no Batman today."

Aditya and Karthik watched their show as the adults got ready. After Batman was Ninja Turtles, and soon enough it was eight o'clock and someone was knocking at the door.

"Karthik, can you get that?" Swapnika Aunty shouted as she put in some stud earrings.

"You look great, dear," Ramesh Uncle said, kissing her on the cheek.

"Ew," Aditya said.

"How did you like the movie, *beta*?" Aditya's mother walked inside immediately when Karthik opened the door.

"It was great, Aunty, thanks for letting us use Uncle's car."

Her eyes twinkled. "Such a sweet boy. No problem, my dear."

Deepika ruffled Aditya's hair as she sat on the bed and lifted him into her lap. "Jason's downstairs for us, Swapnika."

"Really?"

The mere mention of Jason's name filled Aditya's heart. He hadn't heard from the man since his first day of kindergarten, when Jason had gotten him one of those metal lunchboxes covered with pictures of superheroes.

"Kiara just called our room. He says he has something important to tell us. He said to bring everyone."

Ramesh waved the suggestion off. "You go without me, okay? I can't handle that man's enthusiasm this morning."

"Suit yourself," Swapnika Aunty said. "Come boys, let's not leave Jasonji waiting."

It was the only reason Aditya would willingly turn cartoons off on a Saturday morning. Heading down to the connected restaurant, he wondered what the man had bought him this time.

Kiara Aunty was a new hire of his parents to help run Curry in a Hurry, the go-to restaurant for motel guests. She was waiting at the front desk when Aditya and his family arrived, and pointed them to the booth Jason was sitting in. Puli shook the man's hand before sliding into the corner with Aditya and Deepika. The other side of the booth had Jason and Swapnika Aunty.

"Where's Ram?"

Swapnika Aunty offered what Aditya knew was her fake smile. "He woke up with a cold. He's sorry he couldn't be here."

It was just as well he didn't come down, Aditya thought. He wouldn't have been happy seeing Aunty and Jason sitting so close to each other.

Mom got straight to the point, as always. "So, what's this news?"

"First things first," Jason said. He plucked out a bag of groceries from his side. "Brought you all some organic produce."

"Too generous of you, Jasonji."

Aditya heard the embarrassment in his mom's voice. It wasn't the first time he'd brought them groceries. Aditya knew his mom thought organic food was a scam, but he did enjoy the eggs.

"Thank you, Jasonji," Swapnika Aunty said.

"Well, I have to do what I can when I can," he said.

Silence descended. "What do you mean?" Aditya's dad spoke at last.

Jason ran a hand through his shock-white hair. "Ah, let's order first."

No sooner were the words out of Jason's mouth than Kiara Aunty appeared. "Yes, Jasonji?"

"Garden omelets, coffee, hash browns, and milkshakes for the boys?"

Aditya and Karthik's mouths dropped open, stomachs growling in anticipation. "Yes!" Both answered simultaneously and without hesitation.

"Jasonji," his dad whispered, "what is going on?"

After sending Kiara Aunty to put in their orders, Jason responded. "I'm moving back to Sedona."

No one spoke for several moments. Finally, Swapnika Aunty broke the silence. "Why?"

"It's time," he said. "I'll be seventy-five in a couple years. I want to see my nieces and nephews while I can still travel. I want to enjoy summer weather year-round and say goodbye to snow forever."

Aditya's dad nodded. "Thank you for telling us, Jasonji, and for spending some of your final days here spoiling our families. It's good that you return to your family, as that's what makes life worthwhile."

Smiling, Jason took the man's hands and kissed them. "The Shettys and Thakurs are every bit as much my family as who's waiting for me in Sedona."

Aditya pulled Jason's pant leg and smiled when he earned a ruffle of his hair for the effort.

"So, what've my favorite boys been up to?" Jason said.

The boys explained the plot of *Jurassic Park* as Jason listened indulgently. When the hash browns and milkshakes arrived, Aditya took huge gulps of his Oreo shake while Karthik told Jason about the Batman cartoons.

"Is Batman your favorite superhero?"

"Yes," Aditya said. "He's rich and powerful, and one day I will be, too."

Jason laughed. "I'm sure you will be, as long as you listen to your parents."

"And he has a whole cave filled with WP-encrusted weapons and vehicles," Aditya said. "I'm going to buy some myself one day."

Though the adults did their best to hide it, Aditya saw Jason and his parents exchange a look. He wasn't dumb; he'd overheard his parents talking about the magical drug. It was extremely rare to find in their part of town, even among white people, but it was in all the comics and action shows he watched. Superheroes, detectives—

everyone doing cool things used the drug to get ahead. He knew he couldn't hit the big time without the drug at his side.

"How's business going?" Jason asked, changing the subject. "Seems like you've hired some more help for the restaurant."

Aditya turned to his hash browns and omelet, smothering both in ketchup as his dad talked, all interest gone now that the adults had moved on from cartoons and movies.

"They're good workers, Ajeet and Kiara Kaur. One works the kitchen as the other works the front desk and takes orders. And that's not all. I had to replace Bob and Ryan."

"Oh?"

"They took jobs a few years back at the Hilton across town."

Jason sighed. "That's unfortunate, but it seems like you've managed."

Aditya felt his dad's eyes boring into him as he and Karthik blew bubbles into their milkshakes, giggling and kicking each other under the table. "We do what we must to guarantee our family's happiness."

Chapter Three

June 7, 2001

Aditya arrived from the school bus stop with Karthik right behind him. He found his mother sobbing on the phone at the front desk of the motel.

"Mom?" Dropping his bag, he joined her as she hung up. Karthik darted off to find his own mom, no doubt.

"Jasonji has died."

Aditya's face fell, and he dug his nails into his palms so hard it made marks. When he looked back up, his mom was still crying. Her own father's death hadn't impacted her so deeply, as far as Aditya remembered. Of course, he'd never actually met his grandfather. The way he'd overheard his dad tell the tale; the man had refused to visit America after "that damn Puli" had dragged his daughter across the world without consulting him first.

"He was a great man, Mom." Aditya brought her into a tight embrace, stroking her long raven hair.

"That was Emily," she said. Her voice was tight and shook like the wind, but already she was wiping the tears from her eyes.

Aditya saw her mind at work, knew she wouldn't allow herself more than a few moments of despair. It was the Shetty way. He wasn't sure it was a healthy way to grieve, but it was all he'd ever known from his parents. "Who's Emily?"

"Jasonji's niece. She said he never sold his house in Weehawken, that the family is having a small dinner in his honor tonight."

"Tonight?" *On my fifteenth birthday? I have to celebrate some dead white guy?*

His mother knew his mind like the back of her hand. "I'm sorry, *kanne*, but it's an honor that we've been invited. We must go."

He couldn't hide his disappointment, gritting his teeth and looking at the ground again, but when he raised his head again the words came naturally. "Of course, Mom. Whatever you need."

Swapnika Aunty arrived and took his mother in her arms, and as the two planned what dessert to cook for Jason's family, Aditya and Karthik exchanged a familiar look of regret.

Aditya's mom and Swapnika Aunty recruited Ajeet's culinary skills to make enough burfi to fill his bedroom.

"We'll reschedule your birthday for the weekend," his dad said. "It'll be even better on a Saturday."

"That's okay, Puli Uncle," Karthik joked. "It's not like a lot of people were coming anyways."

Aditya punched his best friend's arm.

"No roughhousing," his mom scolded.

"Sorry, Mom," Aditya said.

"You apologize, too," Swapnika Aunty commanded her son.

"Sorry, bro."

"It's cool," Aditya said. "I know we're just joshing each

other."

"Weehawken's a bit of a drive," Ramesh Uncle said. "How will all six of us fit in the Subaru?"

"The boys can sit on their mother's laps."

"Dad!" Aditya whined. "We're in high school; we're too old for that!"

"*Chup*!" Swapnika said. "Be thankful you're alive, big shots. You're never too old to sit with your mother."

"Listen to your aunty and hold the burfi upright," Deepika said, handing her son a carton as his father brought the car around.

Aditya and Karthik grumbled the whole drive over.

Aditya had never seen a house like the one at 39 Liberty Plaza. It had stairs leading up to a porch and a screen door (to keep out riffraff, he guessed). From the outside, he could see A.C. units on the second and third floors. The motel had units like that, but this was all for one family! There was a little garden to the left of the stairs leading to the porch, with purple and blue hydrangeas popping out of some mulch.

Maybe the motel should get a gardener. He considered recommending that to his dad before talking himself out of it.

"You must be the Shettys and Thakurs." A woman in her forties sped down the stairs to embrace them each individually. She had long blonde hair pulled into a bun, and it was clear from her runny eyeliner that she'd been crying.

"Sorry for your loss, Emily Aunty," Aditya said.

"You are just the sweetest thing," she cooed, kissing his forehead.

He shot Karthik what he hoped was a private look of disgust.

"Well come in, come in," she shouted.

"We made burfi," Swapnika Aunty said. At this, Aditya handed the food to Emily.

"It was his favorite," his mom said. "At least, that's what he always told us."

"We're blessed to have had you in his life," Emily said, looking on the verge of tears. "There was so much he didn't tell us, but we know he loved you all as family."

Almost a dozen people had gathered to honor Mr. Cooles. Emily led the Shettys and Thakurs past couples seated in upholstered chairs around the dining table. Draped in black clothing, the guests sipped tea and tried to guess who'd brought the most expensive gift. Emily ushered the two families into the kitchen to store the burfi.

"You're the only ones who brought something homemade," she said. "So thoughtful of you. I can tell why you were Jason's favorites."

"He was a kind and generous man," Puli said. "A giant among mortals, and my model of what an American should be."

Overwhelmed by his words, Emily caught his shoulder and began to cry again.

"I...I'm sorry if I upset you," he said.

"Not at all," Emily said. "You meant a great deal to Uncle Jason. You're in his will, you know."

"Really?" Now it was Puli's turn to grab Emily's shoulder for support.

"We'll talk about it later," she said.

Apparently drawn by the sound of Emily's tears, a man entered the kitchen to hand her a handkerchief. When Emily finished using it, she handed it back. He threw it in the sink for washing before turning to the others. "James Sutton, pleased to meet you." His tone indicated nothing of the sort.

"And how did you know Jason?" Deepika's question drew a smile from James, and Aditya thought the flash of pearly whites might make him go blind.

"Emily and I are half-siblings," he said. "In a way, Jason was my uncle, too. And how did you know Jason? I wasn't aware he had a daughter?" He bowed to kiss Deepika's hand, but she pulled it away and left him smooching air.

"Daughter?!" Puli's hands balled into fists, and Aditya nudged him to keep cool. For her part, his mother let out what he knew was a fake laugh.

"Haven't you met my husband, Puli?" Taking her husband's hands in her own, she brought him next to her. "We're Indian, of course."

"Oh." James bit his lip. "Excuse me. I didn't know."

"Common mistake," Deepika said with another fake laugh.

It *was* common, Aditya knew. She was so fair-skinned that she'd been mistaken for white at more than a couple sleepovers and back-to-school nights. It drove his dad nuts, but he always thought his mom secretly liked it.

"Let's leave the grownups to it," Karthik said, nudging him toward some stairs leading to the second floor. "I want to explore the house."

No need to stick around to see Dad find a reason to punch James in the mouth.

Following Karthik, Aditya took his leave without anyone noticing.

Aditya and Karthik found themselves in a room that smelled of old books and ink. The typewriter pushed against one brown wall and the built-in cabinets at the far end convinced them it was Jasonji's old study.

"Who still uses a typewriter?" Karthik asked, bashing his fingers over the machine's keys as he sat in a big swivel chair at the desk and spun himself around.

Aditya smirked at seeing his friend go about like a bull in a china shop. Wandering around the room, tugging on books to see if any revealed a secret passage, he posed a question. "You think our parents will get enough from the will to afford a second car?"

"He was successful, man, but he wasn't Batman," Karthik laughed.

As Aditya paced, he found a vent and heard his mom and Emily talking.

"Honestly, I think you'd know more about my mysterious uncle than me," Emily said.

Waving Karthik over, Aditya bent closer to listen.

"Jasonji was full of life, but always seemed burdened with something," his mom replied.

Emily sighed. "Mom told me way back about a girl Uncle Jason lived with in Sedona in the '60s, but he never mentioned it himself. I got the sense he never would've returned West except for the fact that I got married. And then when I got divorced in '97, he moved right back here."

Aditya tripped at that declaration, slamming his nose against the vent. Karthik snickered as he got back on his knees to listen.

"He moved back?" He heard the pain in his mom's voice, and if Aditya was honest with himself, he was hurt, too.

"I thought you knew," Emily said. "You mean you haven't seen him since '93?"

Bored with the conversation, Karthik began opening drawers and cabinets. "Whoa! Look at this!"

When Aditya got up to see what the fuss was about, his jaw dropped. He'd never seen brass knuckles in real life, but he knew what they looked like from movies. Karthik was wearing some now, and not just any pair.

Each jagged edge had flecks of white that shined brighter than gold.

"Is that...?" Aditya couldn't even form the words.

"WP," Karthik said. "Looks like something big went down in Tucson. Something Jason wanted to keep secret."

"Guess he was a reformed hippie," Aditya said.

"Kids?!" Swapnika's distant voice jolted them.

Hearing her clamber up the stairs, Karthik took the brass knuckles off and shoved them into his pants just as his mom opened the door. "I've been looking for you guys," she chided. "Come down for dinner."

"Yes, Aunty," Aditya said. "We were just looking around."

After dinner, after the tearful goodbyes and half-hearted promises to keep in touch, Aditya looked back at the house with its garden and three floors and multiple A.C. units one last time before sliding atop his mom's lap in their Subaru.

One day, I'll live somewhere even nicer than Weehawken.

June 9, 2001

Aditya thought there'd be nothing more embarrassing than hosting his classmates at The Śānta Stay for a party and having one of them tease him for where he lived, but it turned out that inviting his whole class and having none of them show up was even more mortifying.

"Maybe they got confused with the change of dates," his mom said.

"It's just as well," Karthik said, arm around his friend as the pair sat in the conference room and watched Ajeet Uncle bring in some wrapped gifts to set atop the tables they'd pushed together in the center of the room. That was where Aditya's friends were supposed to be seated. "You don't want people knowing we live in a motel anyways, especially girls. Can you imagine a girl like Bella Ferrari showing up here?"

Aditya smiled, thinking about the girl whose locker was next to his own. Her freckles and big tits were the highlight of his day, not to mention that thick Italian accent. She was an immigrant, just like him.

Swapnika Aunty scowled at her son's words, slapping him upside the head. "Go help Kiara Aunty bring the cake!"

"I don't know if I feel like cake, Aunty," Aditya said, watching his friend leave, nonetheless.

"Nonsense," she said. "Your mom and I were up all night with Ajeet making it."

"Thanks, Aunty," he said. "And thanks for helping Mom call all those parents. It's not your fault no one came."

"Hey," his dad said, "why don't I head out and pick up that PS2 you wanted? It's still a Saturday night. You and Karthik can stay up late playing and eating cake and even drinking a few sodas."

Aditya frowned. "It's okay, Dad. I know we can't afford it."

Biting his bottom lip, Puli raised his voice. "You let me worry about what we can and can't afford, okay?"

"It's okay, Dad, I don't mean nothing by it. It's just, if we could afford a PS2, why can't we afford some more staff, so Karthik and I aren't spending our nights and weekends cleaning rooms?"

Seeing his dad ball his hands into fists, Aditya

worried his father might hit him. He knew Ramesh Uncle did it on occasion with Karthik. His dad had never done it before, but that didn't mean it couldn't happen. Puli jumped to his feet in the next moment, though, storming past Kiara Aunty and Karthik, who carried a cake made to feed two dozen people.

The table wasn't quite as bare as Aditya had feared it would be when he'd woken up this morning. Ajeet Uncle and Kiara Aunty had bought him a sweater and socks, and one of the other staffers had baked some eggplant parmesan that would last him through Wednesday lunch at school. Luckily, his parents hadn't ordered the pizza ahead of time, and Ramesh Uncle came in with just three veggie pies to share among them. Sitting between Karthik and his mom, Aditya kept quiet as the adults talked.

"You know how Puli gets sometimes," his mom murmured.

"Please." Swapnika Aunty waved her off. "All the men in our lives act like babies once a week. He just needs to cool off."

Aditya did notice Swapnika Aunty was seated between his mom and Kiara Aunty. Her opinion of the Sikh woman had improved considerably over the last couple years, and he chalked it up to Kiara helping them cook and being respectful enough to buy him and Karthik things for their birthdays, regardless of how small or useful the actual items were.

"Do you like pizza, Kiara?" Swapnika Aunty asked.

The woman nodded, her mouth filled with hot cheese.

"You're so lucky you can eat it like that and still keep that slim figure."

"Your family's from Pakistan, right, Aunty?" Aditya said. He suspected Kiara's hourglass figure and birth country were the main reasons Swapnika Aunty hadn't warmed up to her at first.

"Actually, my family's lived in Hoboken my whole life," Kiara Aunty said.

"Really?" Swapnika Aunty leaned toward the woman, putting her elbows on the table.

"My parents came soon after that immigration bill passed in '65 and I was born soon after. I'm a U.S. citizen." The pride in Kiara Aunty's voice was unmistakable.

"And how do you keep your time when you're not here working?" Deepika asked. "You must have so many American friends if you've lived here forever."

"Oh, most of my friends left for college," Kiara said, "but I wanted to stay here, and my parents introduced me to Ajeet, thank god."

At the mention of his name, Ajeet Uncle took over the conversation. "We're blessed to have both our parents here to help out. I go to night school so we can move out of my parents' house one day, and Puliji has been so kind with our jobs here. God's provided us with a good life."

"You didn't want to go to college?" Aditya asked Kiara.

Ajeet Uncle answered for her. "God blessed us with a youthful marriage. Kiara's barely twenty, and so we'll have many years to grow our family. Someone must stay home to watch the kids."

"Right...." Eyeing Ajeet Uncle's dagger, the thing his mom called a *kirpan*, Aditya thought it best to change the subject. "Is there a *gurdwara* nearby?" He'd never seen a Sikh temple.

Kiara's eyes filled with tears as she opened her mouth to respond, but Ajeet cut her off. "Forgive my wife," he said. "She gets emotional about her faith, as all good Sikh women should. There isn't a local temple, so she must take the bus to Princeton weekly."

"That stinks," Karthik said. Getting up, he walked to her side and handed her a tissue from the table.

Smooth bastard. Aditya knew his friend's kindness

was just an excuse to admire Kiara's tawny skin and full lips up close without drawing attention to himself. He cringed at seeing Karthik stow the used tissue in the back pocket of his jeans. As Kiara Aunty hugged Karthik in appreciation, Aditya wondered why, if it was his birthday, Karthik was the one getting to feel the woman's curves against him.

Probably not the only used tissue Karthik will handle today. He smirked at his own cleverness.

"*Rhumba chamata*, Karthik," Kiara Aunty said.

Karthik blushed at being called very sweet. "You know Tamil?"

"I know many things."

"Go back to your seat," Ajeet Uncle said. He said it nicely enough, but Aditya heard the force in the man's voice and wondered if he'd ever used the *kirpan* at his side. "Let's finish lunch and then we can open presents."

As the seven of them finished their pizza and cake in silence, Aditya wondered where his dad was. He hoped he hadn't been dumb enough to actually go out and buy a PS2.

June 10, 2001

Sunday afternoons at The Śānta Stay meant cleanup rounds of all the rooms before another week began. Far from buying him a PS2, Aditya's dad had assigned him extra rooms to clean.

"Why am I being punished, too?" Karthik whined as the two friends scrubbed a toilet and bathtub.

"Your mom probably saw you gawking at Kiara Aunty's tits."

"Worth it." Karthik laughed and blew a raspberry. "I'd motorboat the shit out of those things."

"I was worried Ajeet Uncle would take out his *kirpan* and gut you if you got any closer."

Karthik frowned, growing serious. "He wouldn't, right?"

"My advice? Stop finding excuses to rub against her and don't find out." Done with the toilet, Aditya moved to empty the trashcan next to it, picking it up before dropping it with a shout. "Fuck!"

"What's up?" Karthik left the bathtub and laughed when he saw. Two used condoms lay on the floor, their contents dripping onto the tiled floor.

"Gross," Aditya complained. "Why can't guests ever leave something useful, like WP?"

"Yo," Karthik laughed, "how often you think Ajeet Uncle spears Kiara Aunty with those things?"

Aditya rolled his eyes before answering. "Never. You heard him. He wants babies."

"You need to have sex for that, right? I ain't that dumb."

Aditya sighed, using a towel and trash bag to swab up the condoms and clean the floors. "Sex without protection, moron. You don't even pay attention in sex ed?"

"Ah, school's a racket, anyways," Karthik said, waving his friend off as he moved to the bedroom to fold sheets. "It's not like school is gonna get me into a house in Weehawken."

"That was a dope ass house," Aditya said. "Where'd you store the brass knuckles from Jasonji's office?"

"Jasonji?" Karthik laughed again, so hard he rubbed a hand over his side. "You know our parents aren't here, right?"

"Force of habit," Aditya said through clenched teeth.

"So, where'd you put them?"

Karthik shrugged. "Somewhere safe. I'm saving them for a special occasion. Guys like us get that kind of power, we can only use it once before shit hits the fan."

"Good point," Aditya said.

But one day, I'll build a world where I can use it whenever I want. The shame of knowing they'd stolen from Jasonji's house was nothing compared to the thrill of a possibly writing his own ticket out of life in a motel. Then, he'd marry someone even hotter than Kiara Aunty and they'd live somewhere even nicer than Weehawken.

Chapter Four

September 11, 2001

Aditya got sent home from school after lunch around 12:30, along with Karthik and every other student in the Tri-State area. He knew it wasn't possible, but he swore he could smell the ash and fire of the Twin Towers when he closed his eyes. The school bus was silent as it drove him and Karthik back to the motel. Though it usually stopped a block away, the driver left them right at the front door today.

"*Kanne!*" His mom must've seen the bus drive in. Tears streamed down her and Swapnika Aunty's faces as they thanked the driver and hugged their sons.

"I'm okay, Mom," Aditya said. "Where's Dad?"

Deepika bit her bottom lip, staring at her feet. "He's been on the phone since noon, handling cancellations. Business is always slow after Labor Day, but nothing like this."

"Why?" Aditya raised his voice.

"It's obvious," Karthik said. "Tourists don't want to be around New York right now, not while the country's under attack." Sliding his hands into his pockets, he scoffed. "Besides, I bet some brown people are getting especially worried about other brown people right about now."

"*Chup!*" Swapnika Aunty scolded, her voice rising. "Were these terrorists Hindu or Muslim, huh?"

"That doesn't matter, Mom," Karthik said. "Brown is brown to just about everyone in this country."

"None of this matters," Deepika said, throwing her hands up in exasperation. "All we can do is play with the cards we're dealt."

Swapnika Aunty opened her mouth, but at that moment Kiara Aunty approached, her *chappals* in her hands. Sweat dripped from her face, and long, dark tangles partly covered her puffy eyes.

"What's wrong?" Deepika took the woman's hands, bringing her inside the motel to sit at the front desk. Aditya followed.

"After seeing the news all day on the TV in the restaurant," Kiara said, "I just wanted to go to the *gurdwara* and pray for all those poor souls…"

"There wasn't a bus?" Karthik stepped toward Kiara, but a glare from his mom kept him from hugging her.

"I walked to three different stops," she said. "No driver would take me. One called me a terrorist." New tears fell from her bloodshot eyes.

"People are so awful," Deepika said. "You don't have to work tonight, *beta*. Just go inside and rest. I'll tell Ajeet."

"No," Kiara said. "I want to do my job. I want our guests to see how hard we work as Americans."

"Speaking of working hard," Swapnika Aunty said, turning to the boys, "go up and get your homework done. I have a feeling we'll need help tonight."

Aditya patted Kiara Aunty on the head. "I'm sorry," he said. It was a wholly inadequate response, and yet it was all he could give.

He grabbed his backpack and headed to his room with Karthik.

Aditya didn't believe in monsters anymore, but that night, he saw several. At 8 p.m., only two diners remained at the motel's connected restaurant, Curry in a Hurry. Still, Kiara Aunty refused to go home, insisting on serving the customers free dessert. Aditya could see and hear their conversations through a window as he and Karthik helped Ajeet Uncle wash dishes in the back kitchen.

"Cur?" A fit man in his fifties stood, towering over Kiara Aunty's small frame. "What the fuck did you call me?"

"I didn't call you anything, sir. I was just asking if you wanted some kheer. For free, of course. In appreciation of you coming out tonight."

"It's some Indian sweet," the man's wife said. "She's just being nice, Roger." She was failing at her attempts to pull her husband back into his seat. Aditya could see the veins in Roger's face.

"Yeah, right," Roger said. Spittle flew from his lips. "She's probably waiting 'til we leave so she can go back to celebrating what her friends did today."

Aditya heard a dish rag behind him plop into a sink. Turning his head, he saw Ajeet Uncle move through the double doors to Kiara Aunty's side.

"Is there a problem here?" Ajeet was taller than the average Indian, but still a bit shorter than most fully grown white men. Still, Aditya imagined the *kirpan* at his side made him look intimidating enough.

"I'm so sorry to be a bother," Roger's wife said, pulling out her wallet. "We were just paying and leaving." She took out a twenty-dollar bill along with her card. "Keep the tip. I know it's gonna be tough for you people now."

"It's always been tough," Ajeet Uncle said. "And what do you mean, 'you people?'"

Aditya saw Ajeet Uncle squeeze Kiara Aunty's hand, saw her leaving the restaurant, but after that he lost track of the conversation, his eyes focused on the gleaming, white jewels adorning the corners of the white woman's wallet. He knew people were still talking, but all he saw was the wallet. He thought he was crazy for being able to hear it, but as he moved to the double doors for a better look, he saw Karthik beside him, as well.

"The brass knuckles call to me, too," Karthik said. "Sometimes Sometimes I wear them and I feel like I can do things."

"What kind of things?"

"Things no one should be able to do. I take them off after a few minutes, though."

"Why?" *Why would anyone refuse that kind of power?*

"It gives me hot sweats. Nausea. If I wear them for too long, I can't walk straight after taking them off."

Then just never take them off.

Lost in his thoughts, Aditya toppled over when Ajeet Uncle and Roger crashed through the double doors of the kitchen, their tangled bodies knocking him and Karthik to the floor.

"What the fuck?!" Aditya gaped at the two men wrestling, then caught sight of something even more compelling. Ajeet Uncle had the woman's wallet tucked away in his back pocket.

WP.

"Fucking skin grafter," Roger yelled. The man swung a meaty fist into Ajeet Uncle's side. As Ajeet gasped, Aditya pulled Karthik to the side of the kitchen, as far from the combat as possible.

"You take, and you take, and you think no one will stop you," Ajeet Uncle yelled.

"You're crazy," Roger said. "Just gimme the wallet and I won't even call the cops. We'll just leave."

"Liar!" Ajeet Uncle charged at the man, crouching and picking him up at the legs to throw him into the sink. Dishes crashed to the floor, breaking into a million pieces. Roger took one of the jagged plates and swung it across Ajeet Uncle's head, cutting through his turban and into skin.

"Get back, towelhead!" Roger screamed as he got out of the sink.

Ajeet Uncle leaned back, but only to give himself room to slip his *kirpan* out of its sheath and swing the blade at Roger.

The man's eyes widened to the size of saucers. "You're trying to kill me?!"

Aditya loved action movies, loved watching gun fights, but in that moment, he wished his parents could barge in and put a stop to the madness. Roger had moved to block the doors, and so he just watched as Ajeet Uncle thrust his blade. Aditya couldn't understand how quickly Ajeet Uncle moved.

Is it the drug?

Ajeet Uncle nicked Roger's arms, legs, face. The man wobbled past the entrance, falling to his side. Ajeet's precision with the *kirpan* was such that Aditya couldn't believe he hadn't done this before. It was clear the man wanted to extend the fight, wanted to prolong Roger's humiliation at being bested by a "skin grafter."

Or is it worse to be called a towelhead?

"Are you going to respect me now?" Gone was the jovial inflection that greeted Aditya with a mango lassi whenever he studied in the kitchen. Ajeet Uncle's voice was maniacal. He was sweating so hard it looked as if he'd run through a monsoon. "Are you ready to apologize to my wife?!"

Roger's own wife finally entered the kitchen. Aditya noted her pallor as she found her husband covered in blood. Screaming, she slammed a pot against the back of Ajeet Uncle's head.

He didn't hear her? Sense her?

Aditya crouched, frozen with fear, trapped in a corner and trying to avoid getting hurt, but he couldn't believe the man who'd shown such skill with a blade would tire out so quickly.

I guess Karthik had the right idea taking it off after a few minutes.

"You boys have to tell the truth," Roger said, turning to him and Karthik. "This fucking skin grafter started it and probably would've killed me if she hadn't intervened." Shrugging, he indicated his wife.

"No one's gonna get you in trouble," she said. "We're gonna call the cops and tell 'em how it probably woulda been worse if the two of you weren't around. You both just stay put and answer their questions."

Aditya could only stare as the couple left the room to find a phone. He knew there was one under the front desk.

We should bail before they get back.

Maybe things would've been different if he and Karthik had left then, or if Ajeet Uncle had gone to jail. Instead, Karthik nudged the man awake with his foot. "Uncle?"

"Why are you waking him?" Aditya hissed. "You're gonna get us in trouble."

"Dude, look around. We're already in trouble. But I'm not gonna let some racists hand a hard-working brown guy to the cops."

As Ajeet Uncle stirred, all of Aditya's frustration melted like ice cream on a summer day.

It's not like Roger died. Why should Ajeet Uncle pay for

some racist's mistake? "Uncle, are you okay? We need to get you out of here."

After getting his bearings, Ajeet managed to stand and threw the wallet on the ground before kicking it across the room. In his life, Aditya had never seen another brown man place his foot upon something as valuable as gold. "Uncle?"

"All my life, the only thing I wanted was to be a good American." Ajeet Uncle's voice was as firm as the ground beneath them. "But even being born here wasn't enough to make me one. Even wearing WP didn't make me one..."

He'd thrown the stolen WP away, but sweat poured down his face. It was enough to darken his shirt.

"I'm not going to jail. It'll be worse than ever now, thanks to nineteen assholes and a culture that rewards division over love."

"No one has to go to jail," Karthik said. "We can get you out." There was a raw pleading in his voice.

"There's only one way out," Ajeet Uncle said.

Aditya screamed a moment before it happened, before the man who'd bought him so many gifts used his *kirpan* and slit his own throat.

The cops took statements from everyone, guests and staff alike, and when they finished, it was past midnight. The moms let Aditya and Karthik watch TV in one of the spare rooms, of which there were now many. The boys liked using one specific room on the top floor, where they'd learned months ago how to finagle the antennae to get free porn. Karthik played it in the background as Aditya threw up in the toilet for the third time that night.

"You okay, bro?"

"Of course not," Aditya rasped between heaving fits. "How can you be?"

Karthik pointed at the TV as if that was sufficient

explanation.

"Twenty-three is too young to die," Aditya said, flushing and then rinsing his mouth.

"On the bright side, Kiara Aunty is single."

"Dude!"

"I'm kidding," Karthik said. "It's a coping mechanism."

"Kind of nuts it happened today, you know," Aditya said. "First the Towers, and now this."

"Yeah?"

"I mean, it's that girl's birthday, right? Bella? Sucks to have it associated with this forever now."

"Bella Ferrari?" Karthik muted the porn and turned. "You're hot for this girl, aren't you?"

Aditya brushed a hand through his hair. "She's cute, right? Those freckles, I mean. And that thick accent. She smells like honey, too."

Karthik smirked. "She's not related to the car family, but you want her to ride you, huh?"

"Shut up," Aditya said, punching Karthik's arm. "Anyways, she may be a Ferrari, but I'm an Audi 5000."

"Hey, I was just joshing you, man. Stick around. We don't have to watch porn."

"I wanna see my mom. You stay here a bit longer, though."

"Yeah, okay," Karthik said. "Just tell my parents I need some more alone time to deal with the trauma of it all."

Headed to the exit, Aditya noticed Karthik turn up the volume. "I can tell the trauma's really getting to you." He rolled his eyes before leaving.

Swapnika Aunty sounded relieved when Aditya told her Karthik needed more time alone. She hadn't opened the door fully when he'd knocked, and as he walked away, he heard Ramesh Uncle shouting. He thought he heard crying, too, but why wouldn't there be crying today?

Everyone was unusually stressed, that was all. No use mentioning this to Karthik.

That night, Aditya slept in fits, waking up in cold sweats every half hour, gasping for air as if he too had OD'ed on WP. He hadn't shared a room with his parents since he was eight, but his mom had insisted on it tonight. His dad had given up the bed for him and his mom, sleeping on the couch instead. Nightmares followed Aditya whenever he closed his eyes, though. He heard the gurgling sound of Ajeet Uncle bleeding out, the screams of Kiara Aunty. More than once, he touched his face as if expecting to feel some of Roger's spittle from yelling racist slurs.

It's not like sleep matters, anyways. His dad had told him school was cancelled for the rest of the week.

"You don't have to leave," Deepika whispered into the phone. Another reason he couldn't fall asleep—his mom's whispers were as soft as an elephant blowing its nose. She'd turned on the desk lamp on her side of the bed and punched in some number on the phone to reach another room. Judging by how the conversation was going, he was betting Kiara Aunty was on the other end.

"Puli said it himself tonight, right before bed. He doesn't want you to leave. We certainly don't blame you for what happened, and family is more important now than ever."

Aditya remained as still as a mouse, hoping his mom wouldn't realize he was awake. She'd just worry.

"Ohio? You've never mentioned your family there. Are you even close?"

If he kept really quiet, he could faintly make out Kiara Aunty's voice.

"You think Ohio is going to be safer than New Jersey? Is there even a Patel Brothers nearby?"

His dad's snores made it impossible to hear whatever Kiara Aunty said next, but his mom's reaction gave him a good guess. "No, we aren't moving to fucking Ohio. Nothing bad is going to happen to Aditya or Karthik."

As far as he knew, his mom had never sworn in her life. The day's stress was getting to everyone.

Who would've thought the Towers falling would be the second craziest thing I saw today?

Aditya's mom slammed the phone down and pulled the covers around her, which was enough to let him know the call had ended on bad terms, along with her and Kiara's friendship.

Terrorists don't need to tear us apart when we do it so willingly ourselves.

Waiting for sleep to seize him, Aditya hoped Karthik had those brass knuckles in a secure hiding spot. He had a feeling Kiara Aunty was right, that Ohio would prove safer than New Jersey this week.

Chapter Five

September 15, 2001

Bob Chambers was the kind of thug who'd wind up president of some Fortune 500 company if he lived long enough. Aditya hadn't heard his name in about ten years, not since the man had left The Śānta Stay to join the Hilton across town, but Aditya recognized him immediately as the man parked his red Chevy Camaro in the lot next to Curry in a Hurry.

"Trouble coming," Aditya said, nudging Karthik. The two were sweeping the floor after the last guests had left. Bollywood music played in the background as Bob and what must've been his son filtered through the door.

"Evening, Aditya Shitty."

Aditya winced at the nickname. Guys at Hoboken High called him that occasionally, so he figured Bob Jr. went to his school. It was hard to tell; most white guys looked similar.

"Thrown any parties lately?" Bob Jr. asked. It was clear from his slurring that he'd been drinking with his dad. Both leaned on a booth with one hand, the other hand in their pockets and fingering what Aditya feared were weapons. "I bet if I looked in the back, I'd catch bin Laden, get myself a big cash reward."

Should I call my dad? Aditya's heart pounded in his chest, hard and loud enough that he considered whether it might leap from his body. Looking to Karthik, he saw the boy was the exact opposite, dangerously calm. He'd taken the WP-coated brass knuckles out of his pocket and slipped them on.

"Get back in your car and drive away." Karthik dropped his broom and stepped forward with a tiger's lethal intent. Aditya's skin warmed just being around the magical drug, and for a moment, he forgot where he was.

"What are you doing?" Aditya hissed under his breath.

"I can't protect my mom from my dad, but I can protect everyone from trash like them." Jerking his head in Bob Jr.'s direction, Karthik raised his fists.

"Look at this skin grafter!" Bob Jr. howled with laughter, and then his dad howled, and then Karthik was on them both. He delivered a clean strike across Bob's face, the WP around the edges of the weapon allowing him to jump unnaturally high and connect with the man's nose. A yelp and the copious blood on the linoleum floor convinced Aditya it was broken. His head felt woozy even though it'd been Bob who'd been hit.

"Get the fuck off my dad!" Bob Jr. caught Aditya in a headlock, choking him and tossing him into the table of a booth before checking on his father.

Aditya shrank back as Karthik swung his fist down on the boy's head. A cracking sound preceded the boy's head opening up, like thunder preceding the explosion of rain from a cloud. The brass knuckles were drenched in blood.

Aditya shuddered. *White, Black, brown. All blood is red.*

Karthik showed no mercy, bringing his fists down on the fallen boy as ruthlessly as any gangster from those old movies. Aditya pulled his best friend off Bob Jr. after a few moments, terrified that Karthik meant to murder the boy. "Calm down!" he shouted. "Jesus, you're killing him!"

Sweat poured off Karthik's skin. His shirt was soaked with blood and perspiration, and he was shaking and cold to the touch. He didn't resist when Aditya pulled the brass knuckles off him and chucked them to the side. Karthik fell to the ground, gripped his sides, and cried. They weren't sniffles, but deep gasps that almost convinced Aditya his friend had been on the receiving end of a few blows, too.

"My boy..." The older Bob staggered over.

Aditya had forgotten the man was even there. He sounded like a dog who'd run through a bramble bush. No one stopped him from whipping out a cell phone and calling 911.

As the sound of sirens grew louder, Aditya understood why Karthik had never worn the brass knuckles for long...

Karthik went to jail that night. Even if there'd been a debate as to his innocence, even if he could've made bail, his parents wouldn't have allowed it. Ramesh Uncle sat at a booth in the restaurant, head in his hands, as cops circled the place. They'd actually put up yellow caution tape and drawn a chalk outline where Bob Jr. had bled out, which was pretty cool, since Aditya had assumed that only happened in the movies.

Well, maybe he didn't actually bleed out. The guy had looked terrible as he'd gotten wheeled into an ambulance, but no one had said he was dead. Aditya was amazed a kid's body had so much blood in it. *If he makes it, maybe Karthik has a chance.*

Swapnika Aunty couldn't stop touching her head to the ground, prostrating herself and reciting *slokas* in Sanskrit. She'd already called Barbara, Bob Jr.'s mom, a few times. The woman hadn't picked up.

"We'll have to leave the country," she told Deepika.

"No one's going anywhere," his mom said.

"You think we'll have a choice?" Swapnika Aunty stuck her nose in the air. Even now, she took what opportunity she had to show off. "We're still green-card holders!" She was hysterical, pacing back and forth, in contrast to her husband, who hadn't moved since he sat down. "I knew we shouldn't have delayed our citizenship test. This country wasn't made for people like us. They'll have a trial and make us pariahs. Karthik's ruined everything."

"Karthik saved us!" Aditya balled his hands into fists as his mom and Swapnika Aunty stared at him. How could she say such things about her own son? "Those guys came here drunk, looking for a fight. They'd have done some serious damage if it wasn't for Karthik."

His mom sighed. "That might've counted for something if we were white. What was he doing with WP? Why'd he hit the kid after he hit the floor?"

Aditya couldn't answer because he had the same questions. Closing his eyes to think, he opened them again at the sound of his dad's approach.

"The kid's going to live," Puli said.

"Thank god," Swapnika Aunty said.

"Niket *bhai* confirmed?" Deepika asked.

Aditya knew the man wasn't actually his mom's brother, but Niket was a trauma surgeon at the hospital and over the years, his parents had developed a friendship with him and his wife.

"Niket really stuck his neck out here for us," Puli said. "I'll go tell Ramesh."

"Mom?" Aditya stuttered when he spoke. "Will Karthik really be deported?"

Deepika fought back tears when she answered. "I don't know, *kanne*. But a boy didn't die today, and in addition to that being a great thing, it helps Karthik's odds a lot."

She shooed him off to bed, then, insisting there was nothing to be done until the morning. And while that was probably true, Aditya still looked back at the restaurant for a glimpse of Swapnika Aunty and Ramesh Uncle before heading to his room. The two parents looked as wounded as Bob Jr.

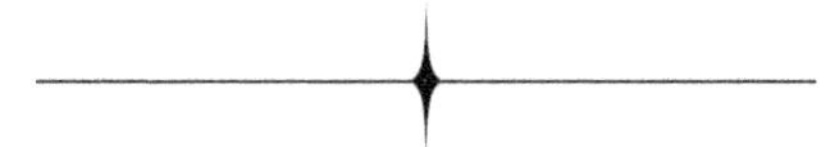

October 9, 2001

Bombs fell across both Afghanistan and, metaphorically at least, Aditya's world that week. Bob Jr. hadn't woken since the night at the restaurant, yet Karthik's trial went on, accelerated by a nationwide fervor to execute swift justice toward any brown man who dared show a propensity toward violence.

"All rise." The Honorable Judge Collins banged her gavel. Each thud against the wooden desk took Aditya to another memory from the past weeks.

Bang. Coming home to find some lowlife had thrown a Molotov cocktail through the front window of the motel.

Bang. Realizing no cop was going to help them find the perpetrators.

Bang. His dad telling him they'd have to sell The Śānta Stay, have to leave the only home he'd ever known.

"Does the prosecution have any final witnesses?"

"We do, Your Honor." A Black woman motioned for a

witness to stand and for the bailiff to move her through the crowd and onto the stand. From his vantage point, sitting between his parents in the third row from the front, Aditya recognized who she was and gasped.

"Do you swear to the tell the truth, the whole truth, and nothing but the truth?"

"I do, your honor," the woman said.

Emily Cooles.

Her long blonde hair was pulled into a bun as it had been the day he'd met her at Jasonji's home, but the tears messing up her mascara had been replaced by crow's feet around stern eyes. She glared at Karthik and his public defender.

"Do you recognize this man?" the prosecutor asked, pointing at Aditya's best friend.

"Yes," she said. "He visited my dead uncle's house months ago."

"And what was the purpose of that visit?"

Emily moved to address the jury, ice in her voice. "I was told the purpose of the trip was so his parents could pay respect to the man who'd hired them, who'd given them a life in America, but it's clear now that the plan was always to steal from my dead uncle."

Audible gasps echoed through the courtroom. More than a few visitors looked toward Ramesh Uncle and Swapnika Aunty, seated in the row right in front of Aditya and bowing their heads as if it made them invisible.

"What did they steal?" the lawyer asked.

To Aditya's surprise, Emily withdrew a photo of the same brass knuckles they'd stolen. This photo was a Polaroid, though. "Karthik stole a piece of the past."

The jurors leaned in, as confused and interested as the rest of the audience.

"What do you mean?" the prosecutor asked.

"There was so much mystery around my uncle,

especially concerning the reason he left Sedona. I'd been searching for explanations since the '90s, and I finally got answers after he died. It was in his will, why the brass knuckles mattered. He wanted them to be destroyed."

Aditya shrank down in his seat. He had goofed off with Karthik in Jasonji's office while the will was being read. *Would Karthik be on trial if we'd just listened?*

"I'd always assumed he'd left Sedona because he couldn't bear to live in the only place where he'd fallen in love with a woman," Emily said. "That was true, but he lost her because of his past life, because of WP."

Will I never be free of its deadly consequences?

"The '60s were a turbulent time, when the drug business was finding its sea legs and gangs ruled parts of Arizona."

"Your Honor, is there a point to this?" The lawyer from the Hudson County Public Defender's office interjected, and, to Aditya's surprise, the judge actually agreed.

"Get to the point, Ms. Cooles."

"Yes, Your Honor," Emily said. "My uncle found work as an enforcer for one of the gangs. Violence was all he'd ever known, having served in WWII. He came home plagued by the memories of those he'd lost, including his younger brother."

She's really laying it on thick, Aditya thought. And it was working. Looking at the jurors, he knew they weren't going to side with this brown guy who'd stolen from a dead vet.

"Uncle Jason was in high demand as the only white guy willing to serve as muscle for the colored gangs. He'd help the Natives, Latinos, anyone who needed some personal security guarantees for meetings. But he drew the line at assassinations. He always just worked to defend lives. He wanted to keep the drug trade civil."

The prosecutor goaded Emily along. "And how did he carry out his...duties?"

"With these brass knuckles," she said, pointing at the Polaroid. Shouts broke out in the courtroom, and Judge Collins banged her gavel for silence.

"My uncle worked jobs for years, until one day..."

The prosecutor handed Emily a Kleenex as she teared up. Aditya couldn't tell if she was faking it or not.

"On one of his days off, he took his girlfriend to the Grand Canyon. He was going to propose to her. In his will, he gave me the ring."

She pulled the ring out from a pocket, and Aditya's mother gasped along with the jury. Ramesh Uncle and Swapnika Aunty slid further down in their seats.

"The woman, Mercedes. She'd learned the truth about his job and confronted him, told him she could never marry a thug. They got into a fight, and, and..."

The lawyer offered Emily another Kleenex. "Yes?"

"Mercedes put the brass knuckles on, said if wearing them made him feel like a tough guy, they would make even a tiny Latina like her tough. She was already worked up, and it was her first time wearing some WP. She never had a chance."

"What happened?" This time it was a juror who called out. The judge warned him another outburst like that would see him dismissed from the case.

"She jumped off the South Rim." Emily broke down into tears, and Aditya knew it was over.

With a heavy heart, Aditya watched Barbara Chambers march up to Swapnika Aunty when the jurors broke to make their decision.

"Stop calling me," she hissed.

"Barbaraji," Swapnika Aunty said, "I cannot ever be sorry enough to make things right, but I do want you to know I disown my child. I'm repulsed by his actions. So is Ramesh. We hate him!"

The vitriol in her words choked Aditya.

"I told Bob that night, the night Puli got promoted." Barbara had worn her blonde hair in a bun, but she yanked it free now so that her curls flared like Medusa's snakes. "I told him he was wrong for using that word in front of your boy, skin grafter. But he was right. Karthik's nothing but a skin grafter." She spat at Swapnika Aunty's feet. "At least now I understand why Jason would hire Puli over Ramesh. He knew the apple doesn't fall far from the tree."

At this last comment, Ramesh Uncle stood to join his wife. "My son is a disgrace, but if you are to damn me for his actions, then I suppose I must believe you're white trash, like your husband."

Barbara's eyes popped wide. "Excuse me?!"

"Ramesh," Swapnika Aunty pleaded, "not now…"

"Bob got your son drunk and then showed up to my work to start a fight."

"Well," Barbara said, "you've got your story and I've got mine. But my version's going to be printed in the *New York Times.*"

"Fucking white people." Ramesh Uncle muttered it under his breath, but Barbara still heard. She shot him one last glare before speeding back to her seat as the jurors returned.

What a joke of a trial.

The judge had special powers when it came to sentencing, given the 9/11 attacks and the fact that Karthik was in America on a green card. Tried as an adult, and with the jurors' consent, Judge Collins revoked Karthik's green card and declared he had to leave the country by October 26. As the crowd funneled out, Aditya waited until the courtroom was empty before hugging Karthik.

"I'll be there to see you off," he said. "And you'll be back one day. I'll bring you back and we'll fucking rule this place."

Karthik laughed. "Smart kid like you? I believe it."

Deepika and Puli patted Karthik on the back before he was escorted back to jail, but the boy's own parents refused to see him.

"Don't ever embarrass me like that," Puli said, ruffling Aditya's hair.

"Will they go back with him?"

"I don't know, *kanne*," Deepika said. "We're selling the motel, and they still have family in Bangalore. It may be best for them to go back. Swapnika will go back for sure."

"But not Ramesh Uncle."

His mom bit her lip. "*Kanne,* I'm telling you this because you deserve to be spoken to with respect, with all the facts."

Puli tried to shush his wife. "Deepika, not here…"

"What's going on?" Aditya pulled at his mom's arm in exasperation.

"Swapnika Aunty's wanted a divorce for a while."

His mom kept speaking, but Aditya stopped listening, taken back to the shouting and half-opened door from the night Ajeet Uncle had died. The night Swapnika Aunty had been happy her son wasn't home because her piece of shit husband was doing god knows what.

It's not right. His nostrils flared and his hands balled into fists.

They left the courtroom without saying bye to the Thakurs. As Deepika went to the bathroom, Puli pulled his son aside.

"I got an offer for The Śānta Stay and I'm going to take

it."

Aditya snorted in derision, looking at the ground. "You were serious? Weren't you looking at expanding into Weehawken with some of the money Jasonji left you?"

"That was before 9/11," Puli said. "That was before your friend put a white kid in a coma!"

"You know it wasn't that simple," Aditya said, raising his voice to match his father's.

"Grow up!" Puli said. "It's always that simple when it comes to white folk. If we're very lucky, we'll get a halfway decent deal for both the motel and the restaurant. That money, combined with the money from Jasonji's will and the insurance money from the fire damage, will be enough to get us an apartment and start a college fund."

College? His grades were pretty good, but he hadn't spent more than a couple hours on school in the last month. Most of his teachers were okay with it, chalking it up to trauma and offering plenty of extra credit.

"I'm serious, Aditya," Puli said. "Use those brains of yours to get us out of this hellhole."

As his mom emerged from the bathroom, Aditya noticed his dad smiling again. As if Puli hadn't just put the weight of the world on his son's shoulders.

"Shall we?" His mom led them past the doors of justice and back onto the street.

Aditya spotted Bella Ferrari on the bus ride home. Saying he needed to stretch his legs, he got up from beside his parents and made his way to where she was seated in the back. "Bella?"

She stayed seated. Aditya leaned over her, grabbing a pole for support. It was difficult not to smell her hair. Even here, amidst the smell of homeless people's piss, she smelled like honey.

"What are you doing here?" he said.

"My parents don't know I'm skipping school," she said. "Don't tell anyone you saw me, okay?"

"Yeah, no problem." Aditya stared at the ground. "You skipped with your boyfriend to see a movie or something?"

Her laughter sounded like a pianist playing scales, capturing all the beauty and complexity of the world. "I broke up with Mark last month."

"Oh?" Aditya met her gaze now.

"He's got a curved dick."

"Oh."

"I mean, that's not why I broke up with him. Just a fun fact."

"Oh…"

She laughed again, the sound as powerful as Karthik's brass knuckles. "I dumped him when he called the Thakurs…well, I don't want to repeat what he called them."

She's not like the others? "Were you at the courthouse?"

"Yeah." Now it was her who found the floor fascinating. Aditya followed her gaze down to her brown leather boots. "I sat in the back. Did my best not to draw any attention."

He wanted to say that was tough to do when she looked so pretty. "You ditched to see Karthik get sentenced? I thought you left Mark for being a racist?"

She ran a finger through her wavy chestnut hair before speaking, eyes still glued to her shoes. "I thought someone from school should be there to support Karthik. I mean, someone like me…"

The bus stopped to drop some people off, and the sudden movement flung Aditya toward Bella. He would've landed in her lap if he hadn't gripped the pole for dear life. Their eyes met and the curves of her lips drew close enough to kiss. He sighed, a sound impossible for her to miss, and in the next moment pulled himself back. "Sorry..."

She giggled; the sound moved his insides. "Don't worry about it."

"Why'd you want to support Karthik?"

She met his eyes again. "There are two sides to every story. Karthik can't be that bad a guy if he's friends with you."

Aditya blushed. Bella cracked a smile, and he knew he had to kiss her.

Now or never. Gathering his courage, he opened his mouth, leaned in, and collided with the pole as the bus stopped again. A tooth came loose.

"Oh my god!" She exclaimed, rising from her seat. "Are you okay?"

He nodded, refusing to open his mouth and reveal the damage.

She smiled again, touching his hand and sending a jolt through his system. "Well, this is me," she said. "Sorry in advance if I'm a bitch to you in school. My parents are pricks who say I'm not allowed to hang out with anyone associated with Karthik. But I'm glad you're still best friends. Nothing's more important than friendship."

Aditya nodded as she squeezed his hand and exited the bus. As it pulled toward his home, he walked back to his parents, hoping it wasn't the last time he'd ever see Bella.

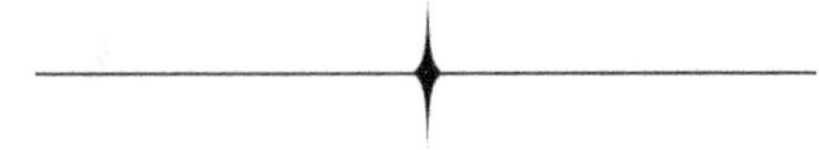

October 26, 2001

Aditya was glad it was a Friday night. He had time to finish his homework (his dad wouldn't take him otherwise) and still make it to the airport to see the Thakurs off. Puli had offered to drive everyone in their Subaru, but Ramesh Uncle insisted his family take the subway.

"These jokers charge four dollars for parking when all we're doing is taking fifteen minutes." Puli took I-678 to avoid paying any tolls, but that'd increased their drive time and led to his sour mood. "I thought a perk of moving from Bangalore was that I'd spend less time in traffic."

"*Chup*," Deepika said, slapping his arm as he got his wallet out to pay the fee. "Catch up to me and Aditya inside."

"You're not waiting for me?"

"*Paavam*," she said, frowning with her eyes and lips. "It's not like the old days. We won't be able to see them past security. Let the boy spend as much time with Karthik as he can."

Leaving his father grumbling under his breath, Aditya ran into JFK and spotted Karthik and his parents waiting to say bye to their oldest friends before leaving forever. The two friends embraced without shame.

"It's not fair," Aditya said.

"Who said any of this was supposed to be fair?" Karthik punched him in the arm. "We'll write letters, yeah?"

"Oh, did you learn how to write?" Aditya punched him back.

"No horse play," Ramesh Uncle said. "That's what got us into this mess."

You're what got us into this mess. Aditya kept his opinion to himself. If he hadn't been afraid to stick up for his friend, if he'd reported any abuse to Jasonji when it'd started all those years ago, maybe his best friend wouldn't be leaving. He made a promise to himself then: no more secrets, no more shame. He'd be an open book with his best friend from now on. He'd have the hard conversations necessary to develop a meaningful, thriving relationship.

Swapnika Aunty pulled Aditya's mom aside to exchange some words in private.

Puli joined the group. "Ramesh."

"It's my own fault," Ramesh Uncle said. "Returning to India wouldn't be an option, legally, if I'd just been faster with that citizenship test."

Karthik turned away, pretending not to hear, but Aditya refused to leave. "Why do you hate your son?" His question drew glares from both dads, but he didn't back down. "He needs his parents."

"Don't talk to me of fatherhood," Ramesh Uncle snarled, and Aditya knew in that moment that Karthik was his father's son, that any capacity for violence the boy had inherited stemmed from this man. "Karthik needs a good kick in the pants. India can give him that, but we'd gotten out. And now we have to go back? Why? Because he can't do anything but use his fists?"

"I only did what you taught me!" Karthik shouted, and Aditya saw Ramesh Uncle draw his hand to slap his son across the face.

"Ramesh?" Swapnika Aunty and Deepika returned in outrage. "How can you slap?" She cradled her boy in her arms, glaring at her husband.

"We'll visit you," Deepika said, trying to break the tension.

Swapnika Aunty's eyes bored into Ramesh Uncle's. "My husband is more badly behaved than my son. If he doesn't shape up quick, you'll be visiting two houses."

"No," Aditya said, "we'd still just go to one."

Sufficiently cowed, Ramesh Uncle tried apologizing, but Karthik just gave Aditya another hug and ran to the security line. He shouted his final goodbye from there. "Use that big brain of yours and bring me back after all this cools down."

"I will," Aditya said. *I promise.* College had renewed meaning, now. He'd solve his parents' problems, Karthik's problems. Everything could be done with the right education.

His parents patted his head as they watched the best friends they'd ever known leave the country. On the TV at the kiosk nearby, Aditya saw footage of President Bush signing the PATRIOT Act earlier that day. He knew Karthik wasn't returning for a very long time, as long as nothing changed. *But one day, it will. Because of me.*

Chapter Six

June 15, 2005

Aditya read another letter from Karthik on the morning of his high school graduation. His mother had given it to him last night, but he'd saved it for today.

We should be graduating together. They'd written each other once a month, sometimes more. Video games. Girls. Food. Karthik couldn't believe how good ice cream and chicken tasted in India. He'd found ways to smuggle meat past his mom. Sure enough, she'd left Ramesh Uncle a couple years ago. Puli hadn't kept in touch with the man as far as Aditya knew.

"*Beta*, we can't be late!" Deepika shouted from her bathroom.

His dad had been right about the insurance money, selling the motel, Jasonji's will. Not to mention the local temple raising some money for them. It'd been enough for a two-bedroom apartment. His dad pulled triple shifts as a bus driver and his mom worked gigs as a part-time teacher, but today proved it was worth it. Aditya knew today was about them even more than him. He was the one going to Princeton in the fall, but only because of their sacrifices.

"I'm just changing into my gown!" Yelling from his room, he tore open the letter from Karthik.

> Aditya,
>
> International postal delivery is ass, so I don't know if this'll reach you before the 15th. Regardless, congratulations on your graduation and getting into Princeton. I knew you were headed for big things, so hurry up and get me back there already. I hear Bella Ferrari is single again. Unless you finally got up the courage to ask her to prom. I'm guessing you didn't cause you're such a pussy.

Aditya rolled his eyes. Karthik had talked this way since they were kids, and so Aditya let it roll off his shoulders. His friend had told him about a year ago about this crew he'd joined to work some jobs. From the way Karthik described it, Aditya thought it was similar to what Jasonji had done in Arizona, serving as muscle for some thugs. He'd considered telling his parents about it, but what would that do? Just get Karthik in more trouble. The money was good (Karthik said he'd pre-ordered an Xbox 360 and helped his mom with groceries a few times), and it sounded like the jobs were limited to property damage, so what did he care? Swapnika Aunty had stopped asking questions the first time Karthik had rescued them from running late on rent.

> My guess was right about who I'm really

working for. The money's as good as ever, but these guys don't fuck around. I'm gonna need an exit strategy sooner or later. I don't wanna go to jail here if I end up having to put another guy in a coma. Pretty sure the Indian police don't know what Miranda rights are.

Aditya laughed. He'd sent a few worksheets and notes to Karthik on occasion, but he hadn't thought the guy would actually study them. Karthik had asked Aditya to do some research on a few names from time to time, guys from his friend's crew. Most of the names were aliases, but Aditya had been able to get Karthik a few real names. On the phone, of course. He wasn't gonna put anything in writing. He'd read a little about these gangs in Bangalore that gamed the real estate market. Some guy would die, and they'd sneak in before a will was read, make enough of a stink that they'd be able to solicit some bribes unless the deceased had left a title or something else legally binding to the house for their descendants. And it was India, so most of these suckers just had to pay up. If they didn't? That's when Karthik got involved, ripping up drywall and convincing them it was better to pay and get eighty percent of a house than not pay and see the place destroyed.

My boss is looking to get some muscle in with the Army. Maybe I can convince him I should let them recruit me. It'd get me out of this racket, at least. And it'd keep me bashing people's skulls in. Seems to be the only thing I'm good at.

Aditya sighed. It wasn't true, but he'd long given up

on convincing Karthik that if he would just apply himself, he could be book smart as well as street smart.

God, I sound like Dad.

Ignoring his mom pounding on his door, he read the end of the letter.

> Anyways, did you catch the latest Star Wars movie? Kinda lame, but it wasn't all bad. That girl I mentioned, Kritika? She gave me a handjob since the theater was pretty dark and empty.
>
> Gangsta for life,
> Karthik

Smirking, Aditya stuffed the letter into a drawer and yelled to his mom, asking for five more minutes. He doubted Kritika existed, but if that made his friend feel like a big man, it was fine by him. Sliding his gown on, tying some tassels to his cap, he opened the door and let his mom fawn over him.

The ceremony itself was nothing special. Some state legislator gave the commencement address. It was the second speech of the day, after Bella Ferrari said some words as valedictorian. Aditya saw her posing for pictures with friends as his family walked to their car from the convention center that'd hosted the event.

"That's the girl you always mention, right?" His mother stopped in front of a fountain where a group of girls were taking selfies.

I don't always talk about her, do I?

"There's a girl?" Puli asked.

"No, Dad, there's no girl."

"Good," he said. "No time for girls at Princeton."

"She's going to NYU," Aditya said.

"So you do know her!" Puli exclaimed.

Aditya cringed. *Me and my big mouth.*

His mom pulled him by the arm to greet Bella, who was, thankfully, not with her parents. Aditya knew they still didn't like him.

Deepika tapped the girl's shoulder. "You're Bella, right?"

"Mrs. Shetty?"

Aditya's mom tensed as soon as Bella touched her hand. A gesture that'd no doubt been intended as friendly turned violent as Deepika bent over and clutched her stomach.

"Mom?!" Aditya said, alarmed.

Puli moved quickly, grabbing Bella by the arm and pushing her aside. "It's the WP," he said, pointing to the bracelet Bella wore on her right hand. "Deepika's overly sensitive."

They were causing a scene, now, with his mom dry-heaving as she knelt on the ground.

"Breathe," Puli said. "Just breathe."

Bella pulled the bracelet off and handed it to a friend before pulling out a water bottle from under her gown and handing it to Aditya's mom. "I'm so sorry, Mrs. Shetty."

"It's...not...your...fault," she said between gasps. "Haven't...had...an incident like...this in years."

Within moments, his mom was good as new. She rose from the ground as if nothing had happened. "All better, see?"

Bella smiled, her wavy hair flapping in the wind now that her graduation cap was off. "I'm sorry to be a bother."

"Nonsense," Deepika said. "It's me who's the bother. It seems the problem's getting worse with age."

"There's still so much we don't know about WP," Bella

said, "especially its effects on people like you."

Aditya winced at that phrase. He knew she didn't mean anything by it, but it still stung.

"So," Deepika said, holding Bella's hands now, "what are your plans, dear? Aditya mentioned NYU."

Bella looked at him for the first time, and when their eyes connected it was like she'd touched him with WP. His heart pounded as his palms became clammy.

"I didn't know he kept such tabs on me," she said. She returned her gaze to Deepika. "I want to become a lawyer."

"Why?" Puli asked.

"I want to be a judge one day," Bella said. "What happened to Karthik, what's happening to minorities all across the country just for having some WP on them, it's not right."

Aditya and his dad fell silent until Deepika broke the tension. "I pray for that kid once a week," she said. "Niket *bhai* tells me he's still in that coma."

Bob Jr. still hasn't woken up?

"That's fucked up," Aditya said.

"Language!" Puli barked.

"Sorry, it's just…it's wrong that Ajeet Uncle couldn't get the mental healthcare he needed, that we've got friends who ration insulin, but at the same time, some rich, spoiled, brain-dead kid is living long past his sell-by date."

No one spoke until Bella began giggling. "Who talks like that?"

"I wish you two had spent more time together," Deepika said, looking Bella up and down. "A good girl like you would've set him straight."

"Oh, I don't know," Bella said to him. "You're straight, aren't you?"

"Yes!" Aditya said.

"Good." She winked before saying goodbye to his parents and heading back to her friends.

Good? What does that mean?

"What's the matter with you?" Puli said, slapping Aditya's head. "You talk to a girl like that? It's a good thing you never dated. And don't date in college. This family can only endure so much trauma."

"Why didn't you ever ask that girl to prom or something?" Deepika asked as they piled into their 1985 Subaru Justy. Despite being nineteen, the oldest in his class, he was still younger than the car.

"Don't encourage him," Puli said, fiddling with the ignition and steering wheel to get the car to start.

"It just never happened, Mom," Aditya said. Hearing the car finally start, surveying the fraying interior, he was glad it hadn't.

May 9, 2009

Aditya decided it was tradition, reading a letter from Karthik the morning before graduation. He'd stayed home to save money his first three years, but in senior year, his parents had surprised him with off-campus housing. After driving to his place last night, they'd handed him the envelope before taking him to dinner.

Aditya knew Karthik had convinced his boss to let him join the Army, but he hadn't heard anything from his best friend in over a year and had wondered if he'd been sent to fight in Iraq or something. Now, as before, his mother knocked on his door for him to hurry up.

"Just wrapping up!" he yelled, tearing the envelope open.

Aditya,

Do I call you the next Bill Gates or the next Mark Zuckerberg? Or maybe even the next Kennedy? Nah, that don't make no sense. Kennedy was drowning in pussy.

Aditya laughed so loud his mom apparently decided he'd fallen. "Did you trip on your gown? Let me in. I can help."

"Two more minutes!" He resumed reading.

I heard you got into business school at Harvard? Congratulations. Learn a lot and then work that magic for me. I hear a degree from there is more powerful than WP. I can't say where I am, but I'm safe. The Indian Army pays ass, but there are some benefits. It's a lot calmer than the last job, and the old boss still tosses me some cash now and then. Of course, I'm still eager for you to get me back to America.

Aditya sighed in relief at learning Karthik was safe.

Oh, by the way, my dad died. Heart attack. No skin off my back, but you should let Aunty and Uncle know. Mom was already seeing this guy in Bangalore, and with this, it makes re-marrying easier. I think I'd like that. Mom deserves happiness after all that's happened, and I like this new guy okay.

Aditya smiled. The guy was still a brute, but he was definitely maturing.

I'll write more when I can. Take care of yourself. And get me the fuck outta here. I'm sick of being shot at.

Gangsta for life,
Karthik

Stuffing the letter into his pocket, Aditya threw his gown over his head and headed out. Today, when he was out there, Karthik would be with him, too. After all, in another life, it could've just as easily been his best friend graduating from Princeton with honors.

Governor Corzine gave the commencement speech. Aditya barely listened, scrolling through Facebook on his phone instead. His dad had scolded him for getting an iPhone, but he'd bought it himself with money from his TA job, so Puli couldn't say that much about it. Scanning the "People You May Know" feature, he saw a woman with green eyes, freckles, and wavy chestnut hair.

Bella?

He spent the next fifteen minutes poring over her profile (luckily made public). They'd lost touch after Hoboken High. Judging from her pics, her tits were still as big as ever and she enjoyed flaunting them at the beach. Engrossed with her profile, he sent her a friend request and it wasn't until his seatmate nudged his ribs that he noticed students were walking to get their diplomas.

"Move, Shitty," the guy hissed. Aditya hadn't outgrown the nickname despite a new school and new friends (well, acquaintances he got drunk with on occasion). Standing up, walking along with the rest of his year, he spotted his parents in the crowd. Deepika was yelling at the top of her lungs as Puli tried holding a camera steady to record the whole thing as she bounced on her feet snapping pictures every thirty seconds. She tried and failed to whistle when his name was called, causing Aditya to laugh so hard he almost tripped over his gown.

This one's for you, Mom.

Aditya didn't complain once as his mom dragged him and Puli around campus to take pictures absolutely everywhere. She already had plenty of shots of him, but "not with your fancy gown on." Sitting at Carnegie Lake, she asked another family to take a picture of them near the water.

"Want to rent a canoe?" Aditya asked. "I've steered one before. It's not that hard, and the weather's nice today."

"Please," Deepika said, rolling her eyes. "Do you want your mother to drown?" She'd worn a red and gold *saree* for this occasion, and it was as majestic as it was difficult to walk in.

"I gotta tell you something." Aditya decided to bring up Karthik's letter only after they'd finished with pictures, as the three walked back to the Subaru. "Ramesh Uncle died."

"What?" Puli generally let his wife and son walk in front of him, content to be overshadowed, but at this news, he pulled ahead. "Karthik wrote that?"

Nodding, Aditya continued. "Heart attack. But that's not all—Swapnika Aunty's been dating some guy. Karthik thinks now that his dad's dead, she'll marry him."

"Wonderful news," Deepika said. "Sad about Ramesh, of course, but I've longed for this day. Swapnika deserves someone who can make her happy."

Puli sighed. "Wonderful, indeed. The dream of every husband is that his wife remarries before he's even been cremated." Opening the door, he started playing with the steering wheel and ignition to start the car. "I hope you at least wait until my body's cold," he told Deepika.

"*Chup!*" she said. "That brute had it coming. Don't worry; I'll mourn you like any good wife."

"How about happier topics for my graduation day?" Aditya asked as the car stirred to life. His phone dinged with a notification he'd gotten an email. When he checked it, he cheered out loud.

"What now?" Puli asked.

"My scholarship came through," he said. Though he'd already accepted Harvard Business School (because come on), the financing was a topic of spirited debate with his parents. They'd used the last of the insurance money and Jasonji's gifted funds to help pay rent for his senior year. Harvard tuition was just one of the reasons his dad thought he was a moron for buying an iPhone. With this scholarship, though, he'd be able to swing it.

"Congratulations!" His mom beamed as they drove toward Hoboken.

"Thanks, Mom."

"Explain this scholarship again," Puli said. "It sounds like a job."

"I work with a professor," Aditya said, trying his best not to sound exasperated. He'd explained the process twice already. "Help him with research, that kind of thing. He's actually writing a book now, so I guess I'll probably be helping him with that, too."

"And you'll get your name on the book?" Puli asked.

"Um...no."

"I see. So, you help this man become a famous author and in return he pays you minimum wage."

"Plus the scholarship," Aditya said.

"It's a good deal, Puli," Deepika said.

"It's a scam. But you're the big shot now. If you want to be scammed, I won't stand in the way."

"Come on, Dad, don't be like that. The education is worth more than any book deal."

Deepika nodded.

"You know how much people will pay someone with degrees from Princeton and Harvard?" Aditya asked. "I can pay you back for Princeton and still have enough to get you a new car."

Puli's hands tightened around the wheel of the Justy. "What's wrong with our car?"

"It's over twenty years old!"

"You thought it was the coolest thing when I took you to Jurassic Park in it," Puli grumbled.

"I was seven!"

Puli grew silent as they sped down 95-South. Finally, the quiet was uncomfortable enough that Deepika spoke.

"Did you meet any cute girls at Princeton?"

"Mom…"

"What use is it going to be if you get so smart and so rich, but I don't have any grandkids to spoil?"

"He's not even twenty-five," Puli grunted as they got off the highway and turned into Hoboken.

"Oh, you've decided to grace us with your voice again?" Deepika joked. "But really," she said, turning back to look her son in the eyes. "No girls? Whatever happened to that Bella girl from high school?"

Aditya adopted his dad's grunt. No matter what either of them said, he knew he was his father's son. "We lost touch. Anyways, it's not like we were ever really friends to begin with."

As they pulled into the parking lot of their apartment complex, Aditya checked his phone and smiled at what he saw—a greater achievement than winning his scholarship and graduating from Princeton combined. Bella Ferrari had accepted his friend request.

Chapter Seven

March 13, 2010

Aditya spent most Saturday nights at the Widener Library at Harvard. The building housed three and a half million books and looked every bit the palace it was meant to be when it had been completed in 1915. Constructed with limestone and with Corinthian pillars forming a colonnade across the front, the outside was just as grand as the inside with its domed ceiling and marble fireplaces.

For Aditya, the week had been spent neglecting homework as he'd worked with Professor Sonorous, but he was glad that if he had to spend the weekend catching up with his coursework, he could at least do so in such a grand library. On his first visit, a librarian had tried to scare Aditya with tall tales of Widener's history. Legend said the reason Harvard had a swimming requirement for graduation was because the lead donor's son had died aboard the *Titanic*. Aditya doubted that was true, given how that'd likely disqualify the physically disabled and lead to countless lawsuits, but it was fun to think about.

Just more proof of how the wealthy hoard their power to dictate to the rest of us from on high.

Spring break had officially started yesterday. He should be at a bar or back in some woman's apartment. He'd messaged back and forth with Bella Ferrari a few times after she'd accepted his friend request, but it was all a bit silly. She'd graduated from NYU, but loved the city and wanted to stay there as she saved up for law school.

Not that I'd have time for her anyways, even if she did live here.

He was busier than he'd ever been. Classes. Homework. Job. Parents. They worried if he didn't call them twice a week, and those calls never lasted less than an hour. He was already developing crow's feet from lack of sleep. He'd found gray hair in his shower on more than one occasion. Typing away at his laptop, he heard a couple giggling in the shelves behind him. He'd chosen a room far below the ground floor to try and get some quiet, but it sounded like the horny teenagers had the same idea. Standing from his desk, he spotted the flash of a purple bra and heard a moan before deciding to close his computer.

Alcohol it is. If someone could even get laid at the library during spring break, there were only upsides to going to a bar.

Aditya frequented a place near Boston University called The Pig's Lick, a modest two-story brick building that, according to city legend, had once served beer to none other than Ben Franklin. Aditya believed that story about as much as the one about the Widener. Entering the bar, he walked up to the quieter second floor and ordered a bourbon and curly fries before finding a round empty table to sit at. When the food and drink arrived, he downed the liquor in one shot and asked for another. The waitress left him, and that's when he saw her.

"Kiara Aunty?"

She was pushing forty, but he'd recognize that hourglass figure and smile anywhere.

"Oh my goodness," she said. "Aditya?!"

She hugged him tight, and he thought back to the days he and Karthik had competed to see who could feel her breasts through her shirt without her noticing. Looking back, he wondered if she'd always known.

Probably not, since she kept hugging us.

She released him from her embrace. Aditya noticed a woman around his age at her side.

"This is my stepdaughter, Mahira," she said.

"Stepdaughter?" Aditya motioned for them to join him, pushing some fries towards them, and getting two chairs from a neighboring table.

"I'm not sure you remember," Kiara Aunty said, "but I moved to Columbus after..." She left the sentence unfinished.

"Yeah..." Aditya said.

"I found a wonderful man there, Jagvir Sidhu. He taught molecular biology at Ohio State. We married in 2005."

"I can't believe Mom didn't tell me," Aditya said.

Kiara Aunty bit her lip, placing her hand atop his. "We didn't leave on the best terms. I was happy to have a new life, new friends, new family."

"You should give her a call," he said. "You can't escape family no matter how hard you try. I guess that's why we're running into each other now."

"Sure, *beta*," Kiara Aunty said, handing him her phone to enter Deepika's number. "You've gotten so handsome."

Aditya blushed. "Can I get you a soda, Aunty?"

Kiara laughed. "I drink now. How about a whiskey, instead?"

"I've got it," Mahira said. Aditya couldn't help but stare as she left for the bar. She had curves in all the right places and a supple chest.

"Knock it off with this Aunty business; it's just Kiara now. I feel old enough at thirty-seven."

Aditya nodded as Mahira returned with two red wines. "What brings you to Boston?"

"Mahira's a junior at Boston University," Kiara said. The pride in her voice made the dark room appear brighter. "I thought I'd visit, since it's spring break."

"For me, too," Aditya said. "I've just started my second semester at Harvard for my MBA."

"Fancy," Kiara said.

"And what are you studying?" he asked Mahira.

"I'm going to be a teacher." The woman wore pink capris, a flowery top, and a "fuck you" frown that somehow made her even more attractive.

"Mahira, be nice," Kiara said. "We'll have our girls' night later. I certainly didn't plan on running into such an old friend."

"And where's your dad? Didn't want to miss the Buckeyes playing tonight?" He'd asked Mahira the question to be polite, but the silence that followed made him wish he'd ordered another bourbon.

"Jagvir passed last year," Kiara said. A wistful smile spread all the way across her lips and into Aditya's chest as a dagger.

"I'm sorry," he said.

"Good can still come from bad," she said. "I found new meaning in life with Mahira."

Sipping her wine, Mahira asked Aditya what her stepmom had been like back in New Jersey. He told her how Kiara had used to dote on him with sweets and tease him about his taste in music. Another hour passed, and Kiara excused herself, saying they'd have to carry her out if she had any more wine.

"You two have fun," she said, hobbling out the door.

They made their way from the bar to a dance club, and by the end of the night Mahira had slipped him her number. Waiting to take the T back into Cambridge, Aditya said, "You were kind of a bitch at the bar with your mom. What changed?"

"She's pretty protective with me," Mahira said. "And especially since she knew you as a kid… I just didn't want her thinking we'd hook up."

He smiled like a fourteen-year-old receiving his first kiss. "Yeah? We're gonna hook up?"

"If you're lucky." Winking, she got on her train, and he watched her disappear.

March 16, 2010

Mahira had the confidence of a mediocre white man and the allure of a dangerous animal. Aditya invited her to Aurora's in the North End for their first date. He'd arrived early to make sure their table was done up real nice, with flowers on it and a view of the bakery across the street where they'd get dessert. He choked on his water watching her arrive in a red dress that showed just enough cleavage to be sexy but not tawdry.

"Wine?" He got up to pull her chair out, using the excuse to brush her smooth arms.

"Trying to get me drunk already?"

He smiled as he sat back down. "I'm a man of ill repute."

She laughed, a snorting sound that told him it was genuine. "At least you're honest."

When the waiter came to tell them the specials, Mahira ordered for the both of them. "You're okay letting a woman take care of you, right?"

"I'm okay with anything that involves you and me spending more time together," Aditya said.

"Famous last words."

Now it was Aditya's turn to laugh. "You aren't like other brown girls."

"How do you mean?"

"Well, for starters, you drink. Aren't you not supposed to, as a Sikh? It's like, disrespectful to God or something?"

Mahira rolled her eyes, dipping some bread into olive oil and answering between bites. "God never had to worry about being popular. You do what you have to do to stay ahead in this country."

He opened his mouth to respond but stopped when he sensed something at his side. A man around his age had just bent on one knee and proposed to a lady. The whole restaurant cheered as the woman said yes, but all Aditya saw was the coat of WP around the diamond ring. He'd been nervous about the date to begin with, but now the drug caused his armpits to dampen with sweat. Undoing his top shirt button to get more air, he noticed Mahira sitting frozen.

"You don't like it, either?"

Mahira's tawny skin turned shock-white as she gripped their table. Aditya saw the veins in her hands stand out.

"Excuse me," he said, interrupting a waitress taking the newly engaged couple's picture. "We need a new table."

The woman scoffed without answering him.

"Please," he begged, "the WP is making me nauseous."

"You didn't have to come here," the waitress sneered. "Stay or leave, but you're making a scene."

The woman wearing the ring spoke. "It's okay," she said. "We've had our moment. I want to walk around, anyways." Telling her fiancé to pay while she waited outside, she suggested they go across the street to the bakery Aditya had picked out for dessert.

"Thank you," he said. "And congratulations."

His muscles loosened moments after the couple left. Looking at Mahira, he saw she was back to normal as well.

"You didn't have to do that," she said. "Say you were nauseous, I mean."

"It affects me, too…"

"It was nice of you," she whispered. "I'm not used to nice guys."

"Forget about it." He ordered them two scotches before asking for the check.

Walking her home, Aditya told Mahira he'd researched this bakery but didn't want to risk running into that couple again.

"It's just as well," she said. "You may not want a second date if I got a few more cannolis in me."

"Don't even joke about that," he said. "You're fucking gorgeous." Pushing her against a building as they walked down a cobble-street path, he kissed her and ran his hands down her skirt. She tasted like sauce and cheese and all the rich things that made life worth living. He moved against her until he knew she felt his erection against her belly. He bit her neck, not caring who saw them. For a moment, they lived on an island in space, and then she was pushing him off her.

"Who needs WP when you're around?" Her eyes told him she wanted more.

"I'm sorry if I got carried away," he said. "It's just that I meant what I said. The Sistine Chapel has nothing on you."

She bent her head back and laughed. "God, does that line work on other girls?"

Aditya stared at the ground. "You're the first one I've used it on. You're the first one…"

She took his head in her hands and kissed his cheek. "Hey, for me, too."

"Really?"

"Yeah," she said. "And I want it to be special. So let's wait. Can you do that for me?"

"Like I said, I'm okay with anything, as long as we're together."

She held his hand as they continued walking to her place. "I know I play the role of confident bitch, but I'm really quite shit around guys. I wish my dad was still around."

"What was he like?"

"Quiet, nerdy…but suave."

"Suave?"

Mahira laughed. "You've seen Kiara. Don't tell me you didn't have a crush on her as a kid."

"Maybe I still have a crush on her," Aditya said. "Maybe this is all a long con to get into her pants instead of yours." He laughed when Mahira slapped his arm. "Yeah, me and my buddy, Karthik, used to like her."

"Well, imagine marrying her despite being over a decade older. You don't do that unless you're pretty suave."

"Or rich," Aditya said.

She laughed again. "We grew up in Columbus, Ohio. He was suave."

"And he taught at the college, right? Is that why you want to teach, too?"

"He taught molecular biology. Some of that involved learning about WP, how it reacts to various body types, how it can be used differently by different types of people."

Aditya nodded. "And if he was still around, maybe he'd have found a way for people like us to use it by now?"

Mahira stopped walking. "It's not like that. I don't want anything to do with a drug that caused my stepmom such heartbreak."

"So, then, what's it like?"

Mahira smiled. "I just know if he was around, he'd be able to convince me I didn't fuck up our first date by being weird around the drug."

"Well," Aditya said, "lemme reassure you that you did not fuck it up. Not even remotely." Kissing her again, he held her hand the whole way back to her place. It was not until his way back to the T, back to Harvard, that Aditya thought maybe Karthik was right, maybe he was a pussy.

Karthik would've scored with her.

June 7, 2010

Indian guilt was an art form as impossible to explain as surrealism. It'd been difficult to for Aditya to admit to his parents why he couldn't come home for the summer, that Professor Sonorous was on the verge of turning in a final draft for his book and insisted that his best assistant stay to help him finish. Staying away from home on his birthday, though, was a bridge too far for Deepika Shetty.

"Take the bus," she demanded. "If you get on the 7:35, you'll be here before midnight."

Aditya gritted his teeth as he boarded the T, headed for Mahira's apartment. "I'll be there next weekend, Mom.

I already told you I can't get off tonight."

When he heard himself, he bit his bottom lip to keep from chuckling. After three months, and with it being his birthday, he certainly hoped he would be getting off tonight.

"Don't spend your birthday alone, at least," Deepika said. "Kiara Aunty said her stepdaughter is in Boston. Did you make friends?"

Me and my big mouth. The two women had reconnected and their friendship was stronger than ever, but Mahira didn't want Kiara knowing about them, so he'd lied to his mom for the first time in his life. "I told you, Mom, she seemed standoffish when we met."

"Puli," she hissed, "talk some sense into your son." Aditya heard her try to hand him the phone.

"Leave him be, Deepika," his dad said. "If the big shot thinks he's too good for brown girls, what are we to do?"

Aditya sighed. "I like brown girls just fine."

"Then what is it?" Deepika asked. "Are you gay?"

"What?! No!" Aditya dropped his phone on the train, picking it up while avoiding the stares of the other passengers.

"Don't get so offended," Deepika said. "I thought your generation didn't mind those things."

"We don't mind," he said. "That's just not the reason."

"I bought an ice cream cake this morning," she said, changing the subject.

"Oh?"

"For your birthday. I thought you'd take the 7:35."

"Mom..."

"I know, I know. I'll just feed it to the neighbor's dog now."

Aditya threw his head back in laughter. His mom would rather light herself on fire than give food to an animal.

"Okay, Mr. Comedian," she chided, "you come next week and see if this cake is still here."

As the T stopped and let him off, he wished Deepika goodnight. "I'll see you soon, Mom. Tell Dad I said bye."

Mahira made him butter chicken for dinner. The naan was from the local Patel Brothers and dessert was a lemon-raspberry cake. He'd told her weeks ago how he didn't care for Indian sweets.

"Is it sweet enough?" she asked.

"I don't know," Aditya said after finishing a slice, "lemme check." Kissing her, his hands on her waist, he brought them from the kitchen to a gray futon that made up her living room. She leaned back and let him move his lips across her neck, her sides, her chest.

"You're ready?" he asked.

Nodding, she helped him slide her jeans off. Aditya surveyed her black thong and felt a tightness in his pants. She pulled him back up until their lips were intertwined and their hands were brushing across each other's backs as if they were harps being played. She giggled as he struggled to unhook her bra.

"Let me help," she said. Throwing it and her blouse to the floor, she leaned back again and allowed him to see her fully for the first time. He was on her like a tiger, kissing her neck and massaging her breasts as she cooed in his ear.

"Just like that," she sighed.

He'd watched porn before, had heard from Karthik what women expected. Dropping between her legs, he slid her panties off and began licking.

"What..."

Any protests were cast aside as easily as her top. She thrashed on the couch, bucking her hips against his face and grabbing at his hair until an earth-splitting moan escaped her lips and he thought he'd hurt her.

"What's wrong?" Licking his lips, he found the taste sour yet intoxicating.

"Nothing," she gasped. She shook so hard she shoved him off her. He fell to the floor, yet he couldn't remember ever seeing someone look so content.

"Your turn," she said. Taking him by the hand, she led him to her bedroom. "Did you bring a condom?"

Fuck. The one thing he'd had to remember. His sheepish look answered for him.

"It's okay," she said. Pushing him to the bed, she undid his slacks. "Just lie back."

He thought women must watch porn, too, for he had no other explanation for how a fellow virgin would be this skilled. He considered closing his eyes, but instead decided to watch as her head bobbed up and down.

"I'm close," he grunted. The men in the videos he'd watched always warned their partners. It seemed like common courtesy. Instead of stopping, though, she dug her nails into his ass and pulled him deeper inside her mouth. Unable to control himself, he released and watched in amazement as she swallowed everything, licking her lips.

"I've been waiting three months to do that." Tucking herself under the covers, she pulled him next to her so that their naked bodies were one.

"I've been waiting twenty-four years to do that," Aditya said.

"You came out of the womb horny, didn't you?" Mahira joked.

As they cuddled in post-coital bliss, Mahira reached for her phone.

"Was I that bad?"

Mahira snorted in laughter. Aditya thought he'd never find that attractive in a girl, but in fact he found it sexy, evidence she wasn't just humoring him. "You were the farthest opposite of bad," she said. "I just haven't checked my emails all day."

"Anything good?" He wrapped his arms around her, looking over her to see the screen. She'd opened a newsletter from someone called Rebecca Steinbeck.

"I follow this blog," Mahira explained. "It's this teenager spouting off her thoughts on WP decriminalization. Kinda cool that some white chick believes in expanding treatment while restricting access."

"I thought you didn't want anything to do with it."

"I don't," Mahira said, "but I also don't want to clean my dishes and do my laundry every week. Sometimes you don't give a shit about something, but you still need to care about it because it's literally an everyday task."

"This isn't my first time over," Aditya joked. "Doing dishes is not an everyday task for you."

"Shut up," she said, kicking him beneath the covers.

"Watch it," he said, "there's sensitive materials down there."

Mahira smiled. "Go get some condoms. We'll do it tomorrow morning."

Grabbing his boxers at the side of the bed, Aditya slid into them and turned to face her. She giggled at the sight of his penis drooping out of its flap. "Guy parts are so strange."

Aditya squeezed his pelvic muscles, making his member twitch.

She snorted again. "That was cool!"

"Don't move," he said. "I'll be right back to show you some other fun stuff."

Kissing his manhood goodbye, she smacked his ass as he threw the rest of his clothes on and raced out the door to get what he needed.

December 13, 2010

Mahira Sidhu's body was as beautiful and volatile as WP. Aditya got a high every time she put his hands on her neck and told him to treat her like a slut, but after they were both sated, the fighting began anew. She wanted him to continue keeping them a secret from his mom. She wanted him to attend anti-legalization rallies with her. He was actually glad the end of the semester meant they wouldn't see each other until January. His last final was this afternoon, and after tonight's goodbye, he'd be on the first bus back to Hoboken tomorrow morning. Standing on Mahira's stoop, he started to ring the buzzer and found she'd opened the door before he could.

"I saw you from my window," she said.

Following her up to her apartment, Aditya caught the outline of a red thong through her tight jeans. He inhaled scents of turmeric and garam masala as soon as they stepped into her place.

Pushing him past the kitchen and onto her bed, she slid out of her bottoms and sat on his face. "I went ahead and cooked, but maybe we should have dessert first."

They took a nap after, Aditya's arms wrapped around Mahira's frame. He didn't stir until he heard his phone vibrating from her kitchen/dining room/living room. Sliding his boxers on, he went to the kitchen and saw his mom had texted him.

Talked to Kiara Aunty last night and we both agree how nice it would be to set you up with Mahira.

He groaned. It'd been like this for months. He was glad his mom had someone in the country to talk to about the old days, but the constant lying was giving him an ulcer. Hearing the toilet flush, he turned to find Mahira behind him. She'd thrown on a pink robe and some insulated slippers he'd bought her for her birthday. Throwing her arms around his neck, kissing it, she read the text.

"Your mom still wants to set you up?"

Giving her a better look at his phone, Aditya scrolled past numerous texts over the last few months to show her it was a common topic of conversation.

Talked to Kiara Aunty today. Doesn't she have family in Boston?

Kiara Aunty wished me happy birthday today. Wasn't she with someone when you saw her?

Planning to visit Kiara Aunty in Ohio sometime. Do you think I'll run into anyone else?

The last two texts were from today: *Make sure you write Kiara Aunty's nice daughter before leaving.* It was followed by the one he'd just received.

"Why's your mom so obsessed with me! Like she's a crazy person!" Mahira's cheeks were flushed, not from sex but from rage. She did this often, became a sex-crazed goddess, and when all that passion was expelled, it transformed to anger. Her temper was as short as her lust was grand, and it confused the fuck out of his horny self.

"Calm down," Aditya warned. He didn't like getting angry, but no one spoke about his mother like that. The only way to quell Mahira's anger was to give in to his own, he knew. She only responded to threats and shouting when she got like this.

"I won't!" she said. Moving to the kitchen, she picked up a plate of the chicken curry she'd made for Aditya's goodbye dinner and threw it at him. Rice and chicken mixed with turmeric stained the furniture as he ducked to avoid the mess.

"Are you out of your fucking mind?!"

"This is what you wanted all along, isn't it?" she screamed.

"What are you talking about?"

"You get to play the role of the good Hindu son and paint me as the crazy woman."

Aditya looked at streaks of yellow food coloring the walls of the one-bedroom apartment. "You're doing a good job with the painting on your own."

She strode toward him and he caught her by the wrists, pushing her onto her futon. "Where is this coming from?"

Mahira started crying. "I don't need another fake mom!"

"...what?" He sat next to her, stroking her hair as she sobbed into a cushion.

"You think I'd ever go out drinking with my real mom? Kiara is fun, but I'm not her daughter!"

Oh. He'd been careless. Kiara wouldn't dare call herself Mahira's mom, but Deepika wasn't concerned with showing such tact.

"And if she knew about us, if we got married, she'd call herself my mom, too."

Marriage? The thought had never occurred to him, though he supposed he shouldn't mention that right now. "I'm sorry..."

When he hugged her, she leaned in for a kiss and Aditya tasted salt on her lips.

"I'm a little overly sensitive today," she said.

Aditya looked at the broken plate on the ground. "Maybe a little...what's up?"

Sniffling, she got up and moved to her bedroom, returning with a newspaper article from the *New York Times.* "Go on," she said, "read it."

She cleaned up the mess she'd made as he read the

piece. By the time he was done, a proper meal had been set for both of them at the table.

"Who's Dr. Jocelyne Clark?" He got up to sit and eat.

"My dad was her mentor at OSU."

"Oh..."

"Yeah...I guess I've just been thinking about family a bit more than usual..."

"This is really good." Aditya smiled, taking a bite of the meal. "Thanks for making dinner."

Mahira sniffled again, wiping snot on her robe. "Thanks."

"She doesn't seem much older than Kiara, this Dr. Clark."

"Yeah," Mahira said. "I guess I always thought if he was gonna shack up with a younger woman, why couldn't it've been her?"

He'd never appreciated how much resentment she had for her stepmom. They had similar body types, same religion. Maybe she'd thought her dad had been trying to replace her mom instead of realizing that was impossible and going for something completely different. Maybe that was the real reason she'd wanted him to marry this Black woman, this Dr. Clark.

"I can't have three Indian moms," she said. "Not when the only one that matters is dead."

"I get it," Aditya said. "So, what about this Dr. Clark? She's doing some WP research in NYC at a place called FAIR?"

FAIR stood for the Foundation for Actions against Injustice and Racism. The article cited her research and wasn't shy about using her quotes to advocate against WP legalization. Dr. Clark believed the cause of furthering equity wasn't worth the risk when there were still so many scientific unknowns about how a nonwhite body reacted to the drug.

"I thought about writing to her..."

"Why don't you?"

Mahira pushed her food around her plate with a fork before answering. "What if she's forgotten about me? She hasn't seen me in a decade..."

Mahira might be damaged beyond repair. "How could anyone forget you?" It seemed like the right thing to say.

"Did you read to the end of the piece?" she asked, ignoring his words. "The anti-legalization rallies in NYC and Boston and DC this weekend? I thought we could go together."

Aditya sighed. "You know I'm headed home tomorrow..."

"It's just a few hours," she said. "I could even get to NYC if that's easier for you."

"And what would I tell my mom?"

Mahira had deflated like a balloon, sinking further into her seat, but at the mention of Deepika, she jumped from her bar stool. "It's always gonna be her over me, huh?"

"What are you talking about? You're the one who doesn't want me to tell her about you!"

"Real easy to make me out to be the crazy one, right?" She was screaming again, and for a moment Aditya considered hitting her. The moment passed, but not before she'd seen him get up and ball his hands into fists. "You think hitting me is gonna make you a man? No wonder you want some WP."

This fight isn't just about family. "Have you been reading my journal?" He'd scribbled some notes here and there about WP laws changing over the years. Obama's election in 2008 had seen a new bill pass that allowed startups to offer funders the drug in lieu of equity, regardless of whether or not those funders were white. With an MBA from Harvard, he'd join a hedge fund and get legal access to the drug in no time. "I deserve WP, just like everyone else in America."

"Kiara was so invested in showing me she could be a cool stepmom," Mahira said, digging her nails into the sides of her robe. "We'd get tipsy at home, and once she told me what really happened to Ajeet."

This was what you got for starting a date with sex instead of ending it, Aditya decided. With all the sexual tension released, nonsense was spilling out of her instead of more enjoyable things.

"She read the third-party reports of Ajeet's final moments. The autopsy report. He was fast, then slow. Strong, then weak. Meanwhile, that boy woke up and resumed living his life."

Bob Jr.'s awake? He hadn't known that. "Are you worried I won't be safe? It won't be like that for me. Science has advanced in leaps and bounds since that night."

"If we tell your parents about me, that means we're a real thing. And I can't afford to lose anything else that's real..."

Aditya's nostrils flared as he moved to put his empty plate in the sink. "We're not real? We've been fucking nonstop for six months!"

"There's more to a relationship than sex," she whispered. "Haven't you ever had a one-night stand?"

He backed away as if he'd been slapped. "You said I was your first..."

"That's just what guys like to hear, right?"

Grabbing the counter, his eyes struggled to focus. "How many?"

"...what?"

"How many before me?"

She gulped, and Aditya relished smelling her fear. "People say great sex is better than being on WP. I don't care for the drug, but I always wanted to see if it was true…"

"While we were together?"

"You blew me off a few times…"

"You blew me more than a few times!" He threw his plate against her fridge, smashing it. "Goodbye, Mahira."

Throwing the door open, he got his coat and walked out, ignoring the frightened faces of her neighbors as he moved like an enraged tiger toward the stairs.

May 8, 2011

Aditya graduated from Harvard Business School on Mother's Day. He'd been successful in limiting his thoughts of Mahira to the final minutes before bed each night, but in an ironic twist, his commencement speaker had been none other than Dr. Jocelyne Clark of FAIR. She'd spoken about the importance of decriminalizing WP for minorities but never legalizing it, drawing ample praise from the old white men who bankrolled the university. He hadn't heard much of the speech. In keeping with tradition, his parents had brought another letter from Karthik and he'd preferred to spend his time reading that, instead.

Aditya,

You're an official brainiac now, huh? I've got another four years here by contract, so that should give you plenty of time to come up with a plan for bringing me home. You know you have to wipe your

ass with water here? I guess toilet paper
is a first-world luxury.

Aditya laughed at the image of his best
friend using a bidet.

Anyways, I heard you finally popped your
cherry? Good to hear you're finally getting
some pussy. Send a pic with your
response. I could use some more material
for my spank bank.

He'd told Karthik about Mahira, but not
that she was Kiara's daughter. There
wasn't a reason for keeping it secret, so he
made a note to send him pics of both her
and Kiara soon, along with the news that
they'd broken up.

I'll call you when I can to congratulate you
in person. Mom sent me a local number I
can use to avoid long-distance charges.

Gangsta for life,
Karthik

The speech was over by the time he finished the
letter, and when his name was called, his mom screamed
so loud he knew exactly where she was in the sea of the
crowd. He wasn't the only brown person in the
graduating class—far from it, in fact. But he was the only
brown person who'd grown up poor in America. It
wouldn't last for long, though. A few chance encounters
with an undergrad girl in one of his classes, Claire
something, had resulted in an invitation to attend a

Fourth of July party in the Hamptons at the summer home of a fellow graduate, Ben Blackstone. The man was CEO of The Blackstone Fund, a hedge fund that'd put Aditya at the center of NYC's power structures. Walking across the stage, posing for a picture with the dean, Aditya smiled at knowing his future was secure.

And soon, I'll get Karthik back and secure his future, too.

Aditya's parents hadn't been able to visit campus since dropping him off. He posed patiently as his mom snapped pictures of him at the Charles River, at the Widener Library, at the art museum and a museum of archeology. Walking around the Peabody Museum of Ethnology (a word his dad described as "as made up as Western innovation"), Aditya startled at the sound of his father's voice.

"So, Harvard steals all these fancy paintings from ancient cultures and then charges you to admire them? What a racket."

Aditya would never admit it, but he agreed. He'd considered telling his mom they couldn't get in when he'd learned three tickets would run him thirty-five dollars.

But Mom deserves to see nice things. He'd told them it was free. His dad would kill him if he ever learned the truth.

"Did you ever end up meeting Mahira Sidhu?" His mom asked the question innocently enough, though Aditya noted they were standing in an exhibit displaying paintings of multi-generational families.

"It just never worked out, Mom," he said. *True enough.*

"That's too bad," she said.

"Leave him be," Puli said. "The best opportunities in life are always found around family. Now that he's returning home, I'm sure you'll get grandchildren soon enough. Regardless, he has more important things to do right now. Harvard didn't give him a degree in raising a family."

Not for the first time, Aditya wondered what his dad would've been capable of if only he'd had access to WP.

Chapter Eight

July 2, 2011

The oldest and largest community within the Hamptons was Southampton. Art museums and vineyards attracted some tourists, but this was the only part of the Hamptons with a hospital, which had established this area of Long Island as the dominant location for the privileged to play in. On this particular Fourth of July weekend, Aditya had been invited to none other than Ben Blackstone's palatial nine-bedroom summer home. Saturdays in July meant guys playing beach volleyball in the backyard while girls in the hot tub nearby gossiped about them. It was men shooting pool and sipping scotch in the basement. Women snorting coke and other drugs in one of the spare bedrooms upstairs on the fourth floor.

"Aditya!" Claire Steinbeck shouted at him as he entered the house. "Did you find the place okay?"

Though she was only twenty, Claire carried herself like a titan of industry, which, he supposed, was fitting for her family's legacy. A Google search had informed Aditya that her great-grandfather had written *The Grapes of Wrath* and *Of Mice and Men.* That history and sense of presence, combined with her blonde hair and alabaster skin, made her more bangable than Bella Ferrari. She walked down a winding staircase to greet him, and he wished he hadn't just stuffed a canapé a waiter had offered him into his mouth.

"Yeah," he said, trying to chew quickly. "I just got an Uber."

He'd bought a Hawaiian button-down from Tommy Bahama for the occasion. Looking around, he saw ladies in summer dresses and bikinis, men in open-collared shirts and swim trunks. And he felt something else, a dull headache growing in his head like a tumor.

He grabbed the side of his head. The shrill noise inside got louder, until it clouded his thoughts and he had to sink into a chair in the foyer. Spitting out his canapé on the floor, he realized the cause of his pain. Whether they were wearing a bikini or a dress shirt, almost every person here had WP embedded in their clothes or jewelry. It glittered from their hands and legs and necks, and when he tried to gulp his fear down, he thought his throat was closing.

"Are you okay?" Only a blind person couldn't see the sweat pouring down his face, Aditya knew, and so Claire had to understand his condition. To his chagrin, she called their host over. "Ben, can we get the doctor? This was the guy I was telling you about."

Aditya saw a man around five-foot nine striding toward him.

Nice shoes. The last thing he remembered before passing out was vomiting on the man's Allen Edmonds.

"Can you hear us?"

Aditya opened his eyes. He was sprawled out on a

bed, slacks on but shirt and shoes off. Claire was there, as was the man who must be Ben Blackstone. Aditya groaned at seeing the man's movie-star face. He looked like Zac Efron.

"Doc, I think he's up." Ben sat on the bed and clutched Aditya's hand. "Don't sweat it, kid. Happens at least a few times a year at these things."

Aditya's eyes grew to the size of saucers at seeing the man's WP-encrusted cufflinks. The drug was so close, and yet he felt nothing more than a dull buzz around his ears. Ben smiled and motioned for his doctor to speak. To Aditya's surprise, the elderly man was Indian.

"You gave me quite a scare, Mr. Shetty." As soon as he took Aditya's hand, Aditya was reminded of his father. Both men had those kind eyes, that immediate acceptance of the cards fate had dealt them. "You see this?" Lifting Aditya's right hand, the doctor pointed to a thin metal band around his wrist. The initials "TBF" were carved into it. "It's called a chameleon band."

"Proprietary tech from TBF," Ben said. "If you come to work for The Blackstone Fund, you'll be required to wear it at all times."

Pushing himself up with his arms, his back pressed against the headboard, Aditya assessed his surroundings. There were paintings worth more than a year's rent on the wall, and windows that showed him the party outside hadn't stopped on his account. "What is it?"

"Dr. Kapadia developed it," Ben said, smiling at the man. "It dulls WP sensitivity. You can move your hands on the band to adjust your tolerance up or down so you can feel comfortable no matter how much WP is present. It's why TBF is the best. We can hire nonwhite workers while others can't, at least not without giving up their WP, which is a death sentence in this industry."

Moving his arm around, Aditya noticed the object's

weightlessness. "This is legal?"

Ben shrugged. "Let's just say it's a gray area. Anyone asks, you tell them it's a company bracelet."

"I don't understand..."

"I've learned that nine times out of ten, genius is simplicity," Ben said. "I'm gonna be frank with you because Claire trusts you and her family are old friends. Guys like you and Dr. Kapadia, you work harder than your average white dude. Because you've got to. When you've got something to prove, you make sure you can rise to the occasion—whatever it takes. And why shouldn't I benefit from that work ethic?"

He laughed and Aditya forced a smile.

"There it is," Ben said, pointing right at him. "Drink some water, do some stretching, and then come downstairs. We got things to discuss, Aditya Shitty."

Aditya wasn't sure if he was mispronouncing his name or just racist. Watching the man walk downstairs, slapping a girl's ass as she waited to use a bathroom, he wasn't sure if he wanted to become Ben or kill him.

Dr. Kapadia kept Aditya upstairs for another half hour. In that time, Claire explained how her and Ben's families had vacationed here together growing up, how her dad had provided Ben with a sizable loan early in his career. That was how she'd obtained such a plum internship as a mere rising college junior. Even for Harvard, it was impressive.

"And you two never..."

Claire laughed. "God, no. Benny sticks that thing in any hole he can find. I've got a little more self-respect."

"Benny?"

"He prefers it." Shooing the doctor away, she got Aditya out of bed and forced him to chug some water. "Come on. Let's go back down. Don't make me regret bringing you."

The party moved on from hors d'oeuvres to plates of spaghetti and veal parmesan. Guys dug into them outside between rounds of volleyball while women nipped at salads that cost more than a payment on Aditya's parents' Subaru Justy.

"Hey, Benny!" one guy shouted. "You motherfucker, you ever gonna become a real New Yorker, or you gonna keep cheering for that shitty-ass team in Boston?"

"Big risk, mouthing off to the boss in his own beach house, you little bitch!" Ben shouted back. "I don't know if you got the balls for something like that. Your girl's been telling Vanessa stories." Smacking a girl's ass (Vanessa?), he laughed at seeing the guy's head droop. "You know I'm just joshing you. Go find your girl and she and Vanessa can measure the size of our balls."

Ben laughed and everyone else laughed and then Aditya started laughing, too, despite thinking nothing could be less funny.

The party moved to the basement after lunch and another round of drinks. Some of the girls put on a romantic comedy in the movie theater. Claire and a couple of her friends were watching with keen interest when Ben invited Aditya to play a round of pool.

"TBF hazing ritual," he said, chalking a cue stick and handing it to Aditya. "Play well, and the job's yours."

Aditya wished he'd spent more time playing at Harvard, but he knew the basics well enough.

"You'll be playing Oliver," Ben said, pointing to a burly guy with a jawline that could cut glass. Aditya noticed the WP-encrusted ring on Oliver's finger.

"Is that fair?"

Ben laughed. "Is life? Stop whining and adapt."

Oliver swung his stick around like a pair of nunchucks before leaning it against his veiny neck. The guy's fingers looked like Polish sausages.

I don't have to knock him out, just beat him at pool.

"I'll give you the break," Oliver said.

Aditya bent over the table, trying and failing to ignore the crowd. He scratched, sending the white ball rolling onto the floor to land at some woman's feet. She picked it up and handed it to Oliver.

"Blow on it for luck, baby," he said. She giggled before doing just that. Aditya groaned again and watched Oliver sink four balls in a row, the humiliation more painful than when he'd thrown up on Ben's shoes. He got lucky with his next shot, sinking one, but then Oliver sank another two so he had only one left before the 8-ball.

"Just focus, Harvard," Claire said, having wandered down after the movie. He wondered if she'd invited him here to humiliate him or if she actually thought he'd be an asset to TBF.

Pool is math. The fact that Oliver could murder him with two good punches wasn't why he was winning. In fact, the man's size should be working against him. Closing his eyes, Aditya called upon his education.

Come on, man. Prove the physics degree was just as important as the finance double-major.

Opening his eyes, he took a slow walk around the table.

"Just hit it already," one of the guys whined.

"Spoken like a true bro," a woman said. "Overly eager to get it in the hole."

Aditya smiled at the Black woman. "You and I understand we need to warm up, first." Tapping the white ball, he sank two balls with one hit. He continued examining the board, lining up his shots, until only the 8-ball remained.

"Your move," Aditya said.

"Yeah, whatever," Oliver said. Calling the corner pocket, he hit the ball as hard as he could and sent it bouncing backwards into a different hole. Aditya won by default.

"Looks like we've got a new team member!" Ben's declaration led to Claire bringing out a cake with Aditya's face on it. "You better watch yourself," Ben told Oliver. "I might have myself a new number two! He's even brown!"

They planned on me winning? No white person had ever shown that level of confidence and trust in him. "You got my profile pic from Facebook?" Aditya laughed at the absurdity of the day. The Hamptons. Vomiting. Beating a guy with WP at pool.

"Now, let's really get this party started!" Ben cut into the cake, handing out pieces before grabbing some himself at the end with his bare hands. "Bro, I better not see you using a fucking plate." Aditya nodded, reaching for a slice.

Dad would approve. Laughing to himself, he admitted Puli did always wish he ate like a real Brahmin more often, without silverware. Ben handed him a whole fifth of bourbon before ushering the party into a different room within the basement where some women were not singing karaoke so much as screaming it.

"Move over," Ben said, "I got something to play."

Shutting down "Party Rock Anthem," Ben waited for his song to load. "You all better rage to this to welcome my new boy!"

Memories of Aditya's grade-school days sent him back in time along with the music. Will Smith's "Gettin' Jiggy Wit It" howled from the speakers as men and women gathered around him and Ben. Lyrics were being projected on a wall, but as they started singing Aditya realized Ben had written his own chorus:

Gettin' shitty wit it
Na-na, na, na, na-na-na
Na-na, na, na, na, na
Gettin' shitty wit it
Na-na, na, na, na-na-na
Na-na, na, na, na, na

As sweaty bodies clashed and drinks spilled onto the sticky floor, Aditya caught Claire winking at him and smiled. If this was what it took to belong, to succeed, he'd be the best of them all. Adjusting his chameleon band to tolerate more WP, he threw his hands up in the air and started belting out the new chorus, too.

December 18, 2013

You could see the Statue of Liberty from the top of the 55th floor at One Bryant Park, where The Blackstone Fund's offices were located. Aditya'd worked there for two and a half years, but the view still filled him with pride. TBF only had five people on payroll, but on the bottom floor, all the businesses were having a Christmas party. He'd seen some poor security guards lugging in a larger-than-life Douglas fir. He got angry just thinking about how long it would take them to clean up the tree's sheddings after their party.

And for what? For some big shots to pretend they're worldly? Ben, Oliver, and the other guys had invited him to go camping twice now. He'd said no both times and thought they probably understood he had no interest in shitting in a hole and foraging for food. His father would disown him if he knew a Harvard graduate was debasing himself with such things.

"Going down?" Claire asked as she held the elevator open for him.

"I don't know," he said. "Are any of your girlfriends gonna be at this party?"

They were the last two in the office. She'd finished her undergrad work in May and was now a winter intern for them until she started up again at Harvard in January to complete her MBA. He wondered if she loved the internship or working with her husband more.

She laughed as he entered the elevator beside her, a shrill noise that gave him a headache. Looking at the pendant around her neck, the diamonds encrusted with WP, he realized the real source of his pain. He'd gotten used to being around the four other male employees and their WP, but adding a woman to the mix changed things. He touched his chameleon band, adjusting the sensitivity.

"You couldn't handle a night with my girls," she said, noticing his actions. "They keep their WP on in bed." She winked, and he was transported back to that dance party in the Hamptons. "Anyways," she said as the elevator door opened, "you don't like brown girls?"

His nostrils flared as he remembered Mahira. "No." Stepping ahead of her, he made a beeline for the bar.

The next hour saw Ben jumping back and forth between three women Aditya recognized from the 23rd, 34th, and 42nd floors. Seeing them swing in and out of bathrooms, he wondered what would happen if they ever met each other.

"He isn't fucking in the bathrooms," Oliver said, clinking his glass of scotch against Aditya's own. "He's doing lines of coke with them."

"Coke and WP?" Aditya whistled. "Isn't that a lethal

combination?”

“Who knows? It’s not like there’s a lot of research about WP.”

“Why aren’t you in the bathroom with them?”

Oliver smiled as Claire walked toward them. “Gotta stay sharp for my wife.” The two pawed at each other. Aditya left, pretending to vomit in hands.

I should call it a night. Walking to the exit, re-adjusting the sensitivity on his chameleon band so he could sleep later, he smelled honey and turned to see where it was coming from.

“Bella Ferrari?”

She had red highlights in that wavy chestnut hair of hers, but there was no mistaking that crooked nose and freckles. He couldn’t help but notice her rack before meeting those eyes. They were green, like her backless dress. The thigh-high slit in the skirt revealed she was still skinny.

“Aditya Shetty.” Her Italian accent was as thick as ever, and yet his last name was pronounced with all the care she’d always shown toward people. Her voice held no surprise, and the only way he knew she hadn’t expected him was the way she bit her bottom lip, something she’d always done in school when faced with an unexpected predicament that required more thought.

“What are you doing here?” His voice hitched up an octave as she moved toward him. Smelling her honeyed perfume, he pretended to drop his phone on the ground to give himself an excuse to readjust his pants.

“I’m an intern for the law firm on the 40th floor.”

He smiled as he placed his phone back into his pocket, pleased she was following her dream. “You finished law school, then?”

“Just my first term, at NYU. This’ll get me experience

and help me pay the bills."

"You know what they say," Aditya said. "As long as you're working on a floor higher than your age, you're guaranteed success."

She laughed, a sound as soothing as a warm bath. "You were always so funny." Brushing her hands against his, she took him by the arm and insisted they dance along to the cover of "Winter Wonderland" Michael Bublé just released.

Is this really happening? Their lips were close enough to touch, and for the first time in his life he threw caution to the wind and leaned in to meet them. He tasted tequila, but also honey, the sour and the sweet mixing together to create something new and dynamic and intoxicating.

When he pulled back, she gave a contented sigh and opened her eyes. "I've wanted you to do that for a long time," she said.

At first, he thought he'd misheard her, that too many years had passed since he'd listened to her thick accent daily and gotten used to it. He asked her to repeat herself, and when she did, he had to laugh. "You were the hottest girl in school."

"No," she whispered, her hands wrapped around his neck.

"Yes," he said. "You had your choice of any guy. How could I compare?"

"You were so sweet, especially to your mother. When you care about family like that, it's a real panty-dropper."

He snorted in surprise, and while he'd be mortified with anyone else, she just smiled and laughed, and he knew he could be himself around her without fear of judgment. It was like she was Indian herself. But she wasn't, and he knew that intellectually, if not emotionally. "Where's your WP?"

She frowned. "You know I never wore that stuff

much."

Pulling her to the side, the song over, he motioned for her to open the clutch purse she'd tucked away.

"Aditya, why don't you just accept nice moments?"

"Because there's always a 'but,' and if I know what it is, at least I can prepare."

She opened the clutch to reveal a necklace with sapphires and emeralds encrusted with flakes of WP. Not a lot, but enough to let everyone know she was special. "My *mamma* gave it to me when I got into NYU. I make sure I have it around just in case, but I don't like wearing it much."

How nice to be able to say no to that kind of power... "Why not?"

"It's not right," she said. "My *nonna* WP was still illegal for her growing up. But the government says it's okay now for Italians but not brown people. Not Black people, who've lived here much longer than my grandmother? It makes no sense. And we still know so little about the science of WP. For all we know, it could be killing us all."

Power is only fatal to those who don't have it. To imagine it could hurt those who wielded it—that was a line of thinking that would dismantle capitalism and all this country stood for.

"Put it on," he said. When she protested, he explained what his chameleon band was. Reluctantly, she donned her necklace. Kissing her again, his senses flared, and when he pulled his lips away, he could still taste her. It was more solid than a memory could ever be. "That's wild."

She leaned in for another kiss, and this time he didn't pull away until he spotted Oliver giving him a thumbs-up from the corner of his eye. Again, when their lips separated, it was as if she was still with him. He looked at his chameleon band and saw it was at the same level as when Claire's presence had given him such pain. "Why?"

"So much unknown," Bella said. "I didn't grow up wearing it. My family doesn't have generations of history wearing it. So much we don't know. Until the science is settled, why trust this magic?"

Because everyone else does. Instead of saying that, he smiled and watched her slip the necklace back into her clutch. "Can I walk you home?"

"No," she said. "I'm a good Italian lady and we don't do that on a first date."

"Date?"

She smiled, and he admired just how white her teeth were. "I just told you I'm a good Italian lady. We don't kiss unless it's on a nice date."

"So, it was a nice date?"

"Think about where you're gonna take me next time," she said. "Christmas only comes once a year."

Aditya laughed. "There's always New Year's."

"That bar downtown is having a thing, The Good Citizen. Meet me there around eight?"

"I'll pick you up," Aditya said. "A proper lady needs an escort."

She smiled. "In my experience, it's men who need escorts." Taking his phone, she put her number in and handed it back. "None of this 'wait three days' nonsense," she said. "You text me tonight when you get home."

"Yes, ma'am," he said.

As she walked away, he followed her out into the cold and called out as she hailed a taxi. "Hey! You've been drinking. You sure it isn't the liquor talking?"

"No," she said. Her eyes twinkled in the moonlight. "It's you."

December 31, 2013

Aditya paced outside Bella's apartment building in SoHo at 7:45, wrapping up a conversation with his mom, careful not to slip on the snow. "I'll be there next year."

"Is the reason you're not with your mother because you're with a girl?"

"It's not always a girl, Mom," he said. "I'm seeing some colleagues."

True enough. Claire would be there.

"Hmph," Deepika said. "It would be okay if it was a girl. You're pushing thirty, Aditya. You're no spring chicken, and I'd like a grandchild before I die."

"In that case, I got plenty of time, since you're gonna live forever." Continuing to pace, he felt a snowball splat onto his head. Looking up, he saw Bella leaning outside her third-floor window, wrapped in a decoratively striped Christmas sweater. "Mom, I gotta go. Happy New Year. I'll call you both tomorrow. I love you."

After hanging up, he opened his mouth to ask Bella if she was insane, but another snowball caught him across the lips. Despite the fact his own sweater was wet now, he couldn't stay mad at her. She giggled before ducking back inside and texting him that she'd be down in minutes.

"Were you born crazy?" he asked as she whistled for a cab.

"Italian girls got big lungs to shout, big appetites to enjoy, big hearts to love, and big balls to prove we won't take any shit." She ruffled his hair as they got in the car, then directed the driver to take them to The Good Citizen.

"Okay, cowgirl," he said.

"Now you got the right idea," she said. "Why you think my last name is Ferrari? No one's gonna give you a better ride."

He blushed. "This is what a good Italian lady does?"

She leaned in, breathing on his neck before whispering into his ear. "This is what a good Italian lady does best."

Adjusting his pants, he suggested they go ahead and skip the party to celebrate inside.

"So funny, as always," she said. "But you gotta work for it. Come on, show me a good time."

Aditya saw Claire wave him over as soon as he entered the bar.

"That's my colleague, Claire," he said. "You go ahead. I'll get us three beers."

"Tequila for me," Bella said. "But I need to pee first."

As she left, Aditya thought to himself that no woman had ever told him she needed to use the bathroom in such explicit terms. He wondered if it was a sign of closeness, a positive indication for the night. Heading to the bar, he struggled to get the bartender's attention until Claire came up and saved him.

"Hey," she said, "my friend's waiting."

Aditya ordered three shots of tequila and two beers before thanking her.

"No problem," she said. "I hate seeing you struggle unless it's something I've done."

He laughed. "Where's Oliver?"

"He was here earlier, but he had to rush off. Perks of a long-distance marriage. Even when we're in the same city, sometimes it feels better to be apart than together."

Her smile made Aditya feel as if he was still outside in the snow. "Must be tough," he said.

"He bought me a vibrator for Christmas. It has one of

those mobile apps so he can tease me from afar."

Aditya wasn't sure if he should laugh or not, so he just stayed quiet.

"What's she charging you?"

"...what?"

"The girl you came in with."

Aditya's arm hair stood up. When the bartender returned with their drinks, he downed a shot and ordered another one to replace it. "How do you know her?"

"You're kidding, right?" Claire bit her bottom lip as she stared at him. "Dude, she's an escort."

Aditya grabbed her arm, so hard it must have hurt her because she shrieked at him as she pulled herself free. "Touch me again and see what happens, Aditya Shitty!"

"Take it back," he snarled. "What you said is a vicious lie."

"No," she said, "It isn't. This long-distance marriage thing? It needs rules to work. Oliver and I are allowed to fuck around when we're apart, as long as we don't keep seeing the same person. And back in September, he was so thirsty I literally called a girl up myself. Looked just like her."

Stunned into silence, Aditya downed the other two shots.

The rest of the night was a blur. Aditya barely listened as Bella explained to Claire how she'd known him since grade school, how they'd both gone to Hoboken High, "Home of the Fighting Yellowjackets." When the ball dropped at midnight, he grabbed Bella's hand and pulled her out the door, ignoring Claire's call that "it was so nice meeting you. You're such a cute couple!"

No one spoke on the cab ride home. Bella mistook his silence for eagerness, squeezing his hand as she kissed his neck. Despite his best efforts, there was a tightening in his groin as well as his heart. When the car stopped outside her place, she whispered in his ear that he should join her upstairs before leaving him to pay the driver.

Mahira. Bella. Are girls even worth it? No guy has ever betrayed me.

Gritting his teeth, he entered the building and took off his chameleon band to store in his pocket. He wanted to be fully alert when he confronted Bella. When he knocked, she answered in a red slip she couldn't have worn outside, thanks to its plunging neckline. She licked her lips in anticipation as he grunted and adjusted his pants in front of her.

"It's been so long…"

"Has it?" He undid the belt of his slacks and folded it in half. He would never hit her, but maybe she'd think that and quiver in fear. He hated that he wanted her to see him that way, but he'd learned fear and anger and hate had its place in sexual relationships.

"What are you talking about?" She stepped back and he relished the uncertainty on her face.

"You probably fucked someone last week, didn't you?"

And just like that, he saw her regain her footing. Her posture straightened as she stepped right up to him, closed the door, and pulled the belt away, throwing it on the couch behind her. "Who told you?"

"You won't even deny it?" He scoffed. "…it was Claire. You fucked her husband, Oliver, in September."

Bella rolled her eyes. "Oh yeah. I remember an Oliver. But a woman made that call…was it her?" She laughed when Aditya didn't answer. He hated that the sound still made his heart and manhood stir.

"I give that marriage another four months, tops. Girls like her think they can handle their guy sleeping around, but they can't."

She'd walked to her kitchen as she spoke, walked right past him as if he was nothing. He punched the wall as she mixed Coffee Negronis in two mugs, as if his staying was a foregone conclusion, as if she knew his rage was as fleeting as the snow outside, guaranteed to melt between the warmth of her legs.

"Are you even an intern at that law firm?" he growled. "Or do you just whore it up wherever you see a fancy party? Trying to sleep your way to the top?"

She picked up the single finished drink and threw it in his face from across the counter separating them. He screamed and fumbled around, trying to find a sink to splash water in his eyes, using his hands to guide him until he made his way into her bedroom and the joined bathroom within. Returning, he found her sipping the second drink.

"I hope you didn't want one, because I'm not making another."

"Are all women fucking insane?!" He stormed toward her, and when they were face-to-face, she slapped him.

"Yes," she said, "I *am* an intern, but you've seen this place. I don't live in a studio by choice, and law school is expensive."

"What about your parents?" Aditya sneered, remembering how they hadn't wanted her to associate with him.

"My parents are immigrants who shied away from WP, so it's not like we have the kind of wealth others have." She sighed at Aditya's confusion. "Didn't you take an econ class in college? The government regularly buys WP from white families to increase their own coffers."

"You'd said we're both immigrants, that we're the same…"

Bella smiled, taking another sip of her drink, holding his hand, and moving them to the couch. He sat down next to her, hating that she could see the outline of his hardness through his slacks. She brushed it with hands soft as silk. "Being an immigrant means making sacrifices to succeed no matter what."

Thinking about that dance party in the Hamptons, about embracing the nickname 'Aditya Shitty,' he knew she was right. With that acceptance, all his anger turned to lust. "I'm sorry," he said.

"You'll make it up to me," she whispered, her fingers unzipping him. "Now, lean back."

Midnight had passed, but when Aditya closed his eyes, he saw fireworks. She swallowed him in her mouth, and when he asked about a condom, she said he didn't need one since she was on the pill.

"I only make clients wear them."

The words infuriated him, and that passionate anger found its way inside her as they rocked her bed and her couch and her walls. Before letting him finish, she had him use his tongue and gripped his head between her legs so hard he thought he'd burst like a watermelon under the pressure. When she was sated, she rode him like a real Ferrari until he exploded, and she collapsed in his arms. The sheets were filled with the scent of lust.

"You can't judge me," she said, hours later as they woke from their post-coital nap.

"Okay," Aditya said. Loving her made more sense than WP, and if he'd been able to change himself to advance his career, he figured he could tolerate this in order to finally be with her.

Do I love her? He'd been burned before, but Bella was different. He'd known her forever. She had WP. Still, he wouldn't say anything. *I bet some of her clients tell her they love her after the first time...* The thought both sickened and excited him, knowing she made all of them wear condoms. Knowing he was having sex with a certified professional.

Do you get certified for things like this?

"I mean it," Bella said, taking him from his thoughts. "You have no right. Your best friend was a murderer."

"Karthik?" Aditya pushed his arms behind him, straightening his back against her bed. "That kid actually woke up, Ben Jr."

"Oh…" She closed her eyes and whispered a Hail Mary. It was only then that he noticed the cross lying atop her dresser on the other side of the room. "How is Karthik?"

"He joined the Indian Army."

Bella leaned in with interest, causing the sheets around her to fall away, exposing her bare chest as she wrapped her arms around his waist. "Does he like it?"

"He likes America better."

"Even after all this time?"

Aditya thought of their phone calls over the last year, of the stories his best friend had told him. The battles Karthik had fought, the people he'd killed. It wouldn't be long before the Indian Army discovered it had a mole in its ranks. Karthik hadn't answered him when he'd asked what would be worse: turning against the real estate mafia or being caught spying in the Army for them. "Especially after all this time."

"It's nice you two keep in touch," Bella said, getting up to go to the bathroom. Though she shut the door, he could still hear her pee. She opened the door after flushing to find he'd kicked the sheets away. Giggling at the proof of his eagerness between his legs, she sat beside him. "You couldn't wait until the morning for round two?"

"You're more addicting than WP."

"Safer, more reliable, and longer-lasting, too." Sitting on his face, she gripped the headboard and bucked her hips as he ran his hands over her naked body.

Chapter Nine

May 2, 2014

Chinatown had absorbed much of the culture around Mulberry Street over the last couple decades, but Aditya thought the historic center point of Little Italy still had the best Italian bakery in the city: Nonna's. He'd told Bella to meet him here after dinner this Friday evening. Already seated outside, he watched as she ran toward him, her purse flailing in the wind behind her. Those freckles got him more excited than her voluptuous chest. That was how he knew this was love and not just lust. The sex was great, but they wouldn't go to bed right after, like he had with Mahira. They'd talk about her work (the law firm, not the other thing), his work (possibly less ethical than the other thing), what books they were reading. She'd tease him about being a momma's boy who called Deepika daily no matter what. He'd joke that she was only Italian from the waist down, that she was a subpar cook at best who'd burned rice on more than one occasion. They'd talk so much he'd be ready for round two by the end of the discussion, something she was always eager for as well. The only problem was the weekends she'd spend doing "the other thing." That was their arrangement: she'd be all his during the week, when she wasn't at the law firm. It'd been tough with her classes on top of work, but the semester at NYU was wrapping up this week so she'd have more time for him. The two basically lived together now. But every third or fourth weekend, she'd book a hotel and get a couple jobs in. It wasn't ideal, but she had slowed down after committing to him.

And she has committed. He knew what they had was special. He stood up to pull her chair out as she sat next to him, the sun illuminating the red highlights in her chestnut hair.

"What's got you in such a good mood?" she teased.

"A night with my lady. What could be better?"

"Dessert." She grinned, biting her bottom lip.

"For now, I ordered zuppa inglese," Aditya said.

"My second favorite."

She didn't like conversation while they ate, so he watched in silence as she attacked the trifle with a fork. Watching her eat was like watching Picasso paint. She showed such vigor, such passion, gulping forkfuls down without stopping for water. He'd learned her sweet tooth wasn't to be ignored, and yet she never gained a pound, as far as he could tell. Perhaps she lived at the hotel gym between appointments when she was on one of her weekends away, but as a pair, they'd never worked out together.

"You attack sweets like they've hurt you," he joked. He'd learned after their second date to order his own dessert and ate it now as she finished her own. "How're finals?"

"All right," she said. "I can't believe my first year's over."

"Just two more to go." *Two more and then she can quit "the other thing."*

"And how's TBF?"

"You were right," Aditya said. "Claire left Oliver last month. She couldn't handle an open relationship."

Bella grinned, moving her fork to take a piece of his tiramisu. "I bet she kept the ring, though."

Aditya laughed, pushing the rest of his dessert to her. "Yeah, no shit."

"Poor girl," she said. "It's really something to be twenty-four and already divorced."

"Claire Steinbeck is a lot of things, but poor isn't one of them. She'll bounce back."

"What about Oliver?"

"He put in his two weeks after it became clear Claire wasn't going anywhere. I should be getting his old job any day now. That'll be a nice promotion after three years of grunt work."

"Claire's interning again for you guys?"

Aditya nodded. "She starts next week. We're gonna be working together on a few projects."

"As long as that's not code for something," Bella said, eyebrows raised. "That woman is trouble."

Is she actually jealous? Aditya's heart warmed at knowing he wasn't the only possessive one in this relationship.

"How are your parents?" Bella asked, changing the subject.

"Dad won't let me replace his 1985 Justy. Mom wants to set Karthik up with 'one of my New York friends.'"

Bella laughed. "Isn't he still in India?"

"He's done with the Army next year," Aditya said. "Then he just needs to find a way to convince the government to re-issue him a green card."

"Tough to swing that."

"Mom and Swapnika Aunty are convinced Ben can. They keep pressuring me to ask him."

Bella bit her bottom lip. "Ben's a dick, but even if he wasn't, Karthik can't change the past. He put that kid in the hospital. It's not like WP can change memories."

"You said it yourself, we don't know what WP can do…"

"I know you want him home," she said. She placed her hand atop his, and he sighed at the touch of her warm skin. Watching her lick some tiramisu from her lips, he smiled as a waiter brought them their check.

It was a half-mile walk back to Bella's apartment. She complained the whole way.

"You may have a world-class metabolism," Aditya said, "but some of us still need to exercise."

"My mother says I'll gain my birthing hips when I'm thirty," she said. "That's what happened with her."

He hadn't seen Mr. and Mrs. Ferrari since they'd graduated high school. *I should ask about them.* She'd asked how his parents were doing. It was only right. *Then again, my parents aren't racists.* The memory of her bus ride after Karthik's hearing still lingered in his mind, how she'd said she wasn't allowed to hang out with him because, in her own words, her parents were "pricks" who wouldn't let her associate with friends of Karthik's.

"That wasn't meant to scare you," she said, breaking into his thoughts.

"Hm?"

"You seemed out of it. I didn't mention birthing hips like I wanted to have your kids or anything. It's just something my mom said."

"Oh…"

"Not that I don't think about it. I do want kids…"

They were outside her building now. He moved her to

the side so the hustle and bustle of the city wouldn't disturb them. *She thinks about it?*

"I love you." He'd wanted to say those words since that night at the Christmas party. *Who am I kidding?* He'd wanted to say them since middle school. She challenged him, excited him, made him better in every way. Talking to her was as exciting as making love, for he knew now that's what they'd been doing, making love.

"Thanks." Her words didn't wound him, for there was genuine affection behind them. She embraced him and pecked his lips before continuing. "Please don't be offended that I won't say it back. It's just that I've said it too early before…"

"I understand." And he did. His father had still not said he loved him, but he knew the feeling was there.

"I want it to be the right moment." She was crying now. He took her head into his chest. "I'm so fucking happy right now and I don't want to screw it up."

"You're not going to," Aditya said. Lifting her chin, he kissed her again. The taste of honey and tears mixed to create that perfect blend of sweet and salty. Guiding her inside, up the elevator, past her front door, he took her to bed for the night.

June 7, 2014

Bella took Aditya to The Good Citizen for his birthday. "Remember to turn your chameleon band onto high sensitivity," she said. "You know people love to wear their WP here."

He adjusted the band on his wrist. "So, why are we here again? We haven't been here since you met Claire."

"And look how well that night turned out." She went through the door first, not waiting as he paid their cab driver, and when he entered the bar, shouts of "Happy Birthday!" greeted him. He hadn't had a birthday since he was eighteen, and certainly never as a surprise. Bella passed him a glass of Japanese whiskey as she introduced herself to his colleagues.

"Hi, I'm Aditya's girlfriend, Bella."

Girlfriend. It was the first time she'd used the term around his friends. *If we're calling these guys friends.* Three years at The Blackstone Fund had padded his bank account, and he'd visited the Hamptons enough times now to know he hated it, but at the end of the day he wouldn't call Ben or Claire or any of the others friends. *Maybe that'll change once I'm promoted.*

"Yo!"

Aditya turned to see his boss. The gel in his slicked-back hair made it shine unnaturally under the bar lights. "This your lady?" Ben whistled as Bella joined Aditya's side. "I might have to convert to Hinduism, because you're more blessed than the Red Sox. Three series wins in a decade, baby!"

Aditya blanked for a moment before remembering they'd won last year. "Yeah," he chuckled. "She's awesome."

"Good to meet you," Bella said. "We'll see you around. I want to meet his other friends." Aditya kissed her in gratitude as she pulled him away.

Claire left after a half hour, saying something about meeting a blind date her parents had set up for her.

"She doesn't waste time," Bella said.

"Maybe she's going for a record," Aditya joked. "Divorced twice before thirty." Bella slapped his arm as Ben ordered everyone to gather around.

"Today is, of course, a special day. And special days require special announcements."

Finally. Ben was going to give him the best present of all: Oliver's job. The man had left in April, and in that time, Aditya'd been given most of his work and none of his pay.

"Two big announcements. Well, three, really," Ben shouted, standing on a table and grabbing Aditya's and Bella's shoulders for support. The man's words slurred together. "First, two rounds of shots, on me, in honor of our friend, Aditya Shitty!"

As soon as I get the job, that nickname's going the way of the dodo.

"Next, Claire will be joining the firm full time starting next year! Is she still here? Let's give her a hand."

Aditya rolled his eyes. It wasn't a large bar, but the man still hadn't noticed her departure.

"Finally, a topic I know many of you have been thinking about. We were sad to see Oliver go, but I'm happy to say we finally have his replacement."

Aditya squeezed Bella's hand for support. Oliver's job was too prestigious to not come with some WP. He'd finally get in the legal way. Forget a new car—he'd get his parents a new house.

"I'm so pleased to announce that I'll be taking on Oliver's duties as Managing Partner as well as CEO for the next year. Then, thankfully, that workload will be off-loaded to Claire."

Bella whispered something in his ear, but Aditya couldn't hear her. He saw people clapping, saw Ben jumping off the table, but all he knew was rage.

That motherfucker. Ben didn't even work five days anymore. He took four-day weekends to the Hamptons to impress models and C-list actresses.

"Babe?" Bella spoke again, and this time he saw the

hurt in her face. Were those tears in her eyes? *Sympathy pain?*

"This guy's a dick," he said. "Let's go."

Nodding, she told him she just needed to use the bathroom first. As he waited for her to return, Ben slapped him on the back. "Sorry, Shitty, I know you wanted that promotion."

Aditya balled a hand into a fist under the counter they sat at. "I was disappointed, sure."

Ben shrugged. "That girl's got killer tits, so I wouldn't say it's all bad. Besides, you don't want to dream too big." Snorting, he clutched Aditya's face. "Happy birthday, bro." The man slid a white packet into his hands. "Go home and both of you do a line of this stuff before hitting the bedroom. You won't believe the results."

Aditya gritted his teeth. "No thanks." He handed the bag back to his boss.

Ben glared at him, and Aditya realized in that moment just how pathetic his boss was. WP, coke, scotch. He was more roasted than a burnt marshmallow. *Jesus.* He masked the disdain on his face, or maybe Ben was just too sozzled to tell.

"Word of advice," Ben said. Aditya tried joining Bella, now at the front door, but the man grabbed his shoulder. "You won't get ahead at Blackstone as long as you're a goody-two-shoes. It doesn't have to be drugs, but you better find a vice soon."

Leaving Ben behind, waiting as Bella hailed them a cab, Aditya knew what his vice would be: he was going to ruin Ben Blackstone. He was going to take TBF by force.

Bella had two orders of zuppa inglese sent up to the apartment by the time they returned.

"You know I hate bar food," she said, overemphasizing her accent the way she did whenever he was down and needed a reminder that she was an immigrant, too, that she understood prejudice better than most. Handing him a fork, she dug in with her own. "Ben is a pig. He was never going to promote you. You're there as his plaything, something he finds interesting enough to show off."

"For six hundred thousand a year, maybe that's enough," he said.

Throwing her fork across the room, she grabbed his face and looked him in the eyes. "You've got the smarts and the degree. Just go work somewhere else."

He hadn't looked closely enough before, but now he saw her makeup was blotchy around the eyes. "Babe?"

"I didn't go the bathroom to pee," she said. "Ben made a pass at me right before giving himself the promotion. If you ask me, he only made that announcement to make himself feel good after I blew him off."

A white rage surged through Aditya, and he had to close his eyes as his hands balled into fists. In the next moment, though, he looked at her and spoke calmly. "You should do it."

"Shut the fuck up." She lifted her plate to throw at him before he caught her arm.

"If Ben's dumb enough to hit on you at my own birthday party, he's dumb enough to leave sensitive information lying around his apartment." Bella opened her mouth to protest, but he cut her off. "I know how it sounds, but you saw what happened today. Three years of profits mean shit to him. You get in his apartment, scan some files, that's real ammo we can use against him."

"To what end?"

"A guy that rich? He's got to be involved in some illegal stuff. You don't get to be a billionaire without doing some seriously shady shit. And you're gonna graduate soon. How'd you like to be Legal Director for Adrsta?"

"Adrsta?"

"It's Sanskrit. It's a term for the unseen power guiding all our lives, like fate." Aditya grinned. "It's what I'm gonna rename TBF after I take over. We'll get some dirt, blackmail Ben to give me my due, and then I'll take care of us."

Silence filled the room, and then Bella laughed so hard she spat out some of her zuppa inglese. The colorful trifle smeared his shirt.

"It's not stupid," he said. "Ben is stupid for thinking WP legalization is never going to happen for nonwhites when we've got a Black president in the White House."

"This is so messed up," Bella said.

"Is it? You already sleep with other men."

Bella had kept her shoes on, but now she took them off and drove a heel into Aditya's head. He grabbed it in pain so that her next blow hit his hand.

"You're gonna stab me with that thing!"

"Good!" She shoved him so that he fell backwards onto her couch. "You think I'm just some whore you can order around? My clients pay eight hundred dollars an hour. What'll you pay me to do this?!" She was on top of him now, ripping his shirt and slapping his whole body until he grabbed her wrists and saw red.

"You're hurting me," she whispered.

"Not as much as you're hurting me." Shoving her into her bedroom, he slid his slacks off so she could see his penis poking through the hole in his boxers. Before tossing his pants aside, he fished his wallet out and withdrew three crisp hundreds. "This is all I got," he said, tossing them to her.

"I think we can work something out." She was breathing heavily, shoulders heaving and lust in her eyes. The anger between them was real, powerful as lightning, but so was the desire. She'd enjoyed roleplaying before, but the prostitute/john thing was always avoided.

"Get on the bed." His voice was raspy, and she obeyed his order without question, letting him slide her dress up and pull her panties down before getting behind her.

After, as they lay covered in sweat, Aditya massaged Bella's naked body above the sheets.

"I haven't done that with anyone," she said.

"No one?"

"I always refuse when guys request anal."

Aditya smiled. "You must really like me."

Hoisting herself on her elbows, she turned on her back to face him, looking him straight in the eyes. "I think I love you."

Bella Ferrari was the woman of his dreams, since childhood. And she'd just said she loved him. *If it's a lie, I'll die of heartbreak.*

They embraced, him pressing his excitement against her chest. He kissed her, hoping she knew what it meant, because his taste was still on her lips. She must've, he thought, because the next words out of her mouth were a stark reversal that filled him with joy. "I'll do this...for you."

"Thank you," he said. The night's activities had been all about him, but now he returned to his massage, bringing his hands from her shoulders down to her thighs. She sighed in pleasure, closing her eyes to let sleep and joy take her.

It wasn't often, but when Bella was especially pleased, she snored. That's how he knew it was safe to open the drawer at her side. Spotting her black book of clients, he opened it and flipped through the pages until he found Oliver. Claire had told the truth—it'd only been once. He intended to put the book away, but something told him to check the most recent entry. May 25, 2014. She'd missed

Memorial Day with his parents. His mom had been so excited to meet her.

Who was she fucking instead?

He saw the name, and a note next to it that said the man was a reporter for the *New York Times.* Harold Mueller, aged 26. "I can use that." Hearing her snore, Aditya put the book away and returned to snuggling her.

Chapter Ten

June 5, 2015

In a perfect world, Aditya would've spent every weekend with his girlfriend. Alas, the world wasn't perfect. Still, the last year had provided him with much to be thankful for. Ben hadn't been the least bit surprised at Bella's change in demeanor, sleeping with her that same month. Since then, Aditya had learned much about how The Blackstone Fund was able to dominate the industry. The chameleon bands helped, but so did owning a slew of shell companies under false names and offering equity to half the state legislature in exchange for them ignoring some regulatory and tax issues. A little WP for the nonwhite elected officials. Cash bribes for the Speaker. Call girls for the Minority Whip, some of whom worked at Bella's agency. And the pièce de résistance: the press. Rich pricks like Ben usually said the pen was mightier than the sword because they couldn't fight, but in TBF's case, it was actually true. Aditya wasn't proud of it, but continuing to read Bella's black book had proved invaluable. She'd seen this Harold Mueller guy fourteen times since February 2013, and soon after each liaison, Aditya'd found a *New York Times* article by him slamming one of TBF's competitors. Harold accused one of stealing from a state pension fund. He wrote a takedown piece profiling the CEO of a rival firm. He never had a positive thing to say about TBF—the firm wasn't even mentioned in any of his pieces—but it was clear he was pushing their agenda on Ben's orders through Bella.

And now the final piece comes into play.

Bella had rented a hotel room last weekend, and Aditya had used the time to take a trip to Boston. Back at Harvard, he'd visited the Widener Library. Karthik was leaving the Army within a few months. He'd done so well for himself that he'd been promoted to major. They'd last spoken a few weeks ago, and sure enough, the real estate mafia in Bangalore had discovered Karthik was feeding his superiors information on how best to break up their illegal enterprise. Realizing that killing a senior officer was impossible, they'd gone after his mom and stepdad, instead. Swapnika Aunty had been evicted from her house and then fired, forced to flee to Chennai and stay with relatives. Aditya had learned at the library how to bring her back. He was going to bring everyone back.

Things will be just as they were growing up, only even better with Bella and my own firm.

Karthik had enough money tucked away to steal aboard a cargo ship bound for NYC. Once here, he'd help Aditya take TBF by force. With Ben neutralized, they'd have enough WP to alter some memories, re-issue some documents, and get Karthik's parents here.

Mom will be so happy.

Bella had been wrong about WP not being able to change memories. After hours of reading, Aditya had found the answer at Harvard. Some Citibank alum had started his own firm in 1999, right before the dot-com burst. He'd been making money hand over fist, and when the SEC had started looking into his company, they'd found him guilty of insider trading. It should've been a big trial, the kind a guy like Harold Mueller would've written about. Only no report of the guy breaking a law existed in any New York paper. The firm had instead been written up by the *Wall Street Journal* in 1999 for being run by some wunderkind, and the man's name had been mentioned again in a 2001 article about how the guy was retiring after making some shady investments and losing his Series 63 license. But there'd been no mention of insider trading, no mention of anything illegal. He'd lost his company, but he'd hidden millions in offshore accounts he could still access. Really, he'd lost nothing.

Even if I get caught, Ben won't be able to prove anything, as long as we get enough WP.

The chess board was set. Bella was the pawn that'd made it across the board to become a queen, and once Karthik was home, Aditya would checkmate that fucker Ben with a knight. Smiling, he sipped a scotch in his apartment and looked at a text on his phone. Bella was done at her law office, finally back at her place. It was time to head over and start his birthday weekend off right.

June 6, 2015

Aditya had given Bella a massage upon reaching her place last night. It being so close to his birthday and all, she'd been so grateful she'd let him stick it in her ass. The thought of using her other hole, the one men had frequented over the last week, made him gag. It was hard enough to not break Ben's nose every time he saw him at work. And yet, the more he thought about how many men used her, the hornier he got. She'd promised him from the beginning that only he got to use her ass, and he woke her this Saturday morning by rubbing his hardness against it.

"Uhn." Though she sounded aggravated, he saw her reach for some lube. "Okay, birthday boy." Handing him the bottle, she arched her back into downward dog.

"Twice in a row?" he asked. "This doesn't mean you get to peg me again, right?"

She laughed so hard she collapsed onto the bed. "No. You said you didn't like it, so it's fine. Thank you for experimenting."

He smiled before slapping her butt and lubing himself up. "Thank you for a great birthday." He kissed her neck as he slid inside her.

Aditya made frittatas as Bella cleaned up in the bathroom. She hadn't mentioned any plans for his actual birthday, and he was hoping she'd finally meet his parents tomorrow.

"Babe?" He'd set two plates and made them mimosas after turning off the burner on the stove, but when she arrived from the bedroom, she was pulling a suitcase behind her. "Going somewhere?"

"Ben texted me last night," she said. "He hasn't seen me all week and wanted a weekend away in Southampton."

"And you said yes?" Aditya gulped down the drink in his hand before setting the glass aside so he wouldn't crush it.

"Of course," she said. "We've done so much spying at his place here, but a whole weekend at the summer house? Who knows what good intel I'll find."

He'd planned on filling her in on the grand plan on their way to meet his parents, but now knew he'd never tell her. He was unable to hide his narrowing eyes, his flared nostrils, the fists at his side. "You can just tell me if you prefer fucking him to me."

"What are you talking about?" she said, shrill. "Who just put it in my ass twice?!"

"You know why I prefer your ass?" He was screaming now. She did this to him, brought him down to her level of volume and violence. He stepped toward her, and she slid the suitcase between them. "I want something no other guy gets to touch."

"I thought you'd be happy," Bella said. "This was your fucked-up plan to begin with."

They'd fought like wild animals at least once a month during their relationship, both in and out of the bedroom, but nothing hurt Aditya quite like his logic used against him. He knew it was his fault, but he'd rather stab himself than admit it. Stepping back, he unclenched his fists and motioned to the door. "Whatever. Call me after if you want. Or don't."

Bella slapped him as she walked to the door. "I still love you, Aditya Shetty." Her thick accent dragged like a knife across the chest. "Even though something's real messed up about you."

"What's messed up is ditching your boyfriend on his birthday to be with another man."

She frowned, opening the door and stepping outside. "What did you think was going to happen when you suggested this stupid plan? I screamed and threw things when you mentioned it, but because I love you, I obeyed." When Aditya tried to follow her outside, she pushed him back inside. "Eat the frittata. Clean my dirty dishes. Watch porn on my TV if you want. But after you grow up, why don't you call me?"

She left him behind as he tried to think of a witty response.

Aditya found himself at the office an hour later. He wasn't sure if he was single or not, but figured as long as Bella was spying, he may as well, too. Alone at TBF, he rifled through some manila folders but only found personnel files. The latest hire was none other than Claire Steinbeck, who'd graduated summa cum laude before becoming the only woman to ever start at a hedge fund with the title of Managing Partner.

My title. Opening her file, he saw her salary was much higher than his own. *She's got Oliver's old job and I've got Oliver's sloppy seconds.* He bit his tongue at referring to Bella that way. She deserved more than that from him. She was his goddess. He hadn't meant it. He did love her, more than anyone except his mom. *And when you open yourself up to that kind of love, you're just asking for pain.* Perhaps, then, it was best to ensure no one would ever hurt him again.

"Excuse me?"

Careful not to appear startled, Aditya turned his head and saw a janitor. He closed the file cabinet he'd been sorting through as if he did this every weekend. "Do you need me gone?"

"I'm going to be vacuuming," the man said. "It will get loud."

"Thank you," Aditya said. "I was just leaving." On the way out, he glanced into Ben's office. It had a big safe within, with who knew how much WP inside.

I'll be back for you.

Chapter Eleven

December 18, 2015

As the annual Christmas party at One Bryant Park raged, Aditya and Karthik made their way up the elevator to the 55th floor. In the six months since his birthday, Aditya'd moved his focus from Bella to Karthik.

Bros before hos, indeed.

It'd taken two months and seven thousand dollars, but Karthik had finally arrived home at last three days ago. Aditya had mentioned to Ben months ago that he'd been able to find an original work from Matisse, the French painter, for the house in Southampton. The guy had been obsessed with that country at the time and had instructed Aditya to spare no expense procuring it. After advising Ben that an ocean freighter was the safest way to get the art into America, he'd instructed Karthik to stow aboard. According to the manifest, Ben was the guarantor of the art, under a fake name. And if the truth came out? Well, the truth was that his greedy boss had hired an Indian major with ties to the mafia.

"Can't wait to finally meet this prick," Karthik said,

cracking his knuckles.

Aditya had told his boss to wait in his office tonight to view the painting, but all Ben would witness was Karthik's fist breaking his nose. If he didn't want to end up in a coma like Bob Jr., the man would open his safe and they'd be gone within the hour.

Aditya adjusted his chameleon band as the elevator opened. "Karthik…" He held his friend back as they stepped out together.

"Stop messing around," Karthik said. "I want to get this done and get a New York slice already. Indian pizza tastes like ass."

Aditya raised an eyebrow. "You got a lot of experience eating ass?"

"Don't knock it 'til you try it."

Aditya blocked him as he tried walking to Ben's private office. "I'm sorry."

Karthik's nostrils flared. "This again? It ain't your fault, homie. Some white fuckers want to revoke my green card, want to keep me away, ain't nothing a skin grafter like you can do about it. Or so I thought."

"Yeah?" They'd had this discussion five times in three days.

"Yeah," Karthik said. "It's like I said: you brought me home. My own mom had given up on that."

"I'll bring her home, too," Aditya said. "I promise."

"I know you will, dude. Now let's ice this asshole."

Just outside Ben's private office, they heard noises, like *chappals* slapping against the floor, and a woman moaning in the background.

"Wonder who pretty boy's fucking," Karthik said.

But Aditya knew the answer before Karthik kicked in the door. The woman's accent always thickened in bed.

Bella Ferrari's undergarments were strewn across the

floor, along with her skirt and dress and shoes with WP-studded buckles that looked as if they cost ten grand. Aditya didn't see her at first because Ben had her bent over his table. The windows were open, so anyone nearby with a great telescope could see them. The first thing Karthik did was rip the curtains closed.

"What the fuck?!" Ben pulled out and grabbed his slacks. A pop resounded through the room as Bella screamed.

"You asshole!" she cried. "How many times I gotta tell you? Don't pull out so quickly!"

It was only then Aditya noticed the lube around Ben's penis, the dripping off Bella's ass. "You let him fuck you… there…"

He saw her eyes widen like a deer in headlights as she spotted him. He'd told himself years ago that he'd die of heartbreak if Bella had been lying about loving him. But in that moment, he couldn't die, not yet. He had to make Ben pay, first.

There was silence for a moment, and then Ben stumbled backward, trying to fit himself back into his pants. Aditya was on him in seconds, slamming his fist into the man's face as he used his knees to keep the man grounded. "I loved her, you piece of shit!" His knuckles turned red as he kept punching Ben until the man stopped protesting. Only then did he turn to the man's still-unbuttoned shirt and take the WP-encrusted cufflinks for himself. When he stood, Bella had dressed.

"Damn!" Karthik said. "This is the girl you were fucking? I didn't know you had it in you."

"Karthik?"

Aditya heard the fear in her voice. She knew this was the guy who'd worked for the mafia, for the Army, who'd pulverized some spoiled white kid. Seeing the fear in her eyes made him both happy and sad.

"You shouldn't have left him," Karthik said. He turned to face his best friend. "I know you like this bitch, but we can't have any witnesses."

Aditya wasn't paying attention. Just holding the cufflinks physically, wrapping his hand around them...it was like he'd been living with one arm tied behind his back and now could use both for the first time. The restraints that bound his scrawny frame snapped as the drug entered his system. As smart as he was, he knew he was wasting his potential.

There's so much knowledge out there. I can learn it all.

Where before the world had been laid out in black and white, his intuition now saw shades of red, green, yellow, blue, violet, and so much more. The drug wouldn't make him as strong as a god, fine, but he felt the WP making him smarter. Grabbing the edge of Ben's desk, breathing heavily, he noticed his hand was right where they'd been fucking. He pulled it away in disgust.

"Aditya, you never called..." She whispered his name as if he was a ghost.

"Would it have mattered?" His glare made her recoil against the office wall.

"Of course, it would've," she said. "I love you."

"Liar!" Ripping his chameleon band off, he let it fall to the floor and embraced the added jolt to his system. Rage clouded his vision, and while he knew it wasn't natural, he also knew it was the only way to get ahead.

Only monsters win in America.

He sensed Bella's movements before they happened. He shifted to block the door, embracing her when she made a run for it. He shoved her backwards, sending her stumbling over Ben's inert body. Karthik caught her as she fell; the embrace made her cringe.

"Whatever you have planned," she said, sitting on the

floor now, "I can go along with it. Let's get back together, baby."

He wanted to believe her. His mom deserved grandchildren and he deserved love. But in America, for immigrants like them, one had to choose between power and happiness. And he'd made his decision. "I could forgive you sleeping with him, we both said terrible things, but giving him your ass?"

"I thought about you every day," she begged.

"Do you love him?"

"He actually can be very sweet..." Bella overemphasized her accent when she answered. He remembered it was what she did when he needed a reminder that she was an immigrant, too, that she understood prejudice better than most. Maybe her act would've worked if he wasn't wearing WP, or if Karthik wasn't there, but right now all he saw was her betrayal.

"Aditya..." Ben stirred and spoke through swollen lips. Karthik pulled him up by his shirt, tossed him onto the couch by his safe.

"Name's Karthik," he said. "This is a robbery. Now open up or say goodnight forever."

Looking around the room, Ben saw Aditya had his WP-enhanced cufflinks. "Those things're gonna kill you."

"We'll see," Aditya said. "Now, like my friend said, the safe."

Ben glanced to Bella. "All this over some pussy?"

Striding over, Aditya broke the man's nose. "Don't talk about her like that." He was surprised to find Bella's smile still did things to his insides, that he still cared deeply for her. He let her come close and touch his shoulders, coo in his ear.

"There's still time," she whispered. "We can be together forever."

If only that were true...

"You never even met my mom..." Turning around, he threw her to the ground.

"Let's go tomorrow. Tonight, even."

"You're not gonna fall for this horseshit, are you?" Ben sounded like a cartoon character with his crushed septum. "If you are, you really are a moron."

Karthik dragged Ben back by his hair, prepared to throw him out the window.

"Relax," Aditya said. "We can't open the safe without him." It required a voice and fingerprint to unlock.

Ben laughed. "I'm never gonna do that for you."

Walking to Ben's desk, Aditya opened a drawer and retrieved a letter opener. "What if I cut you in ways that'll make you useless to a woman?"

For the first time, Ben's eyes bulged, and Aditya absorbed that fear until it powered through his body like heat.

"Okay, okay!" Crawling to the safe, Ben opened it. The amount of WP inside knocked everyone to the ground but him. "Eat shit, bros. Sometimes getting what you want is the worst thing you could ask for." Standing up, he slipped on a pair of brass knuckles with flecks of white that he'd palmed from the safe.

He leered over Aditya. "You think you could handle WP?" He kicked Aditya in the ribs and laughed as the man collapsed. He stomped on Karthik's fingers and was rewarded with a crunch. "You're just a couple of skin grafters. Not even special enough to be the first ones to try and steal from me." Walking back to his desk, opening it to take his gun out, he turned around just as Bella brought a paperweight down on his head.

Putting the chameleon band back onto Aditya's wrist, she brought up the sensitivity and kissed his lips as he struggled to rise.

"I never stopped loving you," she said. "It's just...you

do what you have to..."

When it had mattered, when she could've left him to die, Bella had chosen him. Had risked her safety for him. Like all things on the path to success in America, finding love was complicated.

"I understand..." He did. But understanding something and agreeing with it were two separate things.

"You shouldn't be here," Karthik said. Standing up, careful not to touch the WP-adorned objects with his bare hands, he kicked the contents of the safe to a side of the room. "You're not in this. Run away and I'll finish these two. We can come back later for the WP."

"I'm done running away," Aditya said. "I'm sorry I wasn't in it from the beginning. It should've been me that night at the restaurant." His voice cracked. "I can do it. I can put him in a coma."

Karthik shook his head. "We gotta put him in the morgue. Her, too."

Aditya's jaw dropped. He didn't retreat when Bella squeezed his hand at his side. "No," he said. "There's gotta be another way."

"Blood is all these people understand. And she's a loose end. I'll always be looking over my shoulder, as long as she's around."

Kissing Bella's cheek, Aditya stepped toward Karthik and nodded. "Then let me do it." Bella tried running, but Aditya shoved her to the ground. Taking the gun from Karthik, he brought it to Ben's fallen body and pulled the trigger twice. Bella shrieked so loudly he thought someone would hear and come running, but after a moment, it was clear the offices were empty.

"Now her," Karthik said.

Raising the gun, Aditya pointed it at Karthik. "You're my brother, but she's my life."

"Dude..."

No one spoke, no one breathed, until Karthik spoke again. "I did things in the Army, in the mafia. Things I never told anyone about. Don't make me show you."

"You said she's a risk as long as she's around. Well, maybe she doesn't have to be around."

"Aditya?" Bella dared to face both men, her back against the desk as if she were a cornered gazelle.

"She'll leave New York, finish law school somewhere else. She's only got a semester left anyways. After that, she'll leave the country."

Karthik's nostrils flared. "It's like that, huh?"

Aditya pointed the gun closer to Karthik's face. "Yeah, it's like that."

"You brought me back," Karthik said. "I guess I owe you one." He turned to face Bella. "Get the fuck out of here. I see you again, I kill you."

They didn't have time to share a goodbye kiss or any words. All Aditya got before she left his life was a touch on his neck and the smell of honey around him.

December 21, 2015

The next couple days were a blur. After Karthik disposed of Ben's body, Aditya called Bella's most reliable client and introduced himself.

"Harold? Bella's going on a vacation, but she told me you should write one last story for her."

Mueller protested plenty, even told Aditya he couldn't do this without bringing himself down in the process—a point Aditya conceded.

"But I've been at rock bottom before," he said. "Have you? Because if you don't do this for me, you're about to be."

Harold wrote the story as it was dictated to him. Ben was paying off half the state government for special carveouts to benefit TBF over its competitors. He'd gotten in too deep and arranged for a rival company CEO to be framed for embezzlement, but when it came time to pay the man, he'd tried to get out of it and the man had killed him before fleeing.

"No one will believe this without enough WP," Harold said.

"You let me worry about that." Aditya had Karthik working on distributing the contents of Ben's safe to Claire, the other staffers, security guards at the building, state legislators. Anyone on Ben's holiday card list had to get a piece of the action. Claire might've fought him more, but she was busy planning wedding number two and was happy enough to accept the change in ownership since she'd get to keep her title of Managing Partner. He'd even given her a raise.

"That's all of it," Karthik said. "Just a few grams left for us. What a waste."

"On the contrary, we got exactly what we needed." The two sat in Ben's old office—Aditya's now. Karthik sat on the other side of the desk, both men propping their feet up and looking out at the Statue of Liberty. "Amassing power takes time, but now all the pieces are in place. We got our fair shot at last, and now the rest is up to us."

"So, what's next?"

"You can only fool people for so long," Aditya said. "Get started on destroying all the chameleon bands. Offer Dr. Kapadia a nice trip back to India or six feet under if he gets difficult. Starting tomorrow, none of my employees will be shielded from the raw strength of WP."

Karthik blinked. "The stuff in that safe knocked us all on our asses without us even touching it. It makes you hurl if you get too close."

Aditya slammed his hand on the desk. "It's a crutch. With the right training and enough time, my people can handle it. Showing that I'm moving the firm toward more lenient WP policies? Embracing the country's tilt toward WP legalization? That's the only way we're gonna be able to fool the press long term. There'll always be trouble, but as long as we have the press and our own staff in our pocket, we'll be okay."

"And the ones who can't manage?"

Aditya grinned, standing up to look at Lady Liberty as the sun rose over her flame. "They'll quit or adapt. That's the American way. That's the key to gaining power and privilege."

Epilogue

December 25, 2016

Even though it was snowing in Hoboken, Puli Shetty waited on the stoop of his house to watch the Thakurs arrive on Christmas morning. Inside, Aditya's face flushed with pride at watching his father, his dad's smile as intoxicating as WP.

I did it. I brought everyone home. Puli had protested at first, but Aditya had said it was only right that he buy his parents a new house. He was thirty and already CEO of his own hedge fund, thanks to their drive to build a better life for him. His dad had accepted that logic, and so the brownstone at Garden and Eleventh had become the Shetty family home eight months ago.

Aditya grinned at the 1985 Justy in the driveway. It would take more WP than he had to convince his father to let him replace *that*.

"Namaskar Ji." Bala Pillai greeted Puli with the respectful honorific once everyone had made it inside.

"This is my husband," Swapnika Aunty said, bringing Puli into a warm embrace.

"And what a blessing," Puli said, "to have the two boys under the same roof again."

Aditya fist-bumped his best friend. Deepika had cooked all of Karthik's favorites from the old days: butter chicken and gobi manchurian and pav bhaji. At Aditya's and Karthik's insistence that Indian sweets sucked, Swapnika Aunty had baked a cake.

"How will we marry these boys off, Deepika?" Swapnika Aunty swatted her son's head. "Both thirty and still scornful of good Indian sweets."

"Kids today, always on the dating apps." Aditya's mom gave him a knowing wink. She knew he was writing to someone but didn't pry beyond that. True to his word, he'd arranged Bella's passage out of the country after she'd gotten her law degree from the University of New Mexico. He'd arranged for her to get a laptop with every encryption known to man on it. He had her email address, but no one knew where she was. It was better that way.

"Next year we can have Christmas in the city," Aditya said, setting the table. "The work on my place in Union Square should be done by then."

"These buggers charge an arm and a leg for running water," Puli complained. "But my big-shot son doesn't mind, so long as he gets his penthouse."

The words sounded mean, but Aditya's heart raced at the affection in them.

"Gimme a tour before we eat?" Karthik asked the question innocently enough, giving Aditya an excuse to take him upstairs into his room.

"I hear you've hired a few people for the new security firm."

"Yeah," Karthik said. "Maybe I'll become respectable yet."

Aditya laughed. "Just remember Adrsta is your most

important client."

"Of course. And on that topic, I needed to tell you that all chameleon bands have now been destroyed."

Aditya's grip tightened on the banister. "The factory that produced them?"

"All workers given generous severance packages."

"Dr. Kapadia?"

"On a beach."

"Chasing girls?"

"Sleeping with the fishes."

Aditya scowled. "That's too bad, but some of these older guys can't be swayed."

Karthik nodded. "Young blood is gonna save the country."

"And how's training?"

"You were right. Employee attrition is twenty-five percent lower than expected. All the nonwhites needed was time."

"The future can't be stopped."

"Hey!" his dad barked from downstairs. "Are the big-shots ready to eat? The food will get cold."

Aditya learned over the course of the meal that Swapnika Aunty and his mom were thinking about going into business together. A rising desi population in the Tri-State area meant an unlimited demand for South Asian bakeries because, in his mom's words, "just because you don't like gulab jamun and rasmalai doesn't mean others don't. Even some white people love it."

Aditya and Karthik snickered. "Just ask and I'll be your first investor, *Amma.*"

"*Amma?*" Deepika laughed. "Since when do you call me *Amma?*"

"Maybe I don't like Indian sweets, but that's not what makes me Indian." Aditya was done rebelling against his culture. Karthik was teaching him Kannada, and in the meantime, he wanted to try out *Amma* and *Appa* instead of Mom and Dad.

"Whatever you say, *kanne*." Deepika laughed again. "I don't need your money, though. Emily Cooles gave us enough to get started."

Karthik stiffened. "What's her agenda?"

Swapnika Aunty hit Karthik's head again. "No agenda. She feels bad for testifying against you, especially after reading about what happened with Mr. Blackstone."

"I can't believe he got caught up in such awful things," Puli said. "How strange that we personally know two men driven to such violence and depression. First our old chef, Ajeet, and now your boss."

Aditya smirked. "Just goes to show you: white, brown, or Black, all men suffer from delusions. Sometimes the only way out is death."

"Well," Deepika said, "it's a good thing Karthik was there to help you expose all that. It's so lucky this Ben joker booked Karthik as the security for that ship."

"Remember what I always say," Swapnika Aunty said. "Luck is just a word the gods gave us to describe their will."

"How right you are, sister." Deepika cut pieces of cake as her friend took the group's finished plates to the sink. "Don't worry about washing them," she said, turning her head to ensure Swapnika Aunty wasn't doing just that. "Puli will take care of it later."

Aditya grinned. The concept of a dishwasher blew his dad's mind.

"Yes," Puli said, "I'll do it later." He turned to Bala Uncle. "Shall we walk around the block? The Pier and Elysian Park are very close."

It was twenty-eight degrees outside. His dad wouldn't last fifteen minutes, but Aditya smiled, guessing the real reason Puli wanted to leave the house: to show off the new thermal sweater and earmuffs he'd gotten for Christmas from his son.

"Yes, go," Deepika said, shooing the men out. "Leave the women to gossip and badger our sons."

Karthik rolled his eyes as the two men left. "Can I go, too?"

"*Chup!*" His mother slapped him again before asking about his love life.

"*Kanne,*" Deepika said, pulling her own son aside, "I'm so proud of you."

"It's all thanks to you, *Amma*. Everything I do in this country is on yours and *Appa's* shoulders."

"And you have found a girl, no? I see you hiding your phone at the dinner table. Did you track down that Mahira woman?"

Mahira. He hoped she'd read Mueller's article, knew Adrsta was his, knew what she was missing. "Who has time for girls, *Amma*? I'm on my phone during dinner because running the company is a nonstop job."

"Just like running a family," she said. "*Kanne*, one day you'll have to choose."

"I know."But that day couldn't come yet. *Not until it's safe to find Bella.*

"I forgot," Deepika said, changing the subject. "You got some mail."

Walking to the kitchen, she handed him an envelope. Ripping it open, he read it and smiled. "It's from a job applicant wishing me happy holidays. Adrsta's got to expand, and this Indian guy's going places, I can tell."

"Very thoughtful of him," she said. "That shows good initiative. We all need to stick together, or who else will?"

"I'll give him a fair shake. The firm needs another Indian, and this guy sounds perfect. I'll see what he has to say next week, this Rakshan Baliga."

Seeing his dad and Bala Uncle returning from their walk, he tucked the letter in his pocket and rejoined Karthik and Swapnika Aunty at the front door. He'd see Bella again, and she'd join his perfect family and help grow it beyond their wildest dreams. Then, at last, he'd be happy. His mom would be happy. After all, with money and WP, a child born in America had unlimited potential.

Afterword

Thanks for reading Skingrafters! The idea for this book was borne from a desire from readers to learn more about Maadhini and Sadiya's journey. And after I wrote their story, I thought it only fitting to delve deeper into Aditya's origins as well. Maadhini and Aditya are perfect foils, in my opinion, with one representing the ideal skingrafter and one representing the skingrafter gone wrong.

And that future project I teased about? It's a sequel to the WP Trilogy. Yes, I've decided to "Star Wars" this series. Consider Privilege as the middle, Skingrafters as the beginning, and the sequel trilogy as the end. I hope it's more satisfying than the Star Wars Sequel Trilogy.

Please leave me a review on Goodreads, and please visit www.bharatkrishnan.com to sign up for my mailing list and check out my other works.